Wedding on Mistletoe Island

Sophie Pembroke

ORION

First published in Great Britain in 2019 by Orion Fiction,
an imprint of The Orion Publishing Group Ltd
Carmelite House, 50 Victoria Embankment,
London EC4Y 0DZ

An Hachette UK company

1 3 5 7 9 10 8 6 4 2

A CIP catalogue record for this book is
available from the British Library.

ISBN 978 1 4091 8979 4

Typeset by Input Data Services Ltd, Somerset

Printed and bound in Great Britain by Clays Ltd, Elcograf S.p.A.

www.orionbooks.co.uk

To Victoria.
For believing in me, calling me, and never
letting this story leave her heart.

2009

Fliss

'Fliss, this place is incredible!'

Fliss grinned as she watched Lara spin around in the entrance hall of Holly Cottage. Her long, wavy blonde hair fanned out behind her, coloured red and green and gold by the streams of sunlight pouring in through the panes of stained glass that framed the front door.

'I knew you'd like it,' she said. Mostly it was great to see Lara outside of the university library where she'd seemed to live for weeks before finals. She needed sunshine and fresh air and fun, Fliss had decided. They all did.

And she'd even managed to convince her parents to help them do just that.

Holly Cottage had been in Fliss's family since she was a baby. So many wonderful family holidays had been spent in the cottage on Mistletoe Island, right off the western edge of the Scottish coast. But Fliss had a feeling this holiday would be the best.

As long as you don't let any of those friends of yours get too wild, her father had said, reluctantly handing over the keys to the cottage. *I know we can always trust you to behave, but I'm not so sure about some of the rest of them.*

Her mother had talked him round, reminding him of how hard Fliss had worked to get her degree, and how this would be the friends' last chance to blow off steam together, before they settled down and got real jobs.

It helped that Fliss had never once done anything to make them think that there was any risk in letting her stay at the cottage with her friends for a week. It helped even more that her parents hadn't heard the stories of what her friends *had* got up to at university.

Fliss shook her head clear of such thoughts. Her parents weren't here; she didn't have to worry about disappointing them. It was just the seven of them, for seven whole days. She looked around. 'Where are the others?'

'Coming, coming.' Neal appeared in the doorway with two suitcases and a huge grin. Apparently, Caitlin's feminist sensibilities didn't go as far as actually carrying her own suit-case when her boyfriend was there to do it for her. That, or Neal was still trying to make up for something. Probably the latter. 'Look at this. An actual holiday cottage. Not a hostel or tent. We must be grown-ups at last.'

'Apart from Harry,' Jon said, leaning his own suitcase against the wall by the old grandfather clock that had chimed every hour since before Fliss was born. 'He's taken a vow of eternal childhood. He'll never age past twenty-one.'

Fliss thought that was entirely possible. Harry was their joker, their player. The Viking-like rugby star who could drink them all under the table. The one who never revised until the last minute at uni – and even then, only when Lara forced him – but still never worried about passing his degree. He probably figured he'd talk his way into a better result if he needed to. Harry always could charm anyone into anything – even examiners.

She could hear him outside right now with Alec trying to find the best place to house the mini-kegs of beer they'd brought with them. At least she could count on Alec to make sure nothing exploded. Alec was solid. They all knew they could rely on Alec for a pint in the evening, to score the winning try on the rugby pitch, to get a proper job straight out of uni. Alec always shrugged and said he wasn't anything special when they complained about his constant winning at life. But Fliss had figured out Alec's secret: he just got on with it. Whatever needed doing, he worked and made sure it happened.

Well, mostly, anyway. He never did seem to master girlfriends. Or cooking.

Her gaze finally settled again on Lara, beaming up at Jon and looking more relaxed than she had in months. If Harry was the party animal, Lara was their workaholic. The one who always had her essays planned and researched almost as soon as they were set, but still ended up working all night the day before the deadline to make sure her work was absolutely perfect.

Of course, all that studying meant that when Lara *did* cut loose and relax, she really knew how to party.

Maybe that was why Jon was such a good match for her. Steady, serious and studious enough to suit that side of Lara, but he also loved to get outside – hiking or climbing, usually – and he tended to drag Lara with him, to make sure she at least saw sunlight. He was the fixer of the group – the one they yelled for when the shower wasn't working, or the front door of their shared student house wouldn't lock.

But all that seriousness fell away when he was with Lara. Fliss had watched them over the last year of their relationship, a little envious of the way they fit together. The quiet, private jokes they shared, her blonde head pressed against his dark curls as they whispered to each other. Or the way that Lara really seemed to listen when Jon went off on one of his drunken, philosophical, deep and meaningful rambles.

They were good together. Happy. Her gaze strayed back to Neal, just as Caitlin appeared behind him in the doorway, nudging him forwards with her handbag.

'I'm glad to be staying somewhere with a working toilet,' she said, running her usual critical eye over the hallway as she tossed a mane of red hair back over her shoulder.

Fliss hid a grin. Ah, yes. That was what Neal was making up for. She'd heard all about Neal's attempt at a romantic weekend away in a B&B in Norfolk. Caitlin had been more upset at the state of the plumbing than the 'serial killer vibe' Neal said the place had.

Caitlin and Neal were the grown-ups – together since first year, and basically married already at this point. They were university mum and dad to the whole group. When they'd all decided to move in together for second year, Caitlin had been the one to ring around all the estate agents and find them the perfect house. The one who decided who owed how much rent each month based on their bedroom size. The one who kept the shopping list updated on the fridge.

And Neal . . . Neal was the one who got sent to do the shopping, or whatever else it was Caitlin decided needed doing.

Caitlin had a plan for life – several, actually. They all knew the details of Caitlin's three-year, five-year and ten-year plans. She knew exactly where she was going and how she was going to get there.

And, it seemed, she planned to take Neal with her.

That was the group. Her friends. The joker, the reliable one, the workaholic, the serious one, the mum and the dad. And her.

She knew exactly what her role was.

'Miss Fliss!' Harry yelled, forcing his way past the others to press a kiss to her cheek. 'This place is perfect! I see wild parties, skinny dipping in the sea . . .'

Fliss raised her eyebrows to cut him off. Harry grinned, sheepishly. 'Sorry, forgot who I was talking to. Obviously, we'll all be on our best behaviour, and only have respectable, non-wild fun.'

She rolled her eyes, knowing he was lying. But worse than that was knowing that was what he thought she wanted to hear – rather than what her parents expected of her.

That was who she was. Miss Fliss. The *nice* one, whatever that meant. The baby of the group, who needed protecting from the real world. The naive one, who didn't even understand Harry's smutty jokes. The one who smiled and baked cakes and tried to make everyone happy.

And maybe that was who she had been, three years ago, when they all met her in Freshers' Week. But hadn't she moved on at all? She caught Neal's eye, and he gave her a sympathetic smile.

'Come on, Miss Fliss,' Alec said, appearing behind Harry. God, how she hated that nickname. 'How about you show us around?'

Fliss smiled and forced herself to focus on the here and now. They were all done with university, at last. Those old roles they'd filled no longer applied.

She didn't have to be Miss Fliss any more, if she didn't want to, once she got out into the real world.

The whole point of this holiday was to let their hair down. All seven of them, together – freed of the pressures of exams and essays and university in general – celebrating graduation before they moved on to the next stages of their lives.

It would, Fliss decided, be the perfect week. She'd make sure of it.

'I propose a toast!' she said, pulling a bottle of supermarket own-brand cava from her bag. She led the others into the kitchen, holding the bottle high.

With a cheer, Lara went to a kitchen cabinet and brought out seven champagne saucers, passing them to Jon, who handed them along the line until everyone had one.

Fliss tore off the foil and thumbed out the cork with a pop, not caring that this wasn't the sensible way to open sparkling wine. She distributed the cava as evenly as possible, and waited for each of her friends to raise their glasses as she held her own in the air. 'To graduation!' she announced, finally.

'To making it through!' Harry added.

'To Mistletoe Island!' That was Neal.

'To indoor plumbing!' Caitlin, of course, making them all laugh.

'To graduation!' Alec cried.

'To all of us!' Lara, leaning against Jon, smiling up at him.

'To the future!' Jon, smiling back, like she was the only person in the room.

Fliss let the rightness of them all being together, here, settle into her as they clinked glasses. And as she sipped the cava, bubbles tickling her nose, she knew deep in her gut that they would all remember this holiday for the rest of their lives.

Thursday 19 December 2019

Four days until the wedding

Fliss

Fliss reached up to the top shelf, her phone clamped between her ear and her shoulder, the chair she stood on tilting perilously. Above her, the champagne saucers glittered in the hazy winter sunlight misting through the cottage's high windows. She remembered those glasses. Remembered the toasts they'd had the day they arrived at Holly Cottage ten years ago. Remembered Jon buying more bottles of fizz to celebrate an engagement that never happened. They'd drunk every last drop of it later that night in an attempt to cheer him up, once Lara had fled into the night after turning him down. Remembered Harry building a leaky champagne fountain out of the glasses. Remembered Alec making stupid toasts to them all, until they couldn't help but laugh at themselves and the others. Caitlin had laughed so hard at Alec's toast to Neal that she spilt champagne all over her boyfriend and he sulked outside until Fliss took him more alcohol to cheer him up.

Fliss bit her lip. She wasn't going to live in the past. This week wasn't about ten years ago. It was about her future.

She focused on the champagne saucers again. Who'd moved them to this ridiculous high cupboard where they'd never get used? Well, they would use them this week. She could almost reach them . . .

'Felicity, darling, are you listening to me?' Her

mother-in-law-to-be's voice had a slight edge behind the endearments, but Fliss was used to that.

'Of course, Martha. You want to change the centre-pieces.' Again. 'I agree. If we can get snowdrops they'd be perfect accents to the winter greenery.' Honestly, it was as if Martha thought she had no experience of weddings at all, despite working for one of the most sought-after bespoke wedding cake designers in London. She'd talked themes and colours and flavours with brides every working day for the last nine years or so, after her degree in English Literature proved to be less than useful, and she'd decided to pursue her other passion instead.

Although, given all the wedding knowledge she had, organising her own had been considerably more of a trial than she'd anticipated. Mostly due to all the other people involved, who apparently felt they needed to be consulted and kept happy. Her parents, Ewan's parents, the bridesmaids, Ewan's gran, her friends, the guests . . . oh, and Ewan, her fiancé. And maybe, at the end of that long list, even herself.

But none of that mattered now. In four days, on Christmas Eve Eve, she'd be marrying Ewan. Four days of celebrations and fun. Four short days, and her whole life would be different. *That* was what mattered.

'Good.' Fliss could hear Martha's efficient nod down the phone line. 'And maybe we could echo them on the cake . . . I was talking with your mother, and we do think a wedding cake needs flowers, don't you?'

No.

She rested her forehead against a shelf and took a deep, calming breath. Fliss knew *exactly* what her wedding cake needed, thank you very much. She'd been picturing it ever since Ewan had proposed, and they'd started planning a Christmas wedding. She'd had the snowflake designs ready for weeks. She'd briefed the staff up at the hotel where the wedding was being held on the actual baking of the cake, but the decorations would be all her.

Martha was *not* messing with her cake.

'The wedding cake is all in hand, don't worry,' Fliss said, as soothingly as she could manage in the circumstances. As long as she could keep Mum and Martha focused on all the other aspects of the wedding, the cake would be fine. Mum had already dismissed her choice of bridesmaids' dresses as 'too casual' and insisted on helping to choose new ones. What were a few centrepieces at this point? But the cake was hers.

'In that case, let me pass you on to my son.' Not 'Ewan', not 'your fiancé', but 'my son'. Just in case Fliss had forgotten who had loved him first – as if she ever could forget, with Martha around to constantly remind her.

Sometimes, Fliss missed the early days of her relationship with Ewan, when they stayed in eating takeaway Chinese and watching movies, and never had to meet each other's families.

'Hey. You okay? Is the Christmas tree still standing?' Ewan's warm voice in her ear made her smile, as she remembered decorating the tree for the cottage with him the night before. It had been just the two of them again, for the first time in what seemed like ages, and probably the last time until after the wedding.

Holding onto the lower shelf, she stretched up on tiptoes again and reached for the champagne glasses one last time. Her fingers wrapped around the delicate twisted glass stem of the nearest one, and she carefully lowered it – and herself – back down. She placed the glass on the nearest counter, and reached back up for the next glass before answering her fiancé.

'The tree is fine, and so am I. Just getting everything ready for the gang arriving.' Seven of them, again, so seven glasses. Except this time it would be Alec's wife, Ruth, making up the seven, with Jon living over in the States and unable to get back for the wedding. 'It'll be strange without Jon, though. Although, you know, I totally understand why he can't come.'

On the other end of the line, Ewan paused for a moment. Then he said, 'I know you're sad he can't be there. But, under the circumstances . . .'

'You mean Lara,' Fliss guessed.

'Maybe it's for the best.'

Fliss sighed. 'You're probably right. But it's going to be weird, having everyone here without Jon.'

Jon. She needed to talk to Lara about Jon. Or maybe Caitlin would do it . . .

She stretched up again and carefully lifted another glass down. They weren't champagne flutes; that would have been boring. No, these were proper, Gatsby-esque champagne saucers, and if they'd survived this long Fliss was damned if she was going to break them now. 'Guess what? I found these champagne glasses we used last time we were here. I mean, they have ten years' worth of dust covering them from being hidden away in the top cupboard, but with a bit of a scrub . . .' She stopped. 'You don't care about glassware, do you?'

Ewan chuckled. 'After a morning of my mother and yours deliberating between several identical choices of napkins, even glassware sounds interesting.'

'Napkins?' Fliss frowned. 'But I already picked the napkins. The white ones with the silver snowflake pattern to match the ribbons on the chairs.'

'Ah. About that . . .'

Deep breaths, Fliss reminded herself as she closed her eyes. 'We have new napkins?'

'And ribbons.'

'Right.' This was the problem with deciding to spend the last few days before the wedding down at Holly Cottage with her friends. It meant her mother and Martha were unsupervised up at the hotel, half a mile or so away. Her mum had caused enough trouble on her own; how much more could she cause now she had help? With four days left, Fliss wasn't sure she'd recognise her own wedding when it actually came round.

The Mothers, Fliss had learned over the last eleven months, both had very firm ideas about what a wedding should be. And they were both determined to prove to the other that their knowledge of exactly what Fliss and Ewan's big day should look like was superior.

As long as they don't touch my cake.

'Well, that's fine. Whatever they want.' She made an effort to sound cheerful, to find the sunshine and silver linings she was famous for. As long as everyone was happy, she could deal with new napkins and centrepieces. 'All that really matters is that I'm marrying you on Monday. Right?'

She'd wanted a Christmas Eve wedding, but with no ferry running off the island on Christmas Day, and no flights home from Glasgow either, she'd settled for Christmas Eve Eve, knowing everyone would want to get back to their own families for the big day itself.

'Right.' Ewan sounded relieved. He always hated a disagreement or fight as much as she did. It was probably why their relationship was so relaxed. They'd fallen together so easily, after being introduced by one of her colleagues two years ago, that Fliss had barely even noticed they were a proper couple until she realised the fridge in her flat was entirely filled with his favourite foods. Normally, her boy-friends let her down gently before they ever got to that point.

'And now, if you don't mind, I'm off to play a rather chilly round of golf with our fathers. Are you sure you don't want to toss again for "babysitting the parents" duties?' Ewan asked.

Fliss rolled her eyes. 'No, thank you. I'm babysitting our friends instead.' They'd split up the wedding tasks fairly evenly, according to the giant Wedding To Do spreadsheet Caitlin had emailed her the day they announced the engage-ment. Well, after they'd deleted all the most ridiculous tasks. Did people really host bridal teas? She hadn't thought so, until the Mothers got involved.

'*Your* friends,' Ewan corrected her. 'My friends are flying in the day before, like normal people.'

'Are you suggesting my friends aren't normal?' Fliss asked, eyebrows raised.

'I've met Harry,' he said, and Fliss laughed. 'So, I'll see you all in the Griffin for dinner tonight?'

'Yes, please. I miss you.' Since they'd got engaged and moved in together, almost a year earlier, she'd never had a night apart from Ewan – and she didn't really want to start now. The idea of Ewan staying up at the Mistletoe Hotel tonight, when she was lying alone in her bed at Holly Cot-tage, felt wrong.

'After Monday, you'll never have to miss me again.'

He was right, Fliss realised as she hung up. By Monday evening she'd be Mrs Ewan Bennett. Her future, her life, would be settled, approved and celebrated by all her loved ones. She wouldn't just be designing and making cakes for other people's happy endings, she'd be living her own. Her mother could move her expectations on from 'When will you ever get married?' to 'When are you going to give me grandchildren?' instead.

She could picture it in her head: her wedding day, and everyone smiling. No one was going to be disappointed about the napkins or the ribbons on the chairs. They'd all be happy and excited to be there sharing it with them. She was marrying a good man who her parents adored and whose family seemed to like her. And she was doing it on the island that had been a major part of her life – and her parents' lives – since she was a child.

Everyone would be happy. That was what mattered most.

And next to that . . . her own, secret wish for that day.

That it would give her the chance she needed to start over again. A new person, with a new name. A wife.

Not Miss Fliss, the university nickname she still hated. Not her parents' perfect only child, with every expectation on her shoulders. Not the unsettled single girl trying to find where she belonged in London, the one who could never make a relationship last more than six months. Not the dreamer who created beautiful wedding cakes for other people's big days. Or at least, not *only* all those things.

She'd be Ewan's wife. Someone new, who didn't even exist until she said 'I do.'

She couldn't wait.

Fliss stepped down from her chair, adjusting her top – a powder pink jumper with sprigs of mistletoe and holly embroidered all over it – and counted the glasses. Seven dusty champagne saucers all safely on the counter. Satisfied, she ran hot water into the butler's sink, smiling at the fairy lights twinkling above the window behind it. Squeezing in a good measure of washing-up liquid, she reached for the first glass, when a flash of movement out the window caught her eye.

A car.

As quickly as it had appeared, it disappeared again behind some trees. Her heart seemed to stutter and stall, waiting to beat again until the car emerged back into view down the twisting road.

The first to arrive.

Ten years gone in a blink, and soon they'd be together again – apart from Jon. But otherwise, it would almost be a re-run of their graduation trip after university.

Only this time, everything was different.

It had to be.

Lara

Ten years on, the ferry port at Mistletoe Island still felt like the portal to a magical new land. One totally apart from everyday life, and ordinary little worries. A place full of fun and adventure and freedom.

Only, this time, the island was full of memories, too.

Jon.

Lara stared out at the island through her windscreen, waiting for her turn to drive along the single-car-width bridge from the ferry to the shore. Last time, Jon had driven; last time, everything had been different.

Mistletoe Island wasn't far from the Scottish mainland, and Fliss said that since the tourist industry had really taken off over the last decade they'd even increased the number of daily ferry sailings across to the island. With its stunning scenery and island walks – and the development of the Mistletoe Hotel under Fliss's father's company – it was a popular summer destination for those who could bear the midges. But apparently it was Christmas and Hogmanay that really drew in the crowds. Lara didn't like to imagine what they'd all be paying to stay here, the weekend before Christmas, if Fliss's parents didn't own Holly Cottage.

But despite the uptick in the island's fortunes since their last group visit, Lara thought that Mistletoe Island still looked the same. Same craggy, cliffy coastline. Same picturesque white cottages sitting above the harbour, and the tiny stone chapel where Fliss and Ewan would be married the day before Christmas Eve; the same local village they'd bought their food and alcohol in; same pub where they'd monopolised the pool table. The Griffin probably still had the same stained upholstery, and that dent on the wall where Harry had misfired the cue ball.

Maybe it was just her that had changed.

A horn sounded, and she realised it was her turn to move forwards. Carefully, trying to look everywhere at once, she eased the car off the ferry and onto the bridge, driving down towards the village then veering right before she reached it, taking the road that circumnavigated the island, leading away towards the woods.

It was practically impossible to get lost driving on Mistletoe Island. Walking, sure – there were hundreds of tiny paths that wound their way around and inland, through the woods or along the cliff paths, down to the coves. But there was only one main road, riddled with pot holes, that made a full circuit of the island's six-mile circumference, far enough inland that there was little risk of cars losing control and going over the cliff, but close enough to the coastline that Lara could still keep the sea in the corner of her eye as she drove. Maybe there were other, smaller tracks that led inland, but everything Lara needed was on the one road – something she was very grateful for.

The road twisted around, showcasing the scenery of the Scottish islands to perfection, even in the chill of a December day. Banks of gorse and heather that edged the inside of the road still held frost in the patches the sun couldn't reach. Beyond them, the land rose again towards the middle of the island, and there were peaks of snow reaching up into the low, grey cloud. Somewhere up there, Lara knew the animals she'd loved seeing before – the deer, the rabbits, the incredible variety of birdlife – must be hiding from the winter, unless they'd flown south. Last time they'd been there it had been high summer, the August after their graduation, when everything had seemed possible and the future open and endless. Yes, this time, everything was different.

Lara smiled to herself. They'd been so young, then, even if they'd felt old enough to own the world. It was the last time they'd all been together that way, and for that, the island would always hold a place in her heart.

Although, to be honest, there wasn't a chance she'd have even *considered* going back there for anything less than Fliss's wedding. Because even now she couldn't think of that week without remembering how it had ended.

Five days on the island that had already changed her life once, with the five people who knew her better than anyone else in the world – plus the one who'd once seen even deeper inside her. Did she really expect to make it through the week without any new scars – or at least some old wounds reopening?

At least Jon wouldn't be there to do the reminding. She'd felt a flood of relief when Fliss had told her that he wouldn't be coming, though she knew how much her best friend had really wanted him there for her big day.

Slowing a little as she reached a familiar stretch of road, Lara focused on the stone wall that rose to her left. Mistletoe Island might not have changed, but the turning off to Holly Cottage was kind of hidden, if she was remembering right. She knew that if she reached the lighthouse she'd gone too far, but otherwise . . . was that it?

Lara braked again, glad she'd swapped her heels for

trainers. She'd planned to have time to change out of her suit, and maybe even grab a shower at the hotel before she left the event she'd been setting up in Glasgow, but her early meeting had run over, then she'd needed to check in with the two junior colleagues she was leaving in charge in her absence, plus a last-minute call to her boss to update him on how things had gone . . . in the end, she'd only just made her late checkout. In fact, she'd been lucky to catch the ferry at all. It was just as well she'd been working in Scotland this last week; she'd never have made it all the way up from London in time.

She should have left earlier, she knew that. If Fliss's wedding had been a work event she'd have been at that ferry port a full hour early with some work reading to do while she waited. As it was . . .

Was that the turning? Lara wasn't sure. It didn't look as she remembered, but then, the turning onto the winding driveway wasn't the most memorable thing about her last trip to Mistletoe Island, and it *had* been ten years. Damn, she was past it now, and she was almost certain it *had* been the right one. Holly Cottage was further out of the village than a lot of the holiday cottages on the island, and not nearly so well signposted as the hotel.

Shifting her car into reverse, Lara twisted to look over her shoulder as she started backing up. At the same time, her phone started vibrating on the passenger seat. Typical! Ignoring it, she reversed far enough to take the turning, and started up the twisting drive, looking out for Holly Cottage through the trees. Her phone stopped buzzing, finally, and she took the last bend.

She'd been right. There! Holly Cottage came into view, and Lara couldn't help but smile at the sight. Old-fashioned lanterns with bright white bulbs hung from the trees that lined the driveway, and from beneath the thatch of the roof. The bright-red front door looked freshly painted and a perfect wreath of winter greenery hung on it, studded with holly berries that matched the paint. A light layer of the snow that had fallen overnight added a magical feel to the gardens surrounding the cottage, and for a moment Lara felt her muscles relax, happy to be back.

Then her phone started buzzing again.

The bright-red door opened and Fliss bounded out, her blonde curls bouncing on her shoulders as she grinned and waved. She looked about twelve in her pink Christmas jumper, and Lara couldn't help but smile at how perfectly Miss Fliss she still was, after all these years.

Fliss looked so happy to see her, Lara felt immediately guilty about her buzzing phone. But not guilty enough not to take the call. Giving Fliss an apologetic look through the windscreen, Lara picked up her phone and answered. Fliss rolled her eyes, and pulled a face at her, sticking her tongue out so far it made her eyes bulge.

'Lara Miller,' she answered, trying to sound professional and not as if she was about to burst out laughing at her friend's expressions. It was payback, she supposed, for all the times she'd tried to distract Fliss when she was on the phone to her parents, back at uni. Sometimes the others had got involved, too; Harry had particularly liked to make it sound like Fliss was in the middle of some sort of debauched student party, rather than watching *Holby City*.

'Lara! Jeremy here. Was wondering if you'd given any more thought to our . . . proposition.' Jeremy could make even a serious job offer sound slightly slimy. Lara allowed herself a small shudder before answering.

'I thought I had until the New Year to consider?' It was

six days before Christmas, after all. Nothing was happening between now and January anyway.

'The thing is . . . Beatrix would really like this all tied up before she heads off for her Christmas break on the twenty-fourth.'

Beatrix Bryce. The only reason Lara was considering the job. If it had meant working for Jeremy it would have been a hard no from the out. But Beatrix . . . Lara liked Beatrix. Admired her. Even enjoyed working for her, before she'd left the company to set up her own, up in Manchester to be nearer her family. She'd taken the smarmy Jeremy with her, for reasons Lara had never quite managed to comprehend.

Now Beatrix wanted Lara to follow her. And Lara had to decide if she wanted that too.

'Tell Beatrix I'm flattered by her offer, and I'm weighing up my options very carefully as I would love to work with her again.' It would mean new opportunities. Space to grow. Maybe even a director's role eventually – something she could never see happening where she was.

'But?' Jeremy pressed.

Lara stared out of the window at Fliss waggling her eyebrows at her. She was holding up a bottle of Prosecco and a vintage-looking champagne saucer that Lara recognised from their last trip.

'No buts,' she told Jeremy. 'I'm sure Beatrix understands it would be a big life change for me, moving away from London. I have to consider all the angles.' She'd moved to London with her first job when she'd got back from her post-graduation travels. Followed her friends to the big city, and never looked back. Could she leave it now? Move away from the group?

Jon did. But that had been her fault.

Jeremy scoffed. 'Come on, Lara. We both know

you're hardly ever in London. Graham has you flying all over the world fixing his mistakes and smoothing client tempers.'

'That's not what I do,' Lara argued, even though it sort of was. Technically, she was the senior account manager for Graham's event-planning service, but lately she seemed to have been doing a lot more crisis management and client liaison than actual event planning.

'Right. Of course not.' Jeremy didn't even try to keep the disbelief out of his voice.

Lara sighed. 'Look, Jeremy, I'm actually on annual leave now until after Christmas. I'm at an old friend's wedding in Scotland. But tell Beatrix . . . tell her I'm seriously considering and I'll get back to her as soon as I can.'

'Will do,' Jeremy said. 'But don't expect me to believe that you won't be working while you're on leave. I know you better than that, remember?'

The knowing lilt in his voice told her he was remembering their ill-fated two dates and one night together. Something she'd worked very hard to forget.

Working with Jeremy again, and having him constantly reminding her of her brief lapse in judgement, was another item in the con column of the list.

A pop, loud even through the car windows, made Lara jump, and when she looked round she saw that Fliss had opened the Prosecco and was gleefully pouring herself a glass. Her friend met Lara's gaze with her own laughing one as she raised the glass in a toast towards the car.

'I'll call you soon, Jeremy. Merry Christmas.' She hung up before he could return the greeting.

Then she watched Fliss down the saucer of sparkling wine, before pouring another one.

Really like old times − only with better alcohol. She

hoped. The beer Alec and Harry had brought last time had been almost undrinkable. Of course they'd drunk it anyway.

Smiling to herself at the memory, Lara got out of the car.

'That one better be for me!' she called, as Fliss finished pouring.

'It can be,' Fliss replied, with a teasing smile. 'But you have to give me your phone first.'

'Fliss . . .' Lara groaned.

'You promised! No work this week.'

Lara winced at the reminder. She'd really hoped that Fliss would have forgotten that promise.

'You caught me at a stressful moment,' she pointed out. Did thinking about a new job count as work? Lara figured probably not.

'What? Making the table plan for my wedding? How was that stressful for *you*?'

'Okay, when I said stressful, I meant emotional.'

'You meant drunk,' Fliss said, smirking.

'That too. You tricked me into making that promise by feeding me wine.' A *lot* of wine, as Lara recalled. It had been the first time they'd been able to get together, just the two of them, in ages, so they'd made the most of it.

'But you *did* promise,' Fliss said. 'And you've already broken it. So hand it over.'

Lara stared at her smartphone, then at her friend. Fliss took promises very seriously. She never understood how people could let others down by breaking them. And it was her wedding week . . . plus, Fliss would probably be so busy she'd forget after the first night and Lara would be able to steal it back again. Just to keep on top of her emails, or anything urgent that came in. Knowing Fliss she'd hide it in her underwear drawer or something, and since they were sharing a room this week it wouldn't be hard to find. Fliss wasn't exactly the queen of subterfuge and secrets.

Lara swapped the phone for the champagne glass. 'The things I do for you . . .'

Fliss pocketed the mobile. 'Excellent. Now I just need to get Ewan's mother to stop rearranging my wedding, and prevent Harry from seducing any of the guests, and we're all set!'

'Sounds like getting me to give up work for the week was the easy part.' Lara took a swig of Prosecco, her fingers already itching for her phone.

'Probably,' Fliss agreed, but she was still smiling, like always.

Her good mood was infectious. Lara bit her lip as she watched her friend, brimming with joy and excitement. Careful not to spill her drink, she scooped Fliss up in a hug. 'You're getting *married*,' she whispered into her friend's ear.

So many nights she'd sat with Fliss after one stupid man or another had broken her heart. Why could they never see what a treasure she was? So many times she'd watched Fliss bravely draw on all that sunshine inside her, decide that it meant they weren't the one, and move on, determined to find the *right* one. All those idiots she'd had one or two dates with, or the even more stupid ones who'd dated her for months and *still* not realised how perfect she was.

They'd all been leading to here. This week. Fliss and Ewan's wedding.

'I'm so, so *happy* for you,' Lara said, pulling back.

'Me too!' Fliss gave a little squeak of excitement. Then her smile faded as she gave Lara a concerned look. 'You're okay with this, though, right? I don't mean the not-working thing, or the wedding thing. With . . .' She glanced around the snow-covered garden. 'With being here again. After last time with . . .'

'Jon.' His name felt strange in Lara's mouth after so many years of not saying it. She noticed she'd started shivering – due to the wintry cold, no doubt. The wind chill was always worse on the island.

'Yeah.' Fliss chewed her lip, a nervous habit she'd had as long as Lara had known her.

Lara forced herself to smile. 'It's fine. It's been ten years, Fliss. A different life. I like to think we've all grown up and moved on since then, right?'

She definitely wasn't the same girl she'd been at uni, that was for sure. She'd travelled the world, explored places other people barely knew existed. She'd managed events involving thousands of people, and pulled them off perfectly. Or at least without letting on what a scrabble it could be behind the scenes.

She was a smart, professional woman with her own life and countless opportunities at her feet. At least, that was what she reminded herself, whenever she felt that old Lara creeping out again. And she tried not to let herself wonder what might have been, or think about other paths she might have taken.

'Besides,' Lara said, taking a deep breath and smiling at her friend, 'it's not like Jon will even be here. I think I can cope with a few awkward memories.'

'Right,' Fliss agreed, although Lara heard the wobble of doubt in her voice.

She widened her smile reassuringly. 'Don't worry about anything.' Lara draped an arm around her friend's shoulders as they stepped inside Holly Cottage. 'It's going to be a brilliant week – and a perfect wedding day for you. Okay?'

For better or for worse, Lara was back on Mistletoe Island for Fliss. And Lara wouldn't let work dramas, their friends, or even history ruin it for her.

Ruth

'And do you remember the night we got kicked out of the pub?'

From the back of the car, Harry stuck his head between the head rests again, and Ruth twisted away to look out of the window, away from the detritus of Harry's snacks since they'd picked up the hire car at Glasgow Airport almost four hours ago. He wasn't talking to her anyway.

'*You* got thrown out,' Alec corrected him. 'The rest of us had to carry you home.'

'Think I'm still banned?' Harry asked, and Alec laughed.

'It's been ten years,' he pointed out. 'Even if the same people are running it, and even if they recognised you, they'd probably figure you'd have grown up by now.'

'Yeah.' Harry flopped back against the back seat. 'People do seem to keep making that mistake.'

Even in her present mood – which Alec would probably categorise as 'bloody grim' – she couldn't help but smile at that. Of all of Alec's friends, Harry was the eternal child – the one who hadn't got married, or settled down, or shown any signs of wanting to. Even Lara, the only other of them who was still single, had her career as an excuse to avoid the whole serious relationship/family thing. Harry seemed to enjoy remaining a permanent adolescent.

Normally, Ruth was happy to ignore or indulge Harry's childish antics and stories. But today . . .

She sighed, and gazed out of the side window again, watching the iron grey sea rolling out between them and the mainland as they left the harbour.

Harry wasn't the child she wanted in the back seat of her car.

As if sensing her thoughts, Alec took one hand off the steering wheel and patted her hand as it rested in her lap. Ruth tensed at the contact, and then immediately regretted it as he pulled away.

Part of her felt sorry for Alec. He was grieving too, she knew, and he was trying. He didn't know what to do to make her feel better, so he kept trying too hard, and in all the wrong ways. Logically, she knew this wasn't his fault.

But that logic didn't stop the rest of her wanting to push him away, to hurt him as badly as she was hurting.

Ruth bit the inside of her cheek to stop the rage – or grief; she'd stopped being able to tell the difference, really – rising up in her again.

It wasn't Alec's fault. It wasn't anybody's fault. The doctor had been very clear on that.

Some pregnancies just weren't viable. Weren't meant to be.

Except to her it hadn't been just a pregnancy. It had been her baby. Her child. Her daughter or her son. Her child whose heart had inexplicably stopped beating at nine weeks. Her child who she'd carried inside her for another month before the doctors scraped it out of her.

Her body that mourned and grieved with every aching and bruised cell.

Which was why she flinched every time Alec touched her. Why the rage came over her again whenever he told her he *understood*.

How could he?

She knew that more than anything, Alec wanted their lives to go back to normal. To the days when they'd both arrive home from work and eat dinner together with a glass of wine, and talk about the hours they'd spent apart. To weekends spent lazily at home, or out with friends, or exploring the city they both loved. Or even to those exciting early days of pregnancy, where her morning sickness was balanced out by imagining their future together as a family.

It wasn't that Ruth didn't want that too. She just knew that it wasn't possible.

She *wasn't* that person any more. Wasn't the woman who Alec had fallen in love with and married.

The pregnancy might not have been planned, and the idea of becoming a mother might have been terrifying. But having it ripped away from her . . .

That had changed her for ever.

'So, did Fliss say how many single women there'd be at this wedding, Ruth?' Harry asked, his head appearing at her shoulder again as Alec turned another corner on the winding coastal road.

Ruth switched her focus to Harry and his simple view of the world. What was it like to be Harry? Maybe she could channel some of his carefree nature to help her get through this terrible week.

Ruth thought back to when she'd first met him. Bless him, he'd immediately welcomed her into the group, treating her like the big sister he'd never had. The others had followed suit. They'd all been perfectly nice to her since she and Alec got together. Caitlin had even organised a 'getting to know you girls only dinner' when the engagement had been announced, in order to help Ruth feel more a part of the group of friends. It had been kind, if awkward.

But Ruth had always understood that these were *Alec's* friends, first and foremost. And she wasn't sure if she'd ever stop feeling like a hanger-on.

Harry was the only one who didn't make her feel that way. Which was why she humoured him.

'Funnily enough, the single woman guest list didn't come up in our conversations,' she said.

'Pity.' Harry sighed. 'Gotta love a wedding for pulling opportunities. All those fancy dresses and glasses of champagne. Not to mention the bridesmaids . . .'

Harry went on to mention many bridesmaids, as it happened, that he'd known and loved – briefly, of course, because Harry never loved anyone for longer than a week – and Ruth went back to staring out of the car window.

She'd heard a lot about Mistletoe Island over the years she'd known Alec. A decade later, the gang's post-graduation holiday there was practically a legend. Their stories had taken on almost mythic properties. Ruth assumed these stories had been embellished over the years. But the fact remained that while their fellow graduates had been sunning themselves in Ibiza or Thailand or Australia, Alec, Harry, Caitlin, Neal, Lara, Jon and Fliss had decamped to a remote Scottish island – and Holly Cottage.

The cottage, Ruth gathered, belonged to Fliss's family – who were also part-owners of the only hotel on the Island, the rather obviously named Mistletoe Hotel. Which explained, she supposed, why they were all being dragged back there in the chill of late December for Fliss's wedding.

When they'd first got the invitation, including a

handwritten note from Fliss suggesting they recreate their youth by spending the few days leading up to the wedding at Holly Cottage, just the gang, Ruth had actually wondered whether the invitation even included her. Alec didn't even know Ruth existed the last time the friends had all gone to Mistletoe Island. She'd arrived on the scene almost five years later, when a colleague had set her up on a Valentine's Day blind date. The date had been a disaster, but she'd met Alec at the bar and they'd got talking . . . The rest was history. Just not as ancient history as Alec's relationship with the others.

It meant a few extra days' leave, and delaying their usual trip to her own family until Christmas Eve, and at first Ruth had been frustrated that Alec's friends could ask for so much from them both, again. She'd agreed to the trip in the end, of course, because how could she say no to the excitement in Alec's eyes when he'd shared the details? But that had been before she fell pregnant. Before everything that happened next. And now . . . now Ruth couldn't think of anywhere in the world she'd less rather be than in a remote island cottage, forcing herself to laugh at impenetrable in-jokes shared by Alec and his friends.

Behind them, she heard Harry roll down a window, letting the freezing air blast through the car.

'Ah!' He took a huge lungful. When Ruth twisted round, she saw that he'd angled his head out of the car window, face lifted to the sky, eyes closed, as though he was soaking up all that he could. 'God,' he said, ducking his head back into the car, 'it's good to be back here again.' When he opened his eyes, he looked at Ruth, apparently surprised to see her glaring at him. 'What?'

'It's freezing!' She watched as he reluctantly wound the window back up, glass juddering against the rubber seal.

'Thank you.' She turned back round, her voice softening. 'What's so special about this island, anyway?' Okay, it was pretty enough to look at, from what she'd seen on the drive from the ferry. And she got that it had good memories for them all – but was that it? Because if so, she didn't imagine catching a chill was going to make her any more kindly disposed to the place.

'It's . . .' Alec shook his head, a faint smile on his lips.

'What?' Ruth pressed, turning to her husband. He looked . . . different, somehow. She blinked. That frown line, the one that had taken up permanent residence between his eyebrows since the scan that had revealed her silent miscarriage. It was gone. It was almost as though Mistletoe Island had blown it away, when she couldn't. Not that she'd really tried.

'It's magic,' Harry said, his voice softer than Ruth had ever heard before. 'Honestly, Ruth, you know me – I don't believe in any of that stuff. Not true love, or witches and fairies, or even homeopathy. But this place . . . it's like nowhere else on earth.'

Ruth turned back to Alec for a more rational description of the place, but he just glanced at her and smiled.

'You'll see,' he said. 'Harry's right. There's something special about this place. They . . . did you know? They call it the Healing Island.'

He glanced quickly at her, then returned his gaze to the road. The hope in his eyes was unbearable. Ruth looked away, pain shooting through her chest again.

Oh, Lord. Alec had brought her here to fix her. Oh sure, they had to be here because of the wedding. But the reason he'd insisted on her coming, when she'd tried to beg off, when she'd told him how tender and awful she still felt, how she'd rather just go straight to her parents' and see him there on Christmas Eve, even when she'd cried and told him she couldn't take it . . . He'd made her come because he wanted to heal her.

Because he didn't realise quite how broken she was.

'There it is!' Harry sat bolt upright, pointing between them towards an almost invisible path off the main road. 'Up ahead, Al. That's the turning.'

Alec laughed, more carefree that Ruth remembered hearing for months. 'How can you remember that?'

Harry shrugged. 'I remember all the important stuff.'

Sure enough, Alec swung the car down the turning, to follow a long, snaking driveway that finally emerged before a bright, white cottage. Ruth took in a front door with a half-rounded transom at the top, painted the same red as the berries of the holly bushes growing all around it. Above the doorway was a stone turret that merged with the thatched roof that was covered with a sprinkling of snow. Even Ruth had to admit, the place looked like something out of a fairy tale – one of those older ones, though. Not Disney. The sort that had people sleeping for hundreds of years.

Sleeping Beauty. Was Alec hoping this island would wake her up?

The car rolled to a stop. As Alec yanked up the handbrake, Ruth was already opening her door to step out, gazing up at Holly Cottage.

Suddenly, the air whipped around her, invigorating rather than freezing. It felt almost as though the wind was trying to blow away her pain and her rage, just as it had blown away the years for Alec and Harry.

As her hair danced around her face, she allowed herself a smile. Maybe the Healing Island could mend whatever was broken between her and her husband. That would be something, at least. Even if she knew that nothing could touch the depth of the pain inside her.

Fliss

Fliss had forgotten the complete mayhem of having seven people crammed into a cottage. Eight, if she included Ewan. Even if he wasn't staying at the cottage, Fliss hoped he'd be spending plenty of time there with them.

She wanted him to get to know her friends better. To grow to love them like she did. They were a huge part of her life; it felt wrong that he knew them so little.

But maybe it was only natural. He was her future, after all, and her friends, well. They were part of her past, of course, and her present. She hoped they'd still be there in the future – of course, she did – but they had their own lives to lead, as well. They weren't all living in each other's pockets the way they had at university, and while they still maintained regular contact – mostly through the message group Caitlin had set up for them – now they were more scattered. Across cities, even across the world in Jon's case. They couldn't get together at the drop of a hat any more. Plans needed to be made, often months in advance, to fit around everyone's busy work schedules and social calendars. They couldn't just pitch up to the student union in the summer and assume the others would follow soon enough, as soon as they heard their designated pub song, 'Living on a Prayer', reverberating out from the ancient jukebox and across the quad to float up through the open windows of their halls rooms. Even now, whenever Fliss heard Bon Jovi it made her mouth water for a pint.

But that was the good thing about getting married: it brought everyone back together again. Neal and Caitlin had arrived fast on the heels of Ruth, Alec and Harry. Fliss had been swept up in hugs and cries of delight. Ruth had given her a faint smile and hug, then retreated to stand by the kitchen door, as though she might flee the scene at any moment, watching from a distance. Neal had hugged her tight before Alec pushed him aside to do the same, and Harry had actually lifted her up and spun her around, holding her against his barrel chest and grinning up at her as she'd screamed in protest, kicking against his legs until he put her back down. Of course, she'd loved it. Then Caitlin had handed her a huge bunch of white roses, presented already in a vase ('In case you didn't have one') and kissed her cheek before moving past her to hug Alec.

In ten short minutes, the entrance hall was piled up with bags and suitcases. Voices echoed around the rooms as people called to each other, chatting animatedly, as they walked beneath the grandfather clock, its chimes ignored. After ten long years, the cottage was full of friends again.

Now, Fliss gazed across the living room to where Neal was catching up with Harry and Alec next to the large Christmas tree she and Ewan had dragged in from the market at the village and decorated the night before with the ornaments Fliss had found at the back of one of the cottage's many cupboards. She wondered if this might be the last time they were all together like this. Maybe they'd be together for christenings or big birthday parties or whatever, but not for nearly a whole week in the middle of nowhere with nothing to do but talk and reminisce and enjoy each other's company.

They'd all moved on. And somehow, this week – her special wedding week – suddenly felt like a farewell to what had been. To *who* they'd been. And while she was more than ready to move on from being Miss Fliss, the idea of them all moving on from the friendship that had been such a defining part of her adult life . . . that caught her in the chest, suddenly.

Fliss frowned. She was being overdramatic. It was just a holiday, really. There'd be others. Maybe not here, and maybe not just them, and maybe not all of them all at once. But they'd happen. This wasn't the end of anything.

In fact, it was supposed to be the *start*.

'The gang's all here!' Harry said, gleefully, throwing an arm over Fliss's shoulders and pulling her to him. He paused and looked around the room. 'Hold on. No, it's not. Where's Jon?'

'He couldn't make it,' Fliss replied vaguely, watching Lara flinch. She really needed to talk to Caitlin. Make sure she talked to Lara about Jon this week. Prepare her for the fact that, even if he wasn't here for the wedding, he might be around a lot more in the future. Caitlin was the one Jon had called, the one who had all the details. It was up to her.

Caitlin and Neal were still the mum and dad of the group, it seemed. Caitlin remained the person they all called first with big news or any problems. Their townhouse in London – funded by a generous inheritance from Caitlin's grandfather – was where they all gathered for birthdays and dinners, whenever they were all in town at the same time. Well, all except for Jon.

In fact, Fliss realised suddenly, this was the first time *she'd* played hostess since the last time they came to Holly Cottage. Had it really been that long? Oh, Lara had been round to Fliss and Ewan's tiny flat for girls' nights, and before that, when she and Lara had flat-shared, Harry and Alec had piled in for movie nights, Neal showing up with a bottle of wine and a takeaway from time to time. But never all of them together, all at once.

Fliss glanced at Neal, taking a suit carrier from his wife without meeting her eye. He hadn't seemed himself lately, although she couldn't quite put her finger on why. Maybe she'd have a chance to ask him later. As an attentive hostess.

Because this week, hostessing was Fliss's job. And after this week . . . she'd be Mrs Ewan Bennett. A new person altogether. Surely they couldn't keep treating her like the helpless baby then, right?

She was still making Caitlin tell Lara about Jon, though.

'Right, shall we get the cases up to the rooms? Lara, I assume you're sharing with Fliss this time?' Caitlin snapped straight into mum mode and started organising them, not even registering the way Lara winced at the words 'this time'. An automatic reminder that, last time, she and Jon had taken the front double bedroom with the great view out over the sea. 'Why don't you two take the back twin room? Neal, grab their bags for them.'

A muscle twitched in Neal's jaw at the order.

'Hang on,' Fliss interrupted. 'I, um, actually already sorted out the rooms.'

Caitlin's face tightened momentarily, then she eased into a smile. 'Of course. It's your cottage,' she said smoothly.

'Um, Lara – you and me are in the attic room.' Smaller than the master bedroom, but more magical, Fliss thought. Tucked away up in the eaves, they'd have somewhere to escape to from the madness if they needed it. Plus the boys wouldn't be able to stand up straight in there. 'Caitlin, I put you and Neal in the blue room at the front of the house, and Ruth and Alec next door in the green room. Harry, you have the smaller back twin, if that's okay?'

'A bed's a bed to me,' Harry said, with a shrug. 'Shall I take up the bags?' He looked to Caitlin for an answer to that one, and Fliss wasn't even surprised.

Caitlin nodded, and the boys started moving, lugging cases and bags up the narrow staircase. Lara grabbed her own bags and followed, while Ruth and Caitlin gravitated back towards the kitchen.

'It's a pretty good set-up here, considering,' Caitlin was saying to Ruth, as she started unloading the food she'd brought into the fridge and cupboards, ignoring all the supplies Fliss had already laid in, of course. 'There's two bathrooms, plus another loo by the back door. This kitchen diner, the lounge, and a small snug with a window seat I seem to remember . . .' She glanced up at Fliss, who nodded, trying very hard not to be annoyed that Caitlin was describing *her* cottage to *her* guests.

It's just her way. And it's not like we don't rely on her to organise everything most of the time. Why would this be any different?

Except the fact that it was Fliss's wedding, of course. And since The Mothers seemed to be doing a great job taking over that, she'd rather hoped that Holly Cottage and this holiday with her friends could be more her domain.

'Are there plans for tonight, Fliss, or can we hit the pub?' Harry asked, arriving in the kitchen doorway minus suitcases. 'I seem to remember a pool table . . .'

'I seem to recall thrashing you in straight games on it,' Alec added, as they both barrelled into the room.

They immediately launched into a heated debate about a ten-year-old pool game. Across the way, Fliss caught Neal's eye as Caitlin said, 'Boys! Save it for the rematch.'

Neal smiled, and mouthed, 'Just like old times.'

Fliss's smile slipped. Yes, it was. And she'd been looking

forward to exactly that for so long . . . but now it was here, she wasn't completely sure if that was a good thing any more.

'Actually, there's a Christmas market in the village this evening?' she said, immediately wishing it hadn't come out sounding like a question. 'I thought maybe we could stop off there first for a bit, on our way to The Griffin?'

'That sounds lovely,' Lara said, with a supportive smile.

Everyone else looked at Caitlin. Of course.

She nodded. 'Good idea. Why don't we all get ourselves sorted and walk down together?'

A walk sounded good. The village wasn't too far but the walk was long enough for Fliss to collect herself and shake off this anxious funk that had settled over her. And maybe for her to find out what was bothering Neal.

She just wanted this week to go well, that was all.

'Then to the pub! The Holy Grail of Holidays!' Harry jumped onto Alec's back, one arm raised like a lance as the pair of them charged forward, more Monty Python than King Arthur. Fliss laughed, despite herself.

Maybe she was worrying too much. Maybe everything would be fine.

As long as Harry didn't get barred from The Griffin again.

Lara

The village on Mistletoe Island must have had a real name, but if it did, Lara didn't know it. To them it was just The Village, like in that creepy sixties TV show her dad used to talk about. She'd remembered it as a sunny, bright place with pastel bunting flapping in the summer breeze and candy-coloured houses shining in the sunlight.

This evening, though, it was a winter wonderland.

It had already been late afternoon when Neal and Caitlin had arrived at the cottage, and by the time they'd settled in, got changed, and Caitlin had finished organising the kitchen supplies to her liking, the island was fully dark in a way that Lara never saw in the city.

But not the village. That was alight with festivity and a buzz of excitement that made Lara grin in anticipation.

At the crossroads in the centre of the village, the war memorial was obscured by the biggest Christmas tree Lara had ever seen. Tiny lights flickered on every branch, glinting off the silver stars that hung from it in a spiral, all the way to the largest, lit star on the top. Every shop front boasted fake snow, fairy lights and presents in the window. Outside the village hall, a small skating rink had been erected, and children were skating in careful circles around it while anxious parents looked on. Clearly, Fliss's report that Mistletoe Island was *the* place to visit for the winter holidays had been correct. Certainly they wouldn't have bothered to put all this up just for the local inhabitants.

Both roads through the village had been blocked off to cars, and log cabin stalls had sprung up along the pavements, selling decorations, festive fare, toys and other wonders. And under a suitably Narnia-esque lamppost on the corner, a small choir dressed in red were singing traditional carols.

Lara had never seen anything that screamed Christmas quite so wonderfully.

Linking her arm through Fliss's, she dragged her towards the stall selling mulled wine. 'This is perfect. I feel like I should have a fur muff to put my hands in.'

Fliss giggled. 'I keep expecting the Muppets to show up in Victorian costumes.'

'Ha!' Lara warbled a couple of lines of 'It Feels Like Christmas' from *The Muppet Christmas Carol*, Fliss's favourite festive movie, until Harry swept past and linked up her other arm.

'I thought we had a rule about you singing?' he said, reaching to take the next cup of mulled wine from the seller with his usual, charming smile. 'Only in desperate circumstances.'

'Like karaoke bars,' Fliss added.

Lara rolled her eyes. So she couldn't sing. She had other talents.

Fliss paid for three cups of wine, and handed one to Lara, who took a sip. Instantly, the warmth spread through her body, spicy and cosy at the same time. It tasted like Christmas and friendship and home and suddenly there was nowhere Lara would rather be than Mistletoe Island.

Or maybe that was the mulled wine talking.

'Where are the others?' Fliss asked Harry, while Lara communed with her drink.

'Caitlin dragged Neal off to look at some handmade tree decorations his mother might like, and Alec and Ruth are pretending they're not arguing over by the Christmas tree.'

'Great,' Fliss said, beaming, but the tension in that desperate smile told Lara that she hadn't missed the 'arguing' bit. Whatever was up, she hoped they sorted it out quickly. Ruth had seemed a bit down at the cottage, now she thought about it. Maybe some mulled wine would help.

Lara glanced around. Sure enough, Alec and Ruth were still locked in a tense-looking conversation by the tree, and Neal was clearly bored by tree decorations at one of the stalls. Harry might mess around, but when it came to his friends there really wasn't much he missed.

Which made her wonder why he was studying *her* so critically. What did he think he saw?

Or was he just remembering who was missing, and whose fault that was? Because she was. Every time she looked around her, she expected to see Jon − laughing with Alec or choosing decorations with Caitlin or stealing sips of her mulled wine . . .

Lara reached into her pocket to check her phone; an automatic impulse, born out from years of urgent calls and emails. Of course, it wasn't there. She shot a quick glare at Fliss, who wasn't looking, so that was okay.

Harry saw it though. In one swift movement, he downed his mulled wine, and slammed the cup back onto the stall counter. 'Come on. We're going ice-skating.'

Lara took a last sip of her wine and passed the cup to Fliss, as Harry grabbed her arm and led her towards the rink.

'You realise there are no other adults skating, right?' she asked, as the bemused attendant found them skates. 'Not without kids, anyway.'

Harry shrugged. 'So?'

When had she last even been ice skating? Lara couldn't remember. She knew she *had* − as a child, with her cousin

Carly, for definite. It had been on their first list – thirteen things to do before they turned thirteen. They'd managed ten of them, as far as Lara could recall. Not being able to persuade their parents to take them to Disneyland had really brought down their average.

For their Eighteen Things Before Eighteen list, they'd stuck to things they had control over, and both managed sixteen, which wasn't bad. And their Thirty Before Thirty list . . . well. Lara had nailed every single one of them before her thirtieth birthday, the year before.

Maybe she needed a new list. Forty before Forty or whatever.

1. Stop thinking about my ex-boyfriend
2. Rewatch The Muppet Christmas Carol

'Are you thinking about Jon?' Harry asked, as he swept her out onto the ice.

'The Muppets,' Lara told him, mostly truthfully.

'Of course.'

Arm in arm, they wobbled their way out onto the ice. As far as Lara knew, Harry wasn't exactly a seasoned skater, either, so they both clung tightly to each other. Which meant that when Lara's feet inevitably slid from under her, she took Harry down with her, both of them laughing too much to get back to their feet for long moments.

Eventually they found their rhythm, and managed a full circuit of the rink, narrowly avoiding taking out any of the small children skating around them. 'See?' Harry said, as he managed to turn and skate backwards with hardly a wobble. 'Just like riding a bike. I used to do this with my big sister every Saturday when she was about twelve . . .'

As he reminisced about his childhood, Lara looked out into the crowd in the village square as they moved, spotting Ruth's dark hair, plaited over her shoulder, under a bright red hat, next to Alec's solid form in his grey wool coat. Neither of them were smiling. She glanced away, before she started imagining that the man next to them, with the dark, curly hair, was Jon.

'So, is the ice taking your mind off whatever was making you look so thoughtful before?' Harry asked.

'Yes.' And then, because the question was still niggling at the back of her mind, 'Why would I be thinking about Jon, anyway?'

'Because we're here,' Harry said, with a shrug. 'We're back where it all started – or ended, in the case of you and Jon. But this is the place where we began our real, adult lives after university, and saying goodbye to Jon was a big part of that. Made sense that you'd be thinking about him, and you were looking pensive. That was all.'

'You really are far more perceptive than you let on, aren't you?'

Harry shuddered. 'Just don't tell the others. Life's much easier when people assume you have the emotional depth of a puddle.'

Lara patted his arm, and rested her head against his shoulder. 'I won't tell. And I might have been thinking about him a bit today.'

'Me too,' Harry admitted.

Biting her lip, Lara wondered how much she should confess to. 'I keep . . . I keep thinking I see him in the crowd. Or rather, I'm so sure he should be here, that I'm looking for him, even though I know he's not there.'

'Hmm. Sounds like a guilty conscience to me.' Harry nudged her with his shoulder, and she almost lost her balance. 'And you shouldn't feel guilty. You made a choice, ten years ago, and it was your choice to make.'

'I know that. It's just . . . this place.' It was so tied up in all their history, in breaking Jon's heart. She wondered if it would even be easier if he *had* come to the wedding. At least that way there wouldn't be this gaping hole in the group where he was meant to be.

They skated in silence for a few more minutes, before Harry said. 'You going to be okay with this week? Being here, I mean. And, well, the wedding?'

Weddings were a bit of an issue for her, Harry knew that. He'd seen her coping mechanisms at the last two they'd been to, when Jon *had* been there.

Thank goodness Harry was an eternal bachelor and, after Monday's Christmas Eve Eve nuptials, they'd be all out of weddings.

She sighed. 'Honestly? It's going to be weird. But I knew that when Fliss told me the wedding plans. And however weird it is, I still wouldn't miss being here for her this week. Even if she has stolen my phone.'

Harry snorted a laugh. 'She stole your phone?'

'So I can't do any work this week.'

'An excellent plan.' Grabbing her hands, he pulled her around so they made a circle with their arms. He spun them into a spiralling move, sending the kids around them scattering for safety.

'Hey!' one of the displaced kids yelled.

Lara kept hold of Harry's hands so he couldn't respond with a hand gesture. 'Oh, shut it, squirt!'

Lara laughed, tilting her head back as they spun, watching the stars start to merge in the black, black sky. As long as she kept hold of Harry, she wouldn't fall.

'This week is for fun and frivolity and friends,' Harry

said, as he spun her. 'And a wedding, I guess. Not worrying about a past you can't change.'

Harry was right. She needed to learn to relax, and let go.

Besides, her out-of-office message had Caitlin's phone number as a second emergency contact just in case. She wasn't completely out of touch.

Harry brought their spin to a stop, and wrapped an arm around her shoulders as he led her back to the assistant with the skates. 'That's more like it.'

'What?'

'You, smiling again.'

While she'd been star-gazing, Neal and Caitlin had come to watch them skate, Lara realised. Caitlin leant over the barriers, grinning, as Neal scanned the square behind them, until Fliss came and joined them. They all pointed towards the Griffin pub, lit up with multi-coloured lanterns and a bright, white-lit reindeer on the roof. Lara gave them a thumbs up, and they started walking away.

Harry tilted his head closer to Lara's again as she unfastened her skates. 'You and me, Lara, we're two of a kind. Well, you work a lot harder than I do, but apart from that . . . we both know there's too much to see in this world, too much to do, to worry about slowing down.'

'You mean settling down.' An uncomfortable feeling prickled down her spine, like Christmas tree needles scratching her skin.

'That too,' he said with an easy shrug. Harry was the consummate bachelor.

She'd never really thought of herself that way. She just . . . hadn't met anyone worth settling down for.

Not since Jon.

And she'd turned him down, too. Gone off to explore the planet without him. To complete her Thirty Before Thirty list out in the big, wide world.

But that didn't mean she didn't *ever* want to settle down. Did it?

Lara nudged Harry's shoulder with her own. 'We're only thirty-one. Plenty of time. You might meet your future wife at Fliss's wedding!'

Harry was still laughing as they caught up with the others, and headed for the pub.

Ruth

'Look, I'm just saying that maybe you'll have more fun without me there,' Ruth said wearily, rubbing a hand over her forehead. The carol singers were giving her a headache, and the overwhelming scent of oranges and cinnamon from the mulled wine stall wasn't helping. Plus she knew that the others would be watching them, wondering what she was doing to make Alec frown like that.

It wasn't that she didn't *want* to go to the pub and watch Alec and his friends get drunk and reminisce . . . well, actually, that was exactly it. It was bad enough when he and Harry got together in London, especially if Neal or the girls joined in. But ever since the moment they'd arrived at the cottage, Alec seemed to have regressed even further. Part of her worried that if he kept moving backwards, she wouldn't even recognise him as the man she married. He'd be *their* Alec again, not hers. 'I've got a headache, I'm tired, and I'm grumpy. Why would you want me there?'

She didn't mention how sore she was, her whole body still aching, weeks after the operation. Maybe it was just ghost pain, now. Not physical but mental, and never healing.

'Um, because you're my wife,' Alec answered, incredulity in his voice. 'Of course I want you there. And I don't want my friends thinking you don't *want* to be there, either.'

Of course. That was what it all came down to, as usual.

His friends. Heaven forbid that they think she'd be shunning them for one evening, even if she had crossed seas and hundreds of miles to spend the week with them for an event that actually only took one day.

She'd questioned that, too, when the invitation came. Why they had to spend almost a whole week on Mistletoe Island. But in the end, the answer was because Alec wanted to. And it was easier to let him have his way.

Just like she knew she'd end up doing with the pub tonight.

'I was hoping I could take a bath and get an early night,' Ruth sighed. 'Do you really think they all want me there?'

'Of course they do.' Alec rubbed her back, reassuringly, sounding on firmer ground now. She supposed he thought that it was still like the beginning, when she hadn't been sure if his friends liked her or wanted her around. When Fliss's Miss Fliss act was intimidating in its perfection, like she'd never had a bad mood in her life. When Caitlin had tried to mother her the way she did all the others, and failed, because Ruth already had a mother, thanks, not to mention the fact that Ruth was two years older than Caitlin anyway. When Neal had been even more of a mystery to her than he was now. When she'd been uncomfortable with Harry's instant adoption of her as another sister, and she'd barely known Lara from her fleeting visits, and never met Jon at all until her and Alec's wedding. Back when she was even more of an outsider than she felt now.

Now, she knew, it didn't matter. She had her own friends, her own family. She had her sisters to text when she wanted an opinion or a night out. She didn't need Alec's friends the way he did.

The question was no longer if they wanted her to join

them. The question now was whether she wanted to be there in the first place.

'Look, why don't you come for a bit.' He took hold of both her hands. 'We'll have a nice dinner and a few drinks, then I'll bring you home early if it looks like things are going to go on late. Okay?'

Alec, leaving the pub early? Well, that sounded like the most unlikely thing Ruth had heard all week. More unlikely, even, than an island that could heal people. But she let him have his little lie. He probably didn't even know that it was one.

'Fine. I'll come,' she said, and Alec smiled, the way she remembered him smiling before, his eyes glowing in the Christmas lights. She missed that smile. Maybe it was worth a night at the pub to see it again.

The Griffin was the sort of back-country pub Ruth had visited in many towns across Britain. Hidden away behind the main square with the Christmas market, it had garishly coloured lanterns strung across the windows, and a tacky reindeer on the roof. Why the others grew so excited at the sight of it – Harry actually gave an honest-to-God cheer – was beyond her. Even Alec beamed as they approached it, a little way behind the others.

Ruth sighed, and resigned herself to an evening of bad wine and conversations that always started, 'Remember the time when . . .?'

At least there would be wine. Two months ago, she wouldn't have even had that. Of course, she also wouldn't be feeling so bereft, so broken. But she couldn't think about that tonight. Not when she had to smile and pretend nothing was wrong for Alec's friends. They'd both agreed not to tell them of their loss: Alec because he didn't want to bring down the mood of the party, or ruin Fliss's special week. And she . . . she wasn't willing to share her grief, not yet. Telling others only made it more real.

She wished she could shake the feeling that it was a . . . a sign, of some sort. Ruth wasn't the superstitious type – she was a scientist, an academic, she believed in facts and evidence. But still the feeling nagged at her.

She'd been so unsure about the pregnancy when she took that first test. Not about the baby, exactly, but about herself. She didn't know how to be a mother. She hadn't ever had that maternal longing some of her friends had succumbed to, where their whole worlds became consumed by trying for a baby. What if she couldn't do it?

And what if, as absurd as Ruth knew it sounded, the miscarriage was a sign that she shouldn't? That she and Alec weren't meant to be parents?

Even if, as those initial misgivings had started to fade, she'd actually started to picture them as a real family at last. Until the scan.

Ruth hurried to catch up with the others. She couldn't think that way tonight. She had to smile and chat and be friendly. Like a low-grade Miss Fliss, or something. That was what Alec wanted from her. To pretend that nothing was wrong.

Harry took to the bar with the kitty they'd all contributed to back at the cottage, leaving the others to find a table to make base camp.

'Something near the pool table,' Harry called after them, and Lara obediently changed course.

Bringing up the rear, Ruth sighed. Drunken competitiveness. Her favourite.

She shook herself as she followed the others across the pub. No. She had to snap out of this. It was Christmas. This was a big week for Alec – and an even bigger one for Fliss. She wouldn't ruin it for everyone by being a misery for the next five days, even if she felt like one inside. Somehow she had to pull herself together and not just get through this week, but find a way to enjoy it too.

She just didn't know quite how, yet.

As the group hustled in through the main bar to the back room, Alec looked back at her and smiled. He was holding a hand out to her.

For a moment, the feeling she'd had when they arrived at Holly Cottage flooded back. The one that whispered to her that there was a chance everything might be okay. The feeling that her husband really was right there, and not a hundred miles away, which was how it felt most of the time.

Ruth gazed at him, at the hope in his eyes, and made a decision.

Whatever mythical magic Mistletoe Island had, imaginary or not, she was going to take every last bit of it and use it to start healing herself and her marriage. Somehow.

She was going to find her way – not back to the person she used to be, because she knew that woman was gone. But find her way forward. To who she wanted to be next.

Returning the smile, Ruth took her husband's hand and held it tight as he led her through the crowded pub, towards the table Lara had chosen. She didn't let go as they shuffled around the bench seat that ran behind the table. Alec's thigh pressed warm against hers, and he inclined his head to murmur in her ear.

'You feeling okay now?'

She nodded. 'Much better, thank you.'

'Good.' Alec pressed a soft kiss to her temple and then—

Turned away to talk to Neal, sitting on his left, about

whether the old guy sitting by the bar had moved in the last ten years, or was actually fossilised.

Neal laughed at some tame joke Alec made, and Ruth sighed. It looked like she was figuring this out on her own.

Lara

'I need to talk to you.' Caitlin swept in and plonked a bottle of white wine on the table between them before adding and then filling the two glasses she was carrying.

Lara took a sip of hers. She frowned as Caitlin followed suit. 'You're drinking?'

'It's Fliss's wedding week, Lara. Of *course* I'm drinking.' Caitlin made it sound like an automatic assumption, a sure thing. As if she hadn't been the designated driver for every get together for the last eighteen months.

'I mean, you're not . . .' Lara tried to find a more tactful way to put it and then gave up. '. . . trying at the moment?' Caitlin and Neal's sex life was officially none of her business now they were no longer doing it in the room next to hers in their shared student house, and she'd been able to stop sleeping with her headphones in to avoid listening. But Lara knew that they *had* been seriously trying for a family, because Caitlin had told her, after she'd confronted her during the second designated driver incident. (Lara, not being designated, had also not been sober, so had lost a lot of her restraint after the third glass of wine.)

Caitlin gave what, to anyone who hadn't known her for over a decade, might look like a casual shrug. 'We're taking a break from it for the time being. You know, it gets stressful, all that pressure to perform. Maybe we'll talk about it again after Christmas.'

'Right.' Lara frowned, not entirely convinced. From the moment that Caitlin and Neal had got together, they'd run their relationship on the officially agreed ideal timeline. They'd met at university, got engaged a year after graduation, when they both had good, steady jobs. They'd got married the following summer, bought a house, done it up, moved forward in their careers. And then, when they were all settled, they'd started talking about trying for a family.

Lara had endured six months of Caitlin checking the ingredients of every restaurant meal for raw eggs or liver, of her drinking only water and giving detailed updates on her cycle, and had been as supportive as she could. But it hadn't happened.

Then Neal had got his promotion, just after Alec and Ruth's wedding, and suddenly everything had been back on hold. He'd started working all hours, and Caitlin had started drinking wine again when she came round to Lara and Fliss's flat for movie night. Lara had been sorry for her friend, but Caitlin had seemed more relaxed than she had in months.

By the time Neal's work had calmed down and he'd wanted to try again, it had been Caitlin's turn for a promotion and too much work. Suddenly, it was Neal showing up on her doorstep on a Friday night whenever she was in town, with a bottle of red and a bag of popcorn. The movies had changed – Neal liked rom-coms a lot more than his wife – but otherwise, it had still felt like old times. By that point, Fliss was always too busy with Ewan to join them, but sometimes Alec made it, or Harry.

Twelve months ago, Caitlin had decided the time was right again. Work had calmed down, they were more financially secure than ever before, and heading into their thirties.

But still nothing.

Lara had stopped asking, in a vague attempt to not make

things worse. But it hadn't escaped her notice that Caitlin's face looked a little more pinched every time Fliss brought it up on their occasional girls' nights, mostly by asking if the bridesmaids' dresses might need to be altered again.

Lara knew better than to push, though. While the three of them were still close, Lara's friendship with Caitlin – and Fliss's for that matter – had never really recovered from Lara driving Jon away by turning down his proposal. Lara had broken up the group, and she knew Caitlin couldn't easily forgive her for that – or forgive Fliss for taking Lara's side. They'd found their way back to friendship easily enough after the initial few months of awkwardness, but it would never be the same as it had been at uni.

If Caitlin and Neal were having problems – fertility-related or otherwise – she wasn't going to tell Lara about it. Maybe she'd talk to Alec, though. They'd always been close. She should suggest it to him . . .

'Anyway,' Caitlin said, brushing the conversation away with a sweep of her hand. 'My sex life isn't what I need to talk to you about.'

'Well, if you want to talk about mine you're going to be disappointed,' Lara joked. Caitlin didn't laugh. She didn't even smile. 'Because I don't have one?' Lara clarified, uncertainly.

Caitlin put down her wine glass and shifted closer. Then she placed her hand over Lara's free one.

With her free hand, Lara took another gulp of wine. It looked like she was going to need it.

'Am I dying and my doctor forgot to tell me?' she asked, when Caitlin still didn't say anything.

'It's about Jon.'

Oh. Well, in that case, everything made sense. This was clearly a difficult conversation, and Caitlin was always in charge of having those with people. Breaking bad news, staging interventions. Being the grown-up.

'Is it about how he's not coming to the wedding because of me? Because I'd guessed that much already.'

Caitlin pulled back with a frown. 'Of course not. It's Fliss's wedding, if he could be here he would. Why would you think he wouldn't?'

Because last time we were all together on this island I refused to marry him and broke his heart and we've barely spoken since?

And not just her and Jon. None of the others had mentioned him *to* her, either. To start with, it had been so bloody awkward. They'd been the first and only ones of the group to split up – and in such dramatic style – none of the others really knew what to say, Lara supposed. But then when Jon moved away, got married to a gorgeous American without any of them being there, made excuses not to come back except for the most important events . . . none of them ever looked at Lara when they talked about it. Because they all knew it was her fault.

If Caitlin was talking about him now, it had to be important.

'And it's not like he missed *my* wedding, or Alec's is it?' Caitlin went on, defending Jon's record as a good friend. And she was right, Lara had to admit.

If it wasn't for their friends getting married, she and Jon might have managed to avoid each other for the rest of time. But they insisted on happy ever afters. And every time it was awkward as all hell – especially Alec and Ruth's, with Jon's wife Phoebe making pleasant conversation with everyone, and clearly not quite being able to make sense of the strange undercurrents within the group. Still, Lara and Jon had at least managed a conversation at that wedding, three years ago. Well, they'd both said 'Hi' then ignored each other for the rest of the evening, but that was almost the same thing, right? It was definitely more than they'd achieved at Caitlin and Neal's, when everything was still too raw and awful and Caitlin had sat them at tables at opposite ends of the room, and Lara had got shamefully drunk and seduced an usher while Jon did tequila shots with Alec at the bar.

What was it about weddings that brought out the worst behaviour in people?

She glanced across the room at where Harry had been playing pool, hoping he might come and save her from whatever it was Caitlin had to tell her, but he was chatting up some pretty redhead in a very skimpy sequinned dress that made her legs look endless. Probably one of the guests from the hotel, here for the wedding. Lara smiled. At least if Harry was right and she *was* like him, she should get to have some fun while staying single.

Caitlin cleared her throat to attract Lara's attention.

Lara took another slug of wine for courage.

'So? What's the problem with Jon?' Something Caitlin had asked *her* ten years ago, after she turned down his proposal. As if she were supposed to say 'yes please' to getting married at twenty-one and having the rest of her life all planned out for her, the same way Caitlin had planned hers and Neal's.

'He and Phoebe got divorced this autumn. And he's moving back to the UK in the new year. That's why he can't make the wedding – he's boxing up his whole life over there right now ready to move home. So he's not here this week . . . but he's going to be around a lot more again after this.' Caitlin watched Lara's face, then pushed the bottle of wine across the table.

Without saying a word, Lara scooped it up, and filled her

glass until the surface of the wine trembled at the brim.

Fuck. Or, as Harry would say, Fuckity fuck fuck, fuck fuck.

Suddenly, this week felt like the calm before the storm.

Fliss

The problem with being the hostess, Fliss realised too late, was that she felt a responsibility to make sure that everyone was enjoying themselves. Actually, she pretty much always felt that responsibility – to make sure her friends were happy and had what they needed from her. Being in charge only made these worries even worse.

On the surface, the evening didn't seem to be going too badly. But then she realised that Harry and Alec were doing shots at the bar before returning to the pool table, and Ruth was looking tired and unhappy. Caitlin and Lara were steadily working their way through a second bottle of white wine, which Fliss took to mean that Lara now knew about Jon's divorce. And Neal . . . where *was* Neal?

Fliss scanned the bar and found him, eventually, leaning against the wall by the fireplace, nominally watching the pool game. He smiled, slowly, as she caught his eye, then looked casually towards the other room, where some locals were belting out The Darkness's single Christmas hit on the karaoke. He smiled again, and she knew exactly what he was planning. The two of them had always been the most in tune that way.

Before she could stop Neal, the pub door swung open and Ewan appeared, flanked by his brother and best man, Ryan, and his sister Betsy. Relief flooded through her at the sight of them. Which was strange because, before then, the idea of her two worlds colliding had been a little unsettling, to say the least.

Ewan had met her friends before, of course, but he'd always been the newcomer, the outsider. Whether they meant to or not, the others had always given Fliss the impression that they considered Ewan a transient addition, probably because all the others before him had been. Fliss wasn't unaware of the fact that every other guy she'd introduced to her friends, or even raved about after a first date, hadn't lasted longer than six months. She supposed it wasn't surprising that the others assumed Ewan would go the same way.

But Fliss had known different. Not at first, of course. At first, she'd been as cautious as anyone – so cautious, in fact, that she and Ewan had hung out as friends only for weeks before she'd even kissed him. But as their relationship had progressed, that small, sure part inside of her had only grown until, by the time he proposed, it seemed inevitable that they would spend the rest of their lives together.

Now he was almost her husband, her friends would have to get used to the idea that he wasn't going anywhere. Even though they weren't always good at outsiders. There were too many years of inside jokes and memories for anyone to just slot into the group. Ruth and Alec had been married for years, and Fliss knew that Ruth still felt it sometimes. Fliss loved her friends, but she knew that Ewan was right when he pointed out that when they were all together they slipped into old habits, finishing each other's sentences, and talking about events from ten years ago. It wasn't exactly welcoming, she supposed.

At least Ewan's family seemed to be on their side. His mother, despite the wedding takeover, had been certain that Fliss was the one for 'her boy' from the first time they'd met. 'A nice, proper, young lady, that's what Ewan needs,' she'd said, approvingly, as Fliss had handed over a bunch of tulips and homemade dessert for that first Sunday lunch at the Bennett house. It had made Fliss feel like she was in a 1950s movie, but if it meant Ewan's mum liked her, she'd go with it.

His dad, Sandy, had been won over by the pudding. And Ryan and Betsy, Ewan's siblings, were as easy-going as he was – a trait all three must have inherited from their father, Fliss had decided. They'd welcomed her instantly, as had Betsy's son, Morgan, when she'd revealed an unexpected knack for video games, courtesy of years of living with Harry and Alec. He hadn't even objected to dressing up in a suit to play page boy for the wedding.

So even though it was strange to have both her worlds in one place, Fliss was glad to see her new family, all the same. The tension that had been building in her shoulders started to release as Ewan smiled at her and made his way across the room, only delayed slightly by welcomes and congratulations from the others as he passed.

'How's it going?' he murmured in her ear as he hugged her hello, smelling of fresh cold air and home. He pressed a kiss to the corner of her mouth, and pulled away smiling.

'Fine, so far. How are things at the hotel?'

Ewan pulled a face. 'A message from The Mothers – they've arranged a final dress-fitting for you and Lara and Caitlin on Sunday, up at the hotel.'

'But the dresses have already been . . . Never mind. I'm sure that will be fine.' Except that Sunday she'd planned to finish assembling the cake, and then had hoped to do some relaxing in the hotel spa with the girls. Because her dress and the bridesmaid dresses had all been fitted and adjusted in London weeks ago.

'I think they wanted to make absolutely sure you were

happy with the dresses,' Ewan said, although she doubted he knew what went on at a dress-fitting. She was lucky she was getting him into a suit at all, really – he was normally far happier in shorts, even in December.

'That was a really kind thought,' Fliss said, charitably stamping down the part of her that whispered that The Mothers didn't trust her to have done it right in the first place.

Betsy laughed. 'Fliss, you are far too nice to be marrying my brother.' Ryan grinned and nodded in agreement.

Ewan covered Fliss's ears. 'Shh! Don't tell her. She might change her mind. Now.' He moved his hands to circle Fliss's waist. 'Did anyone order food yet?'

Fliss shook her head. 'I think we're past dinner at this point. We ordered chips and nachos and stuff to soak up the alcohol, but that's about it.' Ewan looked disappointed, and Fliss laughed. 'You're starving, aren't you?'

Ewan was always starving. Neal had joked once that Ewan was only with her for the easy access to cake trimmings. With any other boyfriend, that would have hit home, made her anxious. With Ewan . . . she'd just gone and fetched him another piece of cake and ignored Neal. He was probably simply jealous of Ewan's fast metabolism, anyway.

'Little bit,' Ewan admitted. 'Why don't I go order some more sharing platters or something. Maybe a burger . . .'

She rolled her eyes at his hopeful tone, but nodded. Ewan headed off back to the bar, leaving Fliss to introduce everyone to her brother- and sister-in-law-to be – marvelling again at how she'd gain a whole new family on Monday. Enough alcohol had been consumed that the gang welcomed them with excessive warmth – well, Harry did, anyway.

Wrapping Ryan up in a giant hug he boomed, 'Welcome to the family, young Ryan!' merrily ignoring the fact that

Ewan's brother was only a few years younger than them. Then he turned to Betsy with his most charming grin and held out a hand for her to shake, in a very respectable, un-Harry-like way. 'And *you* are even more welcome.' Fliss suspected he wasn't having entirely family-appropriate thoughts at that point.

Regardless, soon Ryan was challenging Alec to pool, and Betsy was chatting with Ruth and Harry by the table. Fliss stood back and watched them. Maybe this two worlds colliding thing wasn't so scary after all.

'I've ordered three platters of mixed starters,' Ewan said, handing her a glass of wine as he returned from the bar. 'Plus a burger for me. I figure that should keep us going. Now, I want in on the pool tournament.' He stripped off his coat, and headed over to the pool table.

'Thank you,' Fliss called after him, and he raised a hand in acknowledgement.

Fliss smiled to herself. She'd been silly to worry. Everything was fine. Ewan was here – what could possibly go wrong?

'And next up we have Fliss and Neal singing "Baby It's Cold Outside"!' The karaoke announcer's voice rang out through the pub, and Fliss closed her eyes in denial.

Neal. Neal and his weird love of karaoke. That was what could go wrong.

Lara

It didn't take much to persuade the others to abandon the pool table and take over the small side bar where the karaoke machine was set up. Even Ewan and his brother and sister, who'd all been playing catch up, seemed to have caught up fast enough to think karaoke was a *great* idea. A sure sign of drunkenness. Lara snagged the wine bottle and carried it through, her mind still on Caitlin's news.

Jon was divorced.

She'd spent ten years proving to herself and others that she'd made the right decision in not marrying Jon. She'd travelled the world alone and with friends, built up a career that rarely kept her in the same place for more than a few days, said yes to any opportunity that came her way without having to consult anyone else – all things that weren't exactly conducive to settling down and committing to one person, one place, one future. But the biggest part of that proof had always been that Jon had fallen in love with and married someone else. She *wasn't* the only person for him, and that was a good thing.

Except, apparently, Phoebe wasn't the only person for him either.

And now Jon was coming home. For good.

Lara had no idea how exactly to react to that.

In fairness, she'd never been given the opportunity to make being around Jon seem normal again. To be friends, and to be with their friends, without their past relationship stretched taut between them.

When she'd told him she couldn't marry him, Jon had fled across oceans in order to stay out of her life. They'd never had that chance to see if they could just be friends again.

Until now.

If Jon was moving back to the country, they'd have to see each other. It was inevitable. He wasn't exactly likely to pitch up on her doorstep for Friday movie night, but there'd be other group events. Probably christenings. Birthdays. Definitely New Year. That was the one holiday they all *always* spent together, if they could. Any way she looked at it, they were going to be seeing a lot more of each other than they had over the past ten years.

'Damn.'

'What?' Caitlin automatically topped her glass up with more wine.

'I realised that if Jon is moving back to Britain, I'm going to have to get used to seeing him again. At parties and nights out and stuff.'

'It took you until now to realise that?' Caitlin asked. 'I was, like, twenty minutes at the stupid bar. How much wine have you had?'

'Not enough to get my head around it.' Lara slumped back against the slightly sticky wall of the pub. 'We're going to have to be *friends*. We've never been friends.'

Caitlin frowned. 'Yes, you have. What about before you started dating?'

'We were flirtation buddies.' There'd always been an edge of something – attraction, lust, anticipation – between them. By the time they'd fallen into bed together it had been as inevitable as winter.

But not this time. This time, they'd be Just Good Friends.

And before that could possibly happen, she needed more information.

'What happened? Did he tell you?' She wished she didn't have this morbid curiosity with the failure of Jon's marriage, but as the woman who'd had the chance to marry him and given it up, she needed to know the ins and outs. Maybe because she was wondering if the same thing would have happened with them. If, perhaps, Jon just wasn't cut out for marriage.

Maybe this could be the final vindication of her decision. Proving to everyone that she'd been right, after all.

But Caitlin shrugged. 'As far as I know, they grew apart. It all seems fairly amicable. Sometimes these things just don't work out, I suppose.'

Lara nodded absently, lost in her own thoughts. Until she realised that Caitlin was looking up at the makeshift karaoke stage as she spoke. The stage where Neal and Fliss were performing some Christmas classics. It was funny, really. Karaoke was the only time that Fliss really seemed to let go, to stop worrying about what other people thought and just enjoy herself. Of course, even then, her sweet enthusiasm and bubbly excitement was infectious. Lara knew there was a pretty good chance they'd all be up on the stage by the end of the evening. Probably belting out Bon Jovi, in addition to the festive favourites.

Neal seemed to be enjoying himself too. He always liked a bit of karaoke — much to his wife's embarrassment, Lara knew. Except Caitlin didn't seem embarrassed tonight, even when Neal missed the note or got the words wrong, leaning in to Fliss and acting his part with more gusto than was strictly necessary.

In fact, Caitlin had turned her back on the stage, and didn't seem to care much what her husband was up to at all.

Suddenly a whole new host of worries caught up with Lara.

'How are things with you and Neal?' Not subtle, but Lara found that being subtle rarely got her very far.

'Same as always.' Caitlin flashed her a smile that didn't quite reach her eyes. 'We're both busy, but fine. What about you? How's work?'

Of course she asked about work. Because there wasn't anything else in Lara's life to talk about at the moment.

God, that was a depressing thought. It couldn't be true, could it? Normally she chatted about her travels – the latest adventure she'd tacked onto a work trip, or solo break she'd taken somewhere other people had never heard of. Or she talked about celebrities she'd met at events she'd worked on, or provided glimpses of behind-the-scenes glamour at award shows or parties.

But lately work had been too busy to indulge her love of travel. And she'd been spending more time in meetings about budgets and scheduling than being on the ground at events.

When had work become all she ever did? And what could she do about it?

Take the job in Manchester, maybe. Make a fresh start. A new life.

But that was a thought for another time. Right now, she wanted to find out what was going on with Caitlin. When was the last time they'd sat down together and had a really good catch-up? Lara couldn't even remember. Which meant it had been too long.

Maybe Caitlin needed Lara to give up some of her secrets first.

'Work is . . . interesting.'

Caitlin laughed. 'I should hope so. Otherwise, the amount of time you spend at the office or travelling for work is downright concerning.'

It was a long-standing argument between all of them, but especially with Caitlin. As if Lara didn't know that her friend gave just as much of herself and her time to her own career, really. It was more apparent with Lara because her hours weren't set by office timetables, and it was always more obvious when she was out of the country for movie nights and birthday dinners.

'I love my job,' she reminded Caitlin. And maybe herself.

Because it was always like this. When she was back with her friends, it was hard not to envy their lives, however much she normally loved hers. Their relationships, having someone to come home to at the end of the day, or a phone call when they were working away that wasn't just asking about where a certain spreadsheet had been saved, or when the AV was being set up. Their homes, too – houses and flats that looked lived in and cosy and welcoming, rather than her half-abandoned mess of a flat that even the cleaner had given up visiting.

It hadn't been so bad when Fliss was single, those first years when they were both living in London together. They'd flat-shared for ages, and knowing that Fliss was there when she wasn't somehow made the place feel much more like home. Friends had popped round for movie night, and they'd even managed to throw a sort of birthday party there once, before Caitlin and Neal took over all the group entertaining duties.

Weekends when Lara hadn't had to work, they'd gone out. For brunch or to the movies or just for drinks and dancing. Evenings when Lara had come home late from the office, they'd sprawled out on the giant couch that filled almost the entire living room and watched high-school comedies from the nineties together while eating party food canapés for dinner. It had been cramped but comfortable – and companionable, too.

But then Fliss had met Ewan and moved in with him a year later, after they got engaged. Movie nights had tailed off as she spent more and more time working, and now the flat felt empty, all the time. Lara had thought about moving, but since that involved being in London and not working long enough to actually find somewhere new and then move into it, she'd never quite got around to it. So Fliss's bedroom still sat empty, and Lara still hadn't thrown out the bottle of Angostura Bitters at the back of the cupboard that Fliss insisted was essential for cocktails they never drank.

'So, what's making your job so interesting at the moment?' Caitlin asked, breaking through Lara's thoughts.

Lara bit her lip. She *wanted* to talk about the two paths ahead of her – wanted help figuring out which way to jump. Stay where she was and wait for her boss to realise she was worth more running things on the ground than in meetings he didn't want to go to, or jump ship to Manchester for new opportunities, new challenges . . . just *new* life. Maybe even one that might have space for romance in it.

Except that would mean admitting to Caitlin that she was considering moving out of London, away from the group. Which would make getting together even harder.

Really, Jon had moved across an ocean. Surely she could move outside the M25 without it being a big deal?

She glanced sideways at Caitlin, who was pouring more wine and checking her watch.

Maybe not.

Caitlin saw keeping the group together as her

responsibility. Lara had already fractured it once, when she turned Jon down, and Caitlin had only just forgiven her for it. If she moved away now, when Jon was moving home . . . would that be the beginning of the end? Would he take her place and she'd be exiled for the *next* ten years?

No. Alec had already admitted that he and Ruth were talking about moving out of the city. And Fliss and Ewan's rented flat was so tiny, and Lara knew they couldn't afford to buy in London. Moving further apart didn't have to be the end of their friendships, and it definitely wasn't the only reason she was considering not taking the job. But she had a feeling that Caitlin might not see it like that. Especially here and now, when they were all back on Mistletoe Island together.

So she lied. 'Just the usual. But you know, an interesting life has to be better than a boring one, right?'

Then, as Neal and Fliss burst into a rousing final chorus of 'Last Christmas', the door to the pub opened again, just visible from where Lara sat at the edge of the small side bar. She looked up, idly curious, as watched as the open door let in a small flurry of snowflakes, an icy blast of wind – and Jon.

His dark curls had blown every which way, and he raised a hand to try and smooth them down, a gesture so familiar that Lara's heart contracted at the sight, then expanded again until her chest felt too tight.

'He's not meant to be here,' she whispered.

'What?' Caitlin looked up. 'Who? Oh! Jon!'

Jon turned at the sound of his name, his gaze landing on them in seconds, long before Lara had managed to catch her breath. He smiled, tightly, one eyebrow raised, and for a long moment they just *looked* at each other.

Ten years. Ten years and suddenly it was as if nothing

had changed since the day she'd told him she couldn't marry him.

She'd seen him three or four times since then, of course, but always in a crowd, and never when she'd been able to just *look* without anyone making a thing about it, or his wife noticing.

And now she could, it was strangely hard to stop.

He shucked off his dark wool coat, and held it over one arm, revealing jeans and a jumper over a shirt underneath. Smarter than she remembered him, but ten years would do that. He wasn't close enough for her to tell yet if there were lines around his eyes, or even a few grey hairs smattered through those dark curls. But even from here she could tell he looked tired. Maybe just 'international flight' tired, but Lara sensed it was something more. 'Long year' tired, perhaps.

It hit her in the chest how badly she wanted to know if he was okay. He'd been through a divorce; he had to be hurting, right? Jon felt things, deeply – deeper than most people suspected. But she knew, because she knew him, and so she worried.

Except – she knew Jon ten years ago. Who he was now, deep down inside in that secret place he'd never share with anyone he didn't love, was none of her business.

She looked away.

Caitlin reached past her for the wine bottle and topped up both their glasses. Lara raised her eyebrows at the gesture.

'You really think *more* wine is going to help right now?' Normally, as much as Caitlin liked a drink, she was the one who made sure they all stopped before things got messy. Not tonight, though.

'I figure it can hardly make things worse at this point,' Caitlin replied, with a shrug.

74

From the corner of her eye, Lara saw Jon moving towards the stage first, and Fliss and Neal, as the music stopped.

'Good job you like an interesting life,' Caitlin murmured.

Lara reached for her wine and didn't answer.

Fliss

'Jon!' Fliss leapt the foot or so down from the tiny stage and threw her arms around him, holding him close, the last missing piece of their puzzle. 'I thought you couldn't make it!'

'So did I,' Jon admitted. 'But I managed to tie a few things up sooner than expected and . . . to be honest, I just couldn't bring myself to miss your big day. I tried the cottage first, but when it was empty I figured—'

'Of course we were in the pub!' Harry finished for him, swooping in for a drunken, manly hug. 'Good to see you, mate. I'll go get you a drink.'

'You could have called and told us you were coming,' Fliss said, as Harry headed to the bar. 'I haven't made up a bed for you or anything.'

Jon gave her a crooked smile. 'Figured it would be more fun this way.'

Neal stepped up next for his own welcome hug. 'Good to have you here. It wouldn't have been the same without you.' Then he shoved a clipboard towards him. 'Now, as our surprise special guest, you get to choose the next song. We'll get everyone up – just like old times.'

Jon's smile faded a little at the reminder of old times, Fliss noticed, but he took the clipboard willingly enough. Then his lips twitched into a grin as he held the board out of Fliss's view and pointed to a song. 'That one.'

Neal beamed. 'Perfect! Then we can do Bon Jovi after

that. I'll get it cued up, you can persuade the others to get up onstage.' He disappeared to talk to the guy running the karaoke machine, while Jon turned to greet Alec and Ruth, who had come up behind him. Then, Fliss said, 'And Jon, this is Ewan.'

They'd never had a chance to meet before, and Fliss's heart felt fuller now that they would, now that Jon was here and their group was complete again.

'The lucky groom!' Jon held out a hand, and Ewan took it. 'Fliss tells me wonderful things about you. Congratulations in advance for Monday. I'm sure you'll both be very happy.'

How hard was it for him to say that, Fliss wondered, coming straight off his own divorce? To be here at all for the wedding, even? There was no hint of it in his voice, if it was.

She looked up, microphone dangling from her hand, and saw Caitlin approaching, Lara hanging back behind her. Caitlin and Jon embraced, exchanging whispers she couldn't make out. Probably berating him for looking too thin, or not calling often enough. Then Lara stepped forward and, tentatively, she and Jon embraced.

Fliss could still see Christmas lights twinkling between the two of them, as if they were ensuring they touched as little as possible, but it was progress. She let out a long breath. Maybe they really had grown up and moved on. Maybe she didn't need to worry about them after all.

'Right, all sorted,' Neal said, returning with the clipboard of song choices. He glanced over the top at the newcomer. 'How's Jon doing?'

'I don't know,' Fliss said, still watching Jon. 'I know Caitlin said that the divorce was a mutual decision, but he looks kind of . . . lost, don't you think?'

Neal gave her a sideways look. 'I meant how's he doing getting everyone up onstage?'

'Neal! Come on. He's your friend. How do you think he's doing?'

Neal shrugged. 'Honestly? Too early to tell. I know he's had a lot of long phone calls with Caitlin – she makes him call every week on a Sunday – but that could be her quizzing him. Or more likely working out the logistics for finding a flat in London, or whatever, although I think she wants him to stay with us to start with. But you know Jon. He likes to think about things before he talks.'

'Unless he's drunk.' Then, it suddenly became hard to shut the usually taciturn Jon up. Fliss vividly remembered one terrible morning when the rest of them had been nursing horrific hangovers, and Jon rolled in still drunk – and talked to them all, at length, about black holes. For hours. It was a risk, but . . . 'Maybe you should get him drunk and ask him how he's doing.'

'You've uncovered my hastily constructed but nefarious master plan,' Neal said smirking.

'Good,' Fliss said. Jon was herding the others towards the stage. His presence was a rare enough treat that he'd had no problem persuading everyone. They all wanted to please him, Fliss knew, to make sure he stayed, this time. He'd been away too long already. Ruth remained in her seat, but that was hardly a surprise. Ewan was laughing and shaking his head too, even though Betsy and Ryan were trying to persuade him to go up.

'And you?' Neal asked. 'How are you coping with all this wedding stuff?'

She looked at him, surprised. 'Fine. I mean, it's the happiest day of my life, right?'

'Apparently.' Neal's tone was too dry, and he was looking

at Caitlin as he spoke. Fliss's worries from earlier on came rocketing back, but before she had a chance to ask Neal how things were with him and Caitlin, the others were all pushing onto the stage with them – even though they barely all fit in the tiny space – ready to sing. Later, she promised herself. She'd find out what was going on with Neal later.

There was a buzz on the stage. When had the seven of them last been together like this – having fun and kicking back? Probably the last time they were on Mistletoe Island. It felt good, Fliss thought. It felt right. Whatever else was going on in their lives, they belonged together. Had done, ever since they'd met, that first Freshers' Week at university, when Harry had bowled into the shared kitchen in halls with a mini-keg tied to his back and comically long bendy straws for everyone, declaring that everyone who drank from his keg of friendship would be a mate for life. And they were.

As long as they were all together, everything would be okay.

'Before we sing, a toast!' Harry raised his pint glass, nearly tipping half of it over Lara. 'To us!'

'To Mistletoe Island!' Alec shouted.

'To Fliss and Ewan,' Jon, obviously more sober than the rest of them, put in, and Fliss shot him a grateful look.

'To marriage,' Neal added, raising his own glass. But there was something hard behind his voice as he stared at Caitlin.

Fliss grasped desperately for a toast of her own, something to lighten the mood again. But then the music kicked in – 'Fairytale of New York' – and everyone groaned, the toasts forgotten.

'Really, Jon? Still?' Caitlin gave him a despairing look.

'And to think I actually missed you,' Harry grumbled.

Jon shrugged, doing his best not to look offended. 'It's my favourite.'

'We know,' the others chorused, probably all remembering the year Jon had tried to learn the song on the tinny keyboard he had in his room. Fliss knew she'd never be able to hear the lyrics without remembering that Christmas.

Their first year in the shared house. They'd only been living together, outside of halls, for three months, and they were still learning each other's quirks and idiosyncrasies. Like how Harry never shut the bathroom door. Or how Caitlin bleached the tea stains out of mugs. Or how Lara left stacks of travel books with Post-it notes sticking out all over the lounge. Or Fliss's tendency for midnight baking. Or Jon's attempts at learning the piano.

They'd all cooked a full Christmas dinner together the weekend before term finished. A pre-Christmas, just for them. Full turkey, stuffing, veg and pigs in blankets. Alec had found boxes of crackers on sale at the pound shop in town, and bought enough for all of them to pull at least four, so they'd had them with breakfast the next day, too. They'd sat around in cracker hats, not caring that the stuffing was black or that the bacon had fallen off the pigs in blankets. After dinner, they'd all watched *The Muppet Christmas Carol* together, crammed onto the sofas in the tiny living room. And then Neal had insisted on karaoke, so Jon had brought out his keyboard and made them all sing along to 'Fairytale of New York' until he could play it all the way through. Which, given how much wine had been consumed with dinner, took far longer than any of them had liked.

Harry had sworn he'd never listen to that song again.

But now Jon was back, every one of them dutifully began to sing as the words appeared on the screen – duetting, with the girls on one side, the boys on the other. And for a moment, it was as if no time had passed at all, and they were all back at uni together.

The boys belted out the first line, and the words caught in Fliss's head.

Christmas Eve, babe.

By this Christmas Eve, she'd be married. She'd be a whole new person.

She looked out into the crowd and saw Ewan watching her from the bar, Betsy and Ryan beside him. He'd never seen her sing karaoke before tonight, she realised. It was something she only ever did with Neal, when they were all out together.

But he was grinning, as Betsy leant up to whisper in his ear. And Ryan, the baby of the family at three years younger than Ewan, gave her a thumbs-up. Like she was already one of them.

Fliss was so busy gazing at her future husband that Lara had to elbow her in the ribs as she missed their next entrance. With a start, Fliss scrambled to catch up with the words on the screen.

It was nearly Christmas. She only had four days left to say goodbye to her old life, to enjoy being with her friends again like old times. All her friends, now Jon was here.

Fliss grinned. She was going to make the most of every moment.

Ruth

Alec's arm was warm in hers, and Ruth snuggled against his side as they walked along the beach, back towards Holly Cottage. They'd all agreed that the scenic route home would be nicer than the road. The couple of glasses of wine she'd had at the Griffin (far less than the others) had left her loose and languid, and if she tilted her head against her husband's shoulder, the sound of the sea washing up over the sand and pebbles was almost enough to block out all her thoughts.

'How're you feeling?' She felt Alec's words as a rumble in his chest, more than she heard them. 'Any better?'

'A little,' she admitted. 'I'm glad I came.'

She was, she realised, surprised. She'd have said it anyway, for Alec's sake, but it was actually true. It had been interesting, watching them all interacting again for the first time in so long. They hadn't all been together as a group since her and Alec's wedding, she was sure – certainly not with Jon there as well.

After his unexpected arrival and their initial greeting, Jon had kept his distance from Lara. Given the way Lara was stumbling over the stony beach, Ruth suspected she wasn't entirely comfortable with the situation either. But they'd kept it together and not made a fuss. For Fliss's sake, she assumed. They were all nice like that.

'Good.' Alec squeezed her arm. 'I'm glad you had fun. It never feels right when you're not there too.'

The warm feeling that came over her at Alec's words went a long way towards warding off the chill of the December night, and the uneasy loneliness that had seeped in the longer he'd spent playing pool with Harry and doing shots. But now Harry was clinging onto Lara's arm – Ruth wasn't quite sure which of them was holding the other up – and Alec was all hers again.

Soon, this whole wedding week would be over, and they'd be back on the ferry to the mainland on Christmas Eve. Normally, they'd have spent a few days with her family before the big day, but because of the wedding, this year they were driving straight to Ruth's parents' house to spend Christmas Day, then on to Alec's mum's the day after Boxing Day. They'd hoped to be celebrating their happy news with everyone this Christmas, but instead Ruth knew she'd be deflecting worried looks from her mum and sisters, and awkward hugs from her dad when he couldn't find the right words. But at least she'd be among family again.

Telling them had been like hearing the news herself for the first time, all over again. Maybe she shouldn't have told her sisters about the baby so early on in the pregnancy, but once they knew she'd had to tell their parents too. And honestly, she was glad to have had their support and understanding since. She wasn't sure she'd have made it through without them knowing.

Resting against Alec's shoulder as they picked their way over the shingle, Ruth took the opportunity to watch the group again as they made their way home, illuminated by the moon and the street lamps that ran along the beach road above them, at least part of the way. They'd all dropped everything to be there this Christmas week, too. But then, it was hard not to, when it was Fliss asking. Miss Fliss who, she knew from Alec's stories, was always there with cupcakes after a bad mark, or popcorn and movies after a break-up. Fliss who tried so hard to make everyone happy – and now she was getting her own happy ending.

The figures of Fliss and Ewan were silhouetted against the waves as they walked the shoreline, arms wrapped around each other, their heads close together as they shared secrets. Ewan would be walking back again later, returning to the hotel where he and his family were staying, but he'd insisted on walking Fliss home anyway, even though she obviously wouldn't have been alone. Ruth smiled a little at the thought. That sort of attention boded well for a marriage, she decided.

Neal and Caitlin were walking a short distance further up the beach, with Jon between them. Ruth frowned. That didn't look nearly so good. She wasn't sure she'd seen the couple even talk to each other all evening. In fact, she was pretty sure that Caitlin had spent more time chatting about rugby to Ewan's little brother Ryan than with her own husband.

'Are Neal and Caitlin okay?' she asked quietly, lifting her head to look at Alec.

'Neal and Caitlin? Of course they are!' Alec gave her a puzzled look. 'They're like the— um, like the big brother and sister of us all. In a non-incestuous way.'

That hadn't been what he was going to say, Ruth realised. He'd been going to say mum and dad. That was what they all called them. But he didn't even want to say the words to her right now. Probably in case she cried. Which she probably would.

How were they ever going to move on from this if they couldn't talk about it?

Not now, though. Not here, when Alec was happy and relaxed with his friends, and basically regressing ten years to his university self with tequila shots and pool tournaments. She needed her grown-up Alec, her husband, to deal with this. Not this overgrown student.

Here, he was with *his* family, she realised. The people who meant the most in the world to him. Whose support and understanding he needed right now.

It only made her more homesick for her own family. For her sisters, who'd listen and comfort and fetch chocolate. Her mum, who'd cook all her favourite meals and defend her from anyone's questions. And her dad, who'd put on the old jazz music they both loved and hug her.

And Alec. She wanted the husband who kissed her so deeply that she felt her bones weaken. The Alec who brought her tea in the morning then distracted her so it went cold before she could drink it. The husband who always texted to tell her he was on the train home – then kept the conversation going through the whole journey until they could continue it in person rather than by text message.

Alec was turning to his family, his friends, the same way she wanted to turn to hers.

Ruth turned her attention to Caitlin and Neal again. Someone else's problems seemed much more manageable than her own right now.

'I'm not so sure,' she said, watching as Neal peeled off and wandered closer to the water, alone. 'Neither of them seems exactly . . . happy.'

'Trust me,' Alec said, looking at her, not his friends. Which normally she'd love, but under the circumstances made her wonder if he was trying too hard not to see what she saw. 'Caitlin and Neal are solid. Always have been, always will be. They're just one of those couples that are meant to be. We all knew that, right from first term at university. And nothing has changed.'

'Right.' Ruth bit her lip, as Alec started humming one of the Christmas songs Fliss had sung at karaoke.

But whatever Alec said, people *did* change. She knew she wasn't the same person she'd been at twenty-one, and neither was he. Usually.

But something about this group, these friendships, dragged them into a time warp. Was she, the outsider, the only one who could see that?

Lara

Lara stumbled over a rock, half buried in the sand, and mentally cursed that last glass of wine. She wasn't drunk – among the many benefits her job had given her, an incredibly high alcohol tolerance was probably the most useful – but she was certainly fuzzy enough to be less careful about where she was stepping. And having Harry hanging off her arm wasn't exactly helping, the great lump. This was harder than ice-skating with him.

'So. You and Jon. Actually in the same place again after all this time and nothing exploded. Who'd have believed it?'

Lara tripped again, dragging Harry down with her before she managed to right herself. Maybe it wasn't so bad having him there.

Apart from his annoying questions.

'Fliss, probably,' she said, airily. 'Since she was the one who invited us. She doesn't like explosions. And Jon *was* invited, even if we didn't think he'd be there. Besides, this isn't the first time Jon and I have seen each other since . . . last time we were here.'

Since I broke his heart. Since he asked me to marry him. Since I screwed up and ruined everything.

No. Scratch that last one. That was definitely the wine talking. The wine, and the nostalgia. *He* was the one who'd screwed up, by expecting her to say yes to a marriage proposal straight after university.

He'd known she had plans, known she wanted to see the world – hell, they were supposed to be going and seeing it together.

Being back here, being all together again, and seeing Jon . . . Still gorgeous, and suddenly single. Worrying about him . . . It was messing with her head.

Not marrying Jon at twenty-one had absolutely been the right decision. She just couldn't help but wish it hadn't meant she'd lost him so completely.

'Right, right. You saw each other at Alec and Ruth's wedding, yeah?' Harry's nose screwed up adorably as he tried to figure it out.

'And Caitlin and Neal's.' The moment she said the words, Lara regretted mentioning it.

Harry grinned. 'Yeah! When I pulled that hot blonde bridesmaid—'

'Caitlin's cousin Julie.'

'—and you disappeared with that usher!'

Lara winced. She'd seen Jon's face as she'd left with the guy – Neal's second cousin or something – seen the flash of emotion before the shields came down.

Seen that she'd hurt him again, when she wasn't even trying.

'That was a long time ago,' she said, softly. 'I'm sure we've both changed a lot since then.' Hell, Jon had been married *and* divorced in the intervening years. She was pretty sure her power to hurt him had long since faded.

Thank goodness.

'So,' Harry asked, looking far too knowing. 'Do you think you two will be able to be friends again?'

'I've barely exchanged two words with him this evening,' Lara pointed out. 'How can I be expected to tell?'

'Because he'll follow your lead,' Harry replied, and Lara

remembered again how he always saw to the heart of the matter. No matter how many shots he'd had.

The others always joked that Harry hadn't changed one bit since they met him. He was still the same joker, the same player he'd been at uni. But Lara thought that maybe Harry hadn't changed just because he'd always been so utterly himself. Open and honest about what he could give, and perceptive enough to see past the appearances and personas the rest of them used to try and be cooler, or more liked.

Harry was just Harry. Lara liked that about him.

'I know Jon,' Harry went on. 'He'll be waiting for you to show him what the new status quo is going to be between you. So, what will it be? Friends? Or awkward acquaintances for the rest of your lives?'

Put like that, it was easy.

'I'd like us to be friends. As much as we can be,' Lara said, staring out at the moonlight on the waves instead of meeting Harry's gaze. Harry knew as well as any of them the mess that the fallout of her and Jon's relationship had been. He'd been the first one to visit her at her parents' house up north, after they'd all got home from Mistletoe Island. The one who'd told her that Jon was leaving.

Jon hadn't mentioned the job offer in America when he'd proposed. She wondered if he'd have taken it if she'd said yes. How different their lives might have been . . .

Too many paths never followed. She couldn't think about them all.

'Good,' Harry said. 'Because there are more important things going on this week than you two rehashing your history.'

'You don't honestly think we'd ruin Fliss's wedding like that, do you?'

'I'm not talking about Fliss's wedding.' Harry bent his

head closer to hers, tugging her against his side as they stumbled over the shingle. 'I'm talking about Ewan's sister.'

'Betsy?' All those weeks helping Fliss with guest lists and seating plans had been worthwhile. She had the names down pat.

'Exactly. So, what do you know about her?' Harry asked. 'I know Jon was talking to her at the pub, after the karaoke, but she's not Jon's type, right? He likes blondes.'

'His wife was a brunette,' Lara pointed out. Harry ignored her.

'Besides, he's still getting over a divorce. That'll put him out of the market for at least another six months, I reckon. Which means I have the whole week at my disposal to convince Betsy to prefer strapping blond guys instead.'

'Why, do you know any strapping blond guys?' Lara asked, innocently, and Harry glared at her. 'How do you even know she's single?'

'Instinct. But actually, I was hoping you'd be able to confirm that.' Harry's gaze turned innocent in the moonlight and Lara rolled her eyes. 'I mean, you were in charge of invitations, right? And you helped Fliss with the table plan. So you should know if she has a plus one or not.'

'And here I was thinking that you were keeping me company out of friendly concern for my tipsy state and mental well-being about suddenly being on holiday with my ex-boyfriend.'

'That too. Helpful hint: don't get in any situations where it looks like he might drop to one knee and produce a ring again. That tends to end badly for you two.'

'Thanks,' Lara said, drily. 'I'll bear that in mind.'

'So? Plus one or no plus one?'

Lara cast her mind back over the invitation lists and smiled. 'As it happens, Betsy does have a plus one for the wedding.'

Harry stared at her. 'No way. You're lying.'

'Why would I do that?'

'Because you're mean and evil and I always liked Jon more anyway.'

Lara laughed. 'Yeah, that's why you spent every Friday night for three months after we split up watching horror movies with me while I wept into my popcorn.'

'And your wine,' Harry reminded her. 'Lots of wine. She really has a date for the wedding?'

'Yep.' Lara grinned. 'Her four-year-old son, Morgan. Fliss and Ewan's ring-bearer.'

Harry raised his hands in a silent cheer.

'I knew it. My instinct is never wrong.' Harry's face turned contemplative. He put his hands in his pockets as they made their way along the beach. 'A single mother, huh? I've never had one of those before.'

'They're not a different species, you know,' Lara pointed out.

Harry flashed her a grin, his teeth bright in the moonlight. 'To the women I usually date? They might as well be.'

Lara thought that 'date' might be too strong a word for Harry's relationships, but she didn't mention it. Harry was a good friend, but a lousy boyfriend. She was grateful to have the first, and to never have experienced the second.

'Just bear in mind that by the end of the week she'll be related to Fliss. Which means you'll probably be seeing her again. So don't go screwing anything up there, okay?'

Harry's eyes widened with fake innocence. 'Me? Never. Besides, she might not even be interested.'

'In which case you'll let it lie and find someone else to fixate over?' Lara said, hopefully.

'In which case, I'll have to be doubly charming.' Harry pressed a swift kiss to her cheek, then suddenly broke into a run towards the sea, where Fliss and Ewan were enjoying some besotted couple time.

'Where's he off to?' Alec asked, as he and Ruth caught her up.

'Hell, probably,' Lara said, and sighed. 'At the very least, somewhere he can cause a lot of trouble.'

'Look at all that water!' Harry yelled, suddenly seeming a lot less sober again, as if the news that a shag was potentially on the horizon had reactivated all the alcohol in his blood. 'We should go swimming!'

Fliss

'It's midnight in December, Harry,' Fliss turned as Harry caught up with them. 'We can't go swimming. We'll freeze to death.'

'Ah, but your Ewan is made of sturdier Scottish stuff than that!' Grabbing Ewan's arm, Harry dragged him away from Fliss. Ewan looked back at her with uncertain eyes, and Fliss knew his concern was more for the soft Southerners than for himself. Ewan grew up swimming off the Scottish coast and was usually game for anything. Fliss shrugged helplessly and left him to it. It looked as though they'd reached Harry's manic drunken stage of the evening, something they were all too used to from university. This was the point where you went along with things and tried to make sure he didn't injure himself, or anyone else. And she knew Ewan would look after her friends.

'Come on! Let's show your bride-to-be what a real man you are!' Harry whooped gleefully. He and Ewan kicked off their shoes and stripped off their clothes, bodies glittering beneath the moonlight. The friends gathered as they watched the two men race towards the retreating tide, Ewan outpacing Harry easily.

'Oh, this is definitely going to end badly,' Caitlin commented. Alec had stripped off too, leaving his clothes in a pile on the sand, and was running after them. 'How cold do you reckon it is out there?'

'Too cold for this run to make *any* of them seem more manly,' Lara commented. Fliss glanced at her with a smile, and realised that her friend wasn't actually watching the three men now paddling in the shallows. She was watching Jon, still standing on the shore and laughing at them.

Great. Something else to worry about.

'I'll head up to the cottage and get some towels ready for them,' Ruth said, softly, from a few feet away. 'And get the fire going.'

'Good plan.' Caitlin hugged her arms around herself, as if just watching the boys was making her colder. 'I'll come with you. Come on, Lara. Fliss, are the keys in the same place?'

'Under the third rock on the right,' Fliss confirmed. The spare key to Holly Cottage was probably the worst-kept secret on Mistletoe Island, but they'd never had any problems.

Lara gave a start, then nodded and followed the others. Fliss wondered if Caitlin had seen the same thing she had – the wistful look in Lara's eyes as she stared at her ex.

The last thing they needed this week was Lara getting it into her head that she and Jon should have another go at things. Their friendship group had only just avoiding im-ploding last time – and only then because one of them had moved continents.

Out in the water, Harry and Alec were yelping at the cold. Ewan, meanwhile, was diving between the waves. Fliss shivered, even as part of her wished she had the courage to join him.

It was always like this. Ewan was the adventurous one – or even Harry or Alec, or Lara sometimes. They were the ones who did crazy things at a moment's notice. Like the time Ewan and Betsy jumped off the cliff not far from their parents' home, straight down into the deep of the sea, whooping and shrieking – and leaving Fliss to watch, her heart in her throat.

It hadn't occurred to any of them, not even to Fliss herself, that she might jump too.

And then there was the way that Lara decided to keep travelling after their planned three-month trip was up – and hadn't come back for another half a year. She'd kept moving on alone, to more and more obscure places – but not until she'd put Fliss safely on the plane home, and checked that her parents would meet her at the other end.

Fliss had endured a soggy British winter, seeing picture messages and check-ins from Lara all over the world, and wondered why Lara hadn't asked her to stay and travel with her. Or why she hadn't suggested it herself.

But she knew the answer to all of it now. Miss Fliss didn't jump from cliffs. She didn't take risks or travel without an itinerary and a plane ticket home. She didn't do anything that could get her into trouble, or make her parents worry.

At least, as far as almost everyone else knew.

Suddenly, she sensed a presence behind her. Without looking round, she knew instantly who it was. Neal.

'Not going in?'

'Not a chance. I like my toes unfrozen, thank you.' The others must, too. They'd barely waded in past their knees, and they were already turning around to come back to shore, Ewan appearing behind them through the surf.

Fliss twisted to smile up at Neal, his familiar scent cutting through the salty air. Maybe now was her chance to ask him what was going on with him and Caitlin. He'd always talked to her before – and usually only her. Caitlin wouldn't want any of them to know the truth of their turbulent relationship – the number of times they'd broken up before they got married, for a day or a week, or the number of nights Neal spent on the sofa after a row, even now. But Neal needed someone to let it all go to, and he'd picked her as his confidante years ago. If there was a problem, he would want to talk about it, she was sure.

But then she saw his face. There was something in his smile, and his gaze. Something just for her. A wicked hint of the forbidden. Something she hadn't seen in years.

'Do you remember when you and I went swimming in this sea?' he asked, his voice low and warm and knowing.

Because Neal knew her secrets too in a way that the others never would. Not even Ewan.

'Of course I remember.' Her voice came out husky at the memory. And suddenly, with four little words, it was ten years ago again. She was back on Mistletoe Island in that one week that had changed everything. And not just for Lara and Jon. 'It was summer. It was warmer then.'

'Summer in Scotland? Not much warmer. But a little, I grant you.' His voice dropped to a whisper as Ewan and the others grew closer. 'Which was just as well. Since you were totally naked at the time.'

Despite the freezing air, a shiver of heat ran through her at his words, taking her by surprise. She hadn't thought that was something she could feel any longer.

That heat belonged to a different girl. A Fliss who didn't exist any more. Or who'd been pushed down so deep inside her she might as well not have done.

A Fliss who had only ever existed for Neal.

As Harry and Alec arrived beside them, panting and swearing at their trousers and shoes, Ewan shaking water from his hair behind them, Neal stepped away.

In that moment, Fliss realised that there were much worse things that could happen on the island than Lara rekindling her crush on Jon.

Like her own past coming back to haunt her.

2009

Fliss

Even at the height of summer, night-time on Mistletoe Island was chilly. But Fliss wouldn't let a little cold stop her. Not when she was on a dare.

'Let's sneak back to the lighthouse. Climb the tower. I dare you.' Neal had whispered the words to her as they'd cleared up the dishes after dinner. Soft enough to ensure that no one else heard. Then he'd moved away, smiling to himself.

Fliss felt a shiver go through her at the idea.

I dare you.

Those were their words – their secret. And she already knew she couldn't resist them.

It had started nine months ago, two years into their friendship already. The night she'd snuck out to a party with some guys she barely knew and not told Lara or Caitlin because they'd have insisted on going with her. Because they didn't think she was capable of looking after herself.

And they'd been right. Not that she'd ever tell them that.

The guys who'd invited her had plans. Plans that involved her body but not necessarily her consent. And Fliss had been too drunk and too high on the excitement of not being the good girl for once to notice until it was nearly too late.

She shuddered at the memory, a chill flooding her as she

remembered. She'd wanted to be wild. To be someone other than Little Miss Fliss, the good girl that everyone else saw and teased for her innocence. Just for one night.

If Neal hadn't also gone to the party – behind Caitlin's back, because some girl asked him, and the two of them were on the outs again even if Caitlin wouldn't let any of the others know about it – she hated to think what might have happened.

But he had. He'd overheard the guys talking, realised what they'd intended, told her and then stuck to her side until they could leave. Then he'd taken her home, sat with her while she threw up, waiting until she was sober enough to be coherent. Which was when the cold fear and shock of the night she'd narrowly avoided sunk in and she started to cry in his arms.

Later, when she was calm again, they'd talked, all night, sitting on the bathroom floor, while the others slept on oblivious, their worlds unchanged.

But since then, Fliss's world had never been the same.

She'd told him everything. How hemmed in she felt by all the expectation – from her parents, for whom she was the perfect, only child. From her friends, who would only ever see her as the wide-eyed innocent they'd first met at university. From the guys she dated, that she'd be good and sweet. From her lecturers, who wanted her to keep up those perfect marks that had been easy enough at A level but were something else altogether at degree level. From Lara, who wanted her to go travelling with her and Jon, and Caitlin, who wanted them all to move in together after graduation, too. From everyone who needed something from her in order to be *happy*.

From the world, who seemed to know who she needed to be, when Fliss didn't even know who she *was,* yet.

Was it so wrong to want some space to find that out? To stop being *her* just for a night?

'You can't tell anyone I said this,' Fliss had begged as weak dawn light lit up the bathroom and the alcohol began to wear off.

Neal had raised his eyebrows. 'You don't think you'd feel better if they knew?'

Shaking her head made it ache, so she stopped. 'No.'

'Then it'll be our secret. In fact . . .' He shifted to face her, ducking his head under the sink. 'We'll make a pact. After all, you know some of my secrets too. Like why I was at that party tonight.'

Because living with Caitlin's expectations of perfection had to be exhausting too. Following her ideal plan, even if it didn't lead exactly where he wanted to go. Maybe Neal really did understand how she felt. Fliss nodded slowly. 'A pact?'

'When we're with the others, we'll keep up appearances. We'll be what they need – or what Caitlin expects, in my case. But when it's just us, we can relax. Be whoever we want to be. Okay?'

The idea of letting go of all the smiles and the niceness flowed over her like a warm blanket. 'Yes. Please.'

Someone she could be whoever she wanted with. Why had she never realised she needed that? And Neal was her friend, she trusted him with her secrets. This was the perfect solution.

Neal grinned. 'Good. But that's not enough. You know what else you need? You need a way to cut loose – but without the risk.'

Fliss had raised an eyebrow. 'How?'

His smile had been pure wickedness. 'Well, when it's just the two of us, we can have some fun. Try new things.

You're not the only one who needs to let go and get outside the comfort zone sometimes, you know.'

Could she do it? Throw off Miss Fliss every now and then and go wild? Maybe. If Neal was with her. 'Okay.'

They'd started small. A karaoke night at a tiny bar off campus that students rarely went to. 'Dare you to sing,' Neal had said. And so she'd found herself singing.

From there, things grew. It wasn't often – just once or twice a month. But when Neal gave her a dare, Fliss felt the same shiver of anticipation every time. Whether she was riding a motorcycle with Neal sitting behind her, or partying all night with strangers, knowing Neal had her back, it gave her the same high. The possibility of being someone else for a night.

They'd kept their adventures to themselves, in accordance with the pact. The others wouldn't understand, even though it was all perfectly innocent. Everyone had their role they were expected to play in the group, and this *definitely* wasn't Fliss's. After only two and half years of friendship, already it was too late for any of them to try and be someone else.

But last night, here on Mistletoe Island, the stakes had changed. Because last night, sitting out under the stars outside Holly Cottage, Neal had turned and kissed her. They'd been talking – about the constellations, about nothing at all – and suddenly his hand was on her cheek, his lips against hers, before Fliss could even process what was happening.

Then the others had come barrelling out, and they'd leapt apart before they saw. And now . . .

Neal and Caitlin had been fighting again, Fliss knew. She'd heard them whispering furiously in corners around the cottage even before Neal had stormed outside after Caitlin's barbed comments grew too sharp over dinner. Caitlin never did anything so obvious that the others would figure it out – although Fliss suspected that Harry had noticed. He usually did.

But Neal needed to tell *someone* and with their pact, she was the obvious choice. He didn't pretend with her, and she didn't pretend with him. So she knew how close to breaking up for good he and Caitlin were this time.

And part of her wondered if she wasn't hoping for it. Hoping that he'd tell her tonight it was over with Caitlin for ever. If that was why her nerves were jangling with anticipation.

They waited until the others were asleep before creeping out and retracing their steps back up to the lighthouse, where they'd all picnicked that day. The lighthouse's beam no longer scoured the night sky as it once had, but the clear sky and a bright moon were enough for them to see by.

The door was easy enough to open, the padlock rusty and broken. They climbed the steps in silence, until they reached the railings at the top, looking out over the ocean.

Fliss leant against the rail, her heart pounding at being here with *Neal*.

And suddenly, she knew that they'd been heading here all along. It felt so inevitable, that nothing she could do now would stop it. Not the guilt throbbing inside her, warring with the anticipation and possibility she'd always felt with him.

This was the last time, she promised herself. After tonight, life would move on. They wouldn't be living in each other's pockets like at university. There'd be no more chances for dares.

So they had to make this one a good one.

Neal stood behind her, his chest warm against her back, his hands resting beside on hers on the rails. He bent to whisper in her ear, his mouth hot against her skin.

'Let's go swimming.'

'I didn't bring my swimsuit.'

'So?'

Yes, Fliss thought, as they ran down the steps back towards the beach. This would be a good one.

Friday 20 December 2019

Three days until the wedding

Ruth

Ruth sat with her elbows propped on the kitchen table, watching the rest of the group over the rim of her teacup as they struggled with their hangovers. She'd got into the habit of starting her day with a cup of lemon and ginger tea during those tiring, nauseous months of early pregnancy, and somehow still didn't seem to have dropped the habit.

'Whose ideas were the shots?' Alec asked, rubbing his temples as he winced in the sunlight.

'Yours,' Jon replied, his head on his arms at the kitchen table.

'Next time, someone remind me I'm too old for this?' Alec replied.

I did, Ruth thought. *But you don't listen to me when your friends are there.*

She frowned as she watched Neal fry bacon, while Fliss squirted ketchup onto white, sliced bread. Beside her, Harry was grating cheese by the bowlful. Lara, meanwhile, was fiddling with the coffee maker – without noticeable success. Ruth wondered if that was the same one that had been in situ last time they'd visited; it would explain the dust. And the rust.

'Bacon sandwiches with ketchup *and* cheese?' Ruth asked Caitlin, who was making tea in a cracked, brown pot.

'Oh yes.' Caitlin swirled the teapot around gently, then poured strong, dark tea into matching navy mugs with tiny silver stars on them. She added milk to both, then pushed one towards Jon, who raised a finger in thanks, while his head stayed on the counter. 'Harry invented it our second year at uni. He swears it's the only thing that works as a hangover cure.'

'And he should know,' Lara put in. 'He's had more hangovers than the rest of us combined.'

Ruth laughed as Harry assembled a sandwich and ripped a giant bite out of it with a growl.

'In a hurry, Harry?' Alec asked, from his seat beside Jon.

Harry grunted something unintelligible from around the bacon sandwich.

Ewan, who'd arrived with his brother Ryan, looking surprisingly fresh and alert compared to the rest of them, rolled his eyes. 'You Southerners. If you'd had a proper swim, Har, you'd be feeling like a different man right now.'

That didn't stop Ewan grabbing his own bacon sandwich – with cheese – Ruth noticed. Ryan rolled his eyes at his brother as Caitlin handed him a mug of tea with a smile.

'I just watched you eat a full Scottish up at the hotel, Ewan,' Ryan said, as Ewan added ketchup.

'Yeah?' Ewan said, looking up. 'But that was ages ago. At least an hour.'

'Aren't you worried about not fitting into that fancy kilt The Mothers chose?' Ryan raised an eyebrow. Ruth wondered how bad the kilts really were.

'That would be a bonus,' Ewan muttered around a mouthful of bacon.

Fliss rolled her eyes at her fiancé, but didn't defend the tartan, Ruth noticed. Caitlin muttered something about unfair metabolisms.

'Anyway, what my friend here was trying to say, is that he's playing golf with us and my father this morning, and we really need to get going.' Ewan grabbed a second sandwich, presumably for the journey. 'Dad always says tee time waits for no man.' A muscle flickered in his jaw as he mentioned his father.

Harry took a huge swallow of bacon sandwich. Were his jaws hinged or something? 'See you all later!'

The three of them swept out of the door, Harry slamming it behind him, and the cottage fell into momentary silence.

'So, what's everyone else got planned for today?' Caitlin asked, topping up Jon's mug of tea. Ruth blinked. She hadn't even noticed him lifting his head enough to drink any, but apparently he had.

'Actually, I thought I might take a walk into the village.' The words were out before Ruth could stop them. She needed to get out. Away from all the comfortable familiarity that didn't include her. And maybe, just maybe, hunt out some of that healing the island had promised.

This was her holiday, her Christmas too. So today, she was going to enjoy Mistletoe Island. Alone.

'Perfect!' Caitlin beamed at her. 'I'd already planned to go into the village to get food for dinner. I thought I'd make my beef with ginger and cranberries. Warming and festive. We can go together!'

'Great.' Ruth hoped her smile didn't look as weak as it felt.

'Beef with ginger and cranberries?' Jon lifted his head. 'That's my favourite dish of yours.'

'I know,' Caitlin said, smiling.

'You are an angel.' Jon got to his feet, drained the last of his second mug of tea, and placed a kiss on the top of Caitlin's head. 'And now, I am going for a run.'

'A run?' Lara asked, incredulous. 'Five minutes ago you couldn't lift your head off the table.'

'And a run will help me clear my head,' Jon answered, watching Lara carefully. It was interesting, Ruth thought, observing them develop a new dynamic. *They* at least couldn't just revert to who they'd been ten years ago. They needed to find a new way forward.

Maybe Alec could learn from them.

Neal shook his head. 'America was *not* good for you, my friend.'

'Tell me about it.'

At his words, Lara's cup clattered against its saucer.

'What about you, Fliss?' Ruth asked quickly, changing the conversation as it was clearly unsettling Lara. She liked Lara. She'd probably like Jon if she got to know him.

'Oh, you know. Wedding things. I'll probably be up at the hotel most of the day, sorting things out with The Mothers, and checking on the cake. Ewan gets The Fathers today, I get the Mothers.' Fliss's gaze faltered. She didn't look much like a happy bride-to-be.

'Because *that's* a fair deal,' Lara muttered.

Ruth frowned. Was she reading too much into everything this weekend? Or were things really more strained, more layered that she remembered from previous gatherings?

'Oh! And there's a lantern walk this evening, through the woods and down to the beach,' Fliss went on, looking hopefully around the table. 'If anyone fancies it?'

'Sounds good,' Caitlin said, answering for everyone. 'I can put the casserole in the oven before we go, and it'll be ready to eat when we get back. Now, Lara, what about you?' Caitlin turned. 'Want to come into the village with me and Ruth?'

'And go grocery shopping? No thanks.' Lara stretched, her arms up over her head, exposing a small strip of skin between her pyjama bottoms and her T-shirt. 'I'm going to curl up with a good book and a cup of excellent coffee. If I can ever get this machine to work.' Fliss shot her a suspicious look that Ruth didn't quite understand. What did she think Lara might actually be planning?

Jon, re-emerging down the stairs in his running gear, went to the coffee maker. 'Let me look at it.'

After thirty seconds of fiddling, the machine started to bubble, and dark black liquid flowed into Lara's cup.

'One good thing I got from America, I suppose,' he said, half smiling.

Ruth watched him turn away, plugging headphones into his ears as he stepped out of the door, revealing a crisp, bright morning outside Holly Cottage. Then the door shut, and it was just them again.

Maybe everything *was* more layered. More complex and confusing. She'd noticed the way Jon's gaze had rested momentarily on Lara as he'd waved goodbye from the doorway. If Ruth wasn't wildly mistaken, Jon wasn't as completely over Lara as he wanted everyone to believe.

Fliss

It was a relief to leave the breakfast chaos downstairs and retreat to the coolness of the attic bedroom she shared with Lara.

At least she had a good excuse – she needed to get dressed for a day up at the Mistletoe Hotel with The Mothers, the wedding planner and the wrong napkins. She'd also get to check in on her wedding cake – the one part of the whole event that was most definitely hers.

Given that brides travelled to London from hundreds of miles away to commission the Magical Bakery to design their wedding cakes, and that Fliss herself was their most in-demand cake designer, there was no way in hell that she was letting anyone else take charge of her own cake.

Most of the cakes she designed these days were elaborate, over-the-top masterpieces in fondant. She'd created a fairy-tale castle complete with sugar unicorns for one bride, and a flower meadow with individually crafted sugar wildflowers for another. But for herself, she'd known exactly how she wanted her cake to look since the moment they decided on a winter wedding.

Simple, elegant and stunning. Pure white, in three tall, round tiers. And with a cascade of snowflakes falling from the top tier down one side – each one different from the others, and gently sparkling as if in the winter sun.

She'd prepared the snowflakes her first day on the island, before the others arrived, giving the modelling fondant plenty of time to dry and harden. She'd used the snowflake cutters she'd designed and had made in London, sitting at the kitchen table in the cottage, working in silence as snow fell beyond the window, enjoying the quiet meditation of creating the decorations. As each was cut out, she'd carefully add tiny variations to each one, using a minuscule brush to tweak them.

Today, she'd check the cakes the hotel had baked for her were right, and split, fill and ice them with buttercream, ready for the fondant coating. It would be relaxing, working on something of her own, without any interruptions.

But first, she had to get dressed, then find a new hiding place for Lara's mobile phone. Lara was sure to scour the room, looking for it, and Fliss wasn't convinced her first hiding place was the best. She hadn't bought that 'sitting around with a good book' act for a moment.

Yes, she told herself now. *Focus on the cake and Lara. Forget about last night.*

Fliss shut the bedroom door behind her and leant her body against the stripped wooden panels for a moment, eyes closed, enjoying the quiet. She could still hear the buzz of conversation and clinking of mugs and plates downstairs, but the sound was distant, as though it carried up from another life. She loved them all dearly, but every time they were all together it was as if the last ten years hadn't even happened. Like they were twenty-one again. Up here, she wasn't the same Fliss who'd met most of those people on the first day of university and barely changed at all. She was the older, better Fliss. All grown up and ready to marry Ewan.

No matter what.

Her eyes snapped open. Crossing the room, Fliss flung open the wardrobe door, then froze. Her wedding dress hung before her, layer after layer of tulle and lace, ready and waiting for her big day. Her future.

Her chest felt suddenly tight with . . . what, exactly? Was it excitement or apprehension? Fliss wasn't sure.

She stared at the lace bodice, at the threads that formed an almost snowflake-like pattern if she squinted, flowing down to the glittering tulle skirt. On the floor of the closet sat her wedding shoes, clear and glittering like Cinderella's glass slippers.

She'd spent weeks finding the perfect dress – one that satisfied both her, Caitlin, Lara and her mum. Mostly her mum, who had looked so sad whenever Fliss pulled out a simple, minimalist gown. 'I always dreamed of watching my only daughter walk down the aisle in a magical, fairy-tale dress,' she'd said mournfully. So in the end, that was what Fliss had bought. And it *was* magical. It looked like it had the power to transform her into anything she wanted to be – into Mrs Ewan Bennett. So why, looking at it, was she suddenly thinking about her past? About hopes and dreams and possibilities long gone, but always, always linked to Mistletoe Island?

Maybe getting married here was a mistake. But she loved the island – had since she was a child – and her parents had been so happy at the idea of holding the wedding here. It was a place with meaning for them all. Plus, she suspected now, her parents liked it because it gave them a chance to show off – their hotel, their island, their daughter. Ewan, bless him, had said he'd be happy anywhere in the world, as long as he got to marry her – and had been researching the history and the geology of the place ever since. It really *was* the perfect place for a winter wedding.

Fliss had been back to the island a handful of times since the summer she'd spent there with her friends, after graduation, but it had never been the same. It didn't matter how many memories of childhood holidays she had of the place, or how many times she'd visited since. In her head, Mistletoe Island would forever be connected to that one trip. The one where everything changed.

The first time she ever kissed Neal.

Her friend – best friend. The only person she'd ever been able to be her true self with. Like she'd given him a piece of her soul the night they made that pact, and somehow never got it back. But that night, that kiss, had changed everything between them.

They'd been careful, and she'd laid down rules. After that night, the only times they'd ever been together that way was when Neal and Caitlin had split up. Every time it happened, she'd told herself that it could be for good this time, that maybe he wouldn't go back to her. But she'd known deep down he always would. She was an escape, a refuge – but she wasn't his real life. The same way the girl she was with him didn't exist except when they were alone.

But for her, Neal would always be the life she didn't live.

Fliss quickly shut the door to the wardrobe, then swore, softly. Sighing, she stepped back and sank down to sit on the bed, her trembling hands resting in her lap. She'd thought she could do this. She'd honestly believed that she could step from one part of her life to the next, without it being a big deal. Without having to say or do anything to sever ties with her past. To address what had happened last time they were on the island. Or everything that had happened since.

Even as everyone had arrived, she'd thought it was possible.

She'd smiled and laughed and been *happy* to have everyone together again, there to celebrate her new beginning.

She'd been holding tight her conflicted feelings for Neal, her love for Ewan, and the complicated state of her heart caused by both, for too long. Even though her occasional relationship with Neal had faded back to friendship years ago – and disappeared completely since she met Ewan – it still sat there in the back of her mind, and her heart. They'd never ended it properly; let it ebb away as Neal and Caitlin's relationship grew more stable, and she settled down with Ewan. But they'd never had the closure of a proper ending. And if any of the others knew what had gone on between Neal and herself, not just on that one night but over months, years . . . She felt a dread of judgement. She and Neal had understood the rules they'd had, but would her friends?

It was time to let something fall. And really, there was only one choice as to what. Hadn't she already told herself that this week was a last goodbye to what used to be? To who *she* used to be? Perhaps to Neal's Fliss, most of all.

Her new life was waiting for her.

Decision made, Fliss sucked in a deep breath, stood and crossed to the wardrobe again. Easing the door open, she smiled at her beautiful wedding gown . . . then quickly and efficiently pulled out a denim dress. That would do. If she wore it with tights and heeled boots it would be smart enough for wedding planning, and warm enough for December in Scotland.

'I always like that dress on you.'

Fliss spun round to see Neal leaning against the door frame. The attic door was closed behind him. How had he done that without her hearing? His eyes were full of something she'd *just* promised herself she wouldn't look for any more. The same something she'd seen on the beach last night. 'You shouldn't be up here,' she whispered, as if Caitlin could hear her down two flights of stairs.

They'd put this part of their relationship behind them years ago. She'd thought they'd both outgrown it. Why was it coming back now? *Because of this damned island,* she answered herself.

'Probably not.' Neal gave her a half smile. 'But everyone's busy downstairs – and all too hung over to miss me. I wanted to talk to you.'

'Neal, I don't have time. I have to be up at the hotel—'

'Do you?' He hadn't moved from the door, watching her. This was how he'd been that night at university, too. The night their friendship had changed, deepened, beyond what she shared with the others.

'I'm getting married on Monday, Neal. It's not like there's nothing to do. There's the cake, for a start—'

'I remember.' She couldn't tell if he meant that he remembered how busy the days before a wedding were, or that he remembered she was getting married.

Maybe it was both.

'Do you remember the first time we ever kissed?' he asked, and the memories swirled around her head so clearly they could be happening all over again.

'Of course I do.' Her face flushed. She could still feel his lips on hers if she thought about it too hard.

'Here, at Holly Cottage. Out in the gardens, looking for shooting stars.'

'I know.' Fliss looked away. She couldn't do this if she was looking at him. 'Neal, we need to talk. I know things between us have been . . . confused for a while now.'

'I'm not confused,' Neal said. Then he sighed. 'But yes, we probably do need to talk. Somewhere away from the others.'

Just like they'd used to. They'd become each other's safe place and secret keeper, after that night at the party when both their secrets had come tumbling out. They'd been friends – real, true best friends. Until Mistletoe Island, when everything had changed. And now Fliss needed to change it back.

'How about we take a walk up to the old lighthouse tomorrow,' Neal suggested, the heat in his eyes gone. He smiled at her platonically, as if they were nothing more than friends. 'Just you and me. Caitlin won't be interested, and we'll find a way to put the others off. We can go for a long walk and talk as much as you need. Sound good? You know how much you love the lighthouse. Remember?'

The thought of being out in the fresh air, able to relax and stop watching everyone, to be able to talk to the one person she'd always been able to tell the truth to . . . Fliss had to admit that sounded pretty wonderful. And then, once she'd said everything she needed to say, they could concentrate on putting away everything else that had been between them and rediscovering that easy friendship. It wasn't as if they'd had anything more. She wouldn't call it an affair, though even thinking the word made her wince. After all, Neal had even admitted to Caitlin that he'd slept with someone else while they were broken up, the last time – he'd just never told her who. Caitlin had never even mentioned it to any of them, of course – that would look too much like failure to follow her plan. But Neal had told her, afterwards. Explained how he told Caitlin it was nothing, it meant nothing.

Fliss meant nothing, she knew. She was his friend. Everything else . . . that was meaningless. Especially compared to what Neal had with Caitlin, or she had with Ewan. And regardless, it was over now.

Tomorrow, she'd end things with Neal for good, give them both the closure they needed. Then on Monday she could marry Ewan and start her new life. It was all sorted.

'That sounds perfect,' she said. But she wasn't talking about the lighthouse.

Lara

Lara's memories of Holly Cottage had always been intimate and cosy, but now the place felt enormous without the others crashing around. Everyone had found somewhere else to be that morning, or someone to be with, except her. Neal and Alec had headed up to the golf course to meet Harry and Ewan, presumably in time to join them at the bar after their round of golf. And with Fliss up at the hotel . . . well, there was only one thing left to do. Find her phone!

Lara began to scan the cottage, thinking quickly as she strode from room to room. Fliss was a creature of habit; she used the same recipe for cookies whenever she baked, explaining she'd found one that everyone liked, so why bother experimenting? She lived in dresses and boots in the winter and dresses and ballet pumps in the summer. She'd even worn her hair the same length and style for the last ten years, although she claimed that was because there was only so much you could do with corkscrew curls like hers.

Which meant, Lara was pretty sure, that Fliss wouldn't have suddenly got more creative with her hiding places either. And since she'd managed to find her birthday and Christmas presents every year they'd lived together, Lara was certain she could find her phone.

She ran up to the attic room and started with the chest of drawers in the bedroom, digging her hands between piles of underwear. Nothing. Moved onto the wardrobe, being careful not to disturb Fliss's wedding dress. Still nothing. She looked beneath the beds, behind the curtains – even in Fliss's jewellery box. Still nothing!

She swirled round to face the room. Lara was forced to admit that she might have underestimated Fliss this time. *Outmanoeuvred by Miss Fliss*, she thought, raising her eyebrows. *I'm impressed.*

Resigned to another twenty-four hours without any contact with the outside world, Lara found herself pottering around Holly Cottage aimlessly, running her hands over the rustically worn furniture and imagining all the other people who must have stayed there, lived there even. What would it be like to spend your whole life somewhere like Mistletoe Island? She couldn't imagine.

She shuddered and ran a hand over her arms. The thought brought her out in hives. She wasn't made to stay in one place, to be only one thing. Wasn't that one of the reasons she'd given Jon for not marrying him, ten years ago?

Having finished the washing up from breakfast (and searched the kitchen cupboards while she was at it), Lara grabbed her Kindle from her bedside table, a blanket from the sofa, and curled up on the large, cushioned window seat in the sitting room, a cup of coffee at her side. If she really couldn't work, she might as well make the most of it. She was used to being alone – looked forward to it usually, after busy days at conferences and meetings. Some of her favourite evenings over the past few years had been spent alone in hotel rooms with a good book and a glass of wine and just *peace*.

Which didn't sound quite as exciting as she liked to think her life was.

Shifting uncomfortably on the pile of cushions, Lara made herself remember all the other, better times – nights out with colleagues, movie nights at her flat, visiting her parents up in the north of England . . . lovely memories with people she loved.

But no *one* person she was in love with. Or who was in love with her. Because that hadn't really happened since Jon, had it?

Oh, she'd dated – plenty, as it happened. But that wasn't the same.

Why *hadn't* she found her forever person – the way Fliss, and Caitlin and the others had? Even Jon, for a time, thought he'd found it; had been sure enough to commit to marriage.

Out in the hallway, the grandfather clock chimed, pulling Lara out of her reverie – and giving her another place to look for her phone. She had managed to unlock the front casing and was rooting around behind the pendulum when the door to the cottage banged open, and Jon appeared, sweaty and rumpled – but not red and breathless like she would have been after a hungover winter run in the freezing cold.

Straightening up, Lara quickly shut the grandfather clock door and stood in front of it, in case it creaked open again before she could lock it.

'Back so soon?'

Jon glanced at the clock, but – thank goodness – didn't ask what on earth she was doing. He ran a hand over his hair. 'I run fast, these days.'

'Away from all the women chasing you, I suppose?' Damn. That was more something she'd have said *before* they started dating, when they had a good line in edgy, teasing comments that were half flirting. She didn't want to remind him of those days. Did she?

A crease appeared in Jon's brow, as though he had no idea what she was talking about. He tilted his head slightly to one side, still looking at her. 'You need to get out of here. Quite aside from the fact that if you break that clock Fliss's mum will kill you, you look like you haven't seen fresh air in months.'

'I get outside,' Lara protested, ignoring the bit about the clock, and not adding that 'outside' for her was usually when she was walking between airport terminals and the car to her hotel.

'Air-conditioned conference rooms with windows don't count.' He continued to gaze at her a moment too long, as if he was contemplating something he was almost certain was going to be a bad idea. Then he gave a sudden nod, as though he'd suddenly come to a decision. Crossing towards the stairs, he began to unzip his top. 'Give me five minutes to shower and change. You get your shoes on. And your coat – it's cold out there.'

She followed him to the foot of the stairs, watching him take them two at a time. 'Why? What are we doing?'

Jon paused in his bedroom doorway, staring back at her, his expression unreadable. 'It's a beautiful, crisp winter's day out there, and you're missing it.' Then he disappeared into his room, shutting the door behind him.

She shook her head in disbelief. He couldn't *make* her go outside if she didn't want to! She was perfectly happy with her book and her window seat and her coffee. The last thing she wanted was to go out for a walk with her ex.

She was fine exactly how she was, thank you very much.

Then Lara bit her lip, and thought about all those hotel rooms, those evenings on her laptop, working from home. She tried to calculate exactly how much of the last year she'd spent in airports at midnight, ignoring people, and the world around her, through the power of her sound-cancelling headphones. Too many hours to count.

Then she thought about a lifetime of get-togethers with her on one side of the room and Jon on the other.

And then she went and found her trainers.

'Where are we going?' she asked, as they left Holly Cottage.

'For a walk.' Jon didn't look at her as he spoke, his eyes firmly on the road ahead. It stretched towards the ocean and the blue sky beyond. The snow had stopped in the night and now there was a biting wind that came off the sea, making tears well in her eyes.

Okay. There was definitely something more than walking buddies going on here. And she needed to figure out what it was.

'Why, exactly?' she asked, hurrying to keep up with him. She'd had to pull her trainers on quickly and they were too loose, making her stumble and trip. 'And don't start with the "Lara needs daylight" argument. That's not what this is about, is it?'

He'd wanted to get her on her own, outside of the cottage. Why?

'Because I think we need to talk. Don't you?'

No. Not really. She'd sort of been hoping they could just *never* talk, pretend that she'd never walked out on him ten years ago. But that was probably too much to hope for.

'You look terrified,' Jon said, more gently this time, a faint smile on his face.

Lara straightened her back. She knew what he meant. He meant that she looked like the old Lara again. The one who followed his lead and went wherever he bid her. Who forgot about her list and dreams until it was almost too late – all because she'd fallen in love.

Last night, Harry had told her that Jon was waiting to take her lead – to see if they could become genuine friends again.

But Harry was only right to a point, because as soon as Jon thought he knew what she wanted, he'd go for it. Whether he was right or not. She was remembering that now.

The most important thing, she reminded herself, was that she wasn't the same girl she'd been when she met Jon – when she met them all. She was an accomplished professional, a self-assured woman. One who'd accomplished everything she'd set out to do.

She couldn't go backwards now.

'No. I agree,' she said evenly, ignoring his raised eyebrows. 'Now you're back in the country, we're going to have to get used to seeing each other at these things. We should be friends. Which means figuring out how to move forward.'

'Exactly!' He tilted his head to one side. 'You're okay with that?'

'Why wouldn't I be?' Lara asked, with a shrug. Relaxed, unruffled. That was how she needed to appear. Even if she could almost feel the air between them vibrating. When was the last time she'd been so close to him? The day he proposed, probably. 'Are you?'

Jon's sharp laugh was snatched away by the sea wind that cut above the cliffs to their left. 'You broke my heart once, Lara, but it was ten years ago. We've grown up. Changed. Yes, we can be friends.' The last word was said with thick irony.

She looked quickly away. 'Right. Sure.'

'We're adults. We can exist in the same space. Agreed?'

'Agreed.'

'Good.' Jon gave a nod, and his pace quickened. 'Then let's go and get drunk.'

She stumbled to a halt. Wait. 'What?'

But he didn't stop walking. Lara jogged to catch him up

and, as they turned a sudden sharp bend, saw a small, cosy pub perched on the cliff top, hidden behind the trees that ringed the island.

'I found it on my run,' Jon explained, as they walked towards the door. A sign swung and creaked in the wind: The Shipwreck. 'Seemed like the perfect place for us to get away from the others and talk about all the things we need to talk about.'

Like how things ended between them, she guessed. Their *feelings*. Lara hung back, eyeing the pub sign, with its tall ship crashing against the cliffs, with some trepidation. 'Are you sure this is a good idea? I mean, moving forward, yes, I'm all for that. But raking up the past . . . I don't really think that's going to help either of us.'

'Neither do I,' Jon agreed. 'That's not what we're going to do.'

Catching his eye, Lara realised what he was offering at last, and smiled. 'Okay, so ground rules. We only talk about our lives *since* the last time we were both on this island. No reminiscing, no rehashing the past—'

'No talk about *us*,' Jon summarised.

'Exactly. This is about us finding a way to be friends again, right?' Jon nodded, and Lara stuck out her hand. Maybe this was her chance to find out how he was really doing since the divorce. As a friend. 'In that case . . . Hi! I'm Lara. Nice to meet you. Want to get a drink?'

Jon grinned, and took her hand in his own. 'I'd love to.'

Ruth

Ruth felt her mood lightening as she and Caitlin started down the path to the village, her walking boots crunching through the frozen snow, and her red bobble hat pulled down over her ears. It wasn't a long walk and, since they weren't planning on buying too much in the way of food and supplies, they'd decided they didn't need the car for the trip.

They took the path that ran alongside the road to the cottage, rather than the slightly quicker route across the beach from the night before. Caitlin kept up a running commentary during the walk, mostly about the latest work they were having done to their townhouse – Neal wanted industrial and she wanted shabby chic. Ruth was happy enough to listen.

'Not that it matters since the carpenter for the kitchen cancelled on us *again* last week.' Caitlin sighed. 'So Christmas will be prepared on wood-effect Formica *again* this year.'

Ruth smiled sympathetically, and gazed out towards the horizon. She'd assumed Alec had been exaggerating when he went on about how stunning Mistletoe Island was. She'd always found the Scottish countryside too wild, too rough for her tastes. But now she realised she'd been wrong – or wrong about this place, at least. The craggy coastline with waves crashing against the cliffs suited her mood perfectly. A street ran along the shoreline, with rows of cottages painted in charming shades of pink, blue and yellow. The contrast between the pretty cottages and the bruising shades of the sea took Ruth's breath away.

'Can you imagine living somewhere like this?' Ruth asked, surprising herself, as they turned a corner and entered the village.

Caitlin paused on the pavement beside her, taking in the view. 'Do you know, I've never really imagined living anywhere except London. Not since we moved there straight after university. Before, even. I'd always dreamt of a townhouse in London.'

Ruth knew Caitlin's family had money, and plenty of it. Caitlin and Neal had been doing up their townhouse in Muswell Hill for years now. Of course, the group of friends were lucky, too, treating Caitlin's home as their unofficial London pied-a-terre. So no one had ever had reason to feel jealous.

But for the first time, Ruth found herself wondering. Did Caitlin ever resent the people who descended on her home? Even if they were old friends? Ruth would have, she knew. Who wanted to play hostess at the drop of a hat? But maybe it was different for Caitlin. Ruth remembered overhearing Lara ask, once, if it was really okay that they were all there *again* for the rugby that weekend. Caitlin had shrugged and said, 'It's nice to have the company.'

She'd thought it was strange, at the time. She and Alec had only been married six months or so. Surely, their home was full with just the two of them, and their love?

Now, this winter of all winters, Ruth finally thought she understood what Caitlin had meant – and felt sad that Caitlin had experienced that same terrible loneliness, even in a marriage.

'I never meant to live in London,' Ruth admitted, trading a confession for a confession. 'I always thought I'd move back home to Kent after I graduated. Maybe commute in if I couldn't find a job outside the city. But I never imagined living there.'

'Until you met Alec,' Caitlin guessed, and Ruth smiled ruefully. 'The things we do for men.'

With a shake of her head, Caitlin started walking again, down the hill towards the village shop, passing under the lights strung up between buildings. Ruth followed, still thinking. The problem with considering herself an outsider to the group, she realised suddenly, is that she'd never taken the time to make Alec's friends *her* friends, before. This sense of being excluded – had it partly been her own fault?

And suddenly, as she walked in Caitlin's footsteps along the village high street, past windows filled with gift-wrapped presents and painted with gingerbread houses, she wanted to change things. She wanted to know what made Caitlin as lonely as she was. *I want to become her friend*, she realised with a bolt of shock. *I want to help.*

The village looked even prettier in the daylight than it had the night before. The weak, winter sunlight darted off the sea, over the village wall, and reflected in all the shop windows, each decorated for the season. Although the Christmas market stalls had been dismantled, the ice rink remained, and children shrieked with laughter as they made their way around. Now that the market had been cleared, Ruth could see the layout of the village better. The village centre was laid out along two short streets, which met in a cross in the centre where the war memorial was, hidden behind the oversized Christmas tree. Ruth paused to look over the names of the fallen from the village. It was a shorter list than she'd seen on most memorials – Alec said she had a morbid obsession for always checking them for someone she might be related to – but on an island this size she guessed that the loss must have been felt keenly.

Biting the inside of her cheek, she turned away to find Caitlin watching her, her clear eyes the blue-green of the winter sea.

'The shop's this way,' she said, after a moment. Ruth nodded and made to follow her. 'Last time we were here, there was this gorgeous twenty-something guy behind the counter who always flirted with me. Dark hair, green eyes, accent to die for . . . I think I volunteered for almost every shop run that summer!'

Ruth smiled. *That* particular reminisce hadn't come out before. That was the other advantage of getting to spend time with Alec's friends one-on-one. She got to see the real people they were, not the person they played in the group.

It seemed to Ruth the more time she spent doing that, the more she realised how constrained they all felt by the person they had to be for their friends – the person they'd been when they all met, more than thirteen years ago now. People changed and grew, but not within the group, it seemed. There, you could only ever be who you'd always been.

Caitlin flashed a smile back at her as she pushed open the rickety wooden door of the shop, setting off the bell suspended above it. Inside, the shop was dark and smelled a little musty, but the refrigerated compartments and slightly lopsided shelves seemed to hold more or less everything they needed.

'I brought a few of the more specialist ingredients, like the juniper berries, with me,' Caitlin whispered as they picked out a punnet of cranberries and filled a paper bag with shallots. 'I figured they might not have them here, and to be honest, I'd planned to make this even before I knew Jon would be here. But Fliss said that the meat comes from the local farms, and so does the dairy, so there's a decent selection.' Potatoes were plentiful, and there was even a small basket holding fresh ginger. Ruth supposed a lot of the holiday cottages must be self-catering, and so it paid to have a good selection of fresh food for tourists like them.

Caitlin lingered longest at the meat counter, debating between the packages of braising steak, which all looked more or less the same to Ruth.

'Did you say you were making beef with ginger and cranberries?' It hadn't occurred to Ruth to even think about what they'd cook or eat while they were there, let alone pack specialist ingredients. Left to their own devices, Ruth suspected everyone would have been happy with frozen pizza, or eating at the pub every night. But Caitlin obviously had loftier ideas, and Ruth had to admit her stomach was grateful. 'It sounds delicious.'

Caitlin shrugged. 'It's a great "throw everything in the pot then sit back and drink wine" dish, so I figured it would suit. But it feels a bit special, and it makes the whole house smell Christmassy too. And . . . well, it *is* Jon's favourite. I guess I was thinking about him when I was planning the holiday, and now he's actually here, it's nice to be able to treat him.'

And that, Ruth thought, was Caitlin in a nutshell. She'd planned ahead, thought things through, picked a dish that suited the occasion – and she'd been thinking about her friends at the same time.

Ruth thought that being Caitlin must be exhausting sometimes. Or all of the time.

'You like to cook?' Ruth asked.

'I do,' Caitlin said, simply. 'I like finding new ingredients, new tastes. Neal says I can lose whole days wandering round Borough Market. But hey, he's always happy to wolf down whatever I cook afterwards.'

'That's nice. Neither Alec nor I are great cooks.' Luckily, neither of them were great foodies, either, so they made it through okay. And it meant they didn't have to spend their weekends at farmers' markets, and could curl up for a good pub lunch with the papers instead.

'Sometimes I envy Fliss, following her passion and designing those beautiful cakes,' Caitlin said, wistfully. Then she shook her head. 'But I don't imagine it's exactly lucrative or secure, is it? So I don't think it would have suited me. Better to keep cooking as a hobby, I think.'

Ruth watched as Caitlin carried on down the aisle, leaving her dreams behind her, and wondered if Caitlin had ever, just once, considered deviating from her life plan. She suspected not.

As they carried their baskets to the counter, Caitlin stopped suddenly, almost causing Ruth to crash into her, then started walking again before Ruth could ask what was wrong. But as they reached the till, she thought she might be able to guess.

There, behind the counter, stood an overweight, balding, miserable-looking guy in his late thirties, dark hair rapidly receding and green eyes heavy. *This* was the man Caitlin had had a crush on, all those years ago?

He brightened as he saw them approach. 'Ah, now this is a treat! Are you two lovelies staying on the island for the wedding? Everyone is talking about the Christmas Eve Eve celebrations, you know. I didn't even know that Christmas Eve Eve was a thing!' His lilting accent was charming, at least. She shot a glance across at Caitlin, who was carefully not looking at her. Or him. Ruth held in a snigger, just. She knew if she laughed, Caitlin would too, and how would they explain their sudden hysterics?

Caitlin smiled weakly, hardly looking up from the meat and veg on the counter. 'That's right. Um, just these, please?'

'Right you are!' He picked up the multiple packs of braising steak first, then the cranberries. 'Looks like you're cooking something special here, then.'

'Beef with ginger and cranberries,' Ruth said, helpfully.

'Room for one more at the table?'

As he looked hopefully between their faces, Ruth bit her lip and Caitlin handed over her credit card, shoving their purchases into the recyclable hemp bags they'd brought with them from the cottage. Ruth managed to contain her laughter until after the shop door had swung shut behind them.

Caitlin hustled them a little way down the road, then gave in herself, doubling over as she dropped her bags to the ground and howled.

'That was him?' Ruth asked, between gasps of air.

'Oh yes,' Caitlin replied. 'Quite the catch, huh? Just as well I never ditched Neal and ran off with him ten years ago.'

'Of course, if you'd picked him he probably wouldn't be the same man now, would he?' Ruth pointed out.

Caitlin eyed her, as though she was trying to guess at Ruth's real meaning. 'You're right,' she said. She gazed around. 'Now, how about you and I get some lunch?'

Ruth glanced at the shopping bags. 'Shouldn't we get these back to the cottage?'

'The food's hardly going to go off in this cold.' Caitlin grabbed her bags. 'Besides, all the others are off having fun. And I think you and I should have a nice, long chat. Don't you?'

Ruth smiled. 'Absolutely.'

Lara

Inside, the pub was more rundown than cosy, with carpet that had rotted away to leave sticky underlay underfoot and grimy windows. In other words, it was perfect.

'I think we can be pretty sure that no one will find us here,' Lara murmured, as they surveyed the drinks behind the bar.

They settled for bottles of beer, figuring at least they couldn't have been watered down or tampered with by the grouchy barman.

'So,' Jon said, as soon as they were seated in the far corner, away from the bar, with only a plastic rose in an old beer bottle between them. 'What have you been up to for the last ten years?'

'Mostly?' Lara winced. 'Working.'

'That can't be all,' Jon said, disbelief in his voice.

Lara shrugged. 'What can I say? I'm married to my job.'

She regretted the turn of phrase the moment she said it, but Jon didn't react.

'What about you?' she hurried on. She took a slug of beer. 'What was it like living in the States?'

'Different.' Jon gave her a lopsided smile. 'Phoebe was always amazed by the things I found jarring, or confusing. For all that they speak the same language, it really is a very different country.'

This was safe ground, Lara decided. She should ask more

about living in America. But apparently her mouth had other ideas.

'I'm sorry about your divorce.' What? Wait. Why had she said that? God, she *sucked* at small talk.

'Stuff happens,' Jon said, peeling off the label from his beer bottle. 'We grew apart. It was all very amicable really.'

'That's something, I suppose.' But as Lara studied him carefully, she could see the dark shadows behind his eyes. He might be trying to act like the divorce was no big deal, but Lara knew better. Knew *him* better, even after all this time. 'And now you're moving home? Are you thinking London, or will you stay with your parents for a while?'

Jon's parents lived across the border into North Wales. But given the work he'd been doing over in the States – not that she'd been keeping track of him or anything – she wasn't sure how much demand there was for social policy advisors there. But maybe Jon was ready for a change, or a slower pace of life.

'Probably London, eventually, if only for job reasons, although it would be nice to be around the old gang again. Caitlin's offered up their spare room if I need it while I'm getting settled. But I might look further north too. My dad . . . he's not been well, and I guess it would be good not to be four hours away if they needed me. But anywhere in the country is still closer than a transatlantic flight, so . . .' He raised the bottle to his lips.

'I'm sorry about your dad,' Lara said softly. She knew Jon's relationship with his father hadn't always been easy, but she also knew that deep down they'd loved each other fiercely. She didn't think for a moment *that* would have changed. They were too similar, Jon's mum had told her once. *They both feel things too deeply, and find it too hard to move on. So they hurt each other even when they're not trying to.*

They'd clashed often when Jon was younger, over what his father thought was best for him versus what Jon wanted. She imagined, from what she knew of Jon's father, that Jon's decision to move continents might well have been another pressure point.

'Thanks.' He suddenly seemed to find his beer bottle intensely interesting, but Lara waited. Eventually, Jon took a deep, shaking breath. 'He's taking each day as it comes. Lots of tests, that sort of thing. Hoping to get some answers in the New Year.'

He'd want to be close for that. 'Must be strange, moving back in with your parents after a decade of living thousands of miles away.'

'You have no idea.' Jon leant his elbows on the rickety table. 'But enough about Dad.' He finally looked up at her. 'Tell me more about your job. What makes it so rewarding?'

Rewarding? Was that what it was?

'Um, I guess it's fun?' She cast a glance around the pub; there was no sign of anyone disturbing them. 'I kind of fell into events by accident, but it's a good fit for me. Lots of travel, lots of new places, new faces. New challenges every day. Plus, you know, a lot of parties to attend. It's a great job for someone like me.' Someone who wanted to go everywhere and do everything. Or someone with nothing else in her life except her friends, who all had their own relationships and lives to live.

Jon interpreted her words differently. 'A great job for someone who doesn't want to settle down, huh?' He nodded. 'Makes sense.'

That wasn't what she'd meant at all, she realised. She'd been working for Graham for eight years now – wasn't that settled? Until this offer from Beatrix, she hadn't even thought about going elsewhere. Day to day, her job might be always new, always different. But longer term, she'd settled and then some.

'Well, yes . . . I might be making a move, actually,' she said. 'I don't know yet.'

Jon raised his eyebrows. 'Tell me more.'

Lara toyed with her bottle, holding the neck between two fingers and balancing it lightly on the rim. 'I've been offered a new position. I need to let them know my decision before Christmas Eve. It would mean new challenges, the chance to be part of a smaller team so doing more of everything, not just meetings. Better prospects for promotion, too.'

'So what's the catch?' Jon asked, a knowing smile on his lips.

She flashed him a quick grin. Of course he knew there was a catch. 'Apart from the fact I'd be working with a guy I dated for about two seconds before I realised what a dick he was . . .' Did she imagine the flash in Jon's eyes at that? Probably. He'd been *married* for most of the last decade. Jealousy was long gone for the two of them. Right? 'It's a big move, away from the company I've spent a long time building up a reputation with. And . . . it's in Manchester.'

'Manchester, huh? Long way from London.' She couldn't read any deeper meaning into his words, no hint to what he thought she should do. She was surprised to find she was even looking for it.

'Says the man who moved thousands of miles away! It's like, two hours on the train or something, and I'd probably be in town for meetings often enough anyway.' If she took the job. Which she really wasn't sure about.

'Then take it,' Jon said. 'If it moves your career forward, gives you new opportunities, sounds like a no-brainer.'

'Yeah, except . . .'

'Except it means leaving London. And everyone.'

That was why she needed his opinion. Because Jon was one of only six other people in the world who understood what that would mean for the group, and her. Plus, he was the only one of them that had actually done it – moved away. Far, far away.

'Yeah.' Lara sighed. 'I know, I know. That's ridiculous. But there are other reasons too! It's a newer company, bigger risk. It might mean even more work, more travel, while I find my feet. And I *really* don't want Jeremy getting any ideas about why I decided to take the job.' She shuddered.

'Okay. So, then don't take it. Stay where you are.' There was no emotion in his voice, no attempt to sway her either way. But she knew he must *have* an opinion. Jon was always the thinker of the group. The one who could see both sides and think through all the possible outcomes.

'Yes. But then . . .'

'You'll never know what might have been,' Jon finished for her.

She couldn't help it. She looked up and met his gaze. 'Exactly.'

She'd already made that choice once in her life before – and look where it brought her.

Right back to where she started.

Lara frowned, as something new occurred to her. It was true that Jon thought through everything, every possible permutation before acting. There was no way proposing to her ten years ago had been a spur of the moment thing, especially since he'd had the ring ready. He had to have known the chances of her saying no. So why had he proposed? Why then, when they were twenty-one and planning on travelling the world together? Why on Mistletoe Island, that week?

The question was eating away at her. She'd pushed it

back over the years as she tried to forget the whole miserable experience. Now, she desperately wanted to ask him, but they'd made a deal. No talking about their past. Only everything that had happened since.

Jon held her gaze for a long moment. Then, he raised his beer bottle and drained it in one big gulp.

Lara reached into her pocket for her phone – an automatic action, something to put distance between them and give her some cover. But of course, it wasn't there.

Damn Fliss. I hope The Mothers are giving her hell. Except not really, because no one deserved that. Especially not their Miss Fliss.

'Another drink?' Jon was already on his feet, going to the bar.

Watching him leave the table brought her back to her original question, though.

Why did he propose then? And where might we be now if I'd said yes?

Ruth

Rather than revisit the Griffin, they chose the other pub in the village – the amusingly named Damp Squid – for lunch. Ruth smiled at the pub sign, showing a soggy, tentacled creature, as they entered, not expecting much. But inside, the scrubbed wooden tables and handwritten specials black-board would have been at home in any London gastro pub.

'Well! This place has changed,' Caitlin said, looking around her with her hands on her hips. 'I'll get the wine list.'

Ruth chose a table in the window, looking out over the village square, and settled into a beautifully upholstered wingback chair. She placed the shopping bags on the empty table behind her, away from the radiators, and decided that spending lunch at the Damp Squid was a million times better than traipsing around the island alone, avoiding the others.

'I got us white to start.' Caitlin placed two very large glasses of wine between them, then handed Ruth a daily menu, and the wine list. 'You can choose the red.'

Ruth didn't know if all Alec's friends usually drank as much as they were this week, or if it was just the wedding effect. Or even falling back into bad habits around university friends. It would probably be rude to ask, she supposed. But after months of abstinence, she could feel the alcohol going to her head after only a glass. She'd have to pace herself.

They studied the menu, ordering sandwiches and chips when the waiter came to ask.

And then it was just the two of them.

Ruth looked around the pub, full of people who seemed to know each other. 'It's weird being here – on Mistletoe Island, I mean – at last,' she said. 'I've heard so much about it from Alec since we got the invite.'

Caitlin took a large slug of wine. 'It's a unique place, for sure. And it's nice to have us all together again. It's been a long time.'

'Because of Lara and Jon?'

'Yeah.' Caitlin shifted in her chair. Ruth couldn't help but think that, despite her words, Caitlin didn't seem all that happy to be there. In fact, she seemed almost as miserable as Ruth had felt.

Which got her back to thinking about Alec, and what he'd decided to do with his day, without her. Probably he'd ended up in a bar somewhere with the boys.

'It's funny that their break-up was such a big deal,' Ruth said. 'I mean, it's been ten years, right?'

'Yeah. But I guess . . . they were both so young. We all were. And I think because Lara left so quickly after it happened, and then Jon moved overseas, they've never really had the chance to find any closure. Talk through what happened and move on.'

'Closure is important,' Ruth agreed slowly. But she wasn't thinking about Jon and Lara. She was thinking about the scan photos still in her handbag.

'It is. As is time together.' Caitlin tilted her head as she looked at her, and Ruth tried not to squirm under her gaze. 'I'm sorry. But I couldn't help notice you seemed kind of . . . eager to get away from Alec this morning. And the rest of us.'

'Not . . . exactly.' Ruth winced at the half lie. 'It's a lot, when you're all together. And it's not that I don't like you guys! But you all have this history and it's almost like I . . . I don't recognise the person Alec is when you're all together. It's like he's ten-years-ago Alec, not the one I married. Does that make sense?'

Caitlin's smile was a little sad. 'We all do that a bit, I think. We're all nostalgic for who we used to be.'

'Sometimes I think Alec wishes he could go back to then. Start over.' Ruth felt guilty voicing the thought, but not saying it wouldn't stop her thinking it. She couldn't even really blame him. Life must definitely have been easier back then.

'I don't think he would. Not if it meant risking not meeting you.'

Ruth looked up, surprised at the surety in Caitlin's voice. Caitlin smiled across the table, and placed a hand next to hers. 'The minute he saw you, we all knew that you were the only one for him. He came to the pub that night and told us that he'd found the woman he was going to marry. And you've been the most important thing in his life ever since.'

Heat flooded to Ruth's cheeks. Was that really true? She knew Alec loved her, that he'd fallen for her hard from the start – because she'd fallen just as fast and just as hard. He didn't care that she was a couple of years older, or that to start with they hadn't even seemed to have much in common. But deciding to marry her the first day they met? Well, when he wanted something, he went for it. She knew that much was true.

Her blush faded as something occurred to her. He'd wanted a child, their child. Ever since the initial shock of the pregnancy had worn off, he'd been excited and eager for their baby – and she hadn't been able to give him that. She'd been focusing on her own pain, but what was Alec feeling? Hurt, anguish? Or frustration that she was stopping him achieving his goal? He'd never failed before, at anything, really. He must hate not being able to *fix* this.

To fix *her*.

'Of course, he's still an idiot to give you any reason to doubt that,' Caitlin went on, oblivious to Ruth's thoughts. 'Why is he, exactly?'

Ruth blinked. 'Why is he . . .?'

'Why is Alec hanging back, doing tequila shots with Harry and not offering to take you to lunch instead of me?' Caitlin spoke slowly, spelling out the obvious. She sat back in her chair. 'Is there something going on with you two?'

Ruth reached for her wine glass, buying time. She tried to untangle her thoughts. Could she tell Caitlin? She was Alec's friend, not hers. But then, she hadn't told any of *her* friends what was going on, either. She'd wanted to keep her pain and her grief tied up tight inside of her.

But Caitlin was asking. She'd noticed something was wrong, and cared enough to ask.

Taking a deep breath, Ruth prepared herself to admit the truth, outside her family, for the first time.

'I had a silent miscarriage, a couple of months ago.' Sixty-eight days, to be exact, but she didn't want Caitlin to know she was counting. 'The baby . . . it died inside me weeks before that, but we . . .' She looked down at her hands, gripped tight around the stem of the wine glass. 'We didn't know until the twelve-week scan.'

'Oh God.' Caitlin reached to take one of Ruth's hands, squeezing it tight enough to hurt. 'I'm so sorry, Ruth. That's horrific.'

'Yeah, it's been pretty horrendous,' Ruth admitted, struggling to smile. 'We'd hoped to be telling you all our happy news this week. And instead . . .' She shrugged. What else was there to say?

'You're stuck here celebrating someone else's happiness when all you want to do is hibernate until spring.'

'Basically. Yeah.' Ruth looked away. The sympathy in Caitlin's eyes felt too heavy, too knowing. 'And I can't help but think that it's a sign. That maybe we're not meant to be parents.'

Caitlin shook her head ever so slightly, as if she were arguing with herself. Then she looked up, her eyes bright.

'I can't imagine how awful you're feeling right now,' she said. 'But I can listen, if you like. Be a friend.'

Ruth met Caitlin's gaze again. The sympathy was still there, but this time it was tempered with honestly. Openness.

Friendship.

Her friend. Not Alec's.

'Thank you,' Ruth said, after a moment. For the first time in a long time, she felt a glimmer of hope. 'I might take you up on that.'

Fliss

Neal had been wrong. She really *had* needed to go up to the hotel and check on the cake. As well as she knew the Mistletoe Hotel, she'd never worked with them on a cake before, and was taking a lot on trust for their baking. If she'd been working for a client she'd have always, always baked the cake herself. But her mum had pointed out how much more there was to do this week, how Fliss was the *bride,* not just the cake maker, this time. How it was her big day and there were more important things to think about than the cake.

The decorating, though, that was all her. And given the turmoil inside her, she was grateful for the familiarity of it all. The calming whirr of the mixer as it churned up the buttercream until it was smooth and creamy and light. The meditative motion of smoothing the buttercream over the crumb in an even layer. The focused intensity it took to lay the fondant perfectly over each tier, making sure it sat smooth and flat and didn't rip along the way . . . The habitual actions, the same ones she performed every day at the bakery, had gone a long way to calming her after the conversation with Neal that morning. But now all three tiers were split, filled, buttercreamed and covered in fondant . . . and she couldn't risk adding the snowflakes until closer to the time, so there was nothing else to do.

Which was just as well, as it turned out that The Mothers

had called a last-minute, emergency meeting with Melanie, the wedding planner – without inviting Fliss.

'I'm sorry,' Fliss said, surprised, as she stumbled over them on her way up from the kitchens. They were gathered in the cosy seating area off the hotel lobby. 'Did I forget that we were meeting?'

The Mothers exchanged a guilty look. 'We didn't want to bother you with the details, darling,' Fliss's mum said quickly. 'We know how much you have on this week.'

'All those people to entertain down at the cottage,' Ewan's mum Martha added, with a hint of disapproval.

'Well, since I'm here anyway, I might as well help, right?' Fliss flashed them all a grin and took a seat. Although, twenty minutes later, she was wondering why she'd bothered. Clearly no one had told her about the meeting because she really *wasn't* needed for it, since no one had listened to anything she'd had to say so far. Not on the matter of the welcome drinks, or the timings for the speeches. In fact, it was obvious that The Mothers would have preferred it if she wasn't there at all. After all, it was only *her* wedding. What did she have to do with it?

What was it about weddings that drove people insane? Her mum was always a little intense, perhaps, with high expectations for her only daughter. But ever since the wedding planning started – and especially since she and Martha got their heads together – things had reached another level. Fliss was honestly scared to leave them alone too long for fear of what she'd come back to. A Cinderella coach pulled through the snow by elephants, perhaps. Or a pod of dolphins doing a synchronised swimming routine in the bay outside the chapel as they exchanged vows.

'I just think that plain white on white for the tables just isn't celebratory enough,' Fliss's mum said.

Martha shuddered in agreement. 'Not at *all* celebratory.'

Fliss stifled a sigh, as the wedding planner looked through her notes again.

'Well, we've already changed the white napkins for gold, like you asked for, Mrs Hayes,' the long-suffering Melanie said. 'And then the chair ribbons for gold and white ones to match, as you suggested, Mrs Bennett.'

Never mind that Fliss's theme had been white and silver with snowflakes. Apparently, that was too subtle. Fliss bit the inside of her cheek to keep from lamenting the loss of her simple, elegant white linen. Plain white linen and china with a subtle snowflake print on the napkins and white bows with tiny silver snowflake charms on the chairs. That's what she'd wanted. But apparently, it wasn't what she was getting.

'What about the china?' her mum asked. 'Is there something we can do there?'

'Well, the hotel does have a rather lovely gold and white service we could hire for just a little extra.' Obviously Melanie had anticipated this. After months of working with The Mothers, Fliss wasn't surprised.

Fliss's mum clapped her hands together with joy. 'That would be perfect!'

'But is it *enough* though, Harriet?' Martha asked. 'What about the glassware? Golden champagne flutes would be just perfect for the toasts, don't you think?'

Melanie's smile grew a little more rigid. 'I'll see what I can do.'

Fliss winced at the mental image of her wedding breakfast tables, and then forced herself to let it go. The Mothers were happy. And this was their big day too, in lots of ways. She just wished Ewan was there with her to roll his eyes and whisper jokes about how ridiculous they were both being.

Of course, Ewan had wisely decided to stay well out

of the way on the golf course with his father and Harry, while Fliss's dad caught up with 'some business', which Fliss suspected actually meant a John Wayne movie in his hotel room. She didn't blame him. A little escapism would be great around now. If it wasn't *her* wedding she'd be curled up there with him, the same way she had when she was a little girl, avoiding doing whatever boring chores her mother wanted her to do next.

The Fathers in general hadn't been much help dealing with The Mothers. Sandy, Ewan's father, had little interest in anything besides golf at the best of times. Fliss's dad, meanwhile, seemed to have decided that since he was providing both cash and venue for the big day his work was done – and Fliss couldn't really argue with that. Besides, he'd let her mum make all the decisions in their lives this far, declaring 'I provide, she decides!' to anyone who'd listen. Why would she have thought it would be any different now?

As Melanie dashed around updating the sample table she'd had set up for them with all the latest golden additions, Fliss's mind started to wander. And of course, it wandered straight back to that morning.

Why had she thought for a moment that she could get through this week without having to talk to Neal about the secrets they still kept between them? That she could put all that behind them without ever addressing it, ending it for good?

That stupid pact. A vow to only be their real selves with each other. Who even *was* her real self these days? Fliss wasn't sure that she even knew.

What had started out as friendly reassurance, the comfort of having a true friend she could relax and say anything to, go anywhere with, do anything with, without judgement . . . somehow, over the years, had morphed into something far more constraining than freeing. And Fliss had no idea how to break those bonds now.

'What do you think about the centrepieces, Martha?' Fliss's mum asked, and she tuned back for a moment. 'It's not too late to change them if we're not sure.'

The wedding is in three days! Fliss wanted to yell. *Of course it's too late! And I chose those centrepieces.* A silver mirror topped with white candles, island greenery (no mistletoe, though, in case one of the berries fell off onto someone's plate and they ate it. Fliss didn't want her wedding breakfast to poison anyone) and, as of Martha's latest interference, delicate snowdrops in tiny glass bud vases. Simple, elegant – and completely out of keeping with everything else now The Mothers had changed everything.

'Maybe we *do* need a little more height on the tables,' Martha replied. Both women stood, their heads tilted at an identical angle, studying the sample table.

As if the centrepieces were what really mattered most about the day. As if she wasn't falling apart over here, freaking out about Neal and secrets and memories.

Remember our first kiss?

Remember when we went swimming here?

He was trying to confuse her. He had to be. But why?

Anything between them that crossed the friendship line had been over for years, since before she met Ewan. Since then, there hadn't been so much as an ill-advised drunken kiss.

But before then . . . even if it had only ever been when Neal and Caitlin were split up, Fliss couldn't deny that it had happened.

They'd been so lucky never to be caught out. Fliss shuddered to think of what might have happened if they'd bumped into one of the others on one of their wild nights.

149

For a time, she'd been paranoid that Lara suspected, but she'd never said anything if she did, and eventually Fliss had relaxed about it.

The last thing they needed was to tempt fate again, bring it all back up and risk discovery now, when it was all over.

'What about the cake?' Martha said, and Fliss snapped back into The Mothers' conversation. 'I really do still feel a wedding cake needs flowers on it somewhere. Maybe if we went with the larger white roses for the tables, and used some fresh flowers on the cake . . .'

'The cake is taken care of, Martha,' she said, trying not to grit her teeth. 'Please, don't worry about it when you have so much else to think about.' She waved a hand across the sample table set up the wedding planner had put together for them. It was hideous. And it was all hers. 'In fact, if you two are okay dealing with this, I need to go get some air. Or maybe some coffee.'

'Okay, dear,' The Mothers said. In unison.

It was terrifying. Two women who'd barely even met before this week had now morphed into the same person. A scary, mutant two-headed person who was trying to take over her wedding day. And Fliss couldn't even bring herself to care.

The day itself didn't matter. Well, it did. But not as much as what came after. After, she'd be Mrs Ewan Bennett. *That* was what mattered.

Because then, she'd be free.

She wouldn't be the innocent baby the rest of the group had to coddle. The girl who had crept out and got caught and kept secrets to make sure they didn't see her differently. That they didn't see the parts of her they wouldn't like.

She wouldn't be the Fliss who had kissed her best friend's boyfriend, or slept with him the night they broke up, before they got back together again two days later. Which was just as well. She didn't like that Fliss very much, anyway.

She wanted to move on. It was past time. And Neal *had* to be her past, not her future, now.

Fliss pushed open the door to the hotel bar. Maybe she'd grab a latte, take it out on the terrace and drink it watching the tiny flurries of snowflakes drifting down, now the early morning sun had given way to more clouds and snow. They had heaters out there, and blankets, and it was sheltered from the wind.

But as she entered the bar, she heard a familiar voice, and knew that her past wouldn't be left behind that easily.

'Harry! Where's Harry gone now?' Neal called. 'He didn't tell me what he wanted to drink.'

'I think he's chatting up my daughter out on the terrace,' Ewan's dad said. 'Should I be worried about that?'

'Probably not,' said Alec, sounding very relaxed about the whole thing. 'Harry likes to flirt, but he never makes promises.'

Didn't he realise that only made it worse? Probably not. Alec was such a . . . man sometimes. She didn't know how Ruth could stand it.

'Fliss?' Neal had spotted her. And moved closer. 'Bored of the wedding preparations already?'

'No,' she lied. 'Just tired after last night. I thought I'd grab a latte. Where's Ewan?' She glanced belatedly around the bar, looking for her fiancé.

'Popped back up to his room to get changed,' Neal replied. 'It transpires golf in the snow wasn't as much fun as anticipated.'

'Told him he needed waterproofs! That boy's been living down south too long,' Ewan's dad called over from the bar.

'Shall I get you a drink?' Neal asked, watching her

carefully. Nothing more than long-standing friendship there, now.

Fliss's gaze flicked to the terrace, where Harry was right now working his charms on poor, defenceless Betsy. Fliss liked Ewan's sister – and her little boy, Morgan. But given everything Betsy had been through with her ex, and now trying to make it as a single mother, the last thing she needed was Harry messing her about.

Harry never meant to hurt anyone, and Alec was right – he never made promises. But that didn't seem to stop women falling for him anyway.

'Or would you rather I go have a word with our friend out there?' Neal said, following her gaze. Because, like always, he knew exactly what she was thinking.

The same way she knew exactly what was on his mind, too, however well he hid it.

'Would you?' She felt bad for asking, but Neal was always the best choice for smoothing things over, finding a way for everyone to back down without losing face. It was a skill they'd all taken advantage of over the years, when inevitable tensions rose. Neal wasn't just Caitlin's enforcer, putting her plans into action. He was the negotiator and the counsellor when she overstepped the mark, and started giving orders rather than making plans. He was the one who talked Caitlin down when her high expectations of others – and herself – led to disappointment sometimes. He was the calm head, the peacemaker.

He wasn't able to soothe his own tensions, though. He needed Fliss for that.

'You want me to put him off for good? Or warn Betsy off?' Neal shrugged, like it was no skin off his nose either way. Which it probably wasn't.

He'd always been so good with people. Harry charmed,

but Neal made people feel understood. Jon got too deep, too serious, too soon, with every conversation, and Alec barged through them all with the grace of a rhino. But Neal listened, and heard what people weren't saying.

It was how he'd seen past the image she'd tried so hard to keep up for the rest of them. Well, that and seeing her at that awful party one Christmas night. Getting her out of there when she couldn't stand or stand up for herself.

Neal knew all her secrets. It was what made him so terrifying to her.

'Just . . . interrupt them. Get Harry back in here with the others, so he can't seduce and abandon poor Betsy before we get to my wedding day.'

'Don't want your special day ruined by women in tears, huh?' Neal joked.

She glared at him. 'I don't want Betsy to get hurt. I don't want *anyone* to get hurt.' The last was a whisper, almost. A plea.

Neal dropped his voice too, but she still heard him, even as she turned away to join her father-in-law to be at the bar. 'I think it might already be too late for that, sweetheart.'

Lara

They all arrived back to the cottage about the same time. Lara helped Caitlin and Ruth with the bags, and almost regretted not joining them as she heard about their long, boozy lunch.

Or she might have done, if she hadn't had her own pub stop with Jon.

She peeked at him from beneath her eyelashes as he started unpacking the bags onto the counter, mesmerised by his familiar movements. They'd nursed another couple of bottles of beer for hours, and shared a giant bowl of chips, more intent on getting to know each other all over again than on getting drunk. They'd stayed away from any subjects that resonated too closely with their past, and actually . . . it had been fun.

Except now it felt like she had two Jons in her head. Two men who had the same mannerisms, the same way of looking too deeply into her words, her eyes. One had the start of a few grey hairs by his temple and the finest of lines around his hazel eyes, but the light from inside them still gleamed in the same way. His body was still long and lean and lightly muscled. She could still make him laugh, his whole face lighting up in a way that was almost painful to see as the young man inside emerged once again.

But only one of them had an American twang to his voice. Only one went running, instead of hiking or climbing or

rowing. And only one of them had ever touched and worshipped every inch of her bare skin.

Stop thinking about it.

She knew all about his job, his marriage, his father's ill
health, his decision to move home. She knew what he liked
about living abroad and what he missed. Knew what he was
hoping to do back in Britain. Knew he wanted to get a
dog – a rescue, probably. She'd only just managed to hold
herself back from volunteering to go with him to the shelter
to choose. She could already see the life and the future he
had planned for himself, and it would be so, so easy to let
herself imagine herself as part of it – especially when it was
just the two of them, talking about their hopes and dreams,
like they'd always done.

But this wasn't the old days.

She wondered what he made of her life, her choices.
When she'd told him all about her job, and the new job
offer, he'd offered advice, guidance, as he always had. But
he'd stayed detached, uninvolved. Because her choices *didn't*
involve him any more, and that still felt weird, even after all
this time.

The strangest part, though, was only knowing the facts.
Jon had told her everything important that had happened to
him over the last decade. But he hadn't told her how he *felt*
about any of it.

And still bouncing around in her head were the *other*
things she didn't know. Things that hadn't seemed to matter
so much until this week, this place. Why had he proposed
at twenty-one? And a more urgent question: what did he
think of her now, at thirty-one? The person she'd become,
yes. But also the person who'd driven him away. Had he
ever forgiven her? Or did he thank his lucky stars for his
escape?

She didn't know if she'd ever have the courage to ask him those last two questions.

'Are you two still okay to cook?' Alec asked, eyeing Ruth and Caitlin as they giggled over a receipt they'd pulled out of a bag of shopping. It was clear they were slightly tipsy.

The two women exchanged an amused look. 'I think we'll still do a lot better than you, darling,' Ruth said.

Lara grinned. The kitchen was the one place that had defeated Alec in his quest to be excellent at everything. She remembered how he'd once set fire to the microwave in their student house, and twice almost electrocuted himself using the toaster. They'd stopped including him on the dinner rota at that point.

'I'll help,' Fliss said, easing herself down from where she'd been sat on the counter. But there was none of the usual Fliss bounce and sunshine. Lara frowned. Was the wedding stress getting to her? Or, most likely, spending the day with The Mothers. She'd get her alone later and ask.

The men were sloping off towards the sitting room, and the sound of the TV carried out to the kitchen. 'Does it bother anyone else that we're getting stuck with the cooking?' Lara asked the others, as she poured her own, well-deserved glass of wine.

'Nope,' Caitlin said happily.

'Not at all,' Ruth added, laughing.

Lara narrowed her eyes. She was missing something here. 'Is this because you don't want Alec to burn the kitchen down? Because Jon and Neal are actually good cooks, you know.'

'I reckon it's because all the alcohol is in here,' Fliss said, taking the wine bottle from Lara to fill her own glass.

'It's because we did the calculations.' Caitlin pulled herb and spice jars from the cupboard and lined them up on the counter in the order they appeared in the recipe. 'The boys cooked breakfast this morning, right? And since we agreed to cook dinner, they'll do the clear up too.'

'Right,' Lara said, slowly. 'But breakfast is a hell of a lot easier than dinner.'

'Yes, but they're in the habit now. They'll cook breakfast every morning and leave dinner to us.'

'And this is a good thing because . . .?' Fliss asked. Lara was glad she wasn't the only one not getting it. Then suddenly, she did.

'Because tomorrow is the stag and hen dos, so we're all eating out,' she said.

'And Sunday's the rehearsal dinner buffet,' Fliss added.

'And Monday's the wedding.' Lara grinned.

'Exactly,' Caitlin said. 'So as long as we cook this one meal, we're off the hook until we all go home on Christmas Eve. We can bung this in the oven, go get ready for the lantern walk, and relax for the rest of the trip.'

That, Lara decided, was why Caitlin was the planner of the group. And such excellent forward thinking deserved a toast. Topping up everyone's glasses, she raised hers. 'Here's to weddings.'

'And romance,' Ruth added, with the sort of secret smile that told Lara the girls' lunch with Caitlin had been good for her. She seemed almost lighter, somehow. Definitely more relaxed. Although that might be the wine.

'And friendship,' Fliss said, but *her* smile didn't quite reach her eyes. *Definitely need to talk to Fliss.*

They all drank. Caitlin slammed her glass down on the counter. 'Right! Let's get cooking.'

In the end, Caitlin ended up doing most of the cooking, with Ruth acting as sous chef. Ruth chopped up the shallots, garlic and ginger, as Caitlin rubbed flour and seasoning into the beef before browning it in the pot. They worked seamlessly together, Ruth adding the shallots to the pot at Caitlin's nod, then fetching the port from the other room while Caitlin assembled the rest of the ingredients from the recipe's long list. Obviously, their lunch out had helped them bond; Ruth had never made such an effort to be part of the group before.

Lara perched on the counter stool next to Fliss, who was flicking through a cake magazine.

'So.' Fliss shuffled her stool a little closer, and murmured in Lara's ear. 'I couldn't help but notice you arrived back with Jon . . . What exactly did *you* get up to today?'

'We went for a walk. Stopped for some chips and a pint. That's all.'

Fliss huffed a laugh. 'This is you and Jon we're talking about. Breathing the same air is an achievement for you guys. I know how relieved you were when we thought he couldn't make it, remember? So, more details, please. Talking over lunch?'

'We caught up on the last ten years or so,' Lara admitted. 'We decided to start our friendship over again from the beginning.'

'Just friendship?' Fliss asked, eyebrows raised.

'Of course! It's been ten years, Fliss. What else could it possibly be?'

Fliss's gaze was too knowing, like she could read all the thoughts and worries that Lara had been carefully suppressing since Jon had arrived on Mistletoe Island. Maybe longer.

Maybe the last decade.

Like exactly why it was she never could make a relationship stick, and whether that was because she'd let the only one that would ever really matter to her implode right here on this island.

'With you two?' Fliss shook her head. 'I wouldn't dare guess. You and Jon were always . . . I don't know. Different.'

'Well, we're definitely different people now than we were ten years ago.' Even if it didn't feel like it when they were together.

'Are you sure?' Fliss asked, softly.

Lara looked away so she didn't have to admit that she wasn't sure at all.

She had been, before she came here. But maybe the fundamentals of a person didn't ever really change, at heart. And it was her heart that seemed to be the problem.

'What are you two whispering about over there?' Caitlin asked, across the kitchen. The scent of orange zest and grated ginger wafted on the air.

'Lara was telling me about her intimate lunch with Jon today,' Fliss said airily, and Lara glared at her.

'Okay, this is the worst idea ever,' Caitlin said, after a brief moment of stunned silence.

'It isn't an idea,' Lara said. 'Nothing is happening. We were catching up. As friends. All we did was talk.' And that was probably all they'd ever do, ever again.

'They were having deep and meaningful conversations in the pub on the cliff path for hours this afternoon,' Fliss corrected. 'And you know those two and their *conversations*.'

'How can you make *talking* sound so seedy?' Lara asked, but no one else was listening. No one else even seemed to notice how un-Miss-Fliss-like the comment was. Probably because they were too preoccupied with Lara and her terrible track record at relationships.

'They used to spend hours just talking, before they got together,' Caitlin explained to Ruth, as if Lara wasn't even in the room. 'It was totally obvious that they were both crazy for each other, but neither of them would do anything about it.' Caitlin eyed Lara suspiciously. 'You and Jon . . . I think you made the right decision ten years, okay? So don't go screwing it up now.'

Lara felt a jolt of surprise. 'You think I made the right decision back then?' Because that had definitely not been apparent in Caitlin's behaviour after the split. It had taken *months* for them to even be friendly again, after Lara turned Jon down. Caitlin hadn't been able to understand why, if she loved Jon so much, she wouldn't just marry him already. And Lara hadn't been able to find the words to explain.

But *now* Caitlin thought she'd done the right thing? Even Fliss was staring at their friend, open-mouthed.

Caitlin shrugged. 'I mean, you were twenty-one. You'd never met anyone outside of school and university. How many people actually marry their university boyfriend, anyway?'

'You did,' Lara said, before she could stop herself. Caitlin didn't reply to that, busying herself with putting the casserole in the oven instead.

'The point is – you and Jon,' Fliss said, with a pointed look at Caitlin's back as if to say 'don't push it'. Clearly there was something going on with Caitlin and Neal that Lara wasn't in the loop about. 'We've all been there, we've all dealt with the fallout. Do you really want to put us all through that again?'

'Hey!' Put *them* through it? And here she'd thought that she and Jon were the ones whose lives she'd turned upside down. Whose hearts had been broken.

At least she hoped she might have gone a small way to starting to heal that today.

'Sorry,' Fliss said, automatically. 'I've spent all day with

The Mothers, and lost the ability to be subtle.'

That Lara could understand.

'It's fine. Besides, I'm not putting anyone through any-thing,' she said, dully. 'There's nothing happening. We talked, that's all. Maybe got a little closure.'

Caitlin let out a relieved sigh, straightening up from the oven. 'Closure. Closure is good. Closure means moving on.' She set the timer on the cooker – apparently, the stew would take at least three hours to cook. Plenty of time for the lantern walk.

'And it's about time you did *that*,' Fliss said, grabbing an empty wine glass and filling it to the brim. 'I mean, at least Jon went off and started a new life, got married and all.'

'And divorced,' Ruth added in an undertone.

'But you've barely been on a *date* since you and Jon broke up. *Ten years ago.*' Fliss finished with a flourish, spilling wine over herself as she brandished the glass in Lara's direction. What was up with her today?

'I've dated plenty,' Lara replied. It wasn't a lie, either. She'd had more than enough of dating guys who didn't get her. She and Jon might have spent months talking before they got any further, but at least that meant they *knew* each other when they decided to start a relationship. She was sick of guys who were only interested in her for as long as it took to get her into bed.

'But you've never fallen in love again, have you?' Caitlin said, softly. 'Maybe that's the problem.'

Lara carefully placed her glass down on the kitchen coun-ter. 'There is no problem. Everything is fine. And since you've all clearly got things under control in here, I'm going to go put on about seventeen extra layers of clothing before this lantern walk.'

'Will you remind the boys we're going soon, too?' Caitlin

asked. Lara waved a hand to show she'd heard as she headed towards the living room and the men. At least she could be pretty sure none of *them* were going to quiz her on the state of her heart.

Even if she almost wished that one of them in particular would.

Ruth

The woods looked magical in the lamp light.

Trees towered over them, branches spiking the sky and swaying in the coastal breeze, leaves whispering in the dark. Above the whispers, Ruth could just make out the faint sound of a band playing, further into the wood. The lantern walk was a local tradition – one that had expanded as more and more tourists came to the island, it seemed – and stalls and stages were set out in a trail through the trees, for visitors to track.

Ruth shoved her gloved hands in her pockets and stared at the trees to the side of the narrow path, while they waited for all the walkers to congregate on the edge of the woods. The entrance through the trees was marked by two old-fashioned carriage lanterns, hung from wrought-iron poles stuck into the frozen ground. A small icicle hung from one of the curled metal spirals at the end, and the light glinted off it as if it were glowing.

Despite the buzz of chatter from the group – Alec and his friends, a couple of other wedding guests who'd arrived early, tourists and island locals – Ruth felt strangely peaceful, with the sea crashing on the rocks on one side, and the otherworldly lights shining through the trees on the other. It felt as though she was about to step through a portal into a different realm.

She didn't make any effort to keep in step with the others

when they were finally given leave to start, although she made sure she kept the rest of their group in sight. Alec and Caitlin were leading the way up at the front, which didn't surprise her. They were deep in conversation, their heads bent close, and Caitlin's glossy red hair gleamed in the light of the lamps that lined the path. Ruth hoped that meant that Caitlin was sharing at least some of whatever was bothering her this week, since she'd managed to avoid all of Ruth's leading questions on the subject over lunch. But from what she knew of Caitlin, they could just as easily be talking about plans for Neal's birthday in March, or what sort of bathroom they wanted to install for the en suite. Or what Ruth had told her at lunch? She felt a twinge of hurt at the thought that Caitlin might share a secret Ruth had trusted her with, even with Alec, who already knew everything. She wouldn't . . . would she?

Fliss and Jon were a little way behind Alec and Caitlin, the bride-to-be's hand tucked through the crook of Jon's arm, pulling him along. Whatever had been bothering Fliss when they'd been cooking seemed to have been put aside, or possibly drowned in wine, because as far as Ruth could tell, Fliss had kept up a stream of excited conversation, bouncing along on her toes, for the entire walk so far. Maybe the magic of the lantern walk had re-enthused her.

Lara, meanwhile, was staying a good distance behind them, with a couple of locals between them too as a buffer. Ruth didn't pretend to know what was really going on between Lara and Jon, but whatever it was, neither of them seemed comfortable with it. Ewan walked beside Lara, dressed in a fleece over his jumper but no coat, hat or gloves. He seemed comfortable enough, though, chatting easily as he pointed out the different sorts of trees or plants growing around them.

Which left Ruth at the back. She frowned. Who was missing, though?

Harry, she realised. Where was Harry? She glanced behind her and found him bringing up the rear with Betsy and her son, Morgan, who was tugging on Harry's hand as he tried to race ahead. Ruth shook her head. Was there anything he wouldn't do to get a woman into bed? Alec was right: Harry was incorrigible. But there was someone else missing, too . . .

'Pretty lights,' Neal said, falling into step beside her. 'Although the whole thing feels rather more pagan than Christmassy, don't you think?'

'I think that's what I like about it,' she admitted, with a smile.

'Ah, you should check out the well, then.' Neal pointed to a sign as they passed it, leading walkers off the main path and into the darkness of the wood, towards something called 'Tobar na Coilltean' or – the English translation told her – The Well of the Woods. 'Supposed to have magical powers or something.' He squinted into the pitch black of the trees. 'Maybe wait until daytime, though.'

'Sounds like the best plan,' Ruth agreed, turning her back on that midnight land, and sticking firmly to the well-lit path.

Neal. How had she forgotten about Neal? Well, actually, she knew exactly how. She'd always found Neal harder work that the others. He seemed to Ruth more an extension of Caitlin than a friend in his own right, although she knew that he and Fliss were close, and that Alec, too, enjoyed his company. Perhaps it was because she only ever saw him when Caitlin was around too that she couldn't get a handle on who he was without her.

Tonight, though, it was just the two of them, wandering

through the trees behind the others. Perhaps this was her chance to get to know Neal better. Although he seemed distracted, his gaze flickering between his friends up ahead.

Did he see the same things she did? The strange pairings, the deep conversations? Did he know what Caitlin was saying to Alec? Or did he not care?

'Caitlin was telling me that the kitchen remodelling has been delayed again,' Ruth said. DIY had to be a fairly safe topic of conversation, whatever it was that was making Neal frown so.

'Hmm?' He looked over at her blankly, then nodded. 'Oh, yeah, right. The kitchen. Caitlin's in charge of that.'

Seemed to Ruth that Caitlin was in charge of pretty much everything.

While she tried to think of another topic of conversation, Ruth turned her attention back to the walk, and found herself so mesmerised that she almost forgot about Neal altogether.

The trees that lined the route were hung with small white lanterns and miles of sparkling fairy lights, strung through the branches, high above them, but also down at ground level, marking the path. Every now and then the path would widen into a clearing, where there'd be stalls selling hot rolls or mulled wine, or a band of musicians playing folk music, or carol singers performing. Sometimes the lights changed and great shards of coloured lights flew up between the branches, making a whole canopy of light overhead.

When she stopped to admire a display, Neal handed her a cup of mulled wine, and she took it gratefully, wrapping her hands around it to warm her through her gloves. She hadn't even noticed him leave her to go to the stall.

'Thanks,' she said, smiling up at him.

With all the stopping and starting and things to see, she'd lost sight of Alec and Caitlin altogether. They'd passed Ewan and Lara a while back, where he was showing her how mistletoe grew on other trees, a parasitic plant. But Harry, Betsy and Morgan had raced past them early on, too, and Fliss and Jon were just up ahead. Neal started walking again, catching the others up, so Ruth fell into step too, until they were walking behind Fliss and Jon.

'How is work going?' Ruth asked, as the path turned narrower. The forest was plunged into darkness as they turned a corner and the last light display faded out of sight. 'You work in software design, right?'

'More project management, these days,' Neal said. 'But yeah, I started out there.'

'And do you like it?' It sounded indescribably dull.

'I'm thinking of leaving. Starting my own business, doing something completely new,' Neal replied, not looking at her. Somehow, even talking about changing his whole career trajectory, Neal didn't sound particularly excited about the prospect.

Ahead, Fliss spun round. 'I didn't know that.'

He shrugged, as Fliss fell into step with them, making the path uncomfortably narrow. 'It's just an idea right now. Something I'm working on. Meeting people, doing research, that sort of thing.'

'Sounds exciting though,' Jon said, from a few steps ahead.

'Caitlin hates the idea, of course. Too much risk.' Neal drained the last of his mulled wine and crushed the cup between his hands. 'It'll probably never happen.'

'That's a shame.' Fliss's words were neutral, but her eyes were troubled – Ruth could see that even by the light of the lanterns.

'I thought it might be nice to have a fresh start,' Neal said, his gaze fixed on Fliss's.

As Fliss turned and began walking again, Neal hurried to follow. Watching them pull ahead, Ruth wondered if Neal had really been sharing his plans with *her* at all.

Lara

Ewan, Lara had decided, was a hidden gem.

Even though he and Fliss had been dating for a couple of years, between Lara's work travel and Fliss and Ewan's loved-up routine, she didn't think she'd ever spent more than a few minutes alone with him – or heard him talk so much. Usually, Fliss was there with them, shining with happiness and chatting enough for both of them, or they were with the whole group, in which case he'd probably struggle to get a word in edgeways.

She'd sort of assumed he was taciturn, or maybe even a little dull. Turned out he was just letting the rest of them talk themselves out.

So far on the lantern walk, she'd discovered that he knew a lot about nature in general – and mistletoe in particular – and was interested in Norse mythology, weather systems and wanted three kids.

He also worshipped the very ground Fliss walked on, which Lara definitely approved of.

'This whole island is fascinating, you know?' he said, as they strolled between the trees and lanterns. 'I mean, look up there! Mistletoe, just clinging to the trees.' Lara looked up and, sure enough, there was the green plant with the white berries she associated with ill-advised Christmas kisses. 'But it's not just the plant life. It's the geology, the community, even the mythology . . . I've been reading up a lot about the place since Fliss suggested we have the wedding here.'

'I guess it must be a bit strange, getting married some-where you've never been before,' Lara said. She hadn't really thought about it before; Mistletoe Island meant so much to Fliss and to the rest of them, but Ewan had probably never even heard of the place until he met her.

Ewan shrugged. 'It wasn't that, so much. I know how much Fliss loves it here, so I wanted to find out more. Do you know that they call it the Healing Island? Mistletoe is poisonous in large quantities, but actually it's been used for centuries to enhance fertility, treat epilepsy and nervous dis-orders . . . and these days, they even use it for cancer!'

'I didn't know that,' Lara said, with a smile. 'What else did you find out?'

Lots, it turned out. Ewan was so laid-back and easy to talk to, they'd made easy conversation most of the way around the lantern walk before Lara even noticed they'd lost the others. Probably when they stopped to listen to the musi-cians that had caught her attention, and Ewan had fetched them hot chocolates and waited patiently for her to finish listening.

'Will Fliss be worrying about you?' Lara asked, as she picked up her pace. 'You can go on ahead if you like, catch her up.'

Ewan lengthened his stride a little, but somehow still seemed to be strolling at a relaxed pace. Lara realised he must have been ambling along beside her when he could have caught the others up easily if he'd wanted.

'She'll know I won't be far,' he said. 'We'll find them by the time we reach the beach, anyway, I imagine.'

'Thanks for hanging back with me.' There had been so much to see, to take in. And, okay, she might have been avoiding being alone with Jon again a little bit.

'Any time,' Ewan said, smiling. Somehow, Lara got the impression he knew *exactly* why she'd been lingering along the way.

In some ways, he reminded her of Harry, she decided – well, Harry without the commitment issues. And he didn't use his charm as openly as Harry did. Rather, he stepped back and let you discover it for yourself.

He wasn't her type – she was more partial to dark and intense than light and laid-back – but Lara could absolutely see why Fliss had fallen for him.

And she'd never had to ask why someone would fall for Fliss. Miss Fliss was the dream girlfriend: kind and sweet and bubbly and *nice*. The only mystery was why she hadn't been snapped up by someone years ago.

'What made you propose to Fliss?' The words popped out of her mouth before she could stop them, and for the first time Ewan actually looked surprised. 'I mean, I can think of a million reasons off the top of my head why you might want to marry her. I wondered . . . which one of them made you actually do it.'

That was a lie, she realised. What she was actually wondering was what had made *Jon* propose, ten years ago. Maybe Ewan could give her some insight into the male brain, since she couldn't exactly ask Jon without upsetting the uneasy truce they seemed to have reached this week. The one that ignored their past altogether.

Ewan considered his answer carefully, which she liked. For all his easy-going nature, when he spoke he said what mattered to him. 'I guess . . . I woke up beside her one morning and realised that I couldn't imagine my life without her. I bought the ring the next day.'

He made it sound so simple.

Lara walked on, barely seeing the lights, lost in her own

thoughts. Jon hadn't been in her life for ten years, but now he was back, even just as a friend, she couldn't imagine it without him again. He was . . . fundamental to who she was, even who she'd become without him.

Which was why it was so important to keep him as a friend. She couldn't risk anything more, however tempted she might feel. Because Jon mattered. Her friends mattered. And if she wanted to keep them all in her life, then Jon could only ever be her friend.

They all knew what happened when he became anything more.

'Here we go,' Ewan said suddenly. 'Watch your step.'

Lara looked up suddenly and realised they'd walked all the way through the woods and out again, emerging further down the cliff from where they went in, beside steep steps that led down the cliff face to the beach. Each step was edged by a lantern, to make sure no one missed noticing the sheer drop on the other side. All the same, Lara clung close to the wall and kept one hand pressed against the rock as they descended. Ewan, meanwhile, walked down with his hands in his pockets, whistling a Christmas carol – although he did glance back every few steps to check she was okay.

She wondered if Fliss had warned him about her phobia of these type of descents. Probably. It was what had knocked visiting Machu Picchu off her Thirty before Thirty list, for certain. And Fliss had had to deal with it when they'd visited that temple in Thailand on their post-graduation travels.

Still, she made it to the bottom intact without losing her footing and knocking down everyone else on the staircase, which was always her biggest fear. As her feet hit the sand and pebbles of the beach, Lara breathed a huge sigh of relief, even before Ewan pointed to the others, standing over by another food and drink stall.

As they joined them, Jon stepped forward and handed her a cup of mulled wine. 'I thought you'd need this.'

'Thanks.' She took it with a smile.

Yes, this was why she had to keep Jon as just a friend. She needed him in her life again as the person who knew her best – better than Fliss, even.

The only problem, Lara thought, as she watched his profile in the moonlight over the rim of her cup, was how badly she wanted to kiss him.

Fliss

Fliss eyed the empty wine bottles dotted across the dining table, as the others talked and laughed. Ruth had disappeared to bed straight after dinner, so Alec seemed to be responsible for at least one drained bottle. Caitlin and Lara had shared another, Jon and Neal the third, before they moved on to brandy. Fliss was too self-conscious to drink much more. Too afraid to let anything slip, or show how unsettled she felt this week, especially with Neal sitting beside her. If he tried to talk to her again, here, when anyone could overhear them, she needed to be alert enough to distract him, without the others noticing.

The lantern walk had been lovely, the mulled wine on the beach welcome, and Caitlin's beef with ginger and cranberry casserole delicious as always. Ewan had headed straight back to the hotel with the other guests, and now it was just the seven of them again, since Harry returned more than an hour after the rest of them with a grin and a vague excuse for his absence.

Fliss knew she should be worried about that. But it seemed she'd reached her limit of things she could worry about today.

Including Jon and Lara.

Earlier, she'd been reading too much into Lara and Jon's lunch, teasing her friend a little too hard. Probably they really had been catching up. But if watching Lara and Jon for signs of a reunion kept Caitlin distracted from the way Neal was watching Fliss, then was it any surprise Fliss hadn't been able to help herself?

Except then she'd spent the lantern walk with Jon, seeing how his gaze always darted back to where Lara was walking with Ewan, until they lost them completely. She'd tried to talk to him about it, to see what she could do to help her friends, but then she'd overheard Neal talk to Ruth about starting his own business. She'd been annoyed that Neal hadn't talked to her about his plans first. Annoyed enough that she'd forgotten all about Jon and his sad eyes.

So much for supporting her friend. She was a terrible person. She knew this, even if none of the others did. She'd known it longer than anyone, even Neal. And her parents, so certain she was their perfect golden girl who would always obey their wishes, had never even noticed at all.

All she could do now was try and keep those awful parts of her hidden a little longer. The part that wanted to rage against the world, to tell people all the horrible things she'd ever thought about them. The part that wanted to tell The Mothers that it was *her* wedding and they could get their beaky noses out of it. The part, deep inside, that still wanted to run to Neal and ask him to get her away from all of this and take her somewhere she could stop thinking about everyone else and do whatever the hell she wanted to do for a change.

All her life, her parents had stressed the importance of thinking about others. Of being a good girl, doing what she was asked, making people happy. That, she knew, was the only way to truly win love – by being loveable.

Once she married Ewan, she hoped she'd have proven once and for all that she could be the person they loved – and maybe something more, too.

She just had to make it to Christmas Eve Eve without everything blowing up in her face.

A knock on the door made her start, as if it were Blind Justice coming for her, ready to read a list of her crimes. Fliss jumped to her feet to answer it. It was far too late for visitors, though. Unless it was . . .

'Ewan!' She opened the door to find her fiancé waiting on the doorstep. This was good. When Ewan was there, she felt like *his* Fliss again. The one she wanted to be for ever.

Not this strange throwback to a girl she never really was.

Maybe he could stay the night to remind her. Except since she was sharing the room with Lara, that might be a little awkward . . .

Ewan swept in to press a swift kiss to her cheek. 'Hey, love. My mum asked me to bring this down for you. I think she'd like you to wear it on Monday, but was too nervous to ask you herself.'

He handed her a flat box, too large for a garter, or anything else hidden. What else could Martha have sent, though? She knew she already had her dress and everything sorted. And given everything else about the wedding Martha had been perfectly happy to change without consulting her, Fliss was amazed there was anything she'd be nervous to ask. Unless she just figured that if Ewan asked her, Fliss's mum wouldn't be there to up the stakes with another request to outdo this one.

'Come inside.' She shut the door behind him, frowning at the box in her hand. She led him through to the living room. The others were still at the long wooden dining table in the cottage kitchen, so at least she could open her box in peace. If it was awful, she didn't want to hear Lara or Caitlin's views just yet. Or worse, Neal's.

'What is it? Do you know?' she asked.

Ewan shook his head. 'Open it.'

Fingers trembling, she eased back the lid.

'Oh! It's a . . . veil.' A delicate, gossamer, beautiful fine veil embroidered with tiny, tiny snowdrops at the edges.

A veil that would hide her face and her shame, until Ewan lifted it. A shiver ran through her at all the things he might discover if he really did lift the veil. If he ever saw the real Fliss.

This was why she hadn't wanted to wear a veil. It felt too much like hiding, when all she wanted was to finally, finally be – not herself, no, not that. But the person she'd always hoped to become, but somehow could never quite manage.

'It's beautiful,' she said.

'Then why aren't you smiling?' Fliss looked up from the veil to find Ewan watching her, concern in his pale blue eyes. 'If you hate it, you don't have to wear it. I don't even know if you already have a veil—'

'No! No, I don't. And it really is beautiful.' Fliss ran a careful finger along the line of snowdrops. 'Where did she find it? Was it hers?'

Ewan shook his head. 'It must be my grandmother's, I think. She had a winter wedding too.'

'Then I'm honoured to wear it.' What else could she say? Not the truth, that much was for certain.

Ewan beamed, obviously not hearing the uncertainty and confusion in her voice.

'Great. Mum will be really pleased. Thanks, love.' He kissed her again, fast and fleeting. 'Right, I'd better get back to the hotel.'

'Can't you stay for a drink?' She placed the veil back in its box, out of sight and out of mind. She wanted Ewan to stay. As a buffer between her and who she used to be, perhaps.

God, she'd been so excited to have everyone here together

177

again after all this time. Why hadn't she realised that they couldn't go back? None of them were who they used to be.

And some of them never really had been in the first place.

'Sorry, love. Uncle Derek and his new wife arrived tonight while we were out on the lantern walk, and they've been in the bar all evening; if I don't get back to referee, all hell will break lose between them and the cousins. I'll see you tomorrow though, okay?'

'Okay.' At least nobody at Holly Cottage was outwardly fighting. Everything just *felt* wrong. 'Tomorrow.'

This time, the kiss he gave her was longer, lingering, and full of promise. 'Only three more days.'

'Two,' she corrected, as the clock behind her chimed the first of twelve times. 'It's tomorrow already.'

And she was wishing away the next forty-eight hours until her wedding day.

Just two more days until she was safe.

As Ewan left, Fliss closed the door behind him and leant against it, her body heavy with secrets and exhaustion.

'Everything okay?' Neal was leaning through the open doorway, watching her. Fliss jumped at the sound of his voice. How long had he been there? Watching them, listening to them?

'Fine. Just . . . he was bringing me something.'

'Kind of him.'

God, they were talking like strangers. As if she'd never kissed him, never touched him . . . and she knew she should be glad of that. It meant that it was working. She was putting aside that part of herself that had fallen for Neal, all those years ago on this island. Or maybe even before, if she was honest.

For years now, Neal had given her . . . what? Something she needed, she knew, even if she'd never been quite able to put her finger on why she needed it. And all he'd asked in return was that she listen.

She could tell from the look on his face, from the way he and Caitlin had barely spoken since they arrived, from everything he said on the walk, that he needed someone to listen now.

But that couldn't be her any more.

However much her heart told her she owed him.

Fliss pushed away from the door.

'Goodnight, Neal.'

She wasn't that girl any more, either.

She was someone new. At last.

2009

Lara

The summer breeze rustled the grasses along the cliff path and the leaves of the trees in the woods beyond. Lara tipped her head back and let the sun warm her skin, her long blonde hair tickling the small of her back where her top didn't quite meet her jeans.

Mistletoe Island was perfect. She loved Holly Cottage, loved being with her friends, but most of all she loved having the opportunity to put the last few months behind her. Everything seemed to have been so hard, so complicated, since Christmas break. Even Fliss seemed to have been feeling the strain from university. And her family . . . after the funeral, nothing seemed the same for any of them. Least of all her.

She touched the necklace at her throat, a keepsake reminder, and thought of the list stuck in the front of her diary. Thirty things to do before they turned thirty. Except Carly would never do any of them now.

She shook the thought away. Carly wouldn't want her to wallow. She'd want her to get out there and live life for both of them.

And with graduation out of the way, with the world opening up to them, Mistletoe Island felt like a fresh new start. A whole new life, starting now.

'I love this place,' she said, smiling up towards the sun, her eyes closed.

'I love you.' The warmth in Jon's voice heated her blood more than the sun ever could, and she turned back towards him, still smiling.

Then she opened her eyes.

Her heart jumped, stopped, then started again. This had to be a joke, right?

Because Jon, down on one knee on the cliff path, a jewellery box in his hand, was *not* what she'd expected to find on Mistletoe Island.

'Marry me?' Jon said, the hope in his eyes unbearable.

Why? The word ricocheted through her head. *Why now?*

In the space between one heartbeat and the torturous next, Lara saw two futures laid out before her. One that led her down the traditional path of marriage and kids and home and boredom. And one that led . . . anywhere else. Or maybe everywhere else. All the places she and Carly had promised each other they'd go.

She thought about her cousin, gone too soon with no chance for either future. She was the only one who could live it for both of them, now.

Lara brought her hand to her mouth, knowing her eyes were too wide. Knew that Jon was smiling, expecting a 'yes'.

And she knew that she couldn't do it.

'I'm so sorry,' she said, and her future split, for ever.

Saturday 21 December 2019

Two days until the wedding

Lara

Lara woke groggily. As consciousness flickered behind her eyelids, she immediately regretted that last glass of wine. She pulled an arm out from beneath the quilt and rubbed her forehead, wondering why there was a shadowy figure leaning over her in the early morning gloom.

Hold on. A shadowy figure?

She sat up and screamed, short and sharp.

Looming over her, the figure snapped on a torch and shone the beam on his face, casting ghoulish shadows, which did nothing to make the whole experience less terrifying.

'Jon! What are you doing in here?'

'Shhh! Do you want to wake up the whole cottage?' he asked, switching off the torch again.

'Maybe?' She glanced across at the other bed. Fliss was still sound asleep, but then Fliss had always been able to sleep through anything. The sleep of the righteous, Lara assumed. 'Depends what you're doing here.'

'It's a gorgeous frosty morning out there. I thought we could take another walk.'

Lara peered suspiciously at her darkened curtains. 'Is the sun even up?'

'Almost.'

Her eyes adjusting to the half-light, she took in Jon's layers of running gear, and his high-end trainers. 'When you said walk . . .'

'I meant run. Come on. It's good for you.'

With a groan, Lara pulled the duvet back over her head, only to have it ripped off again, leaving her shivering. 'I'll give you ten minutes to get ready. Meet me at the front door.'

With a wicked grin, he disappeared, leaving her sat up in bed in the pre-dawn darkness.

She reached automatically for her phone, but of course it wasn't there. It wasn't anywhere, as far as Lara could tell. She was starting to think Fliss was keeping it in her bra. But she hadn't been missing it as much as she thought she would, figuring that Fliss would tell her if anything truly important flashed up on it. Although what Fliss considered important might not be the same as what she did. And she still owed Jeremy a decision about the job before Christmas . . .

Lara dragged her mind back from her work worries. She needed to focus. Jon was waiting for her.

She knew what Jon was trying to do. He was taking them back to where they'd started. Even before they'd started dating, they'd spent a lot of time outside together. Jon had always been happier outside four walls. He liked hiking and climbing and cycling and camping . . . and Lara had liked the way they talked and connected when they were out in the fresh air. It was so much easier to talk to someone when you were walking side by side, rather than looking them in the eye.

Not so easy to talk while running, though.

With a soft groan, she climbed out of bed and went to the bathroom. Washing quickly, she layered up and met him at the front door. Jon looked up from his stretches, and Lara had to quickly switch her glance away from the hints of long, lean muscles she could make out through his running gear, even with only the fairy lights on the tree to see by.

'Stretch first,' he reminded her. 'It's cold out there.'

'Do we really have to run?' she asked, even as she did as she was told.

'It'll be warmer than walking,' he pointed out. 'You used to love getting out in the cold winter air.'

'It wasn't so damn cold further south,' she reminded him.

He tapped her shoulder lightly. 'Come on.'

Outside, the sun was beginning to creep over the sea, sending orange and pink and red light scattering across the frosty ground and the small patches of snow left from yesterday's flurries. The air was crisp and biting, and woke up her skin better than any fancy spa facial could. She could feel her hangover melting away. In the silence of the early morning, Jon nodded at her, not wanting to break the quiet by speaking, and in silent agreement, they set off at an easy pace, along the road towards the woods further inland.

They kept the sea to their right as they ran, and Lara found herself mesmerised by the colours playing on the water and through the clouds. Maybe she'd been wrong. Maybe he didn't want to talk at all.

Maybe he just wanted to enjoy the early morning with her.

Of course, that thought instantly led her to all the other ways they'd enjoyed early mornings together. Usually in one or other of their beds, tucked up in duvets warm with body heat, naked limbs wrapped around each other.

Suddenly, she wasn't cold any longer.

Focus, Lara. Friends. That's all.

Lara had tried to keep her fitness levels up – usually in hotel gyms while travelling for work or by running through airports for a connecting flight – but she hadn't run outside like this in too long. She remembered now why she loved it. *That's good. Focus on that. Not Jon.*

She sneaked a glimpse at him, keeping pace beside her. He could be running much faster, she suspected, but he was holding back to stay with her. She dipped her head so he wouldn't see her smile.

Mistletoe Island wasn't big; at only a few miles across, they were able to run most of the way through the woods and then back along the beach to the tiny harbour before Lara started to feel she needed a break.

'Come on,' Jon said, as he turned in on the road towards the village. 'We can grab breakfast before we walk back.'

'Food sounds good.' *Walking* sounded good, too. She hadn't realised quite how out of practice she was.

They were both winded enough and hungry enough that they didn't need to make much conversation over sausage sandwiches and giant mugs of tea in the cafe looking out over the harbour. Lara smiled at the sight of the tiny stone chapel where Fliss and Ewan would be married in just a couple of days, the rising sun glinting off the steeple.

The silence between them as they ate was companionable, rather than awkward. Which only made Lara think how far they'd come since they'd last seen each other.

This was good. Even if she was distracted by lustful thoughts, Jon clearly wasn't. He was pushing the friendship path like she should be doing, and all she needed to do was go along with it and not expect or ask for anything more.

Eventually, she'd get used to being around him again, and it wouldn't even be an act. They'd be actual friends, the way they should have been all along.

This was good. This was safe. She was even feeling vaguely optimistic about their future friendship.

At least, until they started walking back towards the cottage.

'What do you think the others are doing?' Lara asked, as

they made their way slowly up the winding path to the top of the cliffs again.

'Neal and Fliss are heading out to the old lighthouse this morning, I think,' Jon said. 'And Caitlin was muttering something about mince pies for pre-Christmas before we left. I think she wants to do it this afternoon, in case there isn't time before the wedding otherwise.'

Every year since first year they'd celebrated pre-Christmas together, since they were never in the same place on the day itself. And this year, by Christmas Day Ewan and Fliss would be married, and spending the holiday at the Mistletoe Hotel, while the rest of them scattered to the wind to join their own families for what was left of the festivities. Still, Lara was pretty sure it hadn't been mentioned in Fliss's plan for the week, and they already had the Bridal Tea, not to mention the hen and stag parties that afternoon.

'Caitlin was already up? I didn't see her.' That was a bad sign. Fliss was normally the stress baker of their group, but if Caitlin was up pre-dawn to prepare for a last-minute pre-Christmas, especially after last night's wine-fest, there was definitely something on her mind.

Something else occurred to her. Did Caitlin know that Lara and Jon had gone out together then? Because Lara didn't like to think what she'd make of that.

Jon shot her a look. 'Why does it matter?'

'Because . . .' Lara bit her lip. 'Caitlin might have expressed some concern about you and me spending time together this week.'

Jon's eyebrows rose towards his hairline. 'I'd have thought Mum and Dad would have been pleased we were all getting along.'

Lara smirked at his use of the old nickname for them. It was true that Neal and Caitlin had always seen themselves as the settled, older, sensible ones of the group. The university parents. The ones who knew best. Just because they'd settled down in first year, been the first to get married, to buy a house . . . in fact, they'd done everything first.

But they were all in their thirties now. Surely at some point they had to give up on the idea that Mother Knows Best. Especially since Caitlin and Neal weren't *actually* their parents.

'I think she was concerned that we might actually be getting on *too* well. Fliss too.'

'Ah.' Jon looked away. 'They're worried you're going to break my heart again?'

Lara's own heart contracted at his words. 'Or maybe that you'll break mine.'

'You'd have to care about me for that to happen.' Jon's smile was twisted, without any amusement in it. 'And if you didn't care ten years ago, I can't imagine you starting now, can you?'

Suddenly, Lara realised she'd read everything wrong. Again.

Because there it was. Everything they hadn't said in the pub yesterday. The words that cut through the delicate facade of friendship they'd been weaving since they arrived on the island. They weren't running partners, or new friends, or even old acquaintances.

They'd always been too much, together, for any of those.

They were Jon and Lara. And however much they pretended, Lara knew they'd never be able to sweep away their past altogether. They both still felt it too much.

Jon might have been the one to get his heart broken when she turned down his proposal, but hers had taken a bit of a bashing too, even if she couldn't ever admit that. Their mutual friends were already too angry, too upset at the changes in their happy social circle, more than with her, Lara liked to think. But if they'd seen a hint of her uncertainty, her constant fear that she'd made the worst decision of her life, she knew they'd have pounced on it, and tried to force them back together.

Which was why she couldn't even let herself think, just for a moment, what it would feel like to kiss him again. To be in his arms. To love him . . .

Stop it, Lara. Caitlin and Fliss were right. This was a *terrible* idea.

She looked up, a sharp breeze catching her in the chest and making her breath come hard and fast. They'd reached the top of the cliff. Up ahead was the old lighthouse, looming over the crashing waves below. Out to sea, boats bobbed defenceless in the surf.

And suddenly, with the best view anywhere on the island laid out before her, Lara realised where they were.

Where they'd been heading all morning.

The spot where Jon had proposed, ten years ago.

With the wind forcing tears to her eyes, she didn't know whether to laugh or cry.

Fliss

Lara was gone before Fliss even awoke that morning and Jon's running shoes were missing from where they'd been dumped by the front door the day before.

Fliss figured there were two likely scenarios here. Either Jon had gone running and taken Lara with him, or Jon was out running and Lara had disappeared up to the hotel alone to check her work emails at the business centre.

She wasn't honestly sure which one of the possibilities bothered her more.

'Ready to go?' Neal appeared in the doorway from the kitchen, a mince pie in one hand, and a travel mug of coffee in the other – breakfast, apparently.

'Ready.' Her own stomach was churning too much with nerves to manage coffee or sugar.

She shouldn't be nervous, she reminded herself, as they set off up the path towards the lighthouse on the headland that faced out to the ocean, and Greenland and Canada beyond. It was just Neal. They'd talk, he'd listen and understand, like he always had, and they'd move on.

It was just one more thing to tick off on the pre-wedding checklist, in a way. Caitlin might not have included it on her spreadsheet, but Fliss thought that 'find closure with your past' seemed like an important step before marriage.

At least, it did until they reached the top, and Fliss realised they'd walked the whole way in silence, and that the butterflies occupying her stomach appeared to be breeding. Rapidly.

She stared up at the looming white structure, balanced on the edge of the cliff, its light dimmed these days. She remembered, as a child, watching the light turn and flash, warning boats away from the island.

She wished, sometimes, she'd been warned away too. Because now she was here, alone with Neal, she was starting to think this whole trip was a huge mistake. *Why* had she agreed to come here to talk? Here of all places? A place with so many memories – and where anyone could follow and overhear?

'Do you remember the first time we visited this place?' The first words he'd spoken since they'd left the cottage, and of course they were about the past. Neal pulled ahead to lean against the lighthouse wall, beckoning her to join him, looking out over the water.

Fliss stayed where she was.

'I remember,' she murmured.

It had been sunny, then – lighter and warmer than today. They'd all hiked up to the lighthouse carrying picnic supplies and bottles of Prosecco. She'd been wearing a bright red top, off the shoulder, with shorts. And the thing she remembered most was the way Neal's eyes had lingered on her shoulders all day. Every time she'd risked a glance over at him, he'd been just looking away. Until the time he met her gaze and she felt her cheekbones flush the same colour as her top.

They'd snuck back again together that night – another of their secret dares to each other. A new way to feel alive, to prove they weren't who the others thought they were. They'd climbed the half-rotten stairs all the way to the lantern, where the light used to flash and shine. Together, they'd gazed out over the ocean.

'Let's go swimming,' Neal had whispered in her ear. And in no time they were down on the beach, slipping naked between the waves.

As the sea had lapped against their bodies, he'd kissed her for the second time, while Caitlin and the others slept oblivious back at Holly Cottage.

Fliss shook away the memories. It wasn't that summer any longer.

This was safe. This was goodbye.

Neal pushed off the wall and headed for the door leading into the lighthouse. She followed him inside; the lock had been broken for ever, and Fliss knew that the island kids would hang out inside there sometimes. Today, it was empty, the only evidence of previous inhabitants the occasional tattered picnic blanket or empty beer can. No one could see them here. No one would follow, would they? It was perfectly safe. Wasn't it?

But then Neal's hand reached for hers, pulling her closer as he pressed one hand against her cheek, and she realised it wasn't safe at all. His fingers were icy on her skin, and she flinched at his touch.

He stopped. 'What is it? Too cold?'

Fliss shook her head. 'No. Well, yes. But that's not . . . Neal, this isn't what we are any more. It hasn't been for a long time.' She took a step back, out of his reach.

'But we could be,' Neal replied. 'And we should be.'

There was something in his gaze – something feverish and bright – that Fliss didn't like. Instinctively, she moved across the room.

'Neal, I said we needed to talk, and I meant it. Talk. Not . . . anything else.'

'I seem to remember you enjoying . . . everything else.

Last time we were on this island. And since.' He smirked, stepping towards her.

'That was a long time ago. Before you were married. Before . . .'

'Before *Ewan*.' Her fiancé's name sounded bitter in his mouth.

'Before I fell in love with Ewan, yes.' Maybe it was harsh, but she needed to speak her truth now. She and Neal had never dared talk of love, of anything beyond what they'd had.

And what *had* they had? A few nights when they were both single and their friendship went too far. When the adrenalin and exhilaration of their freedom got the better of them. What did that really add up to? Not love. God, please not love.

What she felt for Neal was a thousand times more complicated than her feelings for Ewan. And she'd always been careful not to examine the former too carefully. He was Caitlin's; she just borrowed him, a little, now and then, when Caitlin and he weren't together. Which was . . . still awful. She wasn't lying to herself about that.

But marginally better than falling in love with her friend's husband, right?

'In love. With him.' Neal stood beside her, not pressing in, but close. One shoulder against the wall, looking down at her, his eyes still intense and focused. She shifted automatically to mirror him, so they were both leaning sideways against the lighthouse wall, facing each other.

'Yes.' She loved Ewan. That much was certain.

'Are you sure?'

She almost laughed. 'Sure that I love the man I'm about to marry? The man I plan to spend the rest of my life with? Have a family with? Yes. Of course I'm sure.'

'Then why does this still make you shiver?' He ran a finger along her cheekbone, down her throat, across her collarbone. Fliss swallowed hard, trying to control her body's response. But she couldn't. It was ingrained, even after all this time. Neal touched her, and her whole self trembled. With anticipation, with possibility, with freedom. Not with love.

She shook her head as she stepped out of reach, not meeting his eye as she spoke. 'That's not the same. You and I, what we had—'

'Have. It doesn't go away, Fliss, just because it's not convenient for you any more.'

'Well, it's time it did!' she suddenly cried, jerking her head up to meet his gaze. 'Because it's not just *inconvenient*, Neal, is it? It's wrong. It was always wrong. All of it. Not just . . . this. It's . . . God, it's terrible, Neal. What we're doing. What we've done. And we can't keep on ignoring that fact.'

'Ignoring it? Is that what you think I've been doing?' Neal barked a laugh. 'Fliss, I've never ignored it. Not for a moment. In fact, I can't think about anything else.'

For a long moment, they stared at each other, as if they were each waiting for the other to break, to give way.

In the end, Neal looked away first, laughing softly. 'You really think you can marry him and be happy?'

'Yes.' She'd be better than happy. She'd be safe. She'd be the person she needed to be – not the one she had only ever been with Neal. Not Miss Fliss any more, but a more grown-up version, maybe.

'Fliss. Look at me.'

She didn't even try to resist; her gaze automatically rose to meet his, and she saw in his eyes none of the confusion she was feeling. Neal, as ever, seemed certain and sure about what they were doing, in a way she'd never managed.

'You know it's not just friendship between us, right? It hasn't been for a long time, whether we acted on that or not. The moment we made that pact, things changed. The truths you know about me, that I know about you . . . No one else sees us the way we see each other. They think you're Miss Fliss, and that I'm just Caitlin's minion to order around. I can't . . . I can't be myself with anyone except you. Can you honestly tell me that you are your true self only with Ewan? More than the Fliss that I know?'

Could she?

'I'm marrying him, Neal,' she whispered. 'Isn't that enough to prove he knows me?'

'Honestly? No.' Neal gave her a soft smile. 'You've been friends with the others for over a decade and they still don't see you. Not the way I do. They don't see the risk-taker. The girl who swears like a sailor in bed. The girl who drank absinthe and danced burlesque in that jazz bar . . . They're still amazed when I persuade you to do karaoke. They don't know you at all.' He paused. 'Does Ewan?'

'If I say yes, will you believe me?'

Neal's gaze locked onto hers. 'If you tell me, right now, that Ewan knows you – knows the heart of you the way I do – then I'll believe you.'

'He knows . . . he knows the person I want to be. The woman, the wife I hope I can be for him.'

Neal snorted. 'That's not the same thing, and you know it.'

'It could be.' The hope in her voice was almost painful, even to her own ears. This shouldn't be so hard. She loved Ewan. So why was this hard?

Neal's hand reached to take the tip of her chin. 'Be honest,

Fliss. What we have . . . this connection between us . . . do you really want to give that up?'

No.

The word filled her head before she could even think her way through the question.

Of course she didn't. Because that connection, the link she had with Neal, that had been such a vital part of her life for the last decade, she could barely imagine her life without it. The only time she felt truly *herself* was on those rare nights they escaped together and did something *new*.

They'd had to be circumspect, of course, and bloody careful, too. But London was a big city, and there were plenty of secret places for them to hide in, when they needed. It was easy enough for Neal to fabricate a work dinner, or office drinks, to be a few hours late home when Fliss called. And he always did, whenever she asked.

She'd tried not to ask too often. Had promised herself she wouldn't after the first time they were together on the island. But temptation – and the need to cut loose – had proved too great. On the days when the world was too much, or she needed support from the one person who understood her better than anyone else, all she'd needed to do to make life look brighter was call Neal and tell him she wanted an adventure. And he'd come – as a friend. Just as a friend. Her very taken and then married friend.

That was all it was, except for those few times right at the start, when Neal and Caitlin were broken up. Just friendship. Just their pact, to always be themselves with each other, and no one else.

But even without any physical connection, Fliss had always felt they were doing something wrong. Still woken up the next morning with a heart full of guilt and regret.

She'd only called Neal once since she'd started her

relationship with Ewan, and never since their engagement. And Neal never called her. He knew if he waited long enough, she'd do it for him, she supposed.

Maybe all she'd really needed to do to end their pact was stop calling. And she couldn't even manage that.

She liked to pretend that she was under Neal's thrall, that he ran the relationship. But looking at it now, with clear eyes, she saw the truth: she was the one keeping their strange emotional affair alive.

And she still didn't know if she could kill it. If she could say goodbye to the person she was with him.

She wanted to. Really, she did. So what was stopping her? What weird block did her brain have against her walking away and living happily ever after?

'I think that's my answer,' Neal said, his hand falling back to his side. It didn't matter that Fliss hadn't said anything.

He'd heard the truth anyway.

Ruth

'Ruth?'

The tentative knock on the bedroom door sent Ruth jolting up so fast the blood rushed from her head. The headache that had driven her to bed early the night before seemed to have receded, but Ruth suspected that the tensions in the group that had caused it were probably all still there. She'd felt it as soon as they'd returned from the lantern walk: Fliss strangely jumpy, Neal sulky and drinking heavily, Caitlin ignoring all of it to play hostess, and even Alec matching Neal glass for glass. Whatever was going on, no one was talking about it, and it made her head pound.

Alec poked his head around the door and gave her a smile. It had been late when he'd finally come to bed the night before, but she'd woken long enough to murmur a goodnight and submit to a peck on the lips before drifting off again. He'd still managed to get up before her, though.

He came into the room, a tray balanced on one hand – this skill a result of a summer waiting tables between university terms – and shut the door behind him.

'I brought you breakfast. Just croissants and stuff. But there's tea, too.'

So much for her and Caitlin's theory that the boys would cook breakfast every day. 'Thank you. Where are the others?'

She couldn't hear the usual clatter of noise and rising conversation that had filled the cottage since their arrival, so she assumed she must have slept even longer than she'd thought.

'Looks like Jon went running first thing. Neal and Fliss headed up to the lighthouse. Harry's playing golf with Ewan, Ryan and his dad again, and I think Lara must still be asleep. And Caitlin has taken over the kitchen to make a thousand mince pies.' She sniffed the air and detected the spicy aroma of mincemeat. 'God only knows who she thinks is going to eat them all.'

'Harry, probably.' Ruth took a mouthful of buttery croissant, and gave thanks for the peace and quiet.

'Probably.' Alec huffed a small laugh, but she could tell his heart wasn't in it.

'Is something the matter?' she asked, placing the croissant back down on its plate.

'Caitlin . . . she mentioned last night on the lantern walk that you were perhaps feeling a bit blue at the moment.'

Ruth stared at her husband. A bit *blue?* Even allowing for his typical understatement that seemed mild.

But worst was the fact that he was only saying something now because *Caitlin* had brought it up. Otherwise he'd probably have carried on cheerfully ignoring it until she stopped feeling *blue,* and perhaps perked up to a cheery yellow instead.

At least she knew now what Alec and Caitlin had been discussing so intently in the woods. Her.

Alec perched on the edge of the bed. 'Look, I know the last couple of months have been . . . awful,' he started. Ruth was about to interrupt with a biting comment about understatement, but then she saw it. In that slight pause before the last word, she saw what she'd been looking for.

Pain. Etched across his face, just for a moment, that same feeling of exquisitely torturous agony that she lived with every moment.

He felt it too.

He might hide it behind tequila shots and too loud laughter, or a squeeze of her hand intended to show that everything was fine, really, but inside, he was the same as her. As broken as her, even.

In an instant, Ruth was back in that hospital room, remembering the ache and the grief that had flooded her at the doctor's words. That moment she realised her baby was gone for ever.

She remembered Alec holding her hand then, squeezing it so hard that she felt the bones rub together.

She'd known right then that she couldn't fall apart. She couldn't let all that grief out – or there would be nothing left inside her at all. Everything she was, had ever been, was sorrow. It was the only thing holding her body and soul together.

So she'd been brave. She'd blinked away the tears that fell from her eyes without permission. She'd nodded at the doctor to show that she understood, not trusting herself to open her mouth. She'd known all that would come out would be a long wail of loss. But she'd squeezed Alec's hand back, showing him she was still there.

She'd held it together. Held *herself* together, through sheer force of will and desperation, until they were home again. Until he'd made her a peppermint tea and left her to rest, while he checked in at the office.

Then she'd fallen apart. When there were no witnesses, no one to hurt with her misery, no one to tell her that everything would be okay again one day.

And when she was done, she'd scooped all that grief back up inside herself, and carried on living, holding it close to her heart every day. So close that she'd never let Alec see the depth and width of it at all.

So close, it had kept him away from her heart altogether.

It was her grief, her pain, and it was all she had left of her baby.

But suddenly, she knew that it wasn't just hers. Yes, she'd understood that Alec was grieving too, intellectually, but that was something different from sharing her own grief with him. Except she realised, now, that sharing some of it was the only way they'd ever be able to move on, together.

Maybe she could tell him. Could let him in, a little. Tell him how the miscarriage felt like a sign that maybe they weren't ready to be a family. That she wasn't ready to be a mother.

Tell him she didn't know if she could take a risk like this again, could live through that much pain twice.

She opened her mouth to speak, but Alec was already talking again. Ruth pressed her lips together in a thin line and listened.

'We've just got Fliss's wedding to get through, and Christmas, then it's a whole new year soon enough. A fresh start, yeah? We can . . . we can try again. Things will go better this time, I'm sure. We were unlucky, that's what the doctors said. So we need to . . . try again. On purpose this time.'

Eventually, he finished speaking and watched her face.

No, she realised. *I can't tell him. I can't tell him anything at all.* She felt something small and flickering inside her extinguish – the tiny flame of hope.

Try again. Ruth nodded automatically. 'A fresh start.'

He wanted a baby. He wasn't scared, or seeing signs. He wanted this.

'Exactly.' He gave her a sad smile. 'We'll be okay, you and me. Yeah?'

'Yeah.' And now, his eyes lit up with his smile. Just one word of agreement. That's all it took to make him happy again. One little word to assure him that everything would go back to normal soon. Even if normal felt a million miles away right now.

All that grief wrapped around her heart. Now, it felt like the pain was strangling her.

But Alec didn't see that. And she didn't know how to tell him.

He kissed her forehead again. 'I'll leave you to your breakfast. Go check on how the mince pies are doing.'

Or, more likely, tell Caitlin that he'd done as he was told and made his wife feel better.

Either way, she didn't try to stop him. She needed the peace, the quiet, to think through all he'd said. Or all that she'd read in his voice and his eyes, and all she'd realised inside herself.

This was breaking him as much as it was her. And he wanted to try for another baby to fix it.

Could they really do that? Just start over and try again?

Ruth wasn't sure.

But she knew that if she wanted to fix her marriage, she needed to heal herself first. Needed to deal with the grief throttling her heart.

And figure out if the future Alec wanted was one she was even capable of giving him.

Lara

If she closed her eyes, she could see the same landscape, the same view, except with Jon on one knee in front of her, a silver ring with a tiny diamond held out between his fingers.

He'd planned this. He'd brought her here to ask her this very question. And she supposed, after all this time, he deserved his answer.

'You think I didn't care about you ten years ago?' she asked, astonishment in her voice.

'You made me believe you were as in love with me as I was with you.' Jon shrugged. 'Obviously, that wasn't the case. So I can't help but wonder – trust me, I've tried, the last ten years. But I keep coming back to the same question. What did I get wrong? Did you not love me? Was it all an act? Or was it something else, something I did? Or even some*one* else? I just . . . you left, Lara. You ran away that night and I didn't see you again for nearly two years.'

'I ran away? Jon, you left the country!'

'Yeah, yeah, I did.' Jon's gaze was steady, serious, and she knew she wasn't getting out of this so easily. 'Because I couldn't be on the same continent as you and not be allowed to love you.'

His words hit her in the stomach, so hard she almost doubled over. 'You married someone else,' she reminded him.

'Did I tell you when I met Phoebe?' Jon asked. Lara shook her head. 'The month after you went to bed with that usher at Neal's wedding to avoid talking to me.'

'That's not—' Lara stopped. That was *exactly* why she'd started flirting with the usher. Hell, she couldn't even remember his name now, and she'd certainly never called him afterwards. It hadn't been about him at all.

It had been about Jon. Like so much else in her life.

'That was when I knew that there really wasn't any chance for us. Two years after you said no, I finally believed it, and let myself fall for someone else.'

'And marry her.' Why couldn't she let that go?

'Because *she* said yes!' Jon yelled, his words flying out on the wind. 'Because I loved her and she actually loved me back. Because I honestly thought we could have a future together. Be happy . . .'

He turned away, but not before Lara saw the pain in his eyes. Maybe this wasn't about her at all. At least, not entirely. She'd asked herself a few times if he was really dealing with his divorce as well as he'd claimed – maybe this was the proof that he wasn't. Jon had always been the serious one, the one who over-thought everything, who felt things deeper than the rest of them. But he'd been shrugging off the collapse of his marriage the way Harry might shrug off a bad date.

Cautiously, she approached and placed a comforting hand on Jon's arm. 'What really happened? With Phoebe, I mean?'

'The usual,' Jon said without looking at her, his voice dull. 'We wanted different things. Like I told you, we grew apart. All the old clichés.'

Lara hesitated, then dropped her hand. 'You don't have to talk about it if you don't want to. I mean, I can understand I might not be your first choice—'

Jon laughed, low and husky. 'But you were. That's the

point. I chose you first, and you said no. I chose Phoebe, and she said yes – but just for now. As soon as she found something she wanted more – a new job, a new life, a new guy – it was all over.'

'She cheated on you?'

Jon shook his head. 'Not as far as I know. No, she wanted . . . more than me, I guess. She got the chance at a new job across the country, and I couldn't leave my job to follow. So we tried the long-distance thing but the distance just seemed to grow. Got to the point we had nothing to even talk about when we *were* together. We had separate lives, and she preferred it that way. Last I heard, she'd started dating her new boss.'

'Ow.'

'Yeah.' Jon looked up, and reached out for her hand. 'It was amicable enough, much more than it was with us. I guess I was older, more able to cope. But it left me wondering if I'm ever going to be able to do this for real. If I'm ever going to find that one person who loves me enough to stay, to say yes to for ever.'

'Of course you will,' Lara said, but the words hurt coming out around the lump that had formed in her throat.

'Really?' Jon shook his head. 'I hope so. But that's why I need to know. I need to understand . . . what did I miss, with us? What went wrong?'

She'd wanted to never have to say it. But the way he asked . . . Lara knew she owed him the truth.

With a sigh, she moved towards a viewing bench, a little further inland from the path, keeping hold of Jon's hand so he had to follow. Once they were sitting, she began to search for the words to make it all make sense, staring out at the waves as they rose and fell, crashing against the sand and stones of the beach. The cliffs dipped inland then out to sea again, high above the waves, and Lara stared at the old lighthouse around the next bay, a small part of her wishing they could just go back to the day they'd all walked up there for a picnic. Back before everything went to hell.

Why had she turned Jon down? She thought she knew the answers now, even though it had taken her years to truly realise what she'd been doing.

'Do you remember what happened, a month or so before graduation? Just after we finished our finals? I had to go home . . .'

'Because your cousin died,' Jon finished for her. 'I remember. It was a car crash, right? You never really talked about it much.'

Lara sighed. 'I didn't know how to. I mean, Carly was like my sister. We might have grown apart when we got older, but I loved her. And when it was just the two of us, we were as close as ever. I thought we always would be.'

'It must have been hard, losing her so young.'

'It was,' she said simply. 'We . . . we had all these plans, together. Before we came to Mistletoe Island that first time, my aunt gave me a keepsake box of Carly's. One I'd bought her when we went on holiday together one year. And in it . . . there was this list we'd written, as kids. Thirteen things to do before we turned thirteen. It was childish stuff, really – we can only have been about nine when we wrote it. Things like go ice-skating, buy our first bra. But we'd ticked off a lot of them. And then we wrote another one – eighteen things to do before we turned eighteen. We got together in the pub the night before I left for university and ticked off all the things we'd done on that one, and then she must have put it in the box. And—'

Her voice faltered and Jon, looking confused, prompted her to continue. 'And?'

'There was a new list. Thirty things before thirty. We'd joked about some of them in the pub that night, but Carly must have written the list herself. So I took it and pasted it into my diary, and I promised myself I'd do all those things for her. Travel the world, get an incredible job, live in London, have a one-night stand at a wedding . . .'

Jon winced at that.

'When you proposed . . . all I could see was that list. All the things I'd never done. All the things Carly would never get to do.'

'And you thought marrying me would stop you doing them?' Sighing, Jon shook his head. 'I mean, apart from the one-night stand thing . . . you never thought that we might do them together?'

'I panicked, okay?' she said, looking away. 'I was twenty-one, Jon. We both were. And I looked at Caitlin and Neal and how settled they were, and how everyone knew they were going to get married and live happily ever after and I wanted more.'

'More than a happy ending?' Jon asked.

'No. Just . . . more of a chance to be me. To find out who that was, and what I wanted now that rainbow holographic nails and my first bra weren't the most important things in my world. To get out there and find my own life, without knowing where it was going to end – with a white dress and an altar. Was that so crazy?'

'It's not crazy.' Jon sighed again. 'So, did you do them all? Everything on the list, I mean?'

'Every last one.' Lara gave him a sad smile. 'And the moment I finished the last one, right before my thirtieth birthday, I realised I had no one to celebrate with. I was out in San Francisco running an event, the night before my thirtieth, and I'd visited Alcatraz just like Carly had wanted to, and nothing was different. She was still gone, and I . . . I was alone.'

Jon blinked. 'You were in San Francisco for your thirtieth birthday?'

'That's what you're taking away from this story?'

'Sorry. I was there that weekend too. On a conference for work.'

Lara stared at him. How different might that lonely weekend have been if she'd known Jon was in town? Maybe they'd have talked all this out months ago.

'I wish I'd known.'

'I wish you'd told me about Carly's list when I proposed,' Jon said, bringing the conversation back round to what mattered. 'If you'd explained instead of running off, if we could have talked . . .'

'I didn't have the words. And if I had, you'd have said we could wait. You'd have waited for me to figure out what it was I needed from the world – and what if after all that it turned out that it wasn't you? I couldn't . . . that's why I had to leave. I had to get out of your life and start my own – not just for Carly, but for me too. I wanted it too. I'm sorry that it hurt you so much.'

And not just him. Because the part she still couldn't say was the worst of all.

The part where some days, she was almost certain that saying no to Jon was the worst mistake she'd ever make.

'All this time,' Jon said, amazement in his voice. 'I thought it was me. That I wasn't enough, or you didn't love me the way I loved you.'

'I did,' Lara whispered. 'So much. But I couldn't say yes to being that person for you for my whole life. Not when I wasn't sure it was who I was meant to be. I didn't want to say yes, then have things fall apart a couple of years into our marriage, when I realised I still needed to go out and find out who I really was.'

'Like Phoebe did.'

'I guess so.'

There it was. Everything they hadn't said in the pub the other day. Everything they'd spent ten years avoiding.

It was all there now, laid out before them. They understood each other at last. Apart from one last question.

'Why did you propose that day?' The words flew out of her, like she couldn't keep them in any longer.

Jon trained his gaze on the horizon. 'Everything was changing. That week here on the island . . . it was like we were all saying goodbye to who we'd been, what we'd shared. And I . . . I'd just been offered this crazy chance to go to the States to work, and I knew I wouldn't be able to go travelling with you that summer if I took it, and . . . it was the only way I could think of to stop you drifting away as everything changed. The only thing I had to keep hold of you. Except I held on too tight and I lost you completely.'

'Maybe not completely,' Lara whispered, letting the words sink in. *I couldn't imagine my life without her,* Ewan had said, when she'd asked why he'd proposed to Fliss. Jon had been doing the same thing, she just hadn't known it.

They finally looked at each other. Then Jon whispered, 'Come here,' and pulled her against him, his arms wrapped tight around her shoulders. After a second, Lara let herself relax into his hold. It felt so familiar, so warm.

So right.

Except it wasn't.

She couldn't do this to him again – or to herself, either. Friends, that was what they needed to be.

Pulling back, Lara wiped her eyes and gave him a watery

smile. 'So, there you go. All our innermost secrets out in the open at last.'

'I wish you'd told me your reasons then,' Jon said. 'Except, I probably wouldn't have understood. You were right; I'd have insisted on waiting for you to be ready. I was so certain that nothing could change what we had, if we held on tight enough. But now, after my divorce . . . I get it.'

'I'm glad. I'm glad I was able to tell you at last.'

'So am I.'

And then, somehow, they seemed to be drifting closer, closer, until their lip met. Jon's mouth was warm in the bitter cold air, his arms around her protecting her from the wind. Their kiss intensified and for a moment, Lara let herself believe that the last ten years might not have happened at all. That there was still a chance for them . . .

Then Jon suddenly pulled away without warning, breaking the kiss. 'No. We can't . . . This isn't what I came here for.'

The space between them opened up and the cold wind sent goosebumps over her body as Lara's eyes snapped open. Jon was on his feet, peering off into the distance, where the sound of laughter carried over to them.

Caitlin, Alec and Ruth crested the hill towards them, heading around the cliff path.

'Ah! A couple more explorers!' Alec cried, spotting them. 'We were just heading up to the lighthouse to retrieve Fliss and Neal so we can do our pre-Christmas Christmas before we get started on the hen and stag stuff. Ryan's booked quad-biking in the woods for later this afternoon, before the pub. Coming?'

Of course. Jon had said that Caitlin wanted to do their traditional presents and festivity, hence all the mince pies.

Except right now, Lara wasn't sure she'd ever felt less festive.

'Sounds like a plan,' she said anyway, not looking at Jon. 'I'm definitely ready for a mulled wine.'

Lunchtime was acceptable to start drinking, right? Especially if she had to spend the rest of the afternoon with The Mothers at some stupid Bridal Afternoon Tea before the hen party that night. And maybe if she drank enough, she could forget how perfect it had felt to kiss Jon again after waiting for so long. A single kiss, the memory of which she'd treasure.

Because he was right. They absolutely couldn't kiss again.

Fliss

Neal moved closer again, one hand at her waist, the other against her cheek, and she knew he was going to kiss her.

It was so tempting. The idea of losing herself in Neal's arms, his kisses, his body . . . losing Miss Fliss, leaving behind all the wedding stress, just being that girl again. The one who could do anything she wanted, without worrying what anyone else thought, or even caring what they felt.

But she *did* care.

And she knew how she'd feel afterwards too. That familiar combination of guilt, pleasure, and bone-deep satisfaction. She knew how the guilt would take over as the pleasure faded. The satisfaction never lasted long enough to outlast the pain, the loneliness and everything else that followed.

The sound of voices outside, somewhere on the cliff path, tore her from her thoughts. She pushed Neal away, her heart racing. What if it was their friends coming to find them? What if they'd walked in on Neal trying to kiss her?

'No,' she whispered. 'I mean it, Neal. No.'

She trusted Neal. He'd never push her further than she wanted. But he knew her better than herself, sometimes, and he *always* knew when she didn't mean it.

This time, she meant it.

The frustration was clear in his eyes, but he didn't try to kiss her again. Instead, Neal rested his hands either side of her head against the lighthouse wall, and stared deep into her eyes, his forehead brushing hers. God, she had to get away, get this over with, before someone found them.

'Why?' he whispered. 'Why do this to us?'

To us. The words tore at her heart, the idea that there really was an *us,* a them, beyond the friendship, and the crazy nights of wild freedom, and the kisses and the lies. She knew now that she'd kept those boundaries up, kept it from ever being more – from ever falling over the edge into love. But she'd only protected her own heart.

She hadn't even thought about Neal's.

She'd known, from the start, that Neal was Caitlin's, that he loved her, she was his one. But she'd also known that one person couldn't be *everything* to another, that was too much for any one person to bear. Everyone needed more people in their lives – friends, family, colleagues, sounding-boards, drinking buddies – a whole world and community around them. At the start, she'd honestly believed she was just another facet of that. Giving Neal something he needed, but wasn't getting in his marriage. The way he gave her a chance to be the person she could never show the others.

But now? Now, right here at the end, she wasn't so sure.

The voices faded away again, whoever was out there carrying along the path without coming in. Fliss's heart started to beat more normally.

But this wasn't over. Neal was still waiting for an answer.

Fliss sighed. 'Because it's time, Neal.'

'You don't want me any more? Don't want this?'

'No.'

'Then what, Fliss?' Neal slapped the wall with frustration and turned away, pacing over to where the ancient stairs spiralled up inside the lighthouse tower. Sitting on one of the lower steps, he opened his arms up to her as if waiting to welcome her answers. 'Tell me. Make me understand what's happening here.'

Fliss bit her lip, and wrapped her arms around her waist to stop herself running into his arms and telling him to forget it all, that they could go back to how they'd been before. So many years, and that impulse still seemed to be ingrained.

She'd been so sure that she loved Ewan enough that this wouldn't hurt. She'd forgotten the truth about love; that it stretched and grew to encompass more people as they entered the heart – children, family, new lovers – but that it always left an emptiness when a heart had to say goodbye to someone it loved.

The part of her heart that was Neal's already ached, and he was still here, in front of her. Still waiting for her response.

'It's time, Neal,' she said, simply.

'Time for what?'

'To move on. For you to commit to your marriage again, start a family, whatever—'

'And what if I don't want to?'

Fliss tipped her head to look at him, and he had the good grace to look abashed. 'Do you think I don't talk to Caitlin, still? I know you were trying again until recently.' Not drinking on Mistletoe Island was practically impossible, so of course they'd taken a break from it.

'*She* was trying.'

'I think pregnancy is one of those things that requires active participation on both sides.' It had hurt, hearing that news from Caitlin, knowing that there was an area of Neal's life that she could never understand or be part of. Fliss frowned. That conversation with Caitlin had been months ago. And yet . . . were they having trouble? Or was Neal not keeping up his end of the bargain? And if so, why?

'I'm not sure it's a good idea,' Neal said, quietly. 'And

that's not the conversation we're having right now, anyway.'

'Fine.' It wasn't fine. It was all a million miles away from fine. But there they were. 'Maybe *I* need to move on. All these years . . . you've had your own life, your marriage, your future all set out. And what have I had?'

'Freedom to live your life any way you wanted, with me on call whenever you needed me,' Neal answered, too fast for him not to have been thinking that for a while. And he was right, to a point.

'Yes. Okay, yeah, I did. But I didn't have what I wanted most,' Fliss said. 'I didn't have the security of forever. Of a proper relationship. I only ever had you now and then, and only until you changed your mind, decided it was too much of a risk, or that you wanted to focus on your life with Caitlin. I couldn't have those things with you – a family, growing old together.'

'And you wanted that?' Neal asked, sounding honestly surprised. 'You never said.'

'Doesn't everybody want someone to grow old with?'

'No. And as far as you let on . . .' he shook his head, looked down at his feet. 'God, Fliss, we should have had this conversation ten years ago.'

'I know.' Her heart heavy, Fliss crossed the small room and sat beside him on the narrow stairs, her thigh pressed against his.

'That first night I kissed you, we should have talked then.'

'I wouldn't have known what to say,' Fliss admitted. 'And a week later I flew off around the world with Lara for six months, and by the time I came back . . .'

'I was already planning to propose to Caitlin.'

'Yeah.' Fliss rested her head against Neal's shoulder, and didn't fight it when he took her hand in his, turning it over to trace patterns over her palm, following her life line, her heart line. Her entire life etched out in the folds and creases of skin.

'If I'd had any sense, I'd have told you then how I felt.'

'Which was?' She'd never asked. They'd barely ever discussed the emotional side of things. He knew everything about her relationship with her family, her work troubles, her problems with the flat she lived in. But she'd never told him how she felt about him, not really. And she'd never asked how he felt in return. The only time they'd come close – one night after a wild motorcycle ride through the hills, followed by too much wine in a room above a pub somewhere – she'd asked why he risked so much to be with her. Neal had smiled down at her as he stripped off her dress, kissing his way down her body, and murmured, *'Because I never could resist you. Not for a moment.'*

Lust, that was what she'd believed they had. Or even just adrenalin from their adventures together. But how could she have really thought that any of that was enough to make their connection last through so much, over so many years?

She hadn't, Fliss realised. She hadn't wanted to admit the truth, so she'd stuck with the fiction.

'I'd have told you that you mesmerised me,' Neal said, his fingers tightening over hers. 'That you always had, the whole time I'd known you. But you were so bright, so beautiful, I never thought I had a chance. And then I fell for Caitlin . . . but I still felt drawn to you, whenever you were in the room. I'd have told you . . .'

'What?' she pressed, needing to know.

Neal gave her a small half smile. 'I'd have told you that I'd always wondered how it would be with us. How far we could go.'

Fliss looked away. 'I guess we know now.'

'No,' Neal disagreed. 'All we ever had was the start of

something. And if you end things now, we'll never know what more we could have had. Without Caitlin, without Ewan. Just the two of us.'

Fliss's heart stopped in her chest, as sure as if the waves had stopped moving outside the window. For a long, timeless moment, a whole other life played out in her mind – a life she could have spent with Neal, as his wife, having his children, growing and laughing and loving and ageing together.

And then the tides moved again, her heart picked up its regular rhythm, and the moment was over.

That other world was as impossible as truly stopping the tides. Maybe, ten years ago, they could have had that. Before Neal's marriage, before her engagement. Before they'd lived a whole decade of life under a lie. If they'd done things right, admitted what they wanted, spoken to Caitlin before anything had ever happened between them . . .

But not now.

And not just because of all the lies they'd told. But because she was in love with someone else.

'It's too late, Neal.'

'Because you're in love with Ewan.'

Fliss swallowed. 'Yes. Which is why . . . we have to break the pact we made. We can't be this to each other any more.'

He watched her for a long moment, as if waiting for her to take it back. And when she didn't, he launched to his feet, stalking away across the room, his shoulders hunched with anger.

'You'll never be the real you again, you realise,' he told her, turning back to face her. His words were clipped, as if he was barely holding in his temper.

'I know,' she said, simply.

She'd never be the girl Neal knew again after today. She wasn't just saying goodbye to him, she was killing off a whole part of herself. And, yes, it hurt.

But she knew it was for the best.

She'd be Ewan's wife. That was the woman she wanted to be now.

'I barely even remember who that girl you knew was,' she said, as new voices and laughter sounded in the distance outside. Ones she recognised.

Quickly, she stepped further away from him, before anything could be seen and misconstrued.

Neal's mocking glance as he watched told her he didn't believe her. She wasn't even sure she believed herself.

'Well, when you remember, I'll be waiting.' He pushed past her, up the stairs to climb the lighthouse tower, his parting words floating back down the spiral steps, echoing off the bare stone walls. More distance between them. That was good. At least, until his parting words hit her like a knife to the heart. 'When you realise I hold a part of you that you can't ever live without.'

Ruth

When Caitlin had suggested a walk up to the lighthouse, Ruth had almost begged off. She had too much else to work through in her mind. But Alec had given her a pleading look, and Caitlin had offered her a mince pie for the road, fresh from the oven, and Ruth had reasoned that she did most of her best thinking when she was walking, anyway. It was only as they made it to the top of the cliff that she realised she'd fallen into line with Caitlin's plans just like all the others always did.

The lighthouse loomed over the island, sitting on the coastline's highest point. Without a light burning inside, it looked sad and old, Ruth thought. Alec and Jon were rehashing whose fault it was they'd lost a Frisbee last time they were up there, both faking a level of anger that was somewhat undermined by the way they kept laughing.

Fliss was standing in the open door of the lighthouse as they crested the cliff, and for the moment before she spotted them, Ruth wondered if she was actually crying. But then Alec called out to her and she waved enthusiastically, all smiles and sunshine as normal.

'Hi! Gosh, I didn't realise it had grown so late. It must be almost time to be getting back for the Bridal Tea.' Fliss beamed as she linked arms with Jon, starting immediately back down the hill.

'After we do our pre-Christmas,' Caitlin added. 'There

won't be time after today, and it's tradition.'

'Of course.' Fliss's smile never faltered for a moment. Ruth found that suspicious.

'Where's Neal?' Ruth asked, surprised that the question had to come from her.

'Oh, he wanted to go up and admire the view.' Fliss waved a hand back towards the lighthouse. 'Too many steps for me.'

'I'm here.' Neal appeared in the doorway. His face looked ravaged. What had they been talking about up here?

But she had more to think about than the two of them. As the group turned back towards Holly Cottage, she hung back behind the others, meaning to concentrate on her own problems. But frustratingly, she found she couldn't stop thinking about the others in the group, as they pulled ahead. What was it that made these people so compelling to watch?

They'd spread out a bit, ranging either side of the cliff path – Neal a little too close to the edge, Fliss far on the other side in the safest spot. Jon walked with Fliss, while Lara hung back a little chatting with Alec. And right in the heart of the group was Caitlin.

She was the one who kept the group together. Who drew the line the others were expected to toe. From telling Lara to stay away from Jon, to organising who needed to be where and when, even when they celebrated Christmas. She'd even heard her berating Harry the night before for not being around enough. Not making the most of the group's time together.

'This might be the last time we're all together like this, Ruthie.' Alec's words came back to her, from the day before they'd left for Mistletoe Island. The day she'd tried to persuade him to go without her.

'You've been friends for over a decade, Alec. I imagine

there will be more opportunities like this,' she'd replied, sure that he was overreacting.

But now, watching them, she wondered.

They were all in their early thirties. Mostly married. There'd probably be children soon, for some of them – she swallowed at the thought, but forced herself to follow it through – and that changed things. Lara's career had taken off and she was around so much less now. Plus Jon's dad wasn't well, Alec had said. They were all entering a different phase of life. A stage where even the longest-standing friendships took a backseat to other, more pressing concerns.

They were all moving on. But she knew that Alec didn't want to.

Wasn't ready to, maybe.

His friends were more than family to him, she realised. They were a security blanket. They gave him support, comfort, surety – but she couldn't help but wonder if they stopped him from ever moving forward. He said he wanted to. He wanted them to try again.

And she . . . she had never been a part of this. She had her own friends, her sisters for confidences and shared memories. Her nieces and nephews to love and cuddle.

She wanted what came next, she realised, suddenly. However terrifying the prospect . . . she wanted it, as much as Alec did.

She wanted the baby, the family life. She wanted all of that. But realising that didn't take away the fear.

What if it went wrong again? What if this time it broke her completely?

What if it broke *them*, their marriage, their future? If too much loss and pain and failure took them somewhere they couldn't recover from?

Could she risk that?

And if she didn't . . . what sort of a future would she be risking instead?

They could be happy without a child, Ruth knew that for sure, because they'd been happy before. But not if they didn't get back the relationship they'd had before her miscarriage. That easy communication, the loving contact, the connection between them.

If they could get back to there, maybe she could take that risk for something more. Maybe.

But first, she had to figure out how to go back to the marriage they'd had six months ago.

She had to go back before she could go forward.

Maybe they all did.

Back at Holly Cottage, Caitlin ushered them all into the front room, where the fire was banked and presents already sat under the tree. Harry banged through the door a moment after the rest of them, and was collared by Caitlin to help her in the kitchen, bringing out trays of mince pies and mulled wine that they all set upon greedily.

'What did I miss this morning?' Harry asked, without giving any of them a hint of where *he'd* been. Although maybe they didn't need it. Ruth wasn't buying the golf line.

'Not much,' Jon said, without turning his attention away from the fire. In fact, now Ruth looked, she saw that nobody seemed to be looking at each other at all. Lara was staring at her hands, as if she had her phone hidden in her lap, which Ruth knew she couldn't have. Fliss was at the window watching the snow fall, and Neal had picked up a book from the shelf to flick through. Even Alec was studying an antique map, hanging on the wall by the door.

Ruth exchanged a look with Harry, who raised his eyebrows in a question. With a small shake of her head, Ruth shrugged. She had no idea what was going on, either.

'Right, are we ready to do presents?' Caitlin, apron still tied around her waist, bustled in with another, entirely unnecessary, tray of mince pies.

Harry gave a cheer, and dove under the tree to start handing out packages.

'We're supposed to do them one at a time, so everyone can see what they're opening!' Caitlin objected, settling herself on the arm of Ruth's chair.

'No time!' Harry tossed a brightly wrapped parcel at her. 'We need to be up at the woods for quad-biking soon.'

'And we've got that blasted Bridal Tea – sorry, Fliss.' Lara grabbed another small present from the pile and handed it to her.

'Ruth, incoming!' Harry yelled, and she instinctively reached up to grab whatever came flying through the air towards her. 'Good hands!'

Ruth looked down at the parcel in her lap. Exquisitely wrapped in brown paper stamped with holly leaves, and wrapped up in red ribbon, she knew it had to be Caitlin's work.

Soon, the floor was a sea of wrapping paper, and everyone had a small stack of gifts in front of them – except for Jon.

'Sorry, mate,' Harry said, with a shrug.

'If we'd known you were coming . . .' Fliss gave him an apologetic smile.

'Actually, there should be at least one under there for him.' Caitlin pointed towards the back of the tree. 'It's just whisky, but at least he has something to open. I always bring a spare gift, just in case,' she whispered to Ruth.

Ruth nodded, as if that was totally something that everyone did, really. God, her family were lucky if she remembered gifts for all of them in the first place.

Lara lifted another gift from her pile, wrapped in tartan paper with no ribbons but a small tag. She read it, then looked at Jon. 'I owe you an Epiphany gift,' she said, with a wry smile. Ruth frowned, figuring she was missing something, as usual.

'In third year, Jon's gift for Lara didn't show up in time for pre-Christmas,' Caitlin explained in a low voice. ' So he said he'd keep it as an Epiphany gift instead, and drove up to her parent's house on the sixth of January with it.'

Jon just shrugged, but didn't look at Lara. 'No need. It's nothing much.'

But despite his words, everyone watched as Lara unwrapped it, a strange tension in the air. As if this one gift could reset the clock on everything Lara and Jon had been through together, and set the tone for their friendship to come.

Maybe it would, Ruth thought. Something had to, after all.

Lara peeled off the paper and stared at the contents for a moment. 'A travel journal! I love it, thank you.' But Ruth couldn't help but notice that her smile never reached her eyes.

A lull hit the room, a pause full of something Ruth couldn't name. Then Harry reached for another mince pie and yelled, 'Keep opening, people! We have stag and henning to do!' spraying crumbs everywhere.

Ruth laughed, and reached for her next present. The Mothers would be livid if they were late for the Bridal Tea.

Lara

The Mothers had outdone themselves.

The small cafe off the village square had been transformed into a scene that wouldn't have been out of place in a period drama. The tables were laid for a formal afternoon tea, with lace doilies and towers of cakes, scones and cucumber sandwiches. The windowsills each held a small potted Christmas tree, decked out in gold and white. String quartet music was being piped through the speakers. And sat at each of the two tables, The Mothers held court, presiding over the Bridal Tea, as if they were about to marry the girls off to eligible suitors, or hold a ball and score them all for effort, maybe.

The waitresses wore black skirts and tops, with lacy white aprons over them that Lara had a strong suspicion were probably Martha's addition. Martha herself was resplendent in a golden-bronze, shot silk skirt and jacket, with cream pussy bow blouse. Fliss's mum, obviously needing to outshine the mother of the groom somehow, was wearing a feathered hat with her own, simpler, pastel skirt suit. Lara was half excited, half afraid to see what outfits they came up with for the actual wedding.

One thing was very clear: this might be Fliss and Ewan's big day, but The Mothers were hosting. She couldn't help wondering how Fliss felt about that.

'Well,' Lara whispered as they stood in the doorway, taking in the scene. 'This is a new wedding tradition for me.'

'I think they might have made it up to torture us all,' Betsy whispered back. 'You don't suppose there's gin in those teapots, do you?' Lara struggled to contain her grin. Ewan's sister definitely had the measure of The Mothers. And Lara had seen a distinctly mocking look in his brother, Ryan's, eyes when he told them all to have a lovely afternoon – before disappearing to go quad-biking with the boys.

Lara wished she was quad-biking. Stupid wedding traditions.

'I think it's . . . a lovely way for us all to celebrate together,' Fliss said, pulling out her customary optimism. But even Lara could see that her smile looked forced, and the crease between her eyebrows hadn't quite faded away.

Before she could say anything, though, Fliss had moved into the room, thanking her mum and Martha profusely for putting on such a treat for the bridal party and friends. She took a seat diplomatically between both tables, and Lara could hear her praising each individual aspect of the tea.

'She really is actually that nice, isn't she?' Betsy said, sounding faintly astonished. 'Ryan and I put bets on, the first time we met her, that it was all an act for the parents. You know, the first time you meet the in-laws you have to make a bit more of an effort. We've been waiting for it to slip, all this time, but whatever Mum says, whatever tactless remark Dad makes, however many times they changed the guest list for this thing . . .' She shook her head in wonder. 'Fliss smiles and says that's exactly what she would have done if she'd thought of it first. It's astonishing.'

'It's Fliss,' Lara said, with a fond smile. 'She's always been lovely, since the day we all met.' But watching her with The Mothers, Lara wondered how much effort that must take. To smile and let go of everything she wanted for her wedding, allowing other people to live out their dreams instead.

'Harry nicknamed her Miss Fliss. Said she was like some proper lady from an Austen novel or something.'

'Harry has read Jane Austen?' Betsy asked.

'He has hidden depths,' Lara replied. Then grinned. 'And I think he mostly watched the TV adaptations. He has a thing for those dresses that push the actresses' boobs up.'

'That sounds a lot more like the Harry I know,' Betsy agreed.

There was something in her voice that gave Lara pause. 'You and Harry have been getting quite close, haven't you?'

Betsy raised an eyebrow. 'You mean, Harry and I have been having a lot of quality time in bed together, right?'

'Basically, yes.'

'I'm a single mum,' Betsy said. 'It's not often Morgan has his uncle Ryan, uncle Ewan *and* his granddad on hand to entertain him – and trust me, he'd far rather spend time with them while he can than with boring old Mum. Do you think it's wrong of me to make the most of my free time?'

'Hell, no,' Lara said. 'As far as I'm concerned, you should take all the advantage you can. It's just that Harry—'

'Harry is Harry,' Betsy said, gently. 'You're worried he's going to break my heart, but you really don't need to. Trust me. Neal and Ewan and even Ryan have all had the same conversation with me, and Ryan's only played a round of golf with him and had a pint in the Griffin. Harry doesn't hide who he is, you know that. I'm not being seduced under false pretences here.'

There was a slight admonishment to Betsy's voice, and Lara realised she was right. Harry never pretended to be anything more or less than he was – and what he was could be wonderful, as long as a person wasn't expecting more.

'You're right,' Lara replied. 'Harry is always honest about

what he can give, and you're a grown woman. I will stop interfering and hope you forgive me.'

'I will if you have a flask of gin in your bag,' Betsy said, with a grin.

'I wish. But I promise to get you a proper drink later, at the hen do.'

'I'll hold you to that.' She started to move towards Fliss and The Mothers, but then looked back over her shoulder. 'Besides, Harry might surprise you. Or maybe this time I'll break his heart.'

'I hope not – to the second anyway.' Actually, Lara thought that Betsy might be a good influence on Harry. If such a thing were possible.

Ruth and Caitlin had settled at the end of the table furthest away from The Mothers, so Lara and Betsy joined Fliss for moral support.

'Ah, Lara, now, you'll agree with me,' Fliss's mum said, as they sat down. Lara glanced at Fliss for some guidance on whether she did or didn't agree with whatever her mum was about to say, but Fliss was too busy disassembling a cucumber sandwich to meet her gaze.

'What am I agreeing with?' Lara asked, helping herself to a scone and reaching for the clotted cream. Sugar was nearly as good as gin, right? And it wasn't as if it were the afternoon tea she objected to, more the way they'd all been summoned to attend.

'Wedding cakes really need flowers, don't they? It's a tradition,' Martha said, with Fliss's mum nodding along in agreement.

'I think the wedding cake is all settled, isn't it, Fliss?' Lara asked. 'And I'm sure it'll be wonderful. I mean, people pay a lot of money for Fliss to design their cakes. She knows what she's doing.'

Fliss flashed her a quick, grateful smile.

'I think that maybe some fresh flowers—' Martha said.

'And a little more *colour*,' Fliss's mum added.

'Exactly,' Martha agreed. 'White is such a *plain* colour – you need some contrast.'

Except that Fliss had wanted her wedding theme to be white and silver with snowflakes, and snowdrops. A proper winter wedding. And The Mothers, as far as Lara could tell, had already stripped most of that away. Even the bridesmaids' dresses had gone from the midnight navy blue that Fliss had wanted to an unflattering baby blue that everyone hated.

'I was planning on adding the decorations to the cake tomorrow morning, after the final dress-fittings,' Fliss said, softly. 'I suppose that—'

'You will love Fliss's cake when you see it,' Lara jumped in, before Fliss could give away the last thing about her wedding that was actually the way she wanted it. 'She's incredible at cake design, and she *is* the professional. Now, have you tried these scones? They're delicious.'

'Thanks,' Fliss whispered, as Ruth and Caitlin shifted up a few seats to join them, and the conversation drifted to the delicious afternoon tea spread before them.

'It's *your* wedding.' Lara plonked a scone on Fliss's plate. This was no time for cucumber sandwiches. 'You're already putting up with awful bridesmaids' dresses and Bridal Teas.'

'I thought you liked the bridesmaid dress?' Fliss looked faintly hurt which, since she'd had basically nothing to do with the choice of the dress, was weird.

'I love it,' Lara lied, pushing the clotted cream towards her. 'But it's not what you wanted.'

Fliss sighed. 'I know. But they're both so excited about it

all. And I'm grateful they want to be involved. And grateful to you for saving my cake,' she added, as she spread jam on her scone.

'Well, if you're really grateful, you could give me back my phone,' Lara suggested.

'Still haven't found it, huh?'

'I'm starting to think you're hiding it in your bra. In which case I might spot it at the dress-fitting tomorrow . . .'

Fliss burst into laughter, earning confused looks from the others – and a disapproving one from The Mothers. 'Sorry. Nothing. Um, Mum, Martha, are you joining us for the hen celebrations later? I don't know what Lara and Caitlin have planned, but I'm sure it will be fun.'

Lara shot Caitlin a panicked look, which she returned in full. What they had planned would definitely be fun . . . but possibly not if The Mothers joined them.

'We won't, thank you, dear,' Martha said. 'This is plenty wild enough for us.'

Lara looked around the tearoom. Wild it was not.

Thank goodness they weren't joining them at the hotel tonight. Even Lara had been a little stunned at Caitlin's suggestion for a hen-night activity.

'Betsy?' Fliss asked. 'You're still up for it, yes?'

'Hell yes,' Betsy said promptly. 'Besides, Lara owes me a drink.'

'Just the five of us, then,' Caitlin said, looking a little relieved. 'Well, I'm sure we'll manage to have *some* fun tonight, anyway. You know, quiet, refined fun.'

Lara looked down at the table to hide her grin. This was one part of the wedding The Mothers *definitely* wouldn't approve of. And it might even help Fliss relax a bit. If she went along with it.

Fliss

Given that the whole week was basically an extended mixed stag and hen party, Fliss hadn't been sure they really needed to assign a particular night to the celebrations. Caitlin and Lara – and most especially Alec and Harry – had felt differently. Neal had shrugged, as if it was nothing to do with him anyway.

Which was true. Even if it didn't feel it.

Ewan, of course, stuck up at the hotel dealing with the families and the still-arriving guests, was also very in favour of getting out and cutting loose for one night. In fact, he and the boys were back from the quad-biking in the woods Ryan had organised, and at Holly Cottage preparing to head out to the Griffin by the time she, Ruth, Caitlin, Betsy and Lara returned from the Bridal Tea.

'Shouldn't you be up at the hotel with your dad and the others?' Fliss asked, as Ewan kissed her hello in the crowded living room.

'I figure this way I get to avoid our fathers *and* see you,' he said, his eyes twinkling, helping to push away the anxiety the Bridal Tea had brought. 'Definite win in my book.'

'To the pub, men!' Harry announced, breaking the moment as he threw open the front door again, letting the snow back in. 'There is more stagging to do!' Then he winked at Betsy, swooped in to press a swift kiss to her lips, and strode out into the darkness, followed by Alec, Jon and Neal.

'One night of freedom before I have to settle down and be a good little husband for ever,' Ewan joked, as he pressed another kiss to her cheek and followed the others out towards the pub for more tequila and pool. Which was about as wild as Mistletoe Island got in terms of cutting loose and enjoying freedom.

Whereas the women . . . 'What *are* we going to do tonight?' she asked, as the cottage door slammed shut behind the men.

She turned to find Caitlin and Lara exchanging a wicked look. Ruth, bless her, looked as confused as Fliss felt, and Betsy . . . ah. Betsy had slipped outside with the guys and was kissing Harry goodbye outside the front window. Very enthusiastically. Apparently his parting peck on the lips hadn't been sufficient. Fliss looked away.

'Well, it's not exactly your usual sort of thing, Fliss,' Lara said, moving closer to put an arm around her shoulders. 'But it's your hen night. Your last chance to do something a little bit wild . . .'

Fliss swallowed. If only Lara knew how wild she *could* be, in the right company.

'Wild?' Her voice trembled – enough that it probably supported their world view of her as poor, naive, innocent Fliss.

'Yes, wild,' Caitlin said. 'I have decided that everyone should have a chance to cut loose and be a little bit wild before they tie themselves down for life.'

Lara shot her a look. 'You make marriage sound *so* appealing, right before Fliss's wedding day.' She turned to Fliss. 'We just thought it would be a bit of fun, was all. Well, Caitlin did.'

Caitlin laughed. 'Don't worry, Miss Fliss. You're not going to get into any trouble with anyone for it.' The old nickname still stung. Only Neal had ever seen the other side of her – the wild side. The side she'd said goodbye to at the lighthouse that morning.

But . . . A new thought occurred to her now. Did she have to say goodbye to that Fliss completely? Or could she keep a little of that wildness? And if so, could she risk sharing it with Ewan, too? Or even with her friends?

Maybe this was her night to find out.

'If you don't want to—' Lara started, looking worried.

'No!' Fliss interrupted. 'I'm sure if you and Caitlin have planned it, I will love it.'

That was the proper Miss Fliss thing to say, wasn't it? She put back on her sunshine smile.

'Besides, I can't think of anything on Mistletoe Island that could be *that* wild,' Fliss said. 'So, what is it? Risqué board game? X-rated video drinking game? A particularly naughty round of truth or dare?'

'Not quite.' Lara and Caitlin exchanged another one of those smiles. 'Come on. We're going up to the Mistletoe Hotel. We need to get your glad rags on. And make-up!'

'Definitely make-up,' Lara agreed.

Fliss stared at the small staging area that had been set up in one of the Mistletoe Hotel's larger meeting rooms, and at the woman standing on it in impossibly high heels, fishnet stockings and a black-ribboned corset. Her long dark hair flowed over her shoulders, and her smiling lips were painted a bright red.

'Hi! I'm Meredith.' She jumped down from the stage with surprising grace considering the heels, and held a hand out to Fliss. 'And you must be our burlesque bride! I'm so excited to teach you all a little dance. But to start off, we need to get in the right mood. So why don't you all choose some treasures from my chest, and I'll pour us all a glass of bubbles to get us started. Okay?'

Fliss nodded, mutely, and tugged at the short, red dress Lara had insisted she wear tonight. At least the wardrobe and make-up set-up made sense now. She'd been baffled as to why her friends were insisting they dress up so much for a night in the hotel bar.

Caitlin had pulled out a suit carrier filled with short, sparkly dresses, while Lara had unpacked a selection of make-up Fliss had a feeling she'd bought specially for the occasion, since none of it fit the natural look she normally wore. Betsy had cued up some music and Ruth had poured them all wine, and soon, they'd all been putting on lipstick and swapping dresses, even if Caitlin and Lara were still the only ones who knew what they were dressing up *for*.

Burlesque. Lara and Caitlin had organised a burlesque dance session for her hen night.

They couldn't possibly have known that she'd done this before – on stage at a tiny jazz bar Neal knew, hidden in some London back alley one night when he'd walked out on Caitlin because he couldn't face a future of following her perfect timeline, her perfect plan. He'd gone back a few days later, of course, just like he always did. Because he loved her, or because it was easier, or, most likely, a bit of both.

But while he'd been single . . .

They'd headed out together for drinks, for him to wallow and let all his misery out. But they'd both known from the start that there'd be something more. And when Fliss saw the poster for a burlesque night at the bar, and then started talking to the dancers . . . she'd known what she'd wanted to do even before the alcohol took effect.

She would never forget how the feeling of power and control over her own life and body had vibrated through her as she'd danced that night. How free she'd felt. How alive.

Miss Fliss would never have done something like this. But her friends were giving her the chance to. *Caitlin,* of all people, was giving her this chance.

The chance to change, perhaps. To grow up. To be anything she wanted, even if no one outside this room would ever see it. Maybe they *were* ready for her to grow into the woman she wanted to be, too. At least, perhaps they'd support her as she tried.

Even if it wasn't quite the Miss Fliss they were all used to.

'Why are you frowning? Too much?' Lara wrapped an arm around her shoulder as she guided her towards Meredith's wooden chest full of corsets, scarves, heels and stockings. Caitlin was already choosing an emerald green corset that would look incredible with her hair, and Betsy had stripped off her black tights to pull on some fishnets instead, while Ruth was looking speculatively at a pair of red heels.

'Why did we need the dresses back at the cottage if we're changing into corsets here?' Fliss asked.

Lara shrugged. 'We figured the getting ready together was half the fun. Plus we'll look slinky and sparkly in the bar afterwards.'

'Everything okay?' Caitlin asked, as they reached the others. 'Not too much for you, Miss Fliss?'

There was something of a challenge in her voice. One that made Fliss's heart stop as she wondered – not for the first time – if Neal's wife suspected something about her friendship with her husband. Was this some sort of test?

No. Caitlin didn't suspect anything because there was nothing to suspect, not any more. This was probably just Caitlin wanting credit for organising everything better than anyone else could, same as always. Since she'd been told she had to have one, Fliss had asked Caitlin and Lara to organise a proper hen night, so they'd planned the most hen-party-ish hen night they could manage on Mistletoe Island, and Caitlin wanted appreciation for it. That was all.

Whatever it was, it made Fliss swallow any last reservations she had and shake her head. 'Not at all. I was just thinking how glad I am The Mothers didn't decide to join us tonight.' Everyone laughed at that, and Fliss smiled.

Maybe she hadn't said goodbye to that girl Neal knew for good, after all. Because she could already feel that freedom thrumming through her veins again.

And it felt amazing.

Lara

Lara stared at the stage as Fliss tried a new move that swiv-
elled her hips and her shoulders at the same time, with the
fluidity and grace of a belly dancer. And no sign of the Dutch
courage they'd all partaken of that still flowed through Lara's
veins, making her feel just a little wobbly on her high heels.

'Are you sure she hasn't done this before?' Ruth whispered, coming to stand beside her, looking uncomfortable
in the corset and fishnets she'd been obliged to wear. In fact,
Alec's wife didn't look particularly happy to be involved in
the hen-night burlesque workshop that Caitlin had arranged
at all.

Unlike Fliss.

'I can't imagine when she'd have had the chance,' Lara
replied. 'Or her wanting to.' But she had to admit that Fliss
looked surprisingly at home up there with the trainer, laughing as she tried the move again, her own blood-red corset
hugging and outlining her figure perfectly. 'We should have
got Ewan here to watch her.'

'Where do you think Caitlin's gone?' Betsy asked, joining
them. 'The boys came back to the hotel about an hour ago
and they're in the bar. I think Caitlin's going to suggest to
Ewan that he might like to stop by this particular room in
about ten minutes or so.'

Lara laughed. Miss Fliss seemed to be coming out of her
shell tonight. That had to be Ewan's influence, right? Or at

least the idea of becoming Mrs Ewan Bennett. It would be great for him to see his fiancé letting go and having fun.

Lara was enjoying seeing it, too. Fliss was always so concerned about doing the right thing, about keeping everyone happy, Lara worried sometimes that she'd never get to do what *she* wanted. Even when they went travelling after university, Fliss insisted on letting Lara pick the destinations, the tours they went on. She said it was an adventure just to be there.

But now maybe Fliss was growing into the person she really was meant to be all along, even if it had taken a hen-party burlesque class for any of them to notice. Lara hoped that meant she'd be very, very happy as herself.

She bit her lip, the memory of Jon's fleeting kiss flashing through her mind. If Fliss could decide who she wanted to be and go after it, maybe she could too.

She just had to decide. London or Manchester? Alone or . . . not. History or the future? Take a risk . . . or stay safe?

Everything felt up for grabs. She just didn't know which one to reach out for.

'Come on up, girls! Our bride needs some backing dancers!' Meredith clapped her hands. Ruth and Lara exchanged a glance as Caitlin slipped back into the room. Their break was over – and they had a show to put on!

They'd spent an hour or so learning a few specific moves, pulling them together into a sort of loose dance routine. Fliss, as the bride, was definitely the star, and received special attention and instruction from Meredith. She also got the sexiest costume.

Lara grinned at Fliss's wine-red velvet corset with the black piping and lace over the black fishnets and matching red high heels, her blonde corkscrew curls wilder than ever after all the dancing. She barely looked like Fliss at all – but she *did* look glorious. She couldn't wait for Ewan to see her and lose his mind.

She hadn't been sure when Caitlin had suggested the burlesque night for Fliss's hen do. It was so utterly un-Fliss-like. But Caitlin had been adamant that they were the new hot thing for hen parties, and that every bride deserved the chance to 'discover their own inner sensuality' before committing to marriage. Which had made Lara wonder if there was something she didn't know about Neal and Caitlin's sex life. She was probably better off staying ignorant, she decided.

'Besides, I think it's time for all of us to move out of our comfort zones,' Caitlin had said.

Lara hadn't known what she'd meant until now.

Lining up behind Fliss with Ruth, Betsy and Caitlin, Lara tried to remember the simple routine they'd been taught. ('You can perform it at the wedding reception,' Meredith had suggested, and they'd all howled with laughter. The idea of The Mothers watching them perform burlesque in front of friends and family was absurd.)

Beaming proudly at them all, Meredith started up the music – something sensual and classic but with a beat Lara could feel vibrating through the boning of her own corset. *Five, six, seven, eight,* she counted silently, and took the first step.

Beside her, even Ruth seemed to be enjoying herself. As if the costume had allowed her to shed whatever had been consuming her since she arrived.

Maybe this was her first step out of that unhappiness, too.

Feeling lighter, happier, than she had in months, Lara moved with the music, twirling and stretching just as Meredith had taught them. Her hair flew back as she flipped around in a swivel, feeling sexy and in control and free . . .

Until she turned to look over her shoulder, her hands stretched down her legs and running up again from her pointed toe, and saw the door to the reception room open.

Ewan, she realised. That was good.

Except he hadn't come alone.

Lara cast a worried glance at Caitlin, who mouthed *Don't stop* at her. With a deep breath, Lara tried to ignore their audience, and continued.

But she couldn't help glancing over at the growing crowd. Had Fliss spotted them yet? Maybe not. She was facing the back of the stage for now. But any moment she'd—

Fliss spun to the front again, curls flying, glorious in her confidence and joy. Lara, watching, saw the moment she spotted her fiancé and smiled. And the moment she saw the others and missed her step.

And the second she decided to carry on anyway.

Oh, well done, Fliss.

It all happened so fast that Lara barely missed her own steps, and she was so busy being proud of Fliss that she didn't immediately register who the other people were. It wasn't until the music stopped, and they all struck their final poses, that she looked up at the sound of applause.

Ewan wasn't clapping; he was too busy looking starstruck. Alec was clapping enthusiastically as he beamed at Ruth, pausing only to elbow Ewan so he applauded too. Ryan appeared to be staring firmly at Caitlin – to avoid seeing his sister and sister-in-law-to-be dressed in corsets, Lara assumed – while Harry had already pushed past them to reach the stage and was whispering in Betsy's ear. After her conversation with Betsy earlier, Lara was glad not to be able to hear whatever he was saying. Neal stood at the back of the group, one eyebrow raised as he stared at the stage. And Jon . . .

Jon stared back at her, heat in his eyes, and Lara knew in that moment that the accidental kiss that afternoon hadn't been accidental.

It had been inevitable.

Fliss

Oh God, everyone was watching her. Not just watching her, but seeing her in a corset and fishnets. Dancing burlesque.

It had been fun and daring when it was the five of them and Meredith. Fliss had felt for the first time that maybe she could let go a little, show a little more of the self she kept hidden, even with Ewan's sister there. But now she felt entirely exposed, on show. And not just because of the corset and fishnets.

Ewan's eyes were wider than she'd ever seen them, but she hoped that was in appreciation rather than horror. She knew she looked good in the outfit; it was the sort of costume it was almost impossible to look bad in. They all looked voluptuous and sexy.

But it was Neal's face she couldn't tear her gaze away from.

He had one eyebrow raised, arms folded over his chest as he watched her. Of course, he'd seen her dressed this way before, years ago. She remembered the heat in his eyes that night, and how she'd known, even as she danced, that this would be one of those nights when he came home with her, thankful that Lara was away with work again.

But that heat had faded to embers now as he watched, and as Fliss struck her final pose she saw him turn and walk away, without looking back.

Beside her, Caitlin swore under her breath, and Fliss

remembered suddenly that Neal's reactions didn't belong to her alone. That he *wasn't* hers, however it felt when he watched her.

Betsy looked between them all. 'Come on,' she said, taking Fliss's arm. 'Let's get dressed and hit the bar.'

'Good plan,' Fliss said.

'And you can tell me how on earth you picked that all up so quickly,' Betsy went on. 'I swear, you must be a natural!'

Or have experience, Fliss thought. 'Probably just years of ballet classes as a kid,' she lied.

Betsy snorted with obvious disbelief. 'I think it's the whole wedding thing. Brides are always beautiful – maybe hens are always sexy. What do I know? I've never been either.'

'Must be it.' Fliss grabbed for her dress, and the security of being Miss Fliss again, the adrenalin of cutting loose wearing off again. 'Come on. Didn't you say something about Lara buying the first round?'

'Hey!' Lara objected. 'I said I'd buy *Betsy* a drink.'

Fliss turned her best puppy dog eyes on her. 'But it is *my* hen night . . .'

Lara rolled her eyes. 'Oh fine. But hurry up. I've been craving a gin since the mad hatter's tea party this afternoon. Mulled wine and actual wine are both great, but now I'm definitely ready for gin.'

They all hurried to dress and make their way to the bar. The corsets might have gone, but they still had full stage make-up on, Fliss realised, as they walked past a row of mirrors in the corridor, as well as their sparkly dresses. Maybe a touch over the top for the Mistletoe Hotel, but they might as well make the most of looking glam.

Neal was already at the bar ordering drinks, but he didn't look their way. Fliss saw Alec approach Ruth with a smile on his face. Good. Someone should get to enjoy the residual sexiness and adrenalin they were all feeling tonight.

Alec placed his hand on Ruth's hip, his whole body turning towards hers as he bent his lips to her ear, saying words clearly only meant for his wife. From Ruth's answering smile, she liked what she was hearing, too. It was the most in tune she'd seen the two of them since they arrived on the island, Fliss realised.

But then Caitlin crossed the bar and, instead of heading for Neal, swerved to take Ruth's arm instead.

'It's a hen night, remember?' Caitlin said, leading Ruth away to a table in the corner, and leaving Alec looking confused and a little bereft.

Damn.

'That was quite the show you put on in there.' Ewan's voice was low and warm in her ear, and Fliss's frown melted away as she turned into his arms and let him kiss her.

'Glad you enjoyed it.'

'Very much,' he said. 'I wish I could come back to Holly Cottage with you tonight and show you how much.'

'So do I. But I suspect Lara would be less keen . . . I'm sharing a room with her, remember?' Fliss glanced around the bar. 'Where *is* Lara?'

And more to the point, where was Jon?

Lara

'That was unexpected.'

As Lara stepped out of the hotel bathroom, Jon's voice made her jump. She turned to find him waiting for her inside the lobby.

'As are you. Were you waiting for me?'

'No. I just went out to get some air.' He pushed away from the wall. 'And then . . . yes. I waited for you.'

'Why?'

'Because . . .' He shook his head. 'I don't know. I needed to find you.'

Lara swallowed. 'I know how you feel.'

'Just . . . stay with me a minute?' There was a rawness to Jon's voice that she recognised from her own. That exhausted, broken sound that came from fighting something for too long.

'Yeah. Okay.'

She leant against the wall beside him as he slumped back, turning to study him as he closed his eyes. Lara could hear their friends in the bar, talking and laughing and drinking. It could have been ten years ago.

Except it wasn't ten years ago.

Lara made herself focus on the few grey strands of hair at Jon's temples, on the way his shoulders were broader than she remembered, how the expression in his eyes when he opened them was more guarded than back then.

He'd grown up. And she couldn't know that the person he'd grown into was the same boy she'd loved so long ago.

So why was her heart so sure he was?

'You looked amazing tonight,' Jon said, after a long moment of silence.

'Yeah, well. Everyone looks good in a corset,' Lara said, with a shrug.

'It wasn't the outfit.' He suddenly fixed his gaze on her before she could look away. 'You looked happy. Free.'

'It was fun.' Why was her mouth so dry? 'I didn't think Fliss would get so into it, but she really did. And it was nice to do something all together, just us girls. It's been ages since we did that.'

'I'm glad. I'm glad you're all still friends. I know . . . when I left, I know Caitlin took it badly. But I always hoped . . . I didn't want you to fall out with anyone over it all. I wanted you to be happy. That's all I've ever wanted for you.'

'I know.' Her eyes burned. She couldn't look away from his hazel gaze. 'I wanted you to be happy too. Then and now. I'm sorry . . . God, Jon, you have to know how sorry I am that I hurt you. But I hope, now you're back, maybe I can make up for all that. Maybe we can be friends again. Real friends.'

'And that would make you happy?' Jon asked.

'Yes. Very.' Being friends with Jon . . . that was a million miles better than not having him in her life at all. And so much better than hurting him again would be.

'But would it be enough?'

No. It'll never be enough.

But it would have to be. She couldn't risk anything else.

'This is a bad idea,' she said. 'You know we can't go here again. You said it yourself on the cliff top earlier. You don't want this.'

'I know. Just . . .' He hesitated. 'Remind me why?' The roughness in Jon's voice told her everything she needed to know.

He *did* want this. Wanted her, wanted them. But he didn't want to want it. Didn't want the pain again. So he'd hold back as long as she did.

She had to hold the line.

She hoped that she could.

'Because I need you in my life as a friend. And last time we tried for anything more it almost destroyed us both, not to mention our friends. I broke your heart once, Jon . . . but I broke mine too. And I don't think I could survive doing it again.'

There was pain in his gaze now. He gave a slight nod. An acknowledgement more than an agreement. 'We should get back to the others.'

She didn't move. 'We should.'

'I really . . . I really want to kiss you again though.'

'That's just the dress. Or the make-up. Or the corset.' Blame everything on the corset. Stupid burlesque-dancing hen party. She looked down at the sparkly dress Caitlin had forced on her, and wished she was wearing her usual skinny jeans and jumper instead, off-duty clothes that couldn't have half the same effect.

'No.' The strength of that one word took her breath away. 'That's just you, Lara. Ten years, and I don't think I ever stopped wanting to kiss you again.'

She had to look at him. However scared of what she'd see in his eyes she was. Or what he might see in hers.

She raised her gaze to his.

God, the heat in those hazel eyes. The *want*.

She looked away.

'Lara . . .' Jon whispered, and she felt it through every cell in her body.

From the bar, Alec's laugh echoed through the lobby and shook her out of her indecision.

She'd almost destroyed their friendship group once before. She wouldn't do that to everyone again.

She wouldn't do it to the two of them, either. *I want you to be happy.*

'I need to get back,' she said, and walked away

2014

Caitlin

The bar Neal had chosen for his birthday drinks was tucked away in a part of London Caitlin had never visited before. God only knew how he found these places. It certainly wasn't with her.

Still, it was a nice place – a converted chapel – and, from her seat tucked up against the wooden benches, she could see Neal and Fliss debating the merits of the various types of gin arranged behind the bar.

Suddenly, the door blew open and Alec appeared – tall, dark and broad even in the oversized doorway. Caitlin smiled. It had been weeks since she'd seen him, and she was looking forward to catching up. Alec was a good listener after a few drinks, and always discreet the next day. Or maybe he honestly didn't remember what they'd spoken about. Either way, it worked for Caitlin.

She didn't want the others knowing all about her business. But Alec wasn't really others, and she needed to vent a bit. Maybe not the specifics, but the generalities. The way that life wasn't everything it was supposed to be by now.

The way that marriage wasn't.

Caitlin had always had a plan for her life, and she had

followed it meticulously. Which didn't explain why the life she'd planned for didn't seem to be what she'd wanted.

She'd planned to get her degree while also making lifelong friends, meet the love of her life, find a secure, financially rewarding career, buy a townhouse in a part of London that she loved. The house could become a hub for all her friends to visit. In between times, she'd spend her weekends doing it up with her partner. Then, when the time was right, they'd get married in an intimate, personal wedding ceremony for a couple of hundred, and settle down to prepare to start a family. She'd retain her career, obviously, and live happily ever after.

She'd held up her end of the bargain. She'd done everything she was supposed to.

So why did the plan feel so much better than the life she was actually living?

Maybe Alec would have the answers after a few pints. Jon would have, but he wasn't there, of course. Not any more.

But before she could even say hello, or stand for a hug, Alec strode across the bar. 'I met the woman I'm going to marry last night.'

Caitlin blinked. She'd never heard Alec so certain about even a second date.

She wondered if she should warn him. Tell him how plans and expectations so rarely matched up to reality. How 'love of my life' could change so easily into nights in the spare room, or nights where one of them walked out swearing they were never going to come back, but always did.

She didn't. 'Tell me more.' Gathering herself, she patted the seat beside her with a smile, and settled in for a long listen, as Alec started telling her about Ruth.

'She's the only one for me, Caitlin, I know it. I'll wait, of course, before I tell *her* that. But . . . I had to tell someone.

I've waited my whole life for this and now it's here . . . I can't wait to spend the rest of it with her.'

She heard Neal laugh across the bar at something Fliss had said. Glancing over, she wondered if she'd ever felt that certain about him. That sure that he was the only possible person to make her happy for the rest of her life. Or had he just been the first person who fitted in with her plan?

'I'm so happy for you, Alec,' she said, hollowly.

But inside, there was another thought swirling around her brain.

Had Neal ever felt this way about her?

Sunday 22 December 2019

The day before the wedding

Ruth

Ruth woke up the next morning, her head pounding.

She opened her eyes and found the other side of the bed empty. Again.

Pushing herself up to sit against the headboard, she waited for the world to settle into position. Where was Alec? After watching him doing trays of Jägerbombs with Harry the night before, she couldn't imagine he'd got up early to fix her breakfast today.

Which meant he hadn't come to bed at all.

She settled back down against the pillows. It wasn't as if there were many places he could have disappeared to on Mistletoe Island, and she trusted the others to have kept him safe.

She wasn't worried about him. She was bloody furious.

They'd had an agreement. Not a verbal one, exactly, but a tacitly agreed ending to last night. Before Caitlin's 'girls only' insistence had interrupted them at the bar the night before, Alec had been *very* clear about how he hoped the evening would end. And Ruth . . . for the first time in months, she'd felt the same way.

For a moment last night, she'd thought things might have shifted, back towards what they used to be, what they used to have. When she'd seen Alec watching her dance . . . She'd been unsure about the whole thing, especially the costume, until she'd spotted Alec's admiring gaze. It never wavered from her body or face as she danced; her husband still only had eyes for her, and that reminder had felt wonderful.

Or it would have done if it had lasted any longer.

'That was quite some dance,' he'd said when she'd entered the bar, voice low in her ear, his words just for her.

'I don't think you were supposed to see it,' Ruth had replied, feeling the heat hitting her cheeks at the memory. 'It was supposed to be just us girls. Lara was worried that Fliss would freak out about doing the class as it was. But then she seemed to be enjoying it so much that Caitlin went to fetch Ewan—'

'And the rest of us trailed along behind.' He'd pressed a kiss to her cheek, then another, lower, just below her earlobe, making Ruth shiver. 'I'm very glad we did, too.'

'So am I.' Her warm words had surprised even her, and Alec had looked stunned.

It had been so long, she'd realised. She hadn't wanted to be touched since the miscarriage, and before that there was morning sickness to contend with – until the day it abruptly stopped. The day her baby died.

She'd forced herself not to pull back at the memory. And Alec had kissed her again, following it up with hopeful whispers. They'd both been drinking, their inhibitions lowered, and Ruth had started to believe that this was what they needed. To just find a way back to the intimacy they'd shared before they started talking about babies and family.

To find *them* again.

'Tonight,' she'd murmured. 'When we get back to the cottage . . .'

'Yes.' Alec's reply was instant, without her even needing to spell out what she meant. 'Definitely.'

And then Caitlin had walked over and dragged her off

to another table, and Alec had gone back to the bar with the boys, but Ruth had still been smiling. Because she and her husband were back on the same page, for one night at least, and she was on a promise. A promise that had kept her sitting up in anticipation, waiting for him to join her last night.

A promise that he'd broken. Because he'd never bloody shown up.

What hope was there for them if they couldn't even get the basics right? If, when it mattered, she still wasn't enough to stop Alec reverting to his university self and choosing fun with his friends over helping her fix their marriage?

Despite her anger, hung-over exhaustion must have won out because Ruth dozed a while longer, only half hearing the other women grumbling as they headed out for dress-fittings up at the hotel an hour or so later. But the room was much lighter when she woke again, to the sound of the door opening and Alec stumbling in.

'Hey,' he whispered, his voice hangover hoarse. 'Sorry. Ended up crashing up at the hotel last night, in Ewan's room. Harry had us on the Jägerbombs.'

'I saw.'

Alec paused at the edge of the bed. 'Are you mad?'

Was she? She felt some of her anger draining away at the childlike sorrow in his voice. But in its place, a miserable sort of acceptance flooded in. This was who he was. This was how he dealt with things. If she was going to move past what had happened to her, she was going to have to do it alone.

This island wasn't healing her at all, whatever Alec had hoped, and whatever she'd let herself believe. It was breaking her apart – breaking her and, right now, at this moment, breaking her marriage.

How could they move forward when Alec was so stuck in the past?

'I don't think we should try for another baby.' The words were out before she decided to say them.

'I . . . Do you really think this is the right time to talk about this? I mean, I have to admit, I'm not quite at my best.'

'You're hung-over to high heaven.' Ruth tried for a smile to take some of the sting from her words. She wasn't sure if she managed it. 'But I don't think it matters. In fact, it's kind of the point. You're not ready for any of this.'

'Because I got drunk on a friend's stag night?' Alec asked, incredulous.

'Because you want it to be ten years ago!' The words flew out of her, too loud and too fast for Ruth to stop them or pull them back. 'You want to be the Alec who can get drunk with Harry every night and still get up for a ten a.m. lecture. You want to be with your friends, being the person you were then. Not the husband I need you to be now.'

'Ha! Like you need me at all!' Alec paced over to the small window that opened up onto the snowy ground at the side of the cottage. 'Ever since it happened, you don't want me near you, won't talk to me about anything—'

'You can't even say it! How can you expect me to talk to you about something if you won't even say the words?' she cried. 'Our baby died, Alec. Inside me.'

He flinched visibly as she spoke. Good. He should feel this as viscerally as she did. It was only fair.

She'd carried their dead baby inside her. The least he could do was hear the words.

'Do you think I don't know?' he asked in a whisper. Then he shook his head. 'You're wrong, Ruth. I don't wish it was ten years ago. I wish it was six months ago. Three even. Back when we still had hope. And a marriage.'

He didn't look at her as he stalked out of the room. Which was fine, because Ruth didn't want to look at him either.

Fliss

The Mistletoe Hotel was much quieter in the morning frost than it had been last night in the midst of the stag and hen nights. Fliss wrapped her coat tighter around her as she, Caitlin and Lara lugged their dresses in from Lara's car and up the driveway.

'Huh,' Caitlin said, raising her hangover-protecting sunglasses as she looked up at the hotel. 'This place is pretty in the daylight.' Last night, they'd arrived in the dark, and all they'd seen was the lights. In the morning sun, it was very different.

The hotel was of the stately home design, and with the white coating of frost over the roof and the grounds, and the pale twinkling of fairy lights around the trees in pots on the front steps, Fliss had to admit it did look magical. Perfect for a silver and snowflake wedding.

Or at least, a snowflake wedding *cake*.

Which reminded her . . .

Fliss checked her watch. 'We've got a few minutes before the dressmaker arrives. I want to go down to the kitchens and check on the cake before we start, if that's okay?' The chef had assured her yesterday that everything was being stored correctly, and that the fondant icing Fliss had added to the tiers of cake still looked pristine, but that wasn't the same as seeing it with her own eyes. She wanted to double-check the snowflakes had set right, too. They needed a certain amount of rigidity to stand up the way she hoped they would on the top of the cake.

'Of course.' Lara grinned. 'We'll all go. I'm desperate for a behind-the-scenes glimpse of Fliss, Master Baker, at work.'

They didn't pass a soul on their way through reception and down to the kitchens. But once they entered the kitchens themselves, it was a different matter. Breakfast was clearly over, but the staff were already hard at work on lunch. The chef pointed them towards a quiet side room, obviously usually used for storage, where Fliss's cake sat on a long counter above a row of under counter fridges, freezers and cupboards.

Except . . .

'That's not my cake.'

She stared at the stacked tiers – three of them, like she'd planned, and ice white, too. Except instead of the silver-edged white ribbon and cascade of snowflakes Fliss had designed, the cake had been studded with silk flowers, loose plastic pearls and gold ribbon. A dozen of the carefully crafted snowflakes Fliss had created had been haphazardly stuck on in between the flowers, as if as a concession to Fliss's vision.

'The Mothers,' Lara breathed, over her left shoulder. 'They were talking about flowers on the cake. You don't think they'd—'

'I absolutely do,' Fliss said.

Caitlin peered at the cake. 'I mean, it's not awful. Well, the pearls are awful, but the rest . . .'

The colours suited the changes The Mothers had wrought on her colour scheme, Fliss had to admit. And the flowers were . . . floral. If someone had picked up a wedding cake from a bakery that specialised in sausage rolls, they'd probably be quite pleased with it.

But she was a *wedding cake designer*. Everyone at the wedding knew that. They'd look at this and think 'anyone could do that'. Because anyone had.

'They must had slipped down here after the Bridal Tea yesterday,' Lara said. 'No wonder they didn't want to come to the hen night.'

'I'm sure Fliss would rather this cake than seeing her mother in a corset and fishnets, dancing burlesque,' Caitlin joked.

'Actually . . . I'm not sure I would.' Part of her was pressing to let it go. To live with the cake like she was living with all the other changes to her big day. To smile and say it was all fine, even though it wasn't.

But another part was screaming at her to fight back. And that part seemed to be growing larger and louder with every day that passed this week.

'What do you want to do?' Lara asked.

I want to throttle my mother. I want to scream and shout and throw an almighty tantrum. I want to demand that people do things my way for a change. But most of all . . .

'I want to fix my cake.'

'Great.' Lara dumped her bridesmaid dress on a chair in the corner. 'Then tell us how we can help.'

Fliss reached into a cupboard under the counter, and pulled out a large Tupperware box. Opening it, she counted the remaining fondant snowflakes. 'Not enough,' she muttered.

'The dressmaker will be here any moment,' Caitlin pointed out.

'I know. I'm thinking.' She wasn't usually the one of their group who had to come up with the plans, to order other people around. But with this, she was the only one who knew what needed to be done – and the only one who could do most of it. Which meant she needed to come up with the answers.

'Right,' she said, putting down the box. 'Here's what we're going to do. Lara, you're going to go and have your dress-fitting first, because you missed the last one in London so your dress is the one that's most likely to need any slight alterations. Okay?'

'Yes, boss.' Lara picked up her bridesmaid dress again. 'Up in the bridal suite, right?'

'Yep. Now, while you're doing that, Caitlin is going to remove all the decorations from these cakes, and I am going to re-ice them.' The fondant she'd already applied had been ruined by having pearls shoved in it, but fortunately she always made sure she had extra, in case of mistakes. 'If you can save any of the snowflakes, that would be a bonus,' she told Caitlin, who nodded.

'On it.'

'Lara, as soon as you get done with Mrs Gibbons, come back here. You can cut out snowflakes while I have my fitting, then I can start trying to reassemble the cake while Caitlin has hers.' The new snowflakes would be too soft to stand up, but she might have enough left to do the difficult parts anyway. The new ones could be stuck to the cake with icing – probably later tonight, after the rehearsal dinner.

It wasn't ideal, but it could work. And Fliss would have at least saved one part of her wedding that felt like *her*.

'Sounds like a plan.' Caitlin clapped her hands together. 'Let's get to work, then.'

Lara

Why were all bridesmaids' dresses so awful? Lara twisted slightly on the stool in the middle of the bridal-suite dressing room to get a glimpse of herself in the mirror, but it was hard to make out anything but a haze of baby blue tulle.

Fliss had pretty good taste, but even she hadn't managed to find something that satisfied The Mothers and still didn't make Lara and Caitlin look like ugly sisters at Cinderella's ball.

Except that was probably the point, right? So that they didn't outshine the bride. Not that they could. Fliss was delicate, ethereal and beautiful in her ivory dress. Otherworldly, almost – even if she knew it wasn't exactly the dress Fliss would have chosen if her mother hadn't also been in the shop weighing in on the decision.

Although right now, Fliss was mostly determined to fix her cake, which Lara supported wholeheartedly. After everything else The Mothers had taken over for this wedding, Fliss deserved something that was just hers, and Lara had every intention of helping her get it, if it meant cutting out snowflakes until the church bells started ringing.

But first she needed to get out of this godforsaken bridesmaid's dress.

'So, we're done?' she asked Mrs Gibbons, the island's resident dressmaker who, Fliss's mum had informed Lara, 'Does for all the brides at the Mistletoe, you know.'

Mrs Gibbons looked up from where she was checking the already perfect hem. 'I suppose.'

Lara resisted the urge to point out that the dress had already been altered for length in London, and it was unlikely that she'd had a sudden growth spurt at thirty-one, but only just. And only because Fliss needed her.

To be honest, it was nice to have something to focus on today. Something other than that strange moment with Jon the night before. The moment when she'd walked away from him.

Lara stepped down off the stool and flashed a smile at Mrs Gibbons. 'I'll go get changed and bring this back to you.'

Back in her jeans and jumper again, Lara felt much more like herself. She skipped back down the stairs to get to Fliss and her snowflakes – only to crash into a couple embracing at the bottom as she turned towards the kitchens.

'Sorry!'

Harry pulled back with a grin. 'Classic timing, Lara.'

Betsy smoothed a hand over her hair, apparently ignorant to the fact that her lipstick was far more telling of what she'd been up to.

'I need to get back to Morgan.' She pressed a last, lingering kiss to Harry's lips, threw a cheeky smile at Lara, and headed up the stairs.

Lara forced herself to lower her eyebrows as Harry stood, hands in pockets, obviously waiting for some sort of admonishment.

'Well? Aren't you going to berate me for seducing Fliss's sister-in-law-to-be and putting the happy day in jeopardy?' he asked.

'Nope.' Smiling to herself, Lara carried on through the doorway into the hotel lobby, Harry following on her heels.

'Is this because you're up to something even more potentially disastrous with Jon?'

Lara whirled round to face him. 'What? No! What gave you that idea?'

'Um, knowing you two for over a decade? Plus he's been giving you the lusty puppy eyes ever since he arrived.'

'Lusty puppy eyes are not a thing,' Lara said. Even though she knew exactly the expression Harry meant.

'They are when Jon is near you. Look, he's doing it right now.' Harry nodded to the far side of the lobby, where Jon stood ostensibly checking buttonhole flowers.

'Then he must really like those flowers.' Lara turned her back on Jon and focused on Harry. 'And I'm not saying anything about Betsy because I already spoke to *her* about it, and I'm convinced she's far more sensible than to let you break her heart.'

'And are you?' Harry asked, his voice more gentle than teasing now.

'I'm *definitely* too sensible to fall in love with you, Harry.'

'That's not what I meant.'

'I know.'

Slowly, Lara turned around, just in time to see Jon looking away.

'I don't think he ever got over you, you know,' Harry said softly. 'And I *know* you never got over him.' She didn't bother denying it. It wasn't as if the two of them had spent the last ten years pining or anything, but this week had made it clear that there was still *something* unresolved between them. If only she had any idea of how to resolve it without ruining everything again.

'Would it be the worst thing in the world if you two tried again?' Harry asked.

Lara shrugged helplessly. 'Possibly, yes. That's kind of the problem. The risk is too big.' To their friendship – and to their hearts.

'So what are you going to do?'

'I have no idea,' Lara admitted.

And then she crossed the lobby towards Jon anyway.

'Hey! You here to pick up the buttonholes?'

Jon looked up from the flowers and smiled. 'Not really. I think Neal was supposed to be doing that. But everyone else seemed to be here at the hotel and I was at a bit of a loose end, so . . .' He shrugged.

The awkwardness of the moment stretched out as they just *looked* at each other, everything they'd already said hanging in the air between them.

'Are you finished here? With the dress-fitting?' Jon asked eventually, his eyes never leaving hers.

Lara nodded.

'Come back to Holly Cottage with me? We could . . . talk?'

She shouldn't go. They were done talking, and they both knew it. There was no conversation left to be had.

All they had left was action.

Lara started to nod – then stopped. 'I can't.'

'Can't have a conversation with me?'

'Can't leave. I have to go help Fliss cut out snowflakes or something.'

Jon blinked, slowly. Then he tilted his head back to look at the ceiling and raised one hand to rub his temples. 'Snowflakes?'

She understood his frustration. Hell, she felt it too. But this was Fliss's week, and Fliss needed her. 'The Mothers ruined her cake. So I need to help her fix it.'

Jon sighed, then looked at her again with a small smile. 'Then I'll help too. We can talk and bake, or whatever.'

Huh. Maybe he really did mean talking, after all, if he was willing to do it while fixing Fliss's wedding cake.

'Then afterwards . . .' Jon left it hanging. But she knew he wasn't talking about talking any more.

Fliss

'That's *almost* perfect.' The island dressmaker, Mrs Gibbons, was a perfectionist, Fliss decided. This was the second fitting this week – on a dress that had already been altered to fit her perfectly in London. Still, her mother had insisted, and since Mrs Gibbons retired to the island she seemed to have a lot of time on her hands, so Fliss had decided it was easiest to go along with things.

As usual.

Besides, she couldn't really complain about perfection-ism today. Not when she'd left Lara – and Jon, who'd been roped in for some reason – written instructions about how to roll out modelling fondant and cut-out snowflakes.

She just hoped they were concentrating on her snow-flakes, and not on each other.

Straightening, Mrs Gibbons slapped her hands against her tweed skirt and smiled up at Fliss as she stood on the chair.

'And I understand you have a veil to try on as well?'

'Isn't it bad luck to try them on together? The dress and the veil, I mean?'

What was it about the veil? All Fliss knew was that she wasn't ready for it. Wasn't ready to hide herself away behind something else when she was just getting ready to break free, perhaps.

She'd thought marriage would give her freedom from the person she used to be. The chance to be a new, ideal Fliss.

But here, now, in a dress chosen by a committee of mothers and bridesmaids, she suddenly wasn't so sure.

What if Neal was right? What if she was locking herself into being Miss Fliss for ever? What if she was cutting off even the small part of her that stood up and demanded a damned snowflake cake, even if she couldn't demand anything else.

'I wouldn't think a modern girl like you would believe in all those superstitions.' Mrs Gibbons dropped her voice. 'Besides, almost everyone does, you know. How can you know if it'll look right, otherwise?'

'In that case . . . I think I left it in downstairs, with the ushers' buttonholes. The photographer wanted it for some photos . . . Shall I go fetch it?'

'No, no. You stay there.' Mrs Gibbons was already halfway to the door. 'I'll get it.'

Fliss suddenly found herself stranded, balancing on a chair in the centre of an empty room. She looked around, feeling a little lost, and in need of a strong coffee. Thank goodness Caitlin had offered to fetch some from the hotel bar. Last night had gone on rather longer than any of them had anticipated, although Ruth had begged off as soon as they got back to the cottage. The other three women had stayed up with another bottle, Michael Bublé crooning Christmas on the stereo, looking through her old photo books by the light of the Christmas tree until the boys got back. Well, some of them, anyway. Alec and Harry had been mysteriously absent. Jon and Neal declared that leaving Alec to sleep it off at the hotel had been an act of kindness, and she hadn't even needed to ask where Harry had got to.

Another thing to worry about. She needed to try to talk to Ewan again about Harry – and about Betsy.

'Now *that's* a look I haven't seen before.'

Fliss spun on her chair at the words, to find Neal leaning against the doorway.

'What are you doing here?'

'Collecting buttonholes for us ushers down at the cottage.' Neal glanced around the room. 'I guess I'm in the wrong place.'

'Neal.' Fliss stepped down from the chair. 'You need to go. You're not supposed to see me in my dress—'

'Why not? I'm not the groom. Am I?'

'That's not what I meant.' Or was it? This whole week had had her imagining different timelines. A different life she could have lived if they'd made different choices ten years ago. If she'd let go of Miss Fliss sooner. If she'd never kissed Neal. Or if she'd never stopped kissing him . . .

She wasn't in love with Neal any more. But the freedom he represented . . . that was harder to let go of.

'Mrs Gibbons will be back soon,' she said, instead of any of the things she was thinking.

Neal didn't even ask who Mrs Gibbons was. 'You look so beautiful.'

'Caitlin, too. She went to get us some coffee.'

'Are you really going to go through with this?'

The question she couldn't admit she kept asking herself. Hearing it in Neal's voice made her hands shake.

'I'm getting married tomorrow, Neal.'

'Well, yeah, you've got the dress and everything.' He stepped closer. Not threatening, not intimidating, just as if he couldn't bear to be so far away from her any more. The anger from that day at the lighthouse had faded away, and now all she saw in his eyes was a painful honesty. 'Fliss, do you really think it'll make you happy? Being Mrs Ewan Bennett? Being what he expects for the rest of your lives? I'm not . . . I'm not saying you should leave him and run away

273

with me. I want you to be happy. No, I want you to be *you*.'

'So do I.' The words came out in a whisper. 'I'm trying.' Then his words caught up with her, and a spark of anger caught in her chest. 'And what other option do I have? You're not even offering me an alternative! You just want things to be the way they always have – you with the wife and happy marriage, and me on my own.'

Neal shook his head sadly. 'That's not what this is about, Fliss.'

He took her hand, holding it against his chest as he looked down at her, and the anger faded away as fast as it had come. Fliss didn't think she'd ever seen him look so serious. Usually there was always a hidden hint of adventure behind his gaze, just for her.

Now . . . now it was gone. It was just the two of them, staring down the future. No grand adventure, just life.

Unless that *was* the adventure.

A clatter of footsteps and an opening door made him leap away from her.

'Everything okay in here?' Caitlin asked, two cups of coffee in her hands, as Mrs Gibbons brought up the rear with the veil box.

'Fine,' Fliss lied, trying to smile. Could she see? Did she know? Fliss had always wondered how much Caitlin suspected. Some days she liked to tell herself that Caitlin had to know everything and had chosen to ignore it. It helped with the guilt.

But most days she had to admit that Caitlin probably trusted them both too much to suspect anything at all.

'Just looking for the buttonholes for the ushers,' Neal said, with a much more believable smile. 'Apparently they're downstairs. See you all later.'

He was gone too fast to notice, but Fliss watched Caitlin

staring after him, a speculative look on her face.

Maybe that trust they'd relied on was wearing thin.

Caitlin handed Fliss her coffee. 'I'm going to go find Lara,' she said. 'I just had the weirdest call for her on my phone.'

'Okay.' Fliss swallowed. 'Um, you'll come back for your fitting next?'

But Caitlin was already striding down the corridor.

'Right,' said Mrs Gibbons, holding up a cloud of white tulle. 'Let's try on this veil!'

As the veil came down over her head, Fliss prepared to make herself invisible once more.

At least, when she was hiding, she knew it was safe.

Lara

'Well, this looks achingly romantic,' Caitlin announced ironically as she walked in on them.

Lara looked across at Jon in his apron, cutting out fondant icing. The two of them were stood either side of a waist-high stainless-steel counter, icing sugar smudged on their faces. They hadn't even managed to talk about anything more than Fliss's ridiculously detailed instructions for the job at hand: *Use parchment paper. Leave to dry for twenty-four hours. Don't touch!*

'Are you done with your dress-fitting already?' Lara asked.

Caitlin shook her head, placing a takeaway coffee cup on the counter. 'She's still doing Fliss. I went to get coffee, and I had the strangest call.' She pulled her phone from her pocket, pressed a few buttons and handed it to Lara. 'I didn't recognise the number, so I let it go to voicemail. Someone called Jeremy, looking for you?'

Lara took the phone, refusing to make eye contact with either of them, and pressed play on the voicemail.

Lara! Jeremy here. Just wanted to check in and see if you've made a decision about our exciting future together yet . . . Don't want to force your hand, but time is running short. Beatrix really wants an answer by tomorrow. Call me!

Jeremy's voice was so loud the others had to be able to hear. Lara winced.

'Fliss stole my phone,' Lara said, playing the message

276

again after turning the volume down. 'I put your number as an emergency contact on my out of office.'

An answer by tomorrow.

'Of course you did.' Caitlin rolled her eyes. 'Well? Call him back. Otherwise he's going to keep calling me. He sounds . . . persistent.'

'You have no idea,' Lara muttered, pressing to call.

She didn't really want an audience for this call, but Caitlin was blocking the door, and neither of them appeared to be going anywhere.

'Jeremy? It's Lara.'

'Lovely Lara! Now, it's nearly my last day in the office before Christmas. Tell me you have good news for me to give Beatrix.'

Lara took a breath. 'Not yet. Like I told you, I need to think about it.'

'I gave you *days*, Lara. I told you she wants this decided before she goes away for Christmas.'

'I've been a bit busy, Jeremy,' she said, trying her best not to snap. 'I'm at my best friend's wedding, on an island off the Scottish coast, cutting out stupid fondant snowflakes to save her cake, and there's a *lot* going on here. Work really isn't the most important thing on my mind right now.'

Caitlin muffled a sharp laugh at that, and Lara shot her a glare.

'I thought work was what you lived for,' she heard Jeremy mutter.

'Look, is there any chance I could have a few more days? Maybe until after Christmas? I'll have decided by then.'

'Well, I *could* ask Beatrix,' Jeremy replied. 'But I understand that your boss and mine will be attending the same house party between Christmas and New Year, and it would be awful if this came up in conversation before you'd had a chance to talk to him, don't you think? Of course, if I could give Beatrix some good news I could ask her to be discreet at the same time . . .'

'I'll call you tomorrow,' Lara promised, through gritted teeth, and hung up.

'Was he *threatening* you?' Jon asked.

She shook her head. 'Beatrix wouldn't do that to me. Jeremy likes to think that he has more power than he does.' She sighed. 'But I do need to make a decision.'

'About what, exactly?' Caitlin asked.

Lara glanced at Jon, took a breath, then said, 'Whether to take a new job in Manchester.' She braced herself for a traditional Caitlin outburst about talking these things over with friends, keeping the group together, the merits of London, and not working with Jeremy generally. All the things that had been stopping her telling her in the first place.

'I see,' Caitlin said softly. 'Do you think you'll take it?'

Lara couldn't help staring at her friend. This wasn't usually how Caitlin behaved. 'I . . . haven't decided yet.'

'Right.' Caitlin took back her phone and picked up her coffee. 'I'd better get back upstairs for my dress-fitting.'

And then she was gone.

Lara looked at Jon. 'She took that better than I thought she would.'

'Hmm. Or worse.'

'Yeah. I was trying not to think that.' Caitlin was never that calm about something that threatened her plans for the future. Lara didn't like it.

Jon flashed her a reassuring smile and, even though it changed nothing, Lara felt a little better all the same.

'We'd better get these snowflakes finished before Fliss gets back,' Jon said, turning to his icing.

Lara put thoughts of Manchester and Jeremy and Beatrix

278

as far out of her mind as she could, for at least another day. She'd worry about it once the wedding cake was sorted. Fliss was the most important thing right now.

There was something strangely relaxing about rolling out the fondant, then using the stamps to cut out the snowflakes. Admittedly, hers didn't look quite as perfect and even as the ones Fliss had made earlier in the week, but maybe Fliss could fix them when she got back.

The important thing was, with her and Jon on the case, Fliss would have all the snowflakes she could ever want.

And she and Jon had time and space to talk. Since that was apparently what they were doing now – or were supposed to be, before Caitlin's interruption.

'So.' Lara placed another slightly wonky snowflake on the sheet of greaseproof paper to dry. 'How are things? Have you spoken to your dad this week? How's he doing?'

'I called them last night, and he's doing fine,' Jon said. 'Looking forward to having us all together for Christmas.' He glanced over at her, looking unbearably cute with a dusting of icing sugar on his nose. 'But I don't want to talk about my family.'

'What *did* you want to talk about?'

The past again? The last ten years, spent apart? Either way, Lara wasn't sure how much more there was to say.

'I want to talk about us. Now,' Jon replied.

Lara swallowed. 'Our friendship?'

'No, not that.' He wiped icing sugar from his hands onto his jeans and for the first time, she realised he was nervous. 'Do you ever wonder what would happen if we met for the first time now, today? Without all this baggage and history, without our friends weighing in . . . Just you and me, meeting in a bar at a wedding, say. What do you think would happen?'

Lara gently placed down her rolling pin. 'I can't,' she said. 'I can't imagine ever not knowing you.'

'Try. For me.' He reached across the counter and gently ran his hand down her face, closing her eyes. His fingers faintly brushed her mouth before he stepped back.

Lara smiled and licked her lips, tasting sugar. 'Okay. So I walk into the hotel bar tomorrow night after watching my best friend marry the love of her life, right?'

'Right.'

'And I'm wearing the most hideous bridesmaid dress in creation, and I spot you sitting at the bar, waiting for a drink.' She could see it in her head, now she tried. Could picture him in a charcoal-grey suit, his dark curls flopping over his forehead because he hadn't had time to get it cut before he came to the island.

'So, would you come over and sit down next to me, or ignore me completely?' Jon asked, his voice closer than she'd expected.

Lara's eyes fluttered open. 'Would you want me to sit down?'

Because she would. She always would. In fact, she had – those first terms at university, when she'd found herself drawn to him over all the others whenever they went out. Or when they stayed in. Something pulled her towards him, and looking up into his eyes she knew it always would.

'I'd never want you to leave my side,' Jon whispered, holding her gaze. He'd come round to her side of the counter. 'I never did.'

She looked away. 'But I left anyway. Look, if you're asking me, if I met you tomorrow would I be attracted to you? Of course I would. I've never wanted anyone the way I wanted you – back then or now.' There, she'd said it. 'This week has been hell not *touching* you.'

Jon caught his breath at her words, and Lara realised that she absolutely hadn't meant to say that last bit.

Too late now.

'What I mean is . . . yes, I'm still attracted to you. Even standing in that stupid apron with icing sugar on your nose. But that part was never the problem for us, was it?'

'If our history is the problem, what if we forget history. Just for the next few days.' Jon moved closer again. She felt the press of his hands on her waist, and Lara knew she wouldn't step away however stupid and reckless this might be. She'd waited so long to be here again – even if she hadn't realised she was waiting until now. Why else hadn't she really fallen for anyone in ten long years? Beyond a crush, a few dates, and the odd one-night stand . . . She'd blamed work, but she knew now that work was simply the excuse she used to stop thinking about what she'd given up.

There was another dusting of icing sugar across the highest part of his cheekbone, she noticed now. Slowly, she stretched up on tiptoes, and gently kissed it away, the heat of her lips melting the sugar.

Then Jon caught her face in his hands and brought her mouth down to meet his own, and she melted into his kiss with relief. Deepening the kiss, she twisted round to meet him so that the small of her back pressed against the counter, the two of them entwined in each other, the kiss that had been pent up for ten years consuming her.

'Caitlin and Neal have disappeared, so I'm – oh!'

Fliss stood frozen in the doorway, her eyes wide, as Lara and Jon leapt apart.

'Sorry, we were just – um, I think we're done with the snowflakes?' Lara said, looking up at Jon for confirmation. He nodded, mutely.

'Great. Well, thanks. I'll start decorating the cake once

they've dried.' Fliss looked between them, shaking her head. 'I suppose without your phone and work you had to find *something* to do with your time.'

Lara's cheeks burned, but she couldn't help but smile all the same. That was probably the closest to a blessing she was going to get from Fliss, given how many reservations their friends had about her and Jon. And Lara couldn't even blame them.

She couldn't stop herself either.

'In that case, we'll see you at the rehearsal buffet tonight.' Lara flashed a smile at Fliss, and grabbed Jon's hand to pull him out of the room behind her.

If they were giving in to temptation, she wanted to enjoy it for as long as possible before the real world came knocking again.

Ruth

The snow was coming in big, heavy flakes as Ruth stepped out of the cottage, but she needed to get away. To walk and think and unwind.

She had no idea where to go though, she realised, as she reached the end of the long, winding driveway of Holly Cottage. Pulling out a map of the island that she'd found in a desk drawer, Ruth considered her options. If she turned right, she'd follow the road down to the village. That had the advantage of pubs and few shops – but the disadvantage of other people, who she really wasn't in the mood for. And also the Mistletoe Hotel.

The others were all up at the hotel, preparing for the wedding. She had zero desire to be in the cottage when they came back.

So. Away from the hotel, which meant away from the village, too. Okay, then it would have to be the cliff path out into the woods. The same way they'd walked for the lantern walk two nights ago. At least she probably wouldn't get lost, even without the lights to guide her. The path had been pretty well defined, as far as she could remember.

Decision made, she turned left up the hill towards the woods, hoping that it might even be warmer when she was cocooned by the trees. Just get away from the real world for a while. Maybe then she could see her own path forwards.

She walked without thinking anything at all beyond the

refrain running over and over through her head. *Got to get away. Got to get away. Get away. Get away.*

But she was trapped on an island, the sea glittering mockingly through the falling snow, reminding her how stuck she was.

She placed it at her back and entered the woods.

The path through the woods meandered between the trees, their heavy canopies protecting the ground from the still falling snow. The snowflakes were starting to settle, covering the island in a delicate white lace. In the woods, however, green and brown and even a few autumn shades still showed through the frost.

With no desire to head back, Ruth decided it was easiest to keep following the path all the way back down to the beach. It wasn't as if there was enough of Mistletoe Island for her to get properly lost if she took a wrong turn, and she had her phone anyway. As long as she could get reception she could call Alec to come and find her.

Or not. Probably not.

As the trees grew thicker and darker, Ruth forced herself to think about the things she really needed to consider. She was safe here. Cocooned from the rest of the island. Even the sounds melted away, and the worst of the weather. She decided that before she emerged from the wood, she needed to be clear on her next moves.

She loved Alec. She loved being married to Alec. Usually. When he wasn't being a drunken idiot and staying out all night.

And yes, she wanted a family.

Those were the easy bits. And they didn't take into account the fear that was eating through her every moment of every day.

The fear that it could happen again.

The fear that her marriage wouldn't survive if it did.

The fear that *she* might not survive it.

The fear that she might not be up to motherhood.

Was there going to be anything left of her that *wasn't* fear soon? How could she start a new year feeling this way?

She stopped as she realised.

She couldn't.

Something had to change. But what?

Suddenly, she spotted the same sign she'd seen on the lantern walk. The one Neal had said led to some magical well. On impulse, she turned off the path and followed the sign, until the trees thinned out and she found herself in a clearing, one covered in frost and snow despite the tree canopy.

Her breath caught in her throat as she wondered if maybe, just maybe, the magic she'd been seeking was finally about to find her . . .

And then she saw the tourist information board.

'Less magical,' she muttered, as she crossed the clearing to read it, skirting around a badly edged pond in the centre.

The board informed her that it wasn't a pond, or really a well, but a natural spring.

Known locally as Tobar na Coilltean, *or, The Well of the Woods, it has long been said to have healing powers. Legend has it, the spring has the ability to help a person cut ties with the past and find their future.*

Ruth scoffed with disbelief. Then she remembered that no one was watching. If she wanted to believe, she could, without anyone laughing at her. Alec would think it was ridiculous . . .

Except Alec had brought her to Mistletoe Island in the first place. And she remembered suddenly what he'd said on their arrival.

'There's something special about this place. They . . . did you know? They call it the Healing Island.'

Maybe he wouldn't find it quite so funny after all.

And really, what could it hurt at this point? It wasn't as if her walk had given her any better ideas.

Ruth read the instructions carefully.

Take a rag from the basket beside the well. Hold it close to the heart, and imagine your troubles transferring into the cloth. Walk around the well three times, then submerge the rag until wet through. Tie the rag to the nearest tree, then leave your worries here with it.

Ruth glanced up. The nearest tree was indeed festooned with brightly coloured strips of cloth. The basket mentioned had been moved to hang from the tree too, she realised, as she reached up to choose a cloth. They were all frozen solid, which didn't help, but she managed to prise a bright-red one from the pile. Then she turned to the pool and spotted her next problem.

The well was iced over.

She could come back later, maybe with a thermos of hot water or something to melt it. But Ruth knew that if she left now the moment would be over, the remote chance of any magic lost for ever.

It must be a fairly sluggish spring to have frozen over in the first place. But somewhere under the ice, water was bubbling up from the spring. New water, new life, hidden from her right now but still there and waiting for spring.

She just had to get to it.

Casting around her, Ruth found a heavy stone. Then she knelt in the frozen grass and started bashing the ice. With every strike, she felt herself hitting out at the unfairness of the world, taking aim and taking out every fear she still held inside her. Never mind magic. This was *action*. And maybe it didn't change anything in the real world, but it felt *wonderful*.

'Will. You. Just. *Break.*' As she spoke the last work, the ice cracked under her stone in an explosion of frozen shards, and chilly water bubbled up through the fissures. The noise echoed up through the trees, sending birds into startled flight. She'd done it. Sitting back on her heels, Ruth lifted her face to the sky and laughed.

And then she stopped, listening to her laughter echoing back to herself off the trees. Listening to herself laugh. When was the last time she'd laughed? Really, truly, laughed?

She couldn't remember. So she did it again.

Yes, she'd walk around the bubbling spring three times. Yes, she'd soak her cloth and hang it from the tree. She'd do everything she was instructed to in order to make the magic work.

But Ruth knew it wasn't any of that which would fix her world.

It was this place. The space away from reality.

She didn't believe in magic. She didn't even believe in signs and superstitions, normally.

The doctors hadn't been lying. There was nothing portentous about her miscarriage; it wasn't a sign or a warning. Here, in the cold, calm and cruel outdoors, she could see that.

Losing her baby was a sadness she had to live with, for ever. But it could be one that would help her grow and move on, maybe. Could guide her to the person – perhaps the mother – that she hoped to be. Otherwise, all this pain would have been for nothing.

But it wasn't magic that would help her through.

It was her strength. The same strength that had allowed her to break the sheet of ice on a spring in a forest.

And it was Alec. The man who had been by her side all

this time. Yes, he made a stupid, drunken mistake last night. And yes, he needed to grow up and leave his uni past behind sometimes, but the point of marriage was that they should be growing up *together*. If she kept pulling away, of course he'd return to what he knew best and where he felt safest.

She needed to get back to him. She got to her feet and began to walk, then stride – then run! – out of the forest. She needed to find her husband, so that they could start rebuilding their life together.

Starting now.

Lara

Lara woke up again much later that afternoon to find herself still naked, and firmly wrapped in Jon's arms.

God, she remembered this.

The sex itself . . . well, that had definitely moved on since ten years ago, and only in the best ways. Back then, neither of them had had much of a clue what they were doing anyway, but now . . . now they were different. They knew themselves better, and they'd had one hell of an afternoon finding out what the other wanted, needed, these days too.

But this. Lying in Jon's arms, feeling his warmth, his closeness, the connection between them . . . None of that had changed at all. She almost wished it had.

It would have made walking away afterwards a lot easier.

She knew why this had happened. Clarity had hit her the moment the passion had worn off in the seconds before she fell asleep, her body relaxed and at peace for the first time in years.

She'd been wound so tight, all this time. Ten years of trying to live out the dreams she'd shared with her cousin, chasing her dream career, travelling the world. Ten years of proving she did the right thing not getting engaged at twenty-one. And finally, this week, even Caitlin had admitted that she had. And somehow, that validation had set her free to give in to the temptation of sleeping with Jon, one last time.

Or maybe Fliss was right and she was just missing her phone.

But now she'd given in, now that glorious moment of total relaxation and rightness was over, all the old worries were starting to creep in again.

'So,' Jon said, his voice raspy with sleep. 'Do you think we got that out of our systems comprehensibly enough?'

'Probably not,' Lara admitted. She could still feel him; his fingers on her skin, his laugh in her ear, the way they'd moved together under the sheets . . . 'But it might be enough closure to do us another ten years.'

Jon rolled onto his side, propping his head up on his hand as he looked down at her. 'Do you really think so?'

She met his steady gaze with her own, probably rather more conflicted and uncertain one. 'No. But it might have to.'

'Why?'

Because we could screw up everything. Because our friends will be furious. Because I don't think I can take losing you again.

Really, he could pick a reason from the very lengthy list she was composing in her head.

Because wasn't this just falling into the same old trap again? If marrying Jon was a bad idea ten years ago, what made starting a new relationship with him now a good one?

Would she end up choosing to stay in London to be near him, if he was there, limiting her options and scope just as surely as she would have if she'd married him? Not that they'd even *talked* about any of that, but God knew Jon had form. He had expectations, and she wasn't sure she wanted to live up to them now any more than she had then.

However much she wanted *him*.

'Look, you're just coming out of a divorce, dealing with your father's illness, moving *countries,* for heaven's sake. I'm weighing up career options, moving cities, all sorts. This is a bad time for either of us to get caught up in the nostalgia of a relationship that died ten years ago.'

'Is that what you think this is?' His voice was even, but she could see the tension in his jaw.

'What else could it be? We've barely seen each other in ten years, and we've fallen into bed after a few days of trying to be friends.' Four days wasn't enough to know if things would work out this time. And Lara knew that if it didn't, she'd lose him for good this time – and maybe the others, too. He'd be in London with them and this time, she could be hundreds of miles away in Manchester, the one left out in the cold.

She couldn't risk that. But she couldn't stay, either, if he was there and she couldn't be with him.

'This could be our second chance,' Jon said, conviction in his voice. 'Our chance to get it right.'

God, she wanted that to be true.

It wasn't just the sex, or the heat that hummed between them when they were in the same room. It was the comfort. The having someone who truly knew her, who saw deeper inside her than the others, even now, even after so long. Having that person she could turn to and talk to and listen to and feel . . . valued. Understood. Needed.

And they could have all that as friends, couldn't they? Without the complication and confusion of sex or relationships.

She loved Jon. She'd always loved Jon. Whether that love covered friendship or more, didn't matter any more. She wanted him in her life, and keeping him as her friend was the safest way of making sure she never lost him again.

She had to make him understand that. That romance was too much of a risk.

Lara sighed. 'Jon—'

A hammering on the door saved her from having to say more, for now. But then, as the door burst open and Alec stormed in, she realised the reprieve might not have been as welcome as she thought.

'I can't find Ruth. We had a row this morning and nobody has seen her since—' Alec's wild, lost expression settled into something far stonier. 'What the hell is going on here?'

Since she and Jon were both naked in his bed, Lara assumed the question was rhetorical. Or that Alec was asking the same question Jon had been, in his way.

Where do we go from here?

Scrambling to tuck the duvet around her body, Lara sat up as best she could, pushing the hair out of her eyes. She felt her cheeks flaming with colour. 'What did you fight about? Have you tried calling her?'

'Of course I've tried calling her,' Alec snapped. 'Her phone is out of signal, or switched off, or something. Going straight to voicemail. And I want an answer. What do you think you two are doing?'

'Working off ten years of sexual tension?' Jon suggested lightly, as he angled his legs out of the bed to pull on his boxers. He froze and stared at Alec. 'Do you mind?'

Slowly, reluctantly, Alec turned his back to the bed.

'Give me a moment to get dressed,' Jon said, as he reached for his jeans. 'I'll come and help you find Ruth.'

'Thanks.' Alec said stiffly. He went to leave, shutting the door behind him.

Leaving them alone.

'Jon . . .' She reached for him. 'What you said about a second chance . . .'

He shook his head, stopping her words. 'I saw the look on your face. Don't worry, I understand. You have your closure, Lara. Let's leave it at that, yeah?'

Fastening his jeans, he grabbed a jumper, yanked it over his head and walked out.

Ruth

It seemed a longer walk back to the cottage than it had been to get out to the woods in the first place. The possibilities and optimism that had filled her by the spring started to fade as the snow grew heavier and her hands and face grew colder. Even her best leather gloves weren't up to a Scottish winter.

It was starting to get dark, too – earlier than seemed reasonable. She must have been in the woods longer than she'd thought.

Finally, she hit the steps down to the beach, and realised that in this weather they'd be absolutely treacherous. Out to sea, the waves were churning, crashing against the beach and the cliff wall, sending spray flying to mix with the snow.

Ruth eyed the steps, then shook her head. She couldn't risk it. Which meant a long walk back along the cliff path instead, back towards the cottage. At least it was mostly downhill.

Tucking her hands into her armpits, she picked up her pace, fear simmering at the edges of her body – until she saw another figure approaching through the falling snow.

The figure raised a hand, called her name, and Ruth realised it was Jon, wrapped up in coat and scarf and gloves.

From the way he headed straight for her, Ruth guessed he'd been sent out looking for her. Maybe they all had.

She'd been gone much longer than she'd intended.

Jon. The one of Alec's friends she knew least of all.

He jogged towards her, until he could talk at a normal volume instead of shouting. 'Hey. Alec's going crazy trying to find you. Your phone's going through to voicemail!'

Pulling her phone from her pocket she checked the home screen. 'No reception. Must be the snow.'

'Or just this damn island messing with us.' Jon shook the snowflakes from his hair. He looked tussled, as though he'd been dragged out of bed. Goodness, had she worried them that much? 'Sorry. Bad day. Come on, let's get back to the cottage and call him from there. He's searching the village.'

Ruth winced. 'Sorry. I didn't mean to worry anyone. I needed to get out of there, you know?'

'I definitely know the feeling,' Jon replied, and the tone of his voice made her wonder. Maybe she wasn't the only outsider here?

'It must be strange for you,' Ruth said, as they started walking down the hill together. 'Being around everyone again for a whole week, after being away for so long.'

'Something I'll have to get used to, I suppose.' Jon shrugged. 'Or not. I could always look for another job somewhere else, move overseas again.'

'To keep away from Lara,' Ruth said, without thinking.

Jon's gaze shot to hers, his shoulders almost up to his ears under his scarf. Ruth wondered what had happened to make him so tense. Lara, she assumed.

Then he gave her a small, self-deprecating smile. 'It's that obvious, huh?'

'That you're still in love with her?' Where had this boldness come from? Was it something she'd found in the woods? Or something she'd earned when she'd faced her own fears and decided to do something about them?

Jon made a noise that might have been a denial or a confirmation; Ruth wasn't sure. Either way, she ploughed on.

'I'm the outsider here,' she said. 'I think maybe I see you all more clearly than you see each other.'

'And what do you see?' Jon asked, curiosity colouring his voice.

She took a deep breath, thinking. 'I see all the others stuck in an image of ten years ago – either because they want to go back to how things were, or because they don't know how to move on. Except for you. You did move – thousands of miles away. And now you're back and—'

'I'm making the same mistakes I did ten years ago too,' Jon finished for her, with a sigh. 'Trying to push Lara into something she isn't ready for. That I don't even know if she wants.'

'Oh, I don't know. The way she's been looking at you all week I'd say she wants,' Ruth joked. She felt like her whole world had lightened since she left the woods, and not only because of the winter white wonderland around them. Because she could see beyond her own fears and problems at last.

'That's not the same as for ever, though. And when I'm with her . . . that's all I can see,' Jon admitted.

'Don't give up yet.' Ruth tucked her hand through the crook of his arm as they walked down the slope, back towards the cottage. 'Sometimes the future takes a little longer to arrive than we'd like. But we have to have faith in it all the same.'

'I hope you're right. One thing my divorce made very clear was that I never really got over Lara. I can't give up on her now. Except every time I've ever tried to hold onto her, I've lost her.'

'I suppose if something matters so much you have to keep trying, right?' Ruth said.

'Until it breaks you?'

'Until there's no chance of happiness, perhaps.' Ruth thought about the baby, and knew that however much they wanted one, there would have to be a cut-off point. She could be brave, she could try again. But she needed to talk to Alec about other options, too. About IVF, or adoption, maybe. Or choosing to remain childfree, if that was the right decision for them in the end.

But what mattered was that they *talked*. It was time to stop letting life happen to them and make choices instead, as far as they could. Together.

Ruth and Jon walked in silence until Holly Cottage was almost in sight. But before they reached the final turn that would reveal those whitewashed walls and bright-red front door, Jon stopped, and held her still beside him.

'Ruth, you say you're an outsider. But you know, you've spent far more time with my friends than I have over the past five years. If anyone is an outsider, it should be me. But you have to want to be a part of something, to be let in. You know?'

He was right, Ruth realised. She'd held them all at an arm's length all these years because they were *Alec's* friends. But did that really mean they couldn't be hers too?

'Ruth?' A familiar voice rang out through the snow as he searched for her, and Jon flashed her a smile.

'Better get you back to him before he calls out the emergency services. Come on.'

They rounded the last corner together, and Alec appeared along with the cottage.

As soon as he saw her, Alec started running. Ruth slowed, and let him catch up to her. 'I didn't know where you were!

I've had the guys out searching. Oh God, love, you're freezing! I'm so sorry. So, so sorry.'

Jon melted away towards Holly Cottage with a smile, as Ruth turned into Alec's embrace. His arms were warmth and home around her, and Ruth let herself lean against him as the snowflakes landed on his face, his eyelashes.

'I'm sorry you were scared,' she said, her voice scratchy with the cold. 'I've been afraid too. Of everything. But I've decided not to be, any more.'

Alec pulled back, his gaze searching her face as if he were checking she was still herself. In fairness, Ruth had to admit she didn't *feel* like her. Or not the Ruth she'd been, these last couple of months.

Maybe the Ruth she always was inside, though. Behind the fear.

'We've got a lot to talk about, haven't we?' Alec said, finally. Ruth nodded. 'Think Fliss will mind if we skip the rehearsal dinner tonight?'

'I'm sure our friends will understand.' Ruth let Alec tuck her under his arm, his hand tight and warm on her shoulder as they started walking down the hill. 'All our friends.'

And for once, it didn't seem wrong to call them that.

Fliss

The rehearsal buffet was due to be served in fifteen minutes, the pianist in the lobby was playing 'Have Yourself A Merry Little Christmas' for the fourth time already, and so far not one of her friends had arrived. Not even her maid of honour or bridesmaid. While Fliss had spent all afternoon fixing her wedding cake, Harry, bless him, had popped back to Holly Cottage to fetch Fliss her dress for the rehearsal dinner, along with her make-up bag. Since he'd brought her exactly the right things, she suspected that Betsy might have helped him — and she hadn't seen either of them since, which she wasn't thinking about at all.

Caitlin had headed back to the cottage after the dress-fitting, along with Neal and the ushers' buttonholes. Neither of them had looked particularly full of the joys of the season — something else she wasn't thinking about. And Fliss knew *exactly* what Jon and Lara had left the hotel to do. But still, she'd have expected them to be back by now.

Fliss assumed the fact they were *all* missing meant something had gone terribly wrong somewhere. Maybe many things. She prayed that none of them had to do with her and Neal.

And of course, she'd know exactly what was going on if any of them would *answer their bloody phones.*

At least her cake was right — or it would be, once the last few snowflakes had hardened enough to add onto the last tier, hopefully later tonight. Then something in this whole wedding week would still feel like hers, which was good because nothing else did. Not even the rehearsal buffet dinner, which seemed to be entirely full of Ewan's side of the invite list, because all of hers were *missing*.

'Is everyone here now, Fliss?' Martha asked, looking conspicuously around her as if to highlight the people who weren't there. *Fliss's* friends. All of Ewan's friends and family were present and correct. Except one, actually . . .

'I haven't seen Betsy yet this evening,' she commented mildly, and took a sip from her glass of champagne. 'Have you?'

Martha's eyes narrowed as she scanned the room. 'I'll go find her.'

One point to Fliss, she decided. Now she just needed her friends to arrive . . .

The door to the hotel flew open.

'Jon. Thank God you're here at least. Where *is* everyone?'

Jon shrugged off his heavy coat with the fur-lined hood. 'Hell if I know, but it's getting treacherous out there. Worse than that winter of second year when Harry decided to toboggan down the hill onto the frozen-over outdoor swimming pool.'

Wincing at the memory of several hours spent in A&E, Fliss peered anxiously through the nearest window. Thick, heavy snowflakes spiralled and fell, whipped in whirlwinds by the strong breeze.

'Nobody's out in this now, are they?' What if one of them was lost in the snow? Mistletoe Island was welcoming, but it had its treacherous cliff paths and dark corners too.

But Jon shook his head. 'Not any more, anyway, as far as I know. Ruth went for a walk after she and Alec had a row. He spent the afternoon scouring the village for her, but I found her walking back from the woods, and they're now ensconced by the fire at Holly Cottage. I don't think they'll be joining us tonight though – she looked frozen, and he was pretty shaken.'

Okay. She could make excuses for two of her friends.

'What about the others? Are Caitlin and Neal still back at the cottage?'

Jon frowned. 'I haven't seen them. Actually, I thought they were still up here at the hotel.'

Fliss shook her head. 'They left *hours* ago. And what about Lara?' She gave Jon a suspicious look. 'Tell me you two haven't screwed everything up again already? Is she okay?'

Two spots of colour appeared in Jon's cheeks, but from the way his hazel eyes flashed, Fliss got the impression it was more anger than embarrassment. *Interesting.*

'I wouldn't dare to try and guess how Lara's feeling. Or where she is.'

'Right.' Something had definitely gone wrong there, then. Not that Fliss was entirely surprised. It had always been a risk, bringing those two together for the week. So much unfinished business between them.

Just like her and Neal, really.

'Jon, mate, you made it!' Ewan swept in with an easy grin and a welcome drink, and a quick kiss on the cheek for Fliss. 'Got some people desperate to meet you. They're moving Stateside in the New Year and are looking for some advice.'

Fliss shot him a grateful smile, and he winked in return, taking Jon off to meet his friends who'd arrived that day. Ewan always knew what she needed when it came to this sort of thing. He was so good at watching a room and seeing who was uncomfortable, who was short of a drink, or who he should introduce to who because they'd probably hit it off.

It just made the fact that he couldn't see everything *she* needed even harder to bear.

Maybe it was her own fault. She'd played her part so well – the happy little housewife-to-be part, for all that she intended to carry on working. It never occurred to Ewan, or anyone, that she needed something more in her life.

More excitement. More risk. More freedom.

Marriage could be an adventure, right? A whole future opening its doors to her.

So why did it feel like they were only closing?

Fliss eyed Jon over at the bar with a couple of Ewan's friends, ordering drinks. Was this how Lara felt when she turned him down? Fliss wished she knew. But Lara had never talked about her reasons. Fliss hadn't even been sure that *Lara* knew what they were, deep down.

In the bar, her father clinked a fork against a glass and climbed up onto a chair – a little unsteadily, Fliss noticed. This thing had been going on for too long already.

With so many people travelling for the wedding, it felt wrong not to feed everyone the night before – but impossible to hold a formal rehearsal dinner without it feeling like the actual wedding reception. So instead, they'd opted for a more casual buffet in the hotel's large main bar that would give the guests a chance to meet and mingle before the big day. But now Fliss realised it just meant everyone had a chance to get properly smashed the night before her wedding.

'I know tonight isn't the night for long speeches,' her father said, as the party quietened. Apparently this was one of the few things he hadn't delegated to her mother – although Fliss could see her sitting in his direct line of sight, nodding approval for now but ready to intervene if he said anything wrong. 'But I wanted to say a few words before the big day, on behalf of my beautiful daughter Felicity.'

Fliss started suddenly as she looked up at him. He was motioning her into the room to stand beside him.

Forcing herself to cross the room on heavy, leaden feet, she tried to count how many more hours she had to get through before it was all over. Before she was married and safe and the future could start.

Not long now. She just had to make it through one more night.

As she stood beside him, her dad rested a heavy hand on her shoulder, reaching down from his chair. Across the room she saw Ewan beaming at her, so happy to be there, and wondered if he saw any of it at all. Her confusion. Her fear. Her unhappiness.

Probably not. She'd been hiding it too well for too long.

'Now, Fliss has always been my golden girl. Kind, thoughtful, generous.' Was he describing her? It sounded like another person, suddenly. 'And I know she'd be the first to want to say a huge thank you to her mother, and to Ewan's mum, Martha, for everything they've done to make this wedding happen. Couldn't have done it without them, could you sweetheart?'

Fliss told herself to smile and nod, even as The Mothers modestly murmured about it being nothing, and all the other guests clapped.

'So let us raise our glasses to The Mothers!' Fliss's dad said, and his audience obeyed. Fliss saw her aunts, the old family friends her mother had insisted on inviting, and Ewan's family and workmates all lifting their drinks and mouthing the words.

'The Mothers,' Fliss muttered, through gritted teeth,

focusing on the room around her instead of the turmoil inside.

'Well done, baby girl.' Her father patted the top of her head, and Fliss resisted the urge to pull away, to tell him she wasn't a baby any longer. Because to everyone in this room, she knew that she was.

Her dad kept the rest of his speech short, as he'd promised, and Fliss took advantage to escape back to the main lobby while everyone was drinking, just as the hotel door crashed open again, and in walked Neal and Caitlin, a full metre of space between them despite the fact that Caitlin was shivering. Neal, on the other hand, looked decidedly unsteady on his feet. Had they spent the afternoon in the pub? Probably, Fliss realised.

She wished they'd invited her along. Or actually, maybe not.

'Sorry we're late.' Caitlin gave a smile that barely reached her lips, let alone her eyes. Neal didn't say anything.

'No worries.' Fliss beamed brightly, and dug deep for the sunny Miss Fliss she knew everyone expected from her. Surely she had to still be in there somewhere? 'I think they're going to be serving the buffet soon.'

'Great.' Caitlin's smile still wasn't convincing. And Neal still wasn't saying anything at all. Just looking at her. 'Are the others all here?'

Fliss shook her head. 'Jon's at the bar. Alec and Ruth aren't coming. And I have no idea where Lara or Harry are.'

Once more the door opened, a flurry of snowflakes following Lara in. 'Sorry, sorry, I know I'm really late. There was . . . is Jon here?'

'At the bar.' Caitlin eyed her suspiciously. Fliss didn't blame her. Clearly *something* was going on with those two.

'Right. Then I'll . . . go be elsewhere.' Lara flashed them

all a quick smile and disappeared into the reception room, heading away from the bar.

Oh, that didn't bode well at all.

Caitlin sighed. 'I'd better go find out what that's all about.' She set off after Lara.

Not for the first time, Fliss wondered if group-mother was really the role Caitlin wanted to play. Or if she'd just been cornered into it, the same way she'd become Miss Fliss.

She looked at Lara, running away again because that was what she did, and they never let her forget it. Would she and Jon stand more of a chance if they all let them both forget what happened last time?

'I need to talk to you.' Neal grabbed her arm, his eyes unfocused as he looked at her.

'Then sober up first.' Fliss shook him off.

'I'm not drunk. Well, not very. But Fliss—'

'Neal, not tonight.' She sighed as she looked at him. 'It's the night before my wedding. I have guests to look after.'

'There isn't exactly a lot of time left,' Neal pointed out.

'Then maybe what you want to say shouldn't be said at all.' Because she already knew it, didn't she? Had already heard it. Thought it herself, even.

What more was there to say, now?

But Neal shook his head. 'This is important, Fliss. Come with me.'

'I can't.' She wasn't even sure that she wanted to.

And even if she did, the figures walking down the stairs, hand in hand, smiles wide, would have stopped her.

'There you are!' she said. 'Where have you been?' Though even as the words escaped her, she could guess what the answer was.

Harry and Betsy paused halfway down the staircase, grinning at each other. Then Harry looked up and raised his

305

voice. 'Everyone? We have some news.'

The chatter died down around them. Neal took a step away from Fliss's side, to her relief. Maybe everything was going to be okay. Her friends were almost all here now. The rehearsal buffet could go ahead and everything was going to be fine. Just as it should be. Just as it always had been. Fliss could feel her heartbeat start to slow as her body relaxed. Thank goodness. Everything was returning to normal.

But Harry's face was beaming with a joy that seemed . . . not quite Harry. He looked almost delirious and as he straightened up to speak again, Fliss felt a jolt of understanding. *Oh my God, no . . . It can't be.*

But it was too late. The announcement carried over their heads, as the rest of the gathering broke out in cheers.

'Betsy and I are getting married!'

Lara

It hadn't been the most *conventional* rehearsal dinner, Lara conceded, but at least everyone seemed to be enjoying themselves. Well, most people, anyway. From the corner of her eye, she spotted Fliss at the bar, perched on a stool with a large glass of white wine in front of her, while the party went on in the next room.

She'd better go make some apologies. Caitlin had been very clear on that point. But first, Harry.

'You're sure about this?' she asked him. 'I mean, before this week a girl was lucky to get a second date out of you. Now you're jumping into marriage?'

'That's because I hadn't met Betsy.' Harry smiled across the room to where Betsy was presumably having the same conversation with her own concerned family and friends. Lara was glad that Betsy hadn't made good on her suggestion that she might break Harry's heart – but she honestly hadn't expected this.

It wasn't normal to go from single to engaged in less than a week, right? Otherwise, Lara was doing this all wrong.

'So, long engagement?' Lara asked, hopefully.

Harry rolled his eyes. 'Honestly, the lot of you. How many years have you spent telling me to grow up and settle down? Find a nice girl and start being an adult for a change?'

'Me, personally? None.' She wasn't that sort of hypocrite.

'Okay, not you,' Harry allowed. 'But the rest of them.

307

The thing is, when you know, you know.'

'So, you fell in love at first sight across a crowded bar while we all belted out "Living on a Prayer" at the karaoke?'

'No,' Harry replied, with exaggerated patience. 'I saw Betsy and I knew I wanted to get to know her. And once I started talking to her, I knew I didn't want to ever *stop* getting to know her. The more I knew, the more I wanted to know. And the more time I had with her the more I wanted.'

'You haven't really been playing golf all week, have you?' Lara said, although she already knew the answer. She remembered that stage only too well. The part where Jon had been the only person she wanted to talk to, to spend time with. When there was still so much to learn about each other that they'd talked for hours, for days.

Just like they'd done again this week. *Oh hell.*

'I got a few rounds in,' Harry said with a shrug. 'Betsy's much better at it than me, though.'

'What about her son?'

'Morgan's got a pretty good swing for a four-year-old, too.'

'I meant—'

'I know what you meant.' Harry's smile was a little disappointed. 'Did you think it would matter to me that she already had a kid?'

'No. I just . . . you never mentioned wanting a family. Or any of this.'

'Because I didn't, until now. But Morgan is part of Betsy. We're going to be a family.'

'Then I'm really happy for you,' Lara said, feeling the burn of something inside her chest. Not guilt, because she wasn't lying. Maybe regret, for everything she'd given up. Maybe envy.

How did Harry make it look so simple? Fall in love, follow your heart, live happily ever after.

Except her heart had never managed a straightforward message yet.

'Thank you.' Harry grinned. 'That's one of you, then. Caitlin's up next, and I think she's going to take a lot more persuading.'

'Good luck.' Lara wrapped her arms around Harry's broad shoulders and hugged him tight.

'You could have this too, you know,' he whispered into her ear. 'If you'd let yourself.'

Lara pulled back. 'Maybe one day. Right now, I have to go talk to Fliss.'

'And later you can buy me a drink for distracting everyone from whatever the hell is going on between you and Jon.'

If only she knew what that was. 'Deal.'

'But first, I need to persuade that pianist to play something good, instead of this Christmas stuff.'

Laughing, Lara watched him stride across the room towards the piano. Then she went to find the bride-to-be.

Fliss didn't look up from her glass of wine as Lara took the barstool beside her and motioned to the bartender to bring her one too.

'Well, shock announcements notwithstanding, I think most people are enjoying themselves,' she said, trying to sound bright and peppy. Like Fliss usually was.

Except right now Fliss was hunched over the bar, her blonde curls limp around her shoulders, looking less like sunshine and daisies incarnate than Lara had ever seen her. Even though the pianist had taken up the challenge, and Harry was now singing along to 'Living on a Prayer', and encouraging the rest of the room to join in. They should be laughing at Harry's antics. They should be joining in.

But Fliss didn't even seem to have noticed.

'Fliss?' Lara nudged her friend, gently. No response.

Lara sighed. Obviously Fliss was mad with her for sleeping with Jon, screwing everything up in record time, so that now they couldn't even be in the same room again. Understandably, really.

'I'm so sorry,' she said. 'I really didn't mean to ruin your wedding week. I honestly thought Jon and I could just be friends. But then, it turns out we're not so good at that. And then we ended up in bed and Alec walked in, and I told him it was just closure.' God, it hadn't been *just* anything, but Lara was pretty sure that wasn't what Fliss needed to hear right now. 'I know our friendships matter more, and I know how close I came to screwing all that up last time. I won't let it happen again, I promise. I won't let anyone fall out over me and Jon.'

The sound Fliss made could barely be called a laugh. There was too much bitterness in it, and when she finally looked up at Lara, her eyes were rimmed with red.

'Trust me, if anyone is going to screw up this week, it's me, not you.'

Lara blinked, as the whole party joined Harry on the 'Whoa-ohs!' 'What do you mean? Is everything okay? Is it the cake? You seemed happy this afternoon. What did I miss?'

Fliss's smile was sad. 'Everything. But don't worry, you weren't the only one.'

This made no sense at all. If Fliss wasn't mad about her and Jon, then what *was* going on? Was it Harry's announcement, stealing her thunder? Or Alec and Ruth not showing up?

Lara took her glass of wine from the bartender, took a huge gulp, then turned back to Fliss.

'Okay, I'm ready. Start at the beginning. Tell me everything, and I will fix it.'

Whatever it took to put the sunshine and smiles back on Fliss's face, she was ready to do it.

'Oh, Lara.' Fliss bit her lower lip, as tears brimmed in her eyes. 'I don't think you can fix this one.'

'Let me try,' Lara said.

Fliss looked at her for a long moment, then nodded. 'But not here. I need to . . . I need to finish my cake, anyway.'

'Then I will help you.' Lara got to her feet, picked up her glass, and waited for Fliss to follow suit.

'Time for the key change!' Harry yelled, and everyone cheerfully picked a random note to carry on singing. Lara was pretty sure no one was going to notice them disappearing for a while.

She motioned to the barman for another bottle of wine to take with them. Just in case.

2011

Harry

Well, this was the most miserable bloody wedding Harry had ever been to. Oh, Neal and Caitlin seemed happy enough – which was just as well, since they were the ones getting married. But Alec was pouring tequila into Jon at the bar after a long, tense afternoon of Jon pretending he wasn't watching Lara. And Lara . . . Harry had danced with her earlier, and she'd been all sharp angles and prickly edges. She hadn't relaxed all day, from the moment she showed up at the church carrying Caitlin's train.

And she hadn't looked at Jon, either.

Harry had sat beside her as she'd steadily worked her way through a bottle of wine, with barely a word of conversation. And then that damn usher had asked her to dance, and she'd disappeared off with him – which was what had led to the tequila at the bar situation.

Harry knew what the others thought about him, that he was good for fun and entertainment, but he had the emotional depth of a puddle. And a lot of the time, they weren't wrong, especially when it came to his relationships.

But with his friends, it was a different matter.

He knew them. He watched them, and he waited.

Then, when they needed him, he could be there, with a bottle of tequila he found behind the cornflakes, or chocolate

312

cake the bakery just happened to be selling at half price. Or even with just a hug, if that was what was required.

He'd never try and stop his friends from making their own mistakes. But he'd never not be there afterwards, either. Like when Lara turned down Jon's proposal and went into full meltdown back at her mum's house, days before catching a plane to Thailand.

The point was, he didn't miss a lot. And he had a feeling he might need to stock up on tequila to hide behind his cornflakes sometime soon.

Fliss dropped into the chair beside him, a full wine glass in her hand. 'Some wedding, huh?'

She was miserable too, although Harry was having a harder time putting his finger on exactly why. She hadn't brought a date after her last six-monther of a relationship ended in friendship. The way they always did.

Poor Miss Fliss. So lovely that people even broke her heart gently.

'Never get married, Fliss,' Harry said, feeling strangely philosophical after a long day's drinking. 'It only makes other people miserable.'

'Tell me about it,' Fliss said, with a laugh.

But even half cut, Harry couldn't help but notice she was watching Neal as she said it.

Monday 23 December 2019

Christmas Eve Eve
Fliss and Ewan's Wedding Day

Ruth

Ruth woke the next morning with her husband's arms around her, and the knowledge that everything was going to be okay. She didn't know quite how yet, but she felt it deep inside, where it mattered.

They'd talked for hours the night before, long past the time when Ruth would normally have begged off and gone to bed with a headache. Whenever the conversation had grown difficult – and it did – Ruth had drawn on that confidence she'd felt in the woods, that certainty of what she had to do to move forward, however much it hurt.

It still hurt. But she knew that telling Alec everything that she thought and felt – about the baby, about them, about the future – had shifted things. Moved them forward enough to fix things, she hoped.

Because she hadn't just talked. Alec had listened, his gaze focused on her face as she talked, his brow furrowed as if he were committing every word to memory. He'd held her hand, held her close, held her while they both cried.

He'd been her husband again.

And suddenly, she could see a future for them once more. One they'd even talked about – tentatively, fearfully even, but with hope, too.

'I want to be a family with you,' Alec had said. 'I don't care what that family looks like, or how it happens. It could be us and our kids, or us and a dog, or just the two of us, a family unit of our own.'

'I want that too.' Ruth had bitten her lower lip, and forced herself to go further. 'But I want children, if we possibly can. It doesn't matter to me if they're ours biologically. I mean, if it turns out that I . . . can't, if that doesn't work . . . I think maybe I'd like to look at adoption? Maybe even long-term fostering?'

The love in Alec's eyes as he'd listened had almost blown her away. 'That's exactly what we should do, then,' he'd said.

'But I want to set an end date,' Ruth had continued. 'I don't want this to be our whole lives for ever.'

'Agreed,' Alec had said. 'I don't want either of us to feel like we've failed if, in the end, the right thing for us is to stay childfree. Because you are my family. That's all I need. And I'll work my whole life to be everything you need.'

She'd kissed him then. She didn't have any more words to show how much she loved this man.

'I don't think I ever want to leave this island,' she murmured now, in the early morning light, unsure if Alec was even awake to hear her. But then his arms tightened around her, and she knew he had.

'I don't think I ever want to leave this bed,' he growled against her shoulder, before kissing his way up her neck.

After all the talking, they'd found their way back to something else, too.

He'd been so gentle with her, so tentative, in a way he hadn't been since they first got together. But their natural rhythm had soon taken over, and Ruth had realised at last what had been missing between them. This connection.

Not the sex, exactly – although she was pretty sure they'd both missed that. But the way they touched, the way they could almost read each other's minds when their bodies were pressed together. The feel of skin on skin that told her that no one else would ever be as close to this man as she was.

The grounding feeling that came afterwards, in the quiet lull, just the two of them breathing together in the darkness.

It would take time, she knew. But slowly, slowly, she could feel her marriage seeping back in to fill the cracks that had almost shattered her.

She'd let Alec back in. And he'd come to her without hesitation.

Perhaps the Healing Island really had worked its magic after all – even if that magic was only making them face up to everything that had come between them.

Ruth kissed him, deep and long, before pulling away with a smile. 'Fliss might have forgiven us for missing the rehearsal dinner reception thing, but if we miss the actual wedding I'm pretty sure we'll be in a lot of trouble. With everyone.'

Caitlin had stuck a timetable on the fridge with allotted shower times and a breakfast schedule for the morning, to make sure they all had time to get ready and be at the tiny chapel down by the harbour in plenty of time. No one else had been surprised by this, so Ruth assumed it was what Caitlin did on big occasions.

Fliss could have been getting ready up at the hotel, Ruth supposed, but whether she was afraid of seeing the groom before the big moment in church, or if she wanted to be away from the hubbub at the hotel, she'd opted to get ready at Holly Cottage that morning. Which meant all the boys had to be showered, dressed, and heading out before the hairdresser arrived.

Ruth checked the clock on the bedside table. 'You're going to miss your slot in the shower if you're not quick.'

Alec shot her a wicked grin, before disappearing under the duvet. 'I can be very efficient with my time,' he murmured against the skin of her breasts.

Well. Who was she to argue with that? Ruth smiled as Alec kissed his way lower.

She had her husband back. They had a great group of friends. They had a romantic Christmas wedding to attend – and it was snowing.

Today was going to be a wonderful day.

Lara

'Today is going to be a disaster.' Fliss dropped to sit on the edge of her bed, and put her head in her hands. 'I have to talk to Ewan and I have no idea what to say. Something's obviously happened between Neal and Caitlin. I don't think he even came back here last night. Alec and Ruth are still hiding in their room. And Jon—' Fliss broke off, clearly aware that Jon's 'bear with a sore head' routine wasn't actually her fault.

Lara tried to find some reassuring words for her, and failed.

She had no idea what Fliss should do next.

How had she not known? After the first confession at the bar the night before, they'd just kept coming. As the two of them had put the finishing touches to the wedding cake, Fliss's whole secret life had spilled out. A secret life she'd been living for over a decade, and none of them even noticed.

None of them except Neal, that is. Because *they* had a pact.

Fliss was her best friend. But Neal was the only one she'd let see that side of her.

That was the hardest part to swallow. Everything that Neal and Fliss had shared over the years. Lara believed Fliss when she said it hadn't started out as an affair, but it seemed to her it had ended up that way, even if only technically emotionally. What was between them was more than a friendship. And the secrets . . . They were the sort of secrets that ate away at any relationship.

God, poor Caitlin. How was she going to take it?

'You hate me now, don't you?' Fliss had asked, eyeing her warily over her glass of wine and another damn fondant snowflake.

Somewhere upstairs, the rehearsal dinner party was still going on. She could hear the strains of 'Fairytale of New York' on the piano, and Harry yelling, 'Sing, Jon, sing! It's your song, mate!'

Up there, all their friends were drinking, talking and singing, oblivious to the truths Fliss had finally let out. And for a moment, Lara wanted to tell the world, to let all the hurt out.

But Fliss was her best friend.

Lara had seen the fear in Fliss's eyes and shook her head. How could she hate her?

'You screwed up,' she'd said, flatly. 'And honestly . . . I'm not sure what happens now. But I don't hate you. And I'll help you find a way through this.'

Fliss had helped her when she'd split from Jon. She'd taken off and travelled the world with her on a moment's notice so she didn't have to be alone that summer. When Lara got back, she'd let her move in with her, and then put up with Lara being away for weeks at a time with work.

Really, how had she not known what was going on?

Fliss had always seemed like an open book. Sunshine, smiles and optimism. She was the one who baked muffins to get them through exams. Who needed the dirty jokes in movies explained to her. Who was forever searching for her prince and never finding him – until Ewan.

Or until Neal. Lara wasn't sure now.

Lara sat down next to Fliss on the bed and took her hand. Watching the pale sunlight filtered by snow reflecting off her diamond engagement ring, Lara asked the question she knew she should have asked the night before, but hadn't quite been ready to hear the answer too.

'Are you in love with Neal?'

Fliss looked up at her sharply. 'No. Well. Not now, anyway. Maybe I was, a little bit, when all this started. But now . . .' She took a deep breath. 'I don't know how to describe it. He knows me better than anyone else in the world. I love him as a friend. And sometimes when he looks at me, or touches me . . . I see what we could have had, if the world had gone a different way. But I'm in love with Ewan. I just . . .'

She faltered, and Lara squeezed her hand. 'Go on.'

'I don't know if he's in love with me.' Fliss's eyes were huge and afraid. 'I mean, I know he loves the Fliss he proposed to. The one he's lived with for a year. But that isn't all of me, is it?'

'Apparently not.' Lara gave her a tight smile. 'So. What are you going to do?'

Fliss shook her head. 'Get married, I suppose. Hope for the best.'

Always with the optimism. But for the first time, Lara wondered whether they'd all been wrong to mistake Fliss's sweetness for strength. What if it was masking a fear that was eating away at Fliss inside, the worry of what would happen if she let herself *be?*

'Because that's the least scary option?' Lara asked. 'I don't think that's a good enough reason.'

Wasn't that what she was doing with Jon, though? Holding back because the alternative was terrifying? Not even letting herself think about what she might really want?

'Because I love Ewan. And I have to have faith that love is enough to make this work. Right?'

A knock on the door interrupted the moment. Which was probably just as well as Lara was all out of emotional guidance.

Tell the truth. Deal with the fallout. Follow your heart.

All advice she should probably try taking herself, really.

Lara got up and opened the door, not even surprised to find Neal standing there. He looked dreadful. His eyes were rimmed with shadows. His dark hair needed washing, and she was pretty sure he'd missed his slot in the shower on Caitlin's carefully planned-out schedule.

'God, you look terrible.'

Neal gave her a tight smile. 'I feel it. Can I talk to her?'

Lara glanced back over her shoulder, and Fliss gave her a small nod. 'Do you want me to stay?'

Fliss shook her head. 'I need to do this.'

'Okay, then. I'll be downstairs when you need me.'

'Oh, but first . . .' Fliss climbed up onto the bed, then put one foot on the windowsill, and reached up into the eaves and beams above. Then she jumped back down, Lara's phone in her hand.

'No wonder I never found it. Cunning, using my fear of heights against me.' Lara slipped it straight into her pocket without looking at it. Work could wait. There were far more important things going on today. 'You sure you're okay?'

Fliss nodded, and gave her a brave smile.

Lara slipped out through the door, letting Neal in behind her.

Leaning against the wall, she tried to figure out what to do next. She needed to talk to Caitlin – but not before Neal and Fliss did. She had to give them the chance to do this right.

324

She needed to get ready for a wedding that might not even happen.

She needed to stall the hairdresser and the florist and the make-up artist – and definitely the bride's parents.

And she needed to talk to Jon.

Biting her lip, Lara thought of the advice she'd given Fliss over the last few hours.

Then she decided to follow her own advice for a change.

'Lara!' Caitlin yelled up the stairs. 'Your turn in the shower!'

She pushed herself up off the wall. Okay. She'd follow her heart *after* she'd got ready for the wedding.

She wasn't messing with Caitlin's schedule today.

Fliss

Neal looked like a different person.

Gone was the carefree, wicked smirk she was used to from him whenever they were alone. Instead, she saw sad, tired eyes and a vulnerable smile.

'I'm glad you came,' she said, keeping the bed between them, not sure who was most likely to break down if they touched. She pulled the white satin dressing gown with 'Mrs Bennett' embroidered on the back – a gift from Betsy – tighter around her, covering as much of her skin and bridal lingerie as was possible. 'I think we need to talk. Again. Don't you?'

He nodded, a tiny movement. Fliss felt her heart starting to crack.

She hadn't lied to Lara. She was in love with Ewan, and not in love with Neal, any more. But that didn't mean she didn't still love him, as her friend. He was a part of her. He held that bit of her soul that no one else even knew existed until now. He'd always, always been there – her secret support system.

And now she had to let him go.

Fliss really didn't know if she could do that, yet.

But she knew she had to try.

'I'm marrying Ewan today, Neal. I'm moving on. And that means . . . whatever there has been between us, it's over.' There. She'd said it.

'Why?' His reaction was far more subdued than she'd expected.

'Because I love Ewan. I want to be his wife.'

'Even if he doesn't know who you really are?'

'I'll tell him. I'll tell him everything.' She'd have to, right? One way or another. This secret was out; it was only a matter of time before everyone knew.

Including Caitlin. Her chest tightened at the idea. Lara said she'd stick with her, but Fliss knew there was a very real chance she could lose all her other friends over this.

And maybe she'd deserve that. But as long as she still had Ewan, she'd be okay.

'And are you planning on coming clean before or after you say "I do" in . . .' He checked his watch. 'Four hours?'

After. The word rang through her head and she knew it was fear speaking. After, it would be too late for him to change his mind. Once they were married, they could work through everything, right?

If she told him before, he might call the whole thing off.

But she had to give him that chance, didn't she? She couldn't let him marry her thinking she was someone she wasn't.

'Before,' she said quickly, before she could change her mind. 'Which means I need to get going. Wait. You wanted to talk to me last night,' Fliss remembered suddenly. 'Before Harry's announcement.'

'Yeah. I wanted to tell you . . . I told Caitlin.' Neal's words hit like knives. 'Everything.'

Fliss felt her body stiffen. 'She knew last night?'

'Yeah.' He ran his hands through his hair, and sat on the edge of the bed, his back to her. 'But that wasn't . . . we're splitting up. But not because of you or us, not really. Because we're both so damn unhappy. We realised we were clinging onto our marriage because it wasn't as terrifying as figuring out what happened if we left it.'

'The least scary option,' Fliss murmured, Lara's voice in her head.

Had they all been holding onto the past because it was less frightening than the future?

'We're not who we were ten years ago,' Neal said, his words heavy. 'None of us are. And I'm sick of trying to be. I'm ready to start again.' He turned to meet her gaze. 'With you, if you'll have me.'

Her heart stopped beating, as if the snow outside her window had frozen it solid.

Ten years ago, how would she have answered?

She couldn't know. Because that Fliss didn't exist any longer.

She stared at him, taking in every detail of his dear face, the hope in his eyes, and suddenly everything crystallised.

'You don't want me,' she said, slowly, as she worked her way through the realisation. 'If you really did then we'd have talked about this before. Made plans, done it right. If you'd wanted to leave Caitlin you would have done it years ago and then, maybe, afterwards we could have seen about us. But you didn't. Even yesterday when we spoke, you never mentioned leaving your wife.'

'You know why I couldn't—' Neal started, but she stopped him with a raised hand.

'I know all the reasons, Neal. But the fact remains, we had our chance, ten years ago, here on this island, and we didn't take it. And now all you're trying to do is go back to who we were then, to start over and try again, because you're unhappy with how life turned out. And it won't work.'

'How can you be sure?'

'Because I'm not that girl any more, and you're not that

guy, either. You have a picture of who I am in your head, and maybe it was true once, but it's as out of date as all the Miss Fliss assumptions people make about me.' As wrong as even the pictures she had of herself, maybe. 'It's time for me to find out who I am now, not then. And I can't do that with you.'

Whatever else happened, she knew she couldn't leave Mistletoe Island with Neal tonight and still hold onto everything else that mattered to her. And she wasn't even sure he really wanted her to.

Neal shook his head. 'You're wrong.'

'You're imagining a future with the Fliss who sneaked around with you and sought out adventure and mischief.'

'That's who you really are,' Neal pointed out.

Was it? Maybe once. But not now. 'It's part of who I was. But part of me really is Miss Fliss too, you know. I can be both – and a lot more.'

She could be Ewan's Fliss, she hoped. The one she'd imagined being all this time. The wife he wanted.

But first, she needed to close the last chapters of her old life.

She took a breath, and cut the cord. 'I love you, Neal – as a friend, if nothing else. But I can't be with you.'

The words came easier than she'd thought, maybe because they were the right ones. The truth underneath all the secrets and the lies.

'I need to find my own future,' she finished.

She didn't add that he was her past. She suspected he already knew that.

Ruth

The men – minus Neal, who hadn't appeared for his slot on the shower schedule – had all headed up to the hotel to meet Ewan for a pre-wedding pint before performing their usher duties. It was kind of him to have included them, Ruth thought. He seemed like a nice man. A good fit for Fliss, Alec said.

Ruth, dressed and made up, headed down to the kitchen to see if there was anything she could do to help anyone – and found Caitlin sitting at the table in her bridesmaid dress, tearing apart a mince pie with her perfectly painted fingernails.

'Is Lara in the shower?' Ruth asked, filling the kettle.

'Hopefully. It's her turn. And the hairdresser is waiting in the snug.'

'Right. And Fliss?'

A piece of pastry went skittering across the table as Caitlin's mince pie collapsed in on itself.

'I think she's upstairs. Talking to my soon-to-be ex-husband.'

Ruth blinked. Then she grabbed the teapot. 'You and Neal are having problems?'

'Neal and I are separating. As of last night.'

Ruth winced. She and Alec had missed a lot, hiding in their room fixing their own marriage. But she'd known from the start of the week that there was something wrong with Caitlin.

'I'm so sorry. Is it . . . there's no chance of you figuring things out?'

Caitlin tore off another piece of pastry. 'Maybe if either of us cared enough to bother. As it is . . .'

'Ouch.' Ruth popped an extra teabag in the teapot for good measure. Maybe she should have added some whisky, she thought, as she poured two cups and added milk.

'Yeah.' With a sigh, Caitlin took her cup from Ruth. 'It doesn't help that he thinks he's in love with Fliss.'

Ruth spilt her tea over the counter. 'What?'

'To be honest, it might be an early mid-life crisis. Hard to tell. It seems they've had some sort of weird emotional attachment affair thing going on for years. I knew . . . well, not all the details, but he's always been different about her. I never realised how far it went.'

'And is she in love with him?' Ruth asked, mopping up tea.

Caitlin's gaze drifted towards the ceiling. 'I imagine that's what he's finding out right now.'

'Right.'

Topping up her tea, Ruth sat down again, eyeing Caitlin cautiously.

'You seem to be taking this all very calmly.'

Caitlin flashed her an embarrassed smile. 'I did my ranting and screaming last night, in the back room of the Griffin, when he told me everything. By the time we went to the rehearsal dinner I was feeling almost numb, I guess. Now, I'm starting to see the silver linings.'

'Such as?' Ruth couldn't imagine any silver linings to losing Alec, not now. But then, he wasn't in love with her best friend.

'Such as realising how unhappy I was.' Caitlin huffed a laugh as she looked down at her hands. 'Which I get doesn't sound like a silver lining. But just acknowledging the fact that I was miserable. That we both were.'

'It means you can go and find a way to be happy instead,' Ruth finished for her.

'Exactly.' Caitlin looked down at the shredded pastry. 'The thing is, I had a plan. *We* had a plan, I thought. You know the one – find love of life, get married, buy house, have family. The usual stuff. And we followed it exactly until we couldn't bring ourselves to take the next step.'

A baby, of course, Ruth realised. 'Kids aren't for everyone, you know. It's perfectly valid to decide not to have a family.'

'I know that. But I want kids. Just not with Neal.'

Ruth blinked. 'Is there someone else?'

'Oh, no! Nothing like that.' Caitlin pushed her hair off her face. 'When we started talking about trying again – months ago now – for the first time, I pictured my future. The one I'd always planned. I realised I didn't want it. This week, this place . . . it confirmed that for me.'

Whereas it had taken Mistletoe Island to show Ruth how much she *did* want the future she'd always planned.

'So, you're definitely splitting up?' Ruth asked.

Caitlin nodded. 'It's for the best. Neal says he never had the chance to find out who he was, who he might have been, outside my plan. That's why he escaped into his friendship with Fliss. But the thing is, I never got to find out those things either.'

'And now you might?'

'And now I might,' Caitlin agreed, with a small smile. 'It took this thing with Fliss to force us into action, I think. When we were younger, we fought all the time – not that we let the others know. We even split up a few times. But in the end, it was always easier to stay together. We moved in together straight after university and since then everything has been tangled up together. Our stuff, the money, the house . . . our friends.'

For the first time, Ruth saw Caitlin's green eyes brim with tears. 'Your friends will still be your friends though, surely? I mean, *I* will still be your friend.'

Caitlin gave her a grateful smile. 'And that means a lot. It's just . . . I've spent more than ten years holding these people I love together, even when they did their best to fall out of each other's lives. Because this group of people matter to me. They're *family*. And now, after all that, it'll be me and Neal that drives a wedge between us all.'

'Or Neal and Fliss,' Ruth pointed out. 'And maybe it's time. Maybe everyone needs to move on. Not forget each other or lose the friendships. Just loosen the ties a little.'

'Let go of the apron strings?' Caitlin joked.

'Something like that.'

'You know, it's funny. I've spent the last six months, a year, maybe longer even, wondering who I might have been if I hadn't just followed that plan so blindly,' Caitlin admitted. 'And now I get to find out. I get to tell the truth about anything and everything. I get to be unashamedly me. Not the group mum, not the responsible one, the sensible one. Just me.'

'That sounds like a silver lining to me,' Ruth agreed. It wasn't one she wanted for herself – she knew who she was without Alec, and she didn't enjoy that life nearly as much as the one she had with him.

But for Caitlin, whole worlds were opening up.

'I don't know how to tell the others,' Caitlin said, her gaze dropping to her cup of tea again. 'For so long it's always been all of us, together. And now . . .'

'And now things are different. But that doesn't mean

you're not still friends, if you choose to be. And it's okay to choose *not* to be, too.' Ruth reached out to touch Caitlin's arm. 'None of you are the same people you were when you met, and you wouldn't want to be. The world moves on. People change, and so do their priorities.'

Caitlin looked up to meet her gaze. 'You must have found us all unbearable, clinging on to the same group of friends we formed over a decade ago.'

Ruth didn't try to deny it. 'Your friendships mean a lot to Alec. I can see why. But that doesn't mean none of you are allowed to change and move on. Even if it risks that.'

'You're right.' Caitlin's expression lightened a little. 'We'll really still be friends? You and me?'

'Definitely.' Her husband wasn't the only thing she'd won back that week, Ruth realised. She'd found a true friendship, too.

'Good.' Caitlin downed the rest of her tea. 'In that case, we'd better find out if this wedding is going ahead or not.'

'It is.' Fliss appeared in the doorway, looking pale and fragile in her ivory gown, the snowflake lace tight over the bodice, flowing into the fairy-tale tulle skirt that just revealed the glass slipper type heels underneath.

Despite the red rims around her eyes, and the darker shadows below them, Fliss looked determined all the same. 'I'm . . . sorry isn't enough. But I am. And I know there's a million things to talk about. To sort out. And I'll understand if you don't want to be there today, or to stand up with me—'

'No,' Caitlin said, and Ruth looked at her in surprise. 'You've been my friend for over ten years, Fliss. I'll be your bridesmaid today. Because . . .' her voice faltered, full of tears. Ruth wrapped an arm around her shoulder and held her close.

'Because this might be the last time,' Lara said, appearing behind her. 'The last time we're all together.'

'And I won't miss that,' Caitlin said. 'I won't miss my chance to say goodbye.'

Fliss stared at her. 'I'm so, so sorry, Caitlin. And I always will be.'

Caitlin nodded. 'Right. Then we need to get your hair and make-up done, ready to head down to the chapel. Your dad will be here with the car any moment.'

Fliss nodded. 'But I need to talk to Ewan, before the ceremony. And then—'

'And then we'll get you married,' Lara finished for her. 'If that's what you still want.'

'It is,' Fliss said, nodding.

'Then let's get moving,' Ruth said, looking between the three women.

She had no idea how this day was going to end. But if she could help all three of them through it, she would.

She owed Mistletoe Island – and them – that much.

Fliss

Fliss stared at her reflection in the mirror propped up on a side table in the snug, as the hairdresser, Marie, fussed with her curls, pinning them back away from her face and affixing the clip that would hold her veil in place.

She didn't look like herself. She didn't look like anyone. The reflection in the mirror was a bride, but not one she recognised. All the things that had made her *Fliss* seemed to have been stripped away. She was an empty shell, waiting to see who she became after this day. This horrible, wonderful day.

Until today she'd known she *had* to get married, and quick, before her secret came out. Now it was already out there, and she felt like she didn't know anything at all.

She didn't know how Ewan would react. But she had to find out before she married him.

Marie pulled out her make-up bag next, and Fliss was glad they'd found someone who could do both hair *and* make-up. She couldn't have taken more people at the cottage today. As it was, Ruth had left with Alec, who'd collected her in the rental car, and Caitlin was still hiding out in the kitchen with mugs of tea. Lara sat rigid on the window seat, staring at her phone, only glancing up occasionally to meet Fliss's gaze in the mirror to check if she was okay.

She wasn't okay. She didn't even bother smiling to pretend that she was.

That was something Miss Fliss would have done. And she wasn't her any longer.

Marie smoothed creams and concealers across her skin, covering the dark circles under her eyes, highlighting the few parts of her face that didn't show the ravages of a sleepless night, and hiding those that did. Fliss disappeared behind the mask of make-up: the pale pink lips, the long lashes, none of it real.

'There.' Marie stepped back to survey her handiwork, and nodded with satisfaction. Fliss stood, smiling her thanks.

'Is the car here?' she asked.

Lara nodded. 'And Harry will have Ewan waiting for you before we go in,' she promised. 'Come on.'

Caitlin met them at the door. 'Hang on,' she said. Then she reached behind Fliss's head to bring forward Ewan's grandmother's veil to cover her face. 'Perfect.'

Fliss glanced at herself in the mirror by the grandfather clock, still ticking out the minutes until she was married. She couldn't even see her own familiar features at all any longer.

She could be anybody.

Maybe she would.

Fliss didn't know quite how Harry had persuaded Ewan to meet her behind the tiny chapel on the edge of the island, but she was glad he had. The moment she saw him – standing there in that hideous kilt that his mother insisted was the family tartan, broad shoulders beneath his jacket, fair hair neatly combed and his face clean-shaven – she felt better. He was hers. Her perfect match. And she could have him for ever. She just had to say 'I do'.

'Fliss? Harry said you wanted to talk to me? You know we're not supposed to see each other before the wedding.

337

It's bad luck.' Ewan's frown deepened as he looked at her. 'What's the matter? Has something happened?'

How could she tell him? Now, when they were due to take vows in just a few minutes?

'I needed to see you. To ask you something.'

'What?'

'You love me, yes? All of me?' Fliss bit her lip as soon as she'd blurted the words out.

Ewan's eyes softened. 'Of course I do! What's made you think otherwise? I know it's been a difficult week, being apart and dealing with our friends and family—'

Fliss couldn't help it. The laugh burst out of her, harsh and frantic. Ewan stepped forward, taking her into his arms.

'Whatever this is, whatever is bothering you, we'll deal with it after the wedding, okay? Because we love each other, and I know we're going to be okay. I know *you*, Fliss.' She could hear the panic in his voice. 'You've worked so hard to make this wedding happen, to keep everyone happy, and now it's all going to work out. Our wedding. Okay?'

She stiffened at his words; it didn't feel like their wedding. Not any more.

But she knew what he needed to hear. 'Okay,' she whispered.

She wanted to believe him. She wanted to marry him and be safe for ever. From her secrets, from that other Fliss. If she married Ewan right now, her future was certain. Less terrifying.

That was why she'd come here now. Yes, to tell him the truth about everything. But mostly to feel that this was right. That Ewan's wife was the Fliss she was meant to be.

Did she?

'Fliss, we have to go.' He looked past her. 'Guests are already arriving, and you're not supposed to be here yet.' He pressed a quick kiss to her cheek and disappeared around the corner of the chapel before she could stop him.

She'd missed her chance. She'd been too scared to tell him everything, even now, and now it was too late.

'Fliss?' Lara picked her way around the back of the chapel, holding the hem of her bridesmaid dress away from the snow. 'People are arriving, and your dad's getting a bit nervous . . . I'm not sure he bought the last-minute check on the venue thing. Come on. If I sneak you back to the car we can drive out through the village and around a few times, then come back once all the guests are seated for the ceremony. If that's still what you want?'

Why did Lara keep asking her that?

She wanted to marry Ewan. He wanted to marry her. Maybe that was the baseline she had to start from.

Everything else would work out. Right?

She let Lara lead her back to the car, where her dad's relieved smile welcomed her.

From then on, everything seemed to happen on auto-pilot. Or as if she were on the outside somehow, watching a wedding video. One of those old cine-film ones her grand-dad used to show them at Christmas. Jerky, oddly coloured films of people she didn't recognise, all smiling and waving for the camera behind a soundtrack of 'Greensleeves' or whatever. You never heard what they were saying, or knew what they were thinking.

Right now, Fliss couldn't hear or process much of anything either. As if she were separated from the real world by that cinema screen. Just waving and smiling and hoping nobody looked any deeper and saw the turmoil inside her.

And suddenly the movie jumped, and she stood in the doorway of the chapel, her dad beside her, holding her arm, and Lara and Caitlin behind her, lifting their skirts over the snow. Her veil covered her face like a filter, making everything beyond it feel out of reach. Hidden.

All she felt was her own breath against the lace, and the biting chill of the Scottish winter on her bare arms.

Well, that and a sense of impending dread.

She looked around the chapel, at the red flowers on the end of the pews, tied up with gold ribbons. At The Mothers, sat either side of the aisle in the front pews, their hats blocking the view of everyone behind them. At the ushers in their powder-blue-and-gold waistcoats. At everything she'd planned and had changed. And behind her, a bridesmaid in pale-blue tulle who probably – and rightly – hated her right now, and a maid of honour who kept asking if she was sure she really wanted to get married.

With each step down the aisle, the doubts and the dread weighed heavier on her shoulders. Because this wasn't *her* wedding at all. And if she went through with it, she'd be swapping the Fliss she had been – Neal's Fliss, Miss Fliss, all of them – for the Fliss who wanted *this* wedding.

She hadn't told Ewan the truth.

I *know* you, *Fliss,* he'd said. But he didn't. Not really.

And if she married him now, with secrets between them, she'd never have a chance to figure out who she was without them.

Who she was when the truth came out.

Caitlin and Lara, following her, they knew.

Alec and Ruth, smiling at her from the pew at her side. They probably knew too by now.

Harry and Betsy, watching Morgan walk ahead of her with the rings. If they didn't know yet, they would soon.

Neal . . . he wasn't even here. But he already knew.

By the end of the day, whether she went through with

this or not, everyone would know. She'd gathered her friends here to see her get married, but now she realised they were all here to see her secrets.

Only Ewan didn't know, as he stood by the altar in that ridiculous kilt, smiling encouragingly. Just like he'd smiled in the bar the night before, when he hadn't seen how she was cringing inside at her father's words.

Fliss stopped walking, halfway to the altar.

'I'm sorry. I can't do this.' In one movement, Fliss pulled the veil from her carefully pinned hair, and tossed it aside. She couldn't hide any more. It was time to be just her. Felicity Hayes.

Whoever that turned out to be.

'I'm so sorry.' She whispered the apology to her father, who called after her as she turned, pushed past Lara and Caitlin, and walked back up the aisle alone.

'Fliss!' Ewan's voice rang out after her, but she just kept walking. Out of the chapel, and without looking back.

Lara

'What's going on?' Jon asked, grabbing Lara's arm as she tried to follow Fliss before the chapel doors swung shut. They hadn't even made it all the way to the altar. All around them, conversation was humming. Fliss and Ewan's nearest and dearest wondering the same thing Jon was, and speculating wildly. Gossip and scandal and rumour.

Fliss was going to have to bear it all.

'Let's just say it isn't going to be us that tears apart the group, after all.'

Jon frowned. 'What does that mean?'

Caitlin put a hand on his shoulder, gently pressing him to sit back down into the pew. 'Okay, now I know this is going to be hard to hear . . .' She trailed off and shook her head. 'What am I doing? I'm not actually your mother, am I?'

'No?' Jon shot Lara a confused look, and Lara hid a smile. However crazy this day might be, Caitlin seemed to be coping with it far better than Lara thought she would have.

'So, I don't have to baby you through this. Here's what's happening. Neal and Fliss have been having some sort of emotional affair for the last decade,' Caitlin said, ticking off the events of the last twenty-four hours on her fingers, efficient as ever. 'Neal and I are getting divorced – only partly because of that. I'm planning some sort of wild new life to celebrate. And Fliss . . . honestly, I don't much care what

Fliss does now. But in summary, you and Lara should feel free to screw and screw up as much as you like. God knows you can't do any worse than the rest of us.'

She drifted out into the aisle again, towards the altar and Ryan, the best man, painting on her most appeasing smile. Lara mentally wished her luck. After all, the bridesmaid and the best man was kind of a tradition, right? And Ryan *had* been staring at her at the burlesque party . . .

'Is she hitting on Ewan's little brother?' Jon asked, peering over people's heads.

'Looks like it. And good for her.'

'Right. But what now?' Jon looked as baffled as the rest of the congregation. Nobody seemed entirely sure on the etiquette of a wedding that didn't happen. Up in the front pews Fliss's mum seemed to be berating her husband for letting this happen. Martha, meanwhile, was trying to console her son – who shrugged her off as he took a couple of steps towards the door, then stopped, his expression a mixture of confusion, betrayal and devastation.

Lara looked away. 'Yeah. It's been a bit of a day. And I think it's safe to say that things are never going to be the same for our little gang again. I was going to come find you, fill you in. But there wasn't time and Fliss needed me.' She glanced towards the oak door. 'Probably still does need me, actually.'

Jon followed her gaze. 'You should go. I'll see if I can do anything for Ewan. Like help figure out what to do with all these people now.' Family members were whispering in the pews. Someone was going to have to say something soon, and it didn't look like it was going to be Ewan, who had now slumped into the nearest pew, his head in his hands.

Jon turned to leave, and Lara grabbed his arm. 'But later? We'll talk?'

His glance was cool, non-committal. 'If you think there's something to talk about.'

'There is.' She knew it, deep inside. Somewhere that hummed and sang with possibility.

Screw and screw up as much as you like, Caitlin had said.

Maybe screwing up was inevitable, to one degree or another. So maybe they should try living, and finding out what happened next. Take the risk and live with the consequences. Because if it was the *right* risk, it would be worth it.

Time to stop being so damn afraid of everything. Fear of missing out on a life she could have lived had already cost her ten years. Making mistakes might be the only way at all to make progress.

The only way to find out if love lasts.

Lara turned from watching Jon as he made his way towards Ewan. Instead, she slipped through the crush of people milling around the tiny chapel, and headed after Fliss.

'Did you know she was going to do that?' Martha demanded, grabbing her arm. Apparently she'd given up on trying to console her son and was trying to find some answers instead.

'Honestly, no,' Lara said. 'As far as I knew she was going through with it.'

Martha's eyes narrowed. 'But you knew a reason why she shouldn't.'

'I do,' Caitlin put in merrily from the other side of the aisle. Ryan looked thrilled to be consoling her in her time of difficulty, Lara noticed. 'My husband told her he was in love with her this morning. I suspect that had something to do with it.'

Lara's smile turned into a grimace. As much as she applauded Caitlin's new-found openness and honestly, she wished it could have waited a little bit longer.

344

'What?' Ewan's voice rang through the rafters of the chapel. Lara winced, and hoped Jon could hold him back long enough for her to ensure that Neal was nowhere in the vicinity.

Shaking off Martha's arm, Lara pushed her way through the crowds to get outside. She beat Fliss's almost-mother-in-law, but only just. And then she stopped.

There, on the edge of the harbour, stood Fliss – and Neal.

Behind them, the waves crashed against the low wall, and in front of them a crowd of onlookers was exiting the church. What the hell was she playing at?

Then she saw Fliss shaking her head, and pushing Neal away, and ran to get closer.

'I didn't do this for you, Neal. I did it for me,' she heard Fliss say. Time to intervene.

Grabbing Neal's elbow, she pulled him back, and he staggered into her. Drunk or just sleep-deprived, Lara couldn't tell. Either way, she needed to get him out of there.

'Jon's with Ewan, figuring out what to do next with all these guests, but you should know that Caitlin just spilled the beans at the top of her voice in the middle of the church, so . . .'

Fliss pulled a face. 'Great. Well, I suppose I can't really blame her.'

'But I can blame you!' Martha, red-faced and furious under her delicate grey hat, stormed across the harbour path towards the jetty, Fliss's mum right behind her. 'After all I did for you! I saved this wedding, you know! Who knows what kind of a disaster it would have been if I'd left it to you and your mother.'

'Hey!' Fliss's mum shouted.

Martha glanced back at her. 'More money than taste, that's your problem. But you!' She jabbed a finger towards

345

Fliss's chest. 'You've ruined the whole day!'

Fliss faced the older woman, spreading her hands in supplication. Lara suspected it wouldn't do much good.

'We should get you out of here,' she murmured to Neal. 'Everyone wants to punch you right now.'

'*I* want to punch me,' Neal said, mournfully.

Later, Lara would sit down with him and figure out exactly what he'd been thinking. And she'd do the same with Fliss, too. They'd all figure out what happened next – just as they'd all done with her when she turned down Jon's proposal ten years ago.

She hoped her friends would be more willing to listen than she had. She hoped nobody would need to move across oceans to save their friendships.

But she also knew that nothing would be the same after this.

'Come on,' she said, taking Neal's arm. 'Before your wife gets out here.'

They both looked back down at the harbour, where Fliss's attempts at explanation were falling on deaf ears. 'Martha, I really didn't mean to—'

'You broke my son's heart!' Martha jabbed with her bony finger again, and this time, Fliss took a step back.

'Fliss!' Lara cried, her eyes widening, but it was too late.

The heel of Fliss's mock glass slipper caught on the edge of the harbour. She cartwheeled her arms though the air to save herself but then, Fliss was falling, falling – splash! – into the water, her eyes wide and her lips blue, the layer upon layer of tulle of her wedding dress billowing around her on the waves. Everyone froze. She looked more stunned than scared as she trod water.

'Mother!' Ewan yelled as he raced past a satisfied-looking Martha. Kicking off his shoes, he balanced on the stone edge, bringing his arms up above his head, and then in one fluid movement he dived into the choppy waters after Fliss. Swimming to her side, he scooped her up beneath her armpits, and helped her to the side, the wedding dress ruined.

'I should have done that, shouldn't I?' Neal said quietly, watching.

'Given how much alcohol you have in your system right now, definitely not,' Jon replied, coming up beside them.

'It's true,' Caitlin added, watching as Ewan hauled Fliss up onto the jetty, the wedding dress clinging to her body. 'Despite everything, I don't actually want you to drown. Or Fliss, for that matter.'

'Well, at least that's one person not rooting for my untimely death,' Neal replied.

'Guys, Betsy has a question for you.' Harry clapped one arm around Lara's shoulders, the other around Jon's.

'What's the opinion on stealing another couple's wedding? And reception.' Betsy grinned, while Harry looked from face to face, ever the optimist. 'I mean, does it even count as stealing if they're not using it?'

Jon and Lara exchanged a look and for the first time since Alec walked in on them, Lara knew they were in perfect synchronicity.

'I think you need to have filled in forms and stuff,' Lara told Betsy. 'Plus there's a waiting period . . .'

Jon was blunter. 'Harry, no. Forget it.'

'Your mother will never forgive you if you get married without her there, anyway,' Lara pointed out.

'True,' Harry said, glumly. 'Still, it would have saved a lot of hassle, right? Right now, eloping is looking pretty good. But I suppose we could use today as a sort of practice?' He turned to Betsy with eyebrows raised.

She grinned. 'Works for me. I mean, my family's all here anyway.'

'Do you think they're okay down there?' Ruth asked, appearing alongside them to take in the spectacle. 'Oh, Alec asked me to tell you all that Fliss's dad wants the reception to go ahead up at the hotel anyway and everyone's invited. Well, not you, Neal. But everyone else.'

'Perfect!' Harry and Betsy said, in unison.

Lara looked around her other friends. 'Why don't you guys go? I'll take Neal back to Holly Cottage and see you there later.' Caitlin wasn't the only one who could organise them all.

'What about Fliss?' Jon asked.

They all peered over the edge again. Fliss and Ewan appeared to be attempting some sort of discussion, but between the shivering and Martha physically dragging her son away, they didn't seem to be getting very far.

'I think she'll be coming back with us too. And fast – we need to get her out of those wet clothes. Come on. Time to go home.'

Ruth

In the end, only Caitlin, Harry, Ruth and Alec went to the reception for the wedding that wasn't. Someone had to, they decided, and Fliss – teeth chattering as Jon wrapped his hired jacket around her shoulders – had asked that Alec go and make her apologies and excuses.

In the past, Ruth knew that the job of responsible adult would have gone to Neal. Not any more. Since Neal and Caitlin both seemed to be regressing into teenagers, it fell to Alec to be the grown-up now. Ruth smiled up at her husband and knew that he'd do a good job. Not just a good job, a great job.

After all, he knew what mattered most, when it came down to it. She'd learnt that on the island.

Fliss and Ewan's guests didn't really seem to care too much that nobody had actually got married that day. They celebrated all the same, and since Harry and Betsy had decided that it could be a trial run for their own nuptials, there was a first dance and even a couple of drunken, impromptu speeches. The Mothers sat on opposite sides of the room, trading glares, neither willing to leave 'their' wedding before the other.

When Harry lobbied the DJ to play Scissor Sisters' 'I Can't Decide', Alec stepped in and requested *their* song, instead. His and Ruth's. As the strains of 'It Had To Be You' rang out across the dance floor, he took Ruth in his arms, and for a moment it felt like it was three years ago, at *their* wedding. When they had their whole married lives ahead of them, and the possibilities were endless.

Because they were, again. Now.

She rested her head against his shoulder and let the feeling wash over her. Whatever happened with their friends, Ruth knew that *their* future was nothing but opportunities to be happy – as long as they sought them out together.

Then Harry cut in. 'Could I have the next dance?' Ruth laughed and agreed as Alec grinned and sloped over to the bar.

They began to move around the dance floor. 'I'm glad you and Alec worked out whatever was going on,' Harry said, as they swayed to the music. 'You two are made to be together. In fact, it was Alec who gave me the confidence to fall in love with Betsy.'

Ruth looked up at him in surprise. 'Really? How?'

Harry smiled. 'He loves you so damn much, Ruth. He always has, right from the first. And I figured if he could, maybe I could too – if it was the right person. I knew that the day the two of you got married. I just never admitted it to anyone else – or even myself, really – until I met Betsy. Then I knew. I knew I could have that too, if I was willing to work for it, to change for it, and to take a chance on it.'

'So, you did.' Ruth beamed up at him. 'I'm so happy for you, Harry. You and Betsy. You're going to be a brilliant husband.'

Stretching up on her tiptoes, she kissed him on the cheek. Then she gently pulled herself free and went to find Betsy to tell her exactly the same.

There might not have been a wedding today, but as Ruth looked around the crowded room, she couldn't help but feel that love had filled the day, all the same.

By the time the party wound down, and Caitlin had disappeared somewhere with the best man, it was gone midnight.

'It's Christmas Eve tomorrow, you realise,' Ruth said, as she and Alec finally meandered along the road back to Holly Cottage. Mistletoe Island's sole gritter had been out, and the roads were mercifully clear, but the temperature was dropping again and it would be icy out in the morning.

'Nearly time to head home,' Alec replied. They had plans to fly back down to Ruth's parents' house on Christmas Eve. It was a long journey, but they'd have Christmas Day and Boxing Day together, before heading off to spend a day or two with Alec's mum, then home to London for New Year.

'Will you be sad to leave?' Ruth wasn't sure herself, to be honest. Mistletoe Island had brought something back, a part of herself she thought she'd lost. But she knew that she was meant to take that with her back to her everyday life, the real world.

She looked out, over the darkened waves, and back at the blackness of the woods under the stars and the snow. She'd miss the peace, and the friendships she'd grown. But she was ready to head back to her real life.

Alec took a moment to answer. 'I knew when we came here that this would probably be the last time we were all together this way. I never imagined things would fracture quite this dramatically . . . But, no. I'm not sad to go. Life moves on, and so do we. We'll still be friends, in our ways. But we have new adventures ahead, you and I. And I can't wait to live them with you.'

He pulled her closer, under his arm, and Ruth snuggled against his chest.

'Neither can I,' she said, smiling into the snow.

Fliss

This was not how she'd planned for the day to go. Not that she'd really had a plan, after everything went to hell with Neal. But if she had, it wouldn't have involved Martha Bennett pushing her into the ocean. Or poor Ewan having to come in after her.

She'd wanted to talk to him then. To explain everything. But between her chattering teeth and Martha screaming at her, it hadn't been possible.

Maybe it never would, now. Maybe she'd never even see him again, impossible as that seemed. They had a whole life together to disentangle. One Fliss wasn't sure she was really ready to say goodbye to.

She loved Ewan. That much at least she was sure of. But how could either of them be sure that he loved *her*? Whoever she might be?

'Are you okay?' Lara asked from the doorway. She clutched a mug of steaming tea, and placed it by Fliss's side as she huddled under the duvet. A hot shower had gone a long way to washing away the chill of the ocean, but she still wasn't properly warm again. Her wedding dress, still soaking, hung over the back of a chair near the fire. A sad, ruined reminder of what she'd almost had.

'No,' Fliss answered honestly. 'But I think I probably will be. Eventually.'

'You will.'

'You know, it's funny. When we were twenty-one and here on the island, we thought we knew everything. Now I'm thirty-one and only just realising I know nothing at all.'

The twist of Lara's mouth told Fliss she knew exactly what she meant.

Lara perched on the edge of the bed beside her. 'Neal's passed out in his and Caitlin's room. I don't think she's coming back tonight anyway, from Ruth's texts.'

'Not coming back?'

'I think Ruth's text said Caitlin was "snogging the face off Ewan's brother".'

'Oh.' Lucky Ryan. At least one brother was enjoying the day.

'Yeah. Anyway, Neal hasn't slept in about two days so wouldn't notice if she came back or not. He's pretty screwed up about everything right now.'

'And that's my fault.'

'I didn't say that.'

'But it is.' Fliss sighed. 'I didn't mean for any of this to happen, but that doesn't make it less my fault. Neal's too, a bit, I know. But at the heart of it, if I'd been honest about who I was from the start, none of this would have ever happened.'

'Why weren't you?' Lara asked. 'Why didn't you tell us to stop calling you Miss Fliss back at uni? Or ask us to take you out to that party? Whatever you needed?'

'I don't know.' But that wasn't true. And hadn't she learned this week how important the truth really was? 'Yes, I do, now. I don't think I did then. But . . . it was because I wanted to be that Fliss too. I wanted to be the person you all loved, *and* I wanted to be something more, the wild Fliss I could be with Neal. I wanted everything, except the risk of you all not wanting me as a friend if you learned who I really was.'

Lara hugged her tight and warm. 'We'd never not want to be friends with you. Well, apart from possibly Caitlin right now, but I think even she'll come around eventually. Maybe.'

'I know that now,' Fliss said. 'But by the time I figured it out, it was too late. I'd been Miss Fliss for too long. I'd been lying to you all. And it was just . . .'

'Easier to keep lying. Even to yourself. I get that.' Lara looked pensive, and Fliss wondered again exactly what was going on with her and Jon.

'But it's all out in the open now,' Fliss said. 'I wish I had the chance to explain everything to Ewan.'

Lara was looking past her now, towards the door. 'Maybe you do.'

Fliss looked up, and there was her fiancé. The man she loved. The man she'd jilted.

Ewan wasn't smiling, understandably. But he was there, looking far more himself in jeans and a dark red jumper. And that gave her heart more hope than anything else could.

'Before I come in, I need to know one thing,' Ewan said, as Lara slipped out past him, away down the stairs. 'Are you in love with Neal?'

'No,' Fliss replied, firmly. 'I might have been, once. But that was a long time ago. Because since the moment I met you, you're the only man I've truly wanted. You still are.'

Ewan came inside, shutting the door. 'Then I'm listening. If you want to explain what happened today. Because if you love me, I don't understand why you walked out on our wedding.'

It took a long time, and a lot of tears, entirely on her part. By the time she'd finished the story, Ewan's expression had still to change from the stoic, listening face he'd put on when he sat down in the chair opposite her.

She'd used to be able to read all his expressions, but now his thoughts were a mystery to her. Like he'd walled himself off completely.

Maybe he had.

'Why didn't you tell me?' he asked. 'No, I know the answer to that. You got caught up in the perfect couple, perfect wedding, perfect marriage thing. Same as me.'

Fliss froze. 'Same as you?' Was this the point where he confessed he'd been seeing other women all along? Because as much as it might salve her conscience, it wasn't going to do anything for her heart.

He flashed her a tight smile. 'Don't worry. There are no big secrets here. It's just . . . this week. I started wondering how much of any of this was for us, anyway. You wanted the time with your friends and I . . . I've been miserable. All bloody week. I thought it would be better when we were married, but then I realised, it would be more of the same. Family and friends and entertaining and dinner parties and being a perfect couple like, ironically, I thought Neal and Caitlin were. And . . . I didn't want that. I thought *you* did. *I* just wanted you and me and the TV and a take-away. I didn't want to be that perfect couple. I wanted to be us.'

'Except now you know that the Fliss you wanted never really existed.'

'Yes, she did. She does.' Ewan leant forward in his chair, so close she could see the intensity in his eyes. 'Because *my* Fliss – the one who wears the same Care Bears T-shirt to bed that she's worn since she was ten, the one who always wants chicken fried rice when she's sick – she *does* exist. And maybe she's not all of you, but she's real.'

Tears burnt behind Fliss's eyes, just when she thought she was all cried out.

'Nobody ever really knows another person completely, Fliss. It's not possible. But I guess I always thought that a relationship was a chance to find out. Because no one is ever really their finished self. We're all still growing and changing. And for me . . . marriage is about watching that other person grow, and about growing with them.'

Growing together. Finding out who she was now *together*. That sounded kind of perfect. But was it too late?

'What are you saying?' she asked. 'I mean, what do you want to happen now?'

'I want this week to have never happened.' Ewan scrubbed a hand through his hair and sat back with a rueful smile. 'But failing that, I think I'd like to start over. Maybe take some time away. I'll go stay with my parents for a while—'

Fliss shook her head. 'You don't have to move out. I've already got it arranged with Lara. I'll stay back at our old flat for a while with her.'

'Great. Because I was going to throttle Mum within a fortnight,' Ewan admitted. 'So, you'll stay there, I'll stay at the flat and maybe after a few weeks we could try . . .' He looked hopeful.

'Dating?' Fliss suggested. They could go right back to the beginning. Figure out if they could ever be a couple again. If he could forgive her. Love her, maybe. Just as she was.

Ewan nodded. 'Dating. Yeah. I think I'd like to get to know the *whole* Fliss. All of you. And who we can become together.'

Fliss smiled through her tears. 'I'd really like that too.'

Lara

Lara softly shut the bedroom door behind her, and padded down the stairs to find Jon. Fairy lights twinkled in the garland wound around the bannister, a reminder that it was more than just Fliss's non-wedding day. It was almost Christmas Eve. She owed Jeremy a decision about the job today, but today was nearly over. At this point she'd have to hope that Beatrix would still take her decision after Christmas.

Everyone else seemed to be sorted, or sorting themselves out. Or unconscious, in Neal's case, but that was good enough for now.

Which meant it was time for Lara to sort out *her* future. To decide which risk she was willing to take. Because every choice was a risk, she realised, pausing on the stairs.

Marrying Jon at twenty-one would have been a risk. They could have been divorced within six months. But saying no had been a risk, too. She'd been risking never finding the love she had with Jon again, ever.

And now? She could stay in London or move to Manchester. She could force Jon and her to stay just friends, or she could open up the possibility of more.

They all had risks. She simply had to decide which was the *right* risk.

Which road was worth risking *everything* for.

And to do that, she needed to talk to Jon.

She found him in the lounge, crouched in front of the fire he'd banked with more wood. He didn't turn around as she entered, but from the way his shoulders stiffened, Lara was sure he knew she was there.

'I've decided to take the job in Manchester,' she said, figuring she'd start with the practicalities and work up to the emotional stuff. 'I'll need to work out my notice period, but I can be there by February. And I want you to come with me.' Oh hell, just dive right in. She'd never been any good at subtle, anyway.

'Is this because of everything that's happened here this week?' Jon asked, still without turning round. In the corner, the Christmas tree lights twinkled, illuminating the snow still falling lightly outside the window. 'You figure you want to get away from the madness that's likely to follow for the next however many months. Or years.'

'I'll still be at the end of a phone whenever they need me. Hell, I'll probably still be in London most weeks for some meeting or another. And you'd be closer to your dad, so it works for you too. But this isn't about our friends, or even our families. It's about me, taking a chance on a future even if it's scary. Call it my New Year's resolution, or something.'

Jon stood up and turned around at last, and relief flooded through her at the look on his face. 'Are we still talking about the job? Or are we talking about me now?'

'Both,' she said. 'I was too scared to marry you ten years ago. Too scared of what I'd miss out on. And honestly? That was probably the right decision. I wasn't ready.'

'I know that now,' Jon said. 'Neither of us were, really. I was just trying to cling on to you, but we weren't the people we needed to be yet.'

'Exactly. But it started a pattern.' Lara took a step closer, thrilled when he didn't move away. 'I was scared to miss out, sure, but soon that became too scared to commit to anything. I threw myself into my job because I knew I could always leave it – but I never did. And besides, it took me to new places, meeting new people all the time, and I thought that was enough. That it was what I wanted.'

'But it wasn't?' It was Jon's turn to take a step now. He came so close that she could see the firelight gleaming in his eyes. She thought about the mistletoe, hanging outside the front door of the cottage, but she had a feeling they wouldn't need it.

Lara shook her head. 'It was just another way to hide from the scariness of the future. I never met anyone I wanted to get to know properly, deep down. The way I'd known you. And I never knew what my next step would be. Because if I didn't think about it, I didn't have to take it.'

'And now?' Jon asked. Was that hope, dancing between the firelight in his eyes?

'Now, I'm ready to take that step. To take a job that will let me work towards a future. Maybe even a directorship one day.' It was the first time she'd dared to say the words out loud. 'To build a new life somewhere I might want to stay. Nearer to my parents, but still in a city. Somewhere I can make my own. Somewhere I can fall in love, maybe, find someone to spend my life with.'

'Someone to say yes to, this time?'

'Yes.'

He was so close now she could see nothing but him. Not the Christmas tree, or the fire, or the snow falling outside the window, or the candles lit around the room.

Then her phone rang in her pocket, the obnoxiously loud ringtone that had been silenced all week while Fliss had switched it off and hidden it.

Lara winced. Jeremy. 'Hold that thought,' she said, fishing out her phone and pressing answer.

'Happy Christmas Eve Eve, lovely Lara! It's nearly the big day. So do you have an answer for me?' Lara got the impression that Jeremy might have started on the Christmas cocktails a little early. Or late, actually. She checked the clock on the mantle — it was nearly midnight.

'That depends. Do I have to work until midnight two days before Christmas if I take it?'

Jeremy laughed. 'Oh no. Beatrix and I just *happened* to be together tonight anyway, and she was wondering if you'd made a decision so I said I'd check.'

Lara raised her eyebrows. Maybe *this* explained why Beatrix had been so keen to take Jeremy with her when she set up her own company. Interesting.

'Well, I've given it a lot of thought.' She caught Jon's gaze, and he shook his head. This was all on her; her decision, her future. He hadn't actually said that he'd join her, if she went to Manchester. She'd just have to hope that he'd be a part of it.

She took a breath. 'Yes. Tell Beatrix I'd love to take the job.'

Jeremy gave a little whoop, then she heard him cover the phone with his hand, his words muffled as he relayed the news to Beatrix. 'She's thrilled,' he said, uncovering it again. 'We'll be in touch in the New Year to firm up the details. Merry Christmas, Lara!'

'Merry Christmas.' Hanging up, she dropped her phone onto the nearest table, and put her attention back where it mattered.

On Jon.

Jon placed a hand on her hip, and grasped her chin to tilt it so she met his gaze. 'So. What am I going to be doing in Manchester while you're building this new life? Besides visiting my parents and job-hunting.'

Relief flooded through her. He was coming with her.

'Marrying me, I hope.' Oh God, did she really just say that? And *Jon* was the one who was supposed to go too deep too soon. 'I mean, eventually. One day. After, you know, dating and stuff. For ages. Getting to know each other again.'

'I think we know each other already.'

He was right. She knew him better than she knew herself. Which might be the point.

'Maybe I need to get to know who I want to be now. And maybe you do too.'

Jon gave a slight nod, conceding the point.

'But maybe we could figure all this out together?' Lara suggested. 'Start the New Year right, I guess.'

Jon smiled. 'I think I'd like that.'

This time, when he kissed her, it felt nothing like the past, Lara realised.

It only felt like the future.

Tuesday 24 December 2019

Christmas Eve

Jon

Mistletoe Island was bustling on Christmas Eve. Between the guests from the wedding that wasn't, and the locals running last-minute errands, there seemed to be people everywhere – although Jon couldn't see the only person he was looking for. As he stood by the harbour, he saw Ruth and Alec approaching, arms wrapped around each other, her bright-red hat bobbing through the crowds. Harry and Betsy were kissing against the harbour rail, an epic goodbye that had been going on for quite some time. Betsy was staying with her family at the Mistletoe Hotel for Christmas, while Harry had to return home and tell his family to expect a wedding in the New Year. Jon grinned; he could just imagine the screams of disbelief now.

Neal had already left the island, Jon knew. Alec had run him down to catch the first ferry earlier that morning. Caitlin, meanwhile, had yet to return from the hotel after the party the night before. Lara had wanted to go and find her, but Jon had a feeling that letting Neal and Caitlin do their own thing for a while could only be for the best.

And Fliss . . . she had stayed at Holly Cottage. Her family were all up at the hotel, but she didn't seem keen to see them again just yet.

'I have some things to figure out,' she'd told them, as Lara hugged her goodbye one last time. 'Mistletoe Island seems the best place to try and do that, right now.'

Jon knew what she meant. It had taken coming back to the island, ten years after his heart broke there, to figure out what he needed to mend it.

If only he could find her in the crowd . . .

'Where's Lara?' Ruth asked, as she and Alec reached him. 'The ferry will be going soon, won't it?'

Jon nodded. 'She said she had to run and fetch something.'

'She's definitely coming back though, right?' Jon almost laughed at the worry in Alec's voice.

'This time, yes. She's my lift to the airport, apart from anything else. I'm pretty sure she's coming back to me.'

They were both done running, for a while. There were still plenty of things they needed to figure out between themselves. But Jon had faith that this time they'd both stay in one place and keep talking long enough to find the answers.

To find the future they'd each run away from, in their own way, ten years before.

He was done beating himself up for leaving the country, for not fighting harder for Lara back when he still could have. And he was finished feeling angry or confused or hurt by Lara leaving, too.

The past was over. Now he was just looking forward to the future.

'Sorry, sorry!' Lara appeared through the crowds, smile wide and blonde hair gleaming in the winter sunlight. 'I'm here.'

'Just as well,' Jon said, pressing a kiss to her hair just because he could. 'Alec was starting to worry.'

'But you weren't?' she asked, looking curiously up at him.

'I knew you were coming back to me.'

Lara's beaming smile made all the waiting worthwhile.

The next little while was a flurry of activity as they tore Harry away from Betsy, piled into their vehicles and got the cars loaded onto the small island ferry. By the time they all met on deck, Mistletoe Island was already starting to recede into the distance.

'Do you think we'll come back here?' Alec asked, as they all stood at the rail and watched the harbour, the chapel, the pastel houses all grow smaller and smaller.

'I hope so,' Ruth said.

'Then we will,' Lara agreed.

They stayed together until the chill wind off the choppy sea grew too much, and the island was nothing more than an outline in the cloud anyway. Then Alec said, 'Bar?' and Harry shrugged and said, 'You're driving, so sure.'

With one last look back at Mistletoe Island, they all made for the warmer inside of the ferry. Except for Lara, who snagged Jon's hand and held him back.

He raised an eyebrow at her. 'You're not cold?'

'I'm freezing,' she admitted. 'You should put your arms around me to keep me warm.'

Laughing, he obeyed. 'So, are you going to tell me why you had to run off to the village first thing this morning?'

'I had to get your Christmas present.' Lara snuggled against his chest for a moment, then moved away enough to pull a small paper bag from her pocket and hand it to him.

'It's not Christmas Day yet,' he pointed out, taking it.

'Yes, but this is also a present for me. So you should open it now.'

Intrigued, Jon opened the bag, smiling as he pulled out a small sprig of mistletoe.

'It just seemed wrong that we spent four days on Mistletoe Island and never kissed under it once,' Lara explained.

'Well, let's see what we can do about that.' Jon held the mistletoe over their heads and bent his lips to hers, sweet and lingering and secure in the knowledge that he could kiss

Lara every day for the rest of his life and never tire of it.

Then the door to the deck crashed open again and Harry yelled, 'You're going to freeze like that and be stuck at the lips for ever, you know!'

'Might be worth it,' Jon murmured against her lips, but Lara pulled away all the same.

'Come on,' she said, her eyes bright and laughing. 'But don't lose that. We might need it later . . .'

Jon glanced back one last time at where Mistletoe Island had disappeared into the mist in the distance.

Maybe Ruth was right, and they'd all go back to Mistletoe Island again one day. But Jon knew he didn't need to, not any more.

The Healing Island had already fixed his heart.

Humming 'Fairytale of New York' under his breath, Jon walked inside to join his friends, and the woman he loved, ready for Christmas, and everything that came after.

Acknowledgements

There are so many people I need to thank for helping me with this book, I'm terrified I might forget one of them. So, if I've ever talked at you about this book, at any point in the last four or five years, THANK YOU SO MUCH for listening!

To be more specific, I really must say thank you to:
• My editor, Victoria Oundjian, for doing everything in her power to ensure this book saw the light of day – and that it was the best story it could possibly be.
• The whole team at Orion for believing in this book, and for making it look so beautiful.
• My agent, Gemma Cooper, for being, as always, the best in the business. I wouldn't want to be anywhere but Team Cooper.
• My husband, Simon, for his constant support and love.
• My children, Holly and Sam, for the best hugs ever, and for sharing the chocolate digestives.
• My parents, brothers, and extended family, for everything.
• My loyal readers, for every great review, every email, every message telling me you loved a book. You'll never know how much they all mean to me.

But above all else, this is a book about friendship. And while as a rule my friendships have been rather less dramatic than the ones on Mistletoe Island (thankfully!) my friends have, over the years, listened to me, helped me through dark times, made me laugh (and cry – but usually in the good way), and simply changed my life.

From my childhood best friend Beth, through all the school friends I now only keep up with on Facebook (but especially the ones I still see often, like Kate), to the forever friends I made in college (especially Street, Pete, Ken, Chris and Kenzo), to ones who married into the group (like Debs, Anna and Carolyn), to my long-suffering university house-mate (Penny), to work friends, to all the incredible friends I've made at Stevenage Ladies Choir (especially Ann-Marie, Ally, Ali and Tash), all the writer friends who make this job even more fun than it was already (all of Team Cooper and the True Love ladies included), right up to the mum friends who help me laugh through the day to day (especially Hayley, George, Claire, Karen, Lisa and Lynsey).

I love you all. Thank you for being my friends.

Credits

We would like to thank everyone at Orion who worked on the publication of *The Wedding on Mistletoe Island* in the UK.

Editorial
Victoria Oundjian
Olivia Barber

Copy editor
Justine Taylor

Proof reader
Clare Wallis

Audio
Paul Stark
Amber Bates

Contracts
Anne Goddard
Paul Bulos
Jake Alderson

Design
Debbie Holmes

Joanna Ridley
Nick May
Helen Ewing

Editorial Management
Charlie Panayiotou
Jane Hughes
Alice Davis

Finance
Jasdip Nandra
Afeera Ahmed
Elizabeth Beaumont
Sue Baker

Marketing
Jennifer McMenemy
Tanjiah Islam

Production
Ruth Sharvell

If you loved *The Wedding on Mistletoe Island*,

don't miss Sophie Pembroke's next heartwarming novel

SUMMER ON SEASHELL ISLAND

Three estranged siblings. One family-run B&B.
A summer to change everything . . .

Available in paperback, ebook and audio

in Summer 2020